I0741829

ISBN: 979-8-9924767-0-5

EBook ISBN: 979-8-9924767-1-2

Written by Brandi Hudson
Contributions from Stephanie Weber

Cover Design by Debarim Publishing

Publishing by
Debarum Publishing, LLC
807 W Broadway St
Spiro, OK 74959
www.debarimpublishing.com

Acknowledgments

The journey, you as a reader are about to take, is due to the collaborative and contributive efforts of Stephanie Weber. Thank you for your endless labors, for sharing your giftedness and talents, and for your investment in the characters and the world they occupy.

Enlisting the help of these excellent editors has vastly improved the book before you: Gail Delaney, Sarah Williams, and Julie Patterson, thank you all!

At any point during the writing process, these friends were eager and quick to brainstorm, offer wisdom, and pray: Ann Musso, Ashlea Kim, Cindy Throgmorton, Donna Nash, Jolynn Harrell, Mandie Wells-Secret, Markie Murley, and Shelly Siegienski.

To my friends and family too abundant to list here, thank you for entertaining conversations about the characters as I drafted and created. I deeply appreciate your continued support and encouragement.

Every Rare & Pleasing Treasure

One

Stratton Davis, wearing a black and white striped sleeveless jumper with black flats, stood before Washington's Headquarters and the several hundred or so visitors at Valley Forge National Historical Park in filtered morning sunlight cast by tall oak and ash trees. She took in the scene as she felt hundreds of years of history swirl around her. She envisioned her ancestor, Peter Cokerill, who served under Washington in this very place over two centuries ago, before the three-story stone house marching, walking, and living amid the American Revolution. He had witnessed and participated in a pivotal moment in American History that had monstrous ramifications into the present day.

Tour groups and guides moved busily about the park, but Stratton was not part of them. She was here alone, walking the old paths of former family members and absorbing as much as she could about the places they had lived and visited. Valley Forge was her last stop on her current trip.

Her cell phone rang. The name came up: *Finley,* Stratton's second-born daughter.

"Good morning, sweetie," Stratton began, "How are you?"

"Well, I had to find out from Noah that you left the homestead and are in Pennsylvania." Finley had an edge to her voice.

Noah was Stratton's third and final child. He operated the homestead she shared with him in Lynnville, Tennessee.

"I tried calling you last week, but someone was out of the country." Stratton could not keep up with her jet-setting, the-world-is-my-oyster, go-getter, real-estate-mogul-in-the-making daughter.

After Stratton and her ex-husband, Dexter, divorced, Finley left Miami for college in Boston, where she graduated. She then moved to New York and recently moved to Denver. She never stayed too long in one location, and Stratton figured it was about time to move.

"The Caymans are hardly out of the country, Mom. Anyway, my boyfriend wanted to take me to his family's vacation home."

Stratton brushed a few strands of rich chestnut brown colored hair from her face in the small breeze. She was not ready to go full gray and kept her hair color as close to its natural color as possible, relying on a skilled henna colorist to achieve a non-toxic, lush look. She quietly sighed. Finley changed boyfriends as often as she moved, and Stratton had long given up trying to get to know too many details too soon. What was the point in knowing his favorite meal if he had already been replaced thrice over by the time a visit to the homestead came around?

"Mom, are you listening?"

Stratton hadn't been. She'd been watching a man, uniformed in khakis and a green shirt, carry gorgeous flowers from his lily-loaded UTV. He would disappear behind the house and then come back and gather more. Stratton's inquisitive eye noticed the array of colors and told her feet to move in that direction, realizing she had to know what purpose the lilies served at Valley Forge.

"Darling, I am listening. It sounds like," she scrambled to remember Finley's boyfriend's name, "you and Austin had a wonderful time."

"So, you think I'm overreacting about the dolphin thing?" Now, she sounded offended.

What dolphin thing? What could have possibly happened involving a dolphin? But the gardener was back again, lifting up the most beautiful orange and black-dotted lilies. He turned and began his stride back around the house. Stratton could see that he was a burly man with medium dark brown hair sporting a very short, trimmed, dark salt and pepper beard that looked almost like a five o'clock shadow versus a mountain man's beard. She followed his steps behind the house to a lovely garden with an unobstructed river view.

"I think you should talk to Austin about how the dolphin incident made you feel and see if he understands where you're coming from." *Would the standard Mom advice suffice?*

The line was silent for about ten seconds. "I guess I could talk to him. I mean, he's already asked me to visit their house in Napa Valley, and from what I hear, the market is great there. I've already started looking at apartments, ya know, just in case."

Stratton knew Denver would be short-lived, and so would Austin. Finley's next call would probably be about the new swanky city she'd discovered in California and how she absolutely must move there.

"Oh, Mom, I gotta run. I've got a new listing, and I think it's about to sell! I love you!"

"I love you, too, honey. Have a good day. Bye."

"Bye!"

Having spent years striving to accept Yehovah's grace for her mistakes, Stratton still felt guilt and blame settle upon her as it pertained to her children, the next generation. She certainly didn't want Finley marrying the wrong guy, but she also didn't want her serial dating to be extreme, as if courtship were like shoe shopping.

She looked at her phone. The wallpaper was a photo of Harper, her eldest daughter. Harper had followed in Stratton's footsteps, married young, brought two beautiful girls into the world, and discovered firsthand the meaning of the word narcissist. Harper's divorce went quickly, and after four years of mending, healing, and being committed to the tenets of Scripture in ways she had never dedicated herself before, she met and married into a six-generation Arkansas ranching family, who had welcomed all three of them into the fold. Whitten Carter, who was widowed, brought two young sons into their marriage, which was everything Stratton had wanted for Harper. Yehovah had made beauty from ashes, provided joy instead of mourning, and praise instead of despair for both Harper and Whitten when He had brought them together.

Regretting that her choice of Dexter Davis as a spouse had brought disharmony to her children, Stratton hoped and prayed her grandchildren wouldn't feel the sting of that choice.

Stratton, feeling overcome with emotion, felt pools of tears forming in her eyes. Just as a few tears snuck out, dotting her cheeks, the gardener approached.

"Mornin', miss, are you alright?" The gardener pulled a fresh navy-colored handkerchief from his pocket and offered it to her.

"Sorry, I'm fine." She waved it away.

"I know the feeling. It's powerful to be in a place filled with so much history." He stood with perfect posture, looking toward the Schuylkill River, and inhaled, "Sure is turning out to be another gorgeous day."

"It definitely is." She agreed, staring at the river moving swiftly in an easterly direction, and she thought again about Peter, the soldier, and all that he must have endured during the war. Her mind returned to the gentleman next to her. "I am wondering what you're doing with the lilies. I don't recall ever reading about them during Washington's time."

"Oh, those? We're cultivating a sample colonial garden and showing folks which kinds of flowers would have been present during that time."

"We?"

"Everest Galloway, miss." He extended a hand.

As she shook it, he continued, "I've been retained by the historical society to oversee the grounds here. I've been working to create gardens that are true to the historical time line. We've got several different displays throughout the grounds."

"That's a fascinating job." *Finley! Why can't you find someone like this?* Stratton couldn't help but let her mind go there. So what if he was a gardener? This was the kind of guy Finley needed to date; he was thoughtful, helpful, and knowledgeable. He had a few years on her but couldn't be more than thirty-five, and Finley was in her late 20s. How Stratton wished she could get the two of them to meet.

"Dr. Galloway?" A teenage boy approached carrying a shovel. "They told me to come help with the lilies. Where do I start?"

Doctor? Oh, Finley, come on! Baby, I've struck gold for you! Stratton couldn't hide her smile. At sixty, she wanted to see her children living the best versions of themselves and presumed all of them would find a spouse and have a family, even though she remained unmarried all these years after the divorce.

Everest turned his attention to the kid. "Go ahead and dig the same size hole as those planters, and I'll be there to assist you in a moment."

The teen moved on with a nod.

"Doctor?" Stratton asked.

"PhD in Forestry and Arboriculture."

"So, your patients are plants," she said with a smile.

Everest gave a hearty laugh. "I suppose they are. I earned all those credentials just to dig in the dirt." His eyes met hers. "So, what brings you here, Miss…?"

"Stratton Davis." She didn't add that she, too, had a PhD.

"Well, what has brought you here, Miss Stratton Davis? You don't seem to be with a tour group."

"Oh, I'm on sabbatical right now, so I thought I would come do some research on an ancestor who fought in the Revolutionary War and was stationed here under Washington."

"Not everyone has that kind of a connection to this place. That's pretty cool. Who is your relative?"

"Peter Cokerill."

"Captain Peter Cokerill?" Everest asked with a raised brow.

"How did you know that he was a captain?" No one ever knew that.

Everest just smiled. "How long are you here?"

"My flight leaves this afternoon. I just came to the area for a quick trip."

Everest glanced at his watch. "I'll be right back." He walked over to the young man digging, and they spoke. He came back to Stratton. "I know this is going to sound like an opener to a *Dateline* episode, but my cottage is just a short five-minute drive through that hedge, and I have something you need to see."

Zero red flags shot up even though Stratton thought they should. You don't agree to go anywhere with a stranger—ever! That was one of the first lessons she had taught her children, and she continued telling her grandchildren that they should never get in the car with a stranger. *Well, it's not a car; it's a UTV, and it is daylight and five minutes from here, so it has to be within screaming distance.*

"OK."

Two

It wasn't five minutes. It was four minutes and twenty-six seconds to Everest's one-level cottage, dripping with fragrant wisteria. Plants surrounding the cottage evoked memories of a place in the French countryside from the summer that Stratton and Harper took a European venture there. Boxwood edging, hydrangeas, and Russian sage took Stratton back to that wonderful trip abroad.

"This is gorgeous," Stratton mentioned.

"A Frenchman originally owned it, and I just added a few touches to bring it back to its origins." Everest approached Stratton's side of the UTV and opened the door.

She exited the UTV to walk beside Everest along a paved path to the cottage door, not bothered in the least at how secluded they were now.

The small cottage seemed more spacious because of the floor plan and decor. Thoreau quotes flew around Stratton's mind as her eyes adjusted to the indoor lighting. This was his own private Walden experience. There wasn't a separate bedroom, just a desk at the end of a made bed in one of the corners, a vintage record player on top of a small bookcase on one side of the bed with a small nightstand on the other side, a couch and coffee table, a small, immaculate kitchen, a brick fireplace, and a door leading to a tiled room that she assumed was the bathroom.

"It's just as lovely inside."

"I can't take credit for that. I only brought what fit in the truck. My lease is up after this job ends." Everest went to the roll-top desk at the foot of the bed and rummaged around. "Here!" He said as he pulled out some papers. "When I came to the grounds and started working, I found a box of letters under a loose floorboard in one of the cabins. The soldier who wrote them apparently requested they be returned there upon his death. We had to demolish that cabin, so we donated the letters. These are copies of the letters. Here, check out this one." He handed her a piece of paper.

Stratton reached into her purse, removed her glasses from their case, put them on, and began reading.

Dearest Brother,

I trust the good Lord finds you well when you receive this letter and pray you remain as such despite what I am to write. Words fail me. I could not bear the burden of writing to our mother or our sister to explain losing Thomas today in battle. Think me not cowardly for choosing to write to You to deliver the message to our loved ones. I wish it had been me.

The only testimony to bravery is that I did not leave him there on the battlefield. I carried him as far as I could and refused to retreat even when the order sounded. I could not walk away from Thomas. The British soldiers were approaching, and as Captain Cokerill rode his horse, he jumped down. We placed Thomas's body upon his stead, and he told me to march on, not to let the British have the satisfaction of two deaths.

He came to our ranks at camp, sat with me, and offered prayer. It sounds so strange, but I felt the presence of angels surrounding us, and all of those stories Father shared with us from Scripture became truer than ever. I cannot explain what has happened to me, but I am a changed man.

Thomas believed we were throwing off the yoke of oppression and fighting for freedom for future generations. He thought the cause of war was worthy and did all unto the Lord's glory.

I was never as strong in my belief, but the captain's prayer spoke to me, and I felt the hand of the Lord upon my heart, and I know somehow that in Thomas's death, my life has been saved. Captain Cokerill says there is joy coming out of this sorrow to behold and that one day in the Kingdom, I will see it if I so choose to be a disciple of the Messiah.

Dearest Brother Jacob, I do believe and trust in those promises and would like to share this all-surpassing peace with others. Thomas's death has the deepest meaning. I am assured it will not be in vain. He served with honor, and his memory will always be a blessing to our family and future generations.

I will send word when my tenure here is done. Cover our regiment in prayer, especially for Captain Cokerill and his safety and protection. His kindness has meant so much to me, and I have much to learn from his faith.

So, after my kind love to you, I remain your loving brother until death and trust in the glory of the resurrection and promised reunion,

Isaac James Parsons

Her tears flowed freely. It was a powerful and tender letter. Everest had the handkerchief ready for her.

"Everest, this was absolutely touching and wonderful to read. I had no idea." She removed her glasses and dabbed under her eyes. "How did you even remember Peter's name?"

Everest beamed a flawless, his-parents-must-have-paid-good-money-for-such-straight teeth smile. "Isaac was my tenth great-grandfather."

Stratton was stunned. "What?"

"I didn't know it when we found the letters, but after a little digging, since it's what I do, I found out he was my ancestor. When you mentioned Peter, it was all I could do not to explode. From what I discovered about Isaac, he became an ambassador for Yehovah, and his progeny found many serving Him to the fullest."

Using the Hebrew Name of God? Oh, Finley, I've done it. I've found an excellent match for you. Stratton glowed. "Thank you, Everest. It was really sweet of you to share this," she said as she handed him the letter.

"Keep it. I have several copies."

Stratton tucked the paper into her purse. "Thanks. What a delightful ending to my day here. I'm sure my children will appreciate knowing this part of our family history." *Well, Noah and Harper would at least acknowledge it was a neat connection, but Finley would somehow turn it back towards her and her latest happenings.*

"Where are my manners? Would you like something to drink?" Everest walked the short distance to the fridge.

"Oh no, I should be getting back; I don't want to miss my flight." Stratton's phone buzzed. "See?" she said with a smile, "the world beckons me." She pulled out her phone. "Oh, dear."

"Everything alright?"

"My flight was just delayed due to inclement weather."

"I don't mind taking you to the airport later. Since you have a little more time, would you like to see more letters from Great Grandpa Isaac where he mentions Peter?"

This complete stranger made Stratton question her discernment for the second time since she had met Everest, and she again agreed.

"OK."

* * * * *

Stratton expected "weather" to mean rain, not the tempest that quickly brewed after the airline sent another text message canceling her flight. She messaged the Airbnb she had just left, asking about staying another night.

Her phone buzzed, and she took off her glasses to read the notification. "That figures. I can't get the Airbnb for another night."

Snacks of fruit, vegetables, and crackers were sprinkled on two plates atop the kitchen table, where the pair pored over the copious letters and writings Everest had on hand. Stratton felt closer to Peter after hearing how influential he was in Isaac's life. Isaac had even named one of his sons after Peter.

Through Isaac's correspondence, she felt like she was getting to know this wonderful relative better. "Everest, would it be too much trouble to take me to my rental car? I can get a hotel from there."

Everest looked down at his phone. "Stratton, I don't think you're going anywhere. It's coming in fast." He held up the phone, showing the radar on the screen.

Their location was covered in red with some pink and purple in spots.

"Oh nonsense, it's just a little rain. I'm sure I could walk back to my car without issue."

Everest opened the front door. The wind blew wildly, and the rain beat down rapidly. "Care to change your tune?" A loud boom of thunder rumbled in agreement with the wind and rain, eliminating the idea of leaving the cottage anytime soon.

"I can't believe this. How long is it supposed to last?"

Everest closed the door. "At least a few hours based on the radar. Look, since you don't have a place to go tonight, you're welcome to stay here."

Hospitality was a gift of Stratton's, but receiving so much from a stranger felt quite different. However, it would make an ideal story for Finley when she told her about him. Not that Finley was the one to ever agree with her mother's choices for suitors, but this time, it felt different. She texted Noah and told him she would stay another night in Pennsylvania but would be home tomorrow.

"Does the couch pull out?" She asked.

"No, but you can have the bed."

It was a Hallmark or a Lifetime movie in the making. The mother of the girl who ends up with the guy has the chance to meet him first, approving him for her daughter and playing matchmaker. She was tickled at the prospect of figuring out how to tell Finley about Everest.

"It's the least I can do for a descendant of The Peter Cokerill," Everest chortled.

* * * * *

The April cold front brought a chill to the air despite it being spring. As the wind howled outside, rattling the small cottage's windows, rain fell against the roof in a steady, rhythmic pattern.

Everest stood back from the fire he had started in the brick fireplace. "This will keep us warm if we lose power."

The flames from the fire seemed to dance in tune with the rain and wind, spreading their warmth through the room.

Stratton had been texting with Noah and sent a final goodnight text to him from her chair at the kitchen table.

Everest had his back toward the fire. "Are you hungry?"

Stratton wanted to repay him for his hospitality, "Yes, but please let me make something. I have already put you out enough." She stood and started toward the small kitchen.

Everest would have none of it. Instead, he guided her to the couch and handed her a glass of lemonade, saying, "You relax and keep me company while I fix us some dinner." He then went to the record player and put on some classical music before moving back to the kitchen.

Stratton appreciated the nostalgia. It felt like she had taken a step back in time. "Everest, how old are you?" she asked nonchalantly while *Clair de Lune* played in the background.

"Forty-seven."

She was glad she wasn't trying to take a drink of lemonade right then. It might have flown straight out of her mouth.

He wasn't near Finley's age, and though he was more mature than her, it wouldn't have been an impossible match.

"Aren't we about the same age?" He asked.

She was glad she still hadn't lifted that glass to her lips.

"Oh, Everest, I'm sixty!" She laughed.

His look was of genuine surprise. "Well, all I know is I scored a perfect 20/20 at my last eye exam."

Stratton smiled at the compliment—*kind to his elders; what an endearing trait.*

"Here we go. Eggplant parmigiana with some homemade bread." He served her on the couch and sat next to her. "Let me pull the coffee table closer."

Stratton took a bite. *Oh, Finley, don't let this one get away!* "It's absolutely delicious."

"Thank you." Everest swallowed a few bites. "So, tell me more about this sabbatical. What do you do? Let me guess, a university professor?"

Stratton laughed, "Is it that obvious? I'm the history department chair at the university and was granted six months off. I've always wanted to explore my family's history and maybe uncover some family mysteries or secrets, so I'm making it an adventure."

"Like crashing at a stranger's cottage without luggage and only one toothbrush to share?"

"Everest!" She hoped he was teasing.

"I'm kidding. I have a brand new one in the right-side drawer in the bathroom." He laughed.

Stratton stole a glance at Everest. *Finley would love his eyes; they are beautifully blue, endlessly wide and pure, like a clear summer day, and seem to sparkle when he laughs. OK, this is not where I need to go—I just need to gather facts about him to share with Finley. It's time to change the subject.*

"The meal was delicious. Since you cooked, let me handle the dishes." Stratton stood, gathered their plates, and headed to the kitchen.

Three

As soon as the rain would let up some, another round would come right behind it, making it too challenging to fetch Stratton's luggage from the rental car, so Everest offered to let Stratton borrow a change of clothes.

"Sorry, I didn't have anything smaller," Everest said from the kitchen when Stratton emerged from the bathroom.

Her sleepwear for the evening consisted of an oversized long-sleeved shirt and baggy flannel pajama pants. The drawstring was pulled tightly, and the bottoms of the pants were tucked into thick wool socks. Looking down at her roomy yet comfortable attire, she laughed, "It's better than sleeping in my jumper."

Everest walked towards her carrying two mugs of hot chocolate and motioned to the couch. "How about a little hot chocolate as a nightcap?"

"That sounds good. I'm not really tired yet," she replied with a smile.

They sat for a few minutes in the cottage's ambiance, the warmth from the fire blanketing them against any icy chills. Sipping on their steaming delectable beverages, they watched a Tchaikovsky piece dance on the soundwaves. "So, do you often work at national parks?" Stratton asked.

"My work is quite versatile and varied. Outside of traditional landscape jobs, I spent last summer at Hershey Park, an amusement park in Pennsylvania, where I revamped their landscaping. I've also been a consultant for landscaping at a handful of garden parties. I would like to expand into other areas, though."

"Where will you head after the Valley Forge job?"

"My next job is taking me to Tennessee."

"I live in Tennessee! Whereabouts are you going?" She sipped her hot chocolate.

"Lynnville."

Stratton coughed, nearly choking.

"Easy now." Everest handed her a napkin.

She cleared her throat. "Did you say Lynnville, as in Lynnville, Tennessee?"

"I did. Milky Way Farms in Pulaski actually, but they said I'd be closer to Lynnville. They've asked me to come help create some gardens for some festival they are having. Should be a lengthy stay, at least through the Fall."

"Everest, I live in Lynnville!" Stratton laughed. *This had to be His will. He was making a way for Everest and Finley to meet.* The story was getting better and better in Stratton's head. "I've been to Milky Way Farms and taken a tour. If I remember correctly, the grounds are about 1,100 acres with a 25,000-square-foot manor house. It's sprawling, manicured, and much larger than my 75 acres."

"You have 75 acres? Do you take care of it by yourself??"

After receiving a large financial settlement from the judge overseeing her divorce, Stratton purchased the acreage. It was ironic that she had been awarded such a financial windfall since her ex-husband had never wanted to relinquish monetary control or any control. She had developed the land, which Noah now oversaw, through careful planning and management.

"Oh, I don't take care of it alone. My son, Noah, is transitioning from electrical work to farming full-time, so he takes care of it more than I do."

She pulled up a picture on her phone, leaning closer to show Everest. "That's him on his tractor." The day he bought the farm tractor outright was a proud moment for Stratton. "He saved up his money and was able to buy his equipment all on his own. He's my happy homestead guy."

Stratton walked a fine line between helping and enabling her children financially. Dexter would never help his children financially, so she had to teach them to be financially responsible and that hard work would pay off in the long run. However, she knew that she was guilty of enabling them at times.

"Noah learned all the ins and outs about that tractor and started his own business. He cuts hay, brush, trees, and anything else someone needs. He keeps acquiring more tractor attachments so he can continue to help others."

"He's a good-looking kid; you can tell how proud he is. It's great that he's doing something he loves, which is so fulfilling," Everest affirmed.

Stratton eased back on the sofa, feeling the travel fatigue and adrenaline rush of the Peter Cokerill connection catch up. "Will you be staying on the grounds at Milky Way? It's only a few minutes from my home."

"Housing is on my own. I've been in touch with a man, Mister Walters, about a rental he has."

"Oh, not that trailer across from the church?"

Everest nodded. "I think that's the one."

"Just so you know, whatever pictures you've been sent aren't accurate. It's very worn down and not safe structurally. You should just come to stay on the homestead." *Finley, you are going to be so thankful one day.* She had just met Everest earlier in the day, and by nightfall, she had invited him into her home to stay. She had to think of a way to creatively spin this so her children didn't think she had completely lost her mind. But had she lost it? She didn't know much about Everest, only what he had told her about himself and what little she had observed.

If she made it through the night and this wasn't a story for *Unsolved Mysteries*, perhaps it would be safe to host him at her home. She was already trying to figure out where to let him stay. The pool house hadn't yet been built because she hadn't put in a pool, so that wouldn't work. The walkout basement room might be fine. It had its own entrance, a kitchen, and a bathroom. She might never even notice he was there except when she invited Finley to come over and have them meet.

"I couldn't possibly put you out like that."

"It's no trouble at all. It's just Noah and me at the house, and we have plenty of room. At least come by and visit before you commit to anything in town. When will you be there?"

"I expect May or June. I'm going to visit my folks in Pennsylvania for a couple of weeks, then head out thereafter."

Parents. Stratton wished her mother was still alive. She'd lost her years ago, and no matter how much time had passed, it always felt like it had just happened. His parents could potentially be in their 60s, the same age as her. *Well, of course, he could be my son-in-law one day, so I am probably close to his parents' age.*

"Not wanting to be too personal, but I am curious: why did they name you Everest?"

"It's not too personal. It was from when my dad climbed Mount Everest. He said that was where God spoke to him on Mount Everest, and his life was never the same. After grad school, he had the opportunity to train and make the climb with a group of friends. He wasn't sure what to do after graduation, so it seemed like a good idea since he was looking for direction for his future. My dad said he journaled extensively on the excursion to stay focused on God and His will. Though he had always been active in his church, lately, he felt that he had been simply attending church and doing what Jesus would do. Taking in the view and grandeur around him, when my dad reached the top, he felt His presence and heard Him say gardening was the way to feed His flock. So, my dad founded his landscaping company, and instead of competing with the top company in town, he married the owner. My mom liked the smells of evergreens and the forest, so when I came along, my dad offered Everest as a name since it both held sentimental and personal meaning. My parents merged their companies, and even though they are retired, they maintain a 51% interest in the company should yours truly ever want to take it over."

"So, you grew up around landscaping and spent a lot of time outdoors?"

"That I did. When I graduated from high school, I wanted to explore other places, but Dad said I'd have to find a way to make money to pay for the many trips I wanted to take. I decided the best way to make money was to capitalize on my landscaping experience, but I wasn't sure how. One day, I found a book on historic gardens and knew I could take my landscaping experience to the next level. I started small with some locals, offering to recreate period gardens or find out what once existed where they lived. Once my parents saw that I had a talent in this area, they encouraged me to go college, so I completed my undergraduate degree in Pennsylvania and then went on to Yale for my graduate degree."

"Impressive. So, you didn't want to take over the family business after grad school?"

"No, I found that I enjoyed moving about for different projects and haven't been afraid to try new places. Keeps me young." He winked as he tried to stifle a yawn.

"Everest, I don't want to keep you up all night. You go on to bed. I'm fine on your couch, really."

"No, no, no. Let me clean up these mugs, and I'll get you settled."

Stratton was drained and normally would have offered to help, but she was also fading quickly. The dark mahogany sleigh bed and its slate-colored duvet, which housed a down comforter, looked awfully inviting.

Everest quickly finished. "Come on, let's get you tucked in." He extended a hand.

She didn't know why she accepted it. Why it felt like a reflex or a natural inclination to take hold of his hand with hers, she clearly didn't have mobility issues. She didn't need assistance walking a few steps to the bed.

They walked hand in hand and stopped by the bedside.

"I changed the sheets this morning, but if you don't believe me, I will put fresh ones on right now."

"It's fine." She let go of his hand, feeling a little toasty. Why was she feeling warm all of a sudden? She glanced down and noticed her socked feet. *That's it; the wool socks are making me feel slightly warm.* Looking up, she saw an open Bible on the nightstand. She could see highlights and notes made throughout the exposed pages, possibly Genesis, but she didn't get a good look before Everest closed it and picked it up.

"OK, there are plenty of pillows and an extra blanket at the end of the bed. I'll leave the bathroom light on, too."

"Thank you, but I truly don't mind the couch."

"Goodnight, Stratton. Sleep well. I'll be twenty feet away if you need anything."

"Goodnight." Stratton settled in the bed.

Everest turned out all of the lights except a small one in the bathroom, and he left the door partially open. He stretched out on the couch.

Stratton's mind began to replay the events of the day, and as she was drifting off to sleep, she had a sudden thought that sent a chill through her, making her slightly shudder: had Everest ever had another woman in this bed? She immediately dismissed that thought and the chill, blaming it on the cold air coming through a crack in the windowsill, and reached for the extra blanket folded at the end of the bed.

But truth has a way of becoming clearer after twilight. What if when she was talking to Finley in her head, she was actually talking to herself?

She dug up that seed as quickly as it was planted and tossed it away. She wanted nothing more than for the sun to rise so she could vacate this cozy little cottage and return to her homestead, where everything made sense. The place where she didn't talk to strangers, let alone stay the night at their home, wondering how often they had overnight guests.

Four

Drool. Stratton's eyes popped open, and she wiped the side of her mouth, embarrassed that she had slept so soundly. Beams of sunlight filtered through the windows, creating a warm glow in the cottage. She sat up and stretched while looking for Everest. It appeared she was all alone. *Hey, I made it through the night. I'm not gonna be featured on a crime show!*

She stood up and decided she could at least get the sheets in the wash for him. She gathered the laundry and found the washer and dryer in the closet behind the bathroom door. She started a load and then sat down at the kitchen table. The Bible he had taken last night from the nightstand was opened to the book of Proverbs. She touched the pages where he made notations along the margins and smiled. Everest Galloway was a testimony about the good in the younger generation and living proof some still sought righteousness in the world.

The front door opened, and Everest entered carrying a brown paper bag. "Good morning. I thought I'd make us a quick breakfast before you need to head out." He placed the bag on the table, still littered with last night's historical papers. "And if you give me your keys, I'll get your rental for you."

Twenty minutes later, after receiving her luggage, Stratton had finished a hot shower and changed into a simple plumb-colored knit short-sleeved shirt, jeans, and a pair of gray slides. As she finished brushing her teeth, she heard Everest in the kitchen making breakfast. She wondered if she would find traces of female visitors if she opened the medicine cabinet door. She chastised herself and opened her makeup bag, grabbing a little eye makeup and mascara. She glanced at her watch and decided to let her damp hair air dry since she needed to get moving as her flight left in a couple of hours.

"It sure smells delicious," she said as she exited the bathroom.

"Eggs Benedict with turkey sausage and some steamed spinach." Everest presented the mouth-watering meal as they sat down at the table.

"A girl could get used to this." Stratton felt herself turn red the moment she said it. She wasn't a girl in the young woman sense. She certainly didn't mean to imply she wanted to get used to Everest making her breakfast. Nor did she want Everest to get used to playing the role of host. She was so embarrassed.

He appeared not to have even noticed her poor word choice. "Did they reschedule your flight?"

"Yes, I'll need to head out right after breakfast to catch my flight." *OK, Stratton, don't make it awkward. Just extricate yourself from this crazy situation and go home. Don't play matchmaker. I just hope he doesn't show up at your door wanting to stay for the summer.* "Another tasty meal, thank you." She moved quicker than usual through the food.

"I'll let you know if I find any more Peter Cokerill references in the family archives when I visit my folks."

"Yes, that'd be great. Let me write down my contact info." Stratton pulled a small notepad from her purse and jotted down her information. Her phone buzzed. "I should go. Thank you for being such a wonderful host, Everest. It was a memorable evening, and I appreciate the copies of your family letters and the time you spent with me reading them." She stood and gathered her belongings.

"I assure you that it was my pleasure. Let me show you out." Everest took her suitcase and walked her outdoors towards her car.

The air was fresh and filled with the fragrant scent of rain-soaked earth from the night's storm. As the sun slowly climbed over the tops of the trees, light shone brightly through the leaves that shimmered from the droplets of water on them, creating a sense of renewal and revival.

Everest loaded her suitcase into the backseat of the car. "You're all set. Thanks for trusting me so I could share about our family's connection. I'll look you up when I'm in town."

"I look forward to it." *Get in the car, Stratton. Go to the airport, Stratton. Quit standing there and making it awkward, Stratton.* "Thank you for sharing your time, home, and food." She stopped before she said bed or clothes. She at least stopped before she said that. What had started as a normal, casual goodbye quickly became uncomfortable. Despite how awkward Stratton felt, she silently thanked Yehovah for their ancestors for forging a bond that was still being honored through their connection. Stratton sighed. "I'm a mom and a grandma, which makes me a hugger. You've been so sweet, and I feel a proper goodbye would include a squeeze."

Everest smiled and enveloped Stratton's frame.

During the embrace, Stratton felt the sun warm her skin by at least two degrees. She breathed in deeply, smelling the fresh scents of bergamot and sage. *Stratton, you need to take a step back and leave.* But she didn't. Like she had said, she was a mom and a grandmother. She was used to affection, which was one of her love languages. She was usually the one with a stronger hold, but she could feel she wasn't taking the lead in this one. She figured he just needed a little extra, but eventually, his arms slackened, and the goodbye hug ceased.

They parted with smiles, and he waved as she backed down the drive, headed to the airport and a return to normalcy.

* * * * *

What had Everest just experienced?

He knew it had been outlandish to ask a stranger, especially a female stranger, to stay with him at his cottage, and he still wasn't sure why he had done it. Stratton didn't seem like the kind of woman who would normally have accepted such an invitation, but she had, and now she was driving away and out of his life.

He thought back to when he had first noticed her. His eyes had singled her out of the crowd of hundreds, and he had decided to approach her.

When he walked up, he noticed that her blue eyes were filled with tears, and he knew he had to come to the aid of this woman in need. Everest painted himself as chivalrous and told himself that he surely would have done that for anyone, not just Stratton, and not just because she was so beautiful to him at that instant, standing there, gazing out at the river with tears in her eyes.

He was astonished to learn they had a historical connection. He smiled as he remembered how touched and moved she had been by the letter. Everest was honored to have shared that experience with Peter Cokerill's relative. So why had he taken things a step further and offered her to stay the night and sleep in his bed? He was simply a nice guy, and the weather was too dangerous for anyone to be out and about.

He had been surprised that she had agreed to stay at his place. Maybe she was just tired and not up for fighting the raging storm outside or fighting him when he'd insisted on her staying.

He couldn't explain his desire to protect her from the storm. He wasn't sure how to gauge his motives. *Why did I reach out and hold her hand as we walked to the bed? How long would we have held hands like that if she hadn't pulled away?* Why couldn't he stop smiling when he thought about everything that had transpired between them since meeting Stratton? What might his future summertime excursion to Tennessee hold? *Will I see her again? Will she remember me and our evening?*

Whenever he needed a reset on his emotions, Everest knew there was only one place to turn: Scripture. He would go to Scripture and seek His will and advice through reading and prayer.

His interest in Stratton was most certainly piqued, but he had to sift through the reasons why.

Five

"I'm home!" Stratton announced as she entered the kitchen from the garage.

Noah got up from his charcoal gray recliner in the living room and carried his empty plate into the kitchen.

"Care to explain why there's a herd of Highland cattle out front, Noah?"

"I got a good deal. Ol' Jasper down the road said he was gettin' out, and I should get in, and he said he'll mentor me with 'em."

"Well, I don't want to see any calves in this house come winter, do you hear me?"

"I'll have that wood stove in the barn by then." He adjusted his overall strap.

He wasn't what Stratton would call burly, not like Everest. Noah was stout. Strong as an ox, and she'd noticed since he'd switched to full-time farming, his activity level was making those overalls looser.

"Besides, you left out all that ancestry paperwork, and I saw that we had an ancestor who was a cattleman. Figure I'm just followin' in the family business." He smiled.

Stratton shared the smile. "You are." She readied a glass of water and took a few sips. "I met someone in Pennsylvania who knew about our relative from the Revolutionary War."

"Oh, cool."

"Yeah, and he will be working a gardening job close by in a couple of months so he may stop in."

"Uh-huh," Noah nodded.

She knew she'd tipped her hand, and Noah was suspicious. He would tell Harper. Harper, always the protector, would call to check on her. He would then tell Finley, who would call in worry mode. Ever since the divorce, their roles had reversed, and the kids were very protective of anyone entering their mother's life. Any nice man at the grocery store, church, or included at dinner with her friends was suspect. She understood that deep down, none of them wanted to see her hurt, so she tried never to worry them. She realized she needed to scale it back and get him off the scent quickly. Besides, nothing was going on between her and Everest anyway. It was legitimately a dead-end trail, but it was better to squash suspicions before rumors could develop.

"Anyway, I was thinking of introducing him to Finley."

"Finley? She doesn't want some guy with a job like that. She likes 'em, fancy fellas." Noah laughed. "But you do you, Mom."

A flash of white raced across the kitchen and turned the corner.

"Noah, what was I just saw running through the kitchen?".

"Oh, that's Cully. We found him in a culvert, and he acted like he wanted to come home with me." Mister Nonchalant explained. "I got him set up with a litter box in the laundry room. He's a sweet boy and won't be any trouble."

"Noah, I can't have you turning this place into a zoo while I'm traveling this summer."

"I won't, Mom, and if you want, I'll move him to the barn."

"It's OK for now, but let's discuss any future additions."

Stratton noticed a piece of notebook paper lying on the counter. "Happy Birthday? Who sent that?" Stratton could barely make out the chicken scratch on it.

"Oh, Dad did."

She noticed Noah's solemnity.

"My birthday was last month. I don't know why he even bothered."

Typical Dexter. He lived by his own timeline and expected everyone to follow suit. How hard would it have been to stop at any number of stores and pick up an actual card?

"Told me he's got my present, but I have to come to Miami to get it. I'm not going to Miami. He probably got me something dumb, anyway. He doesn't even know how old I am."

Noah was 25, which made him three years younger than Finley and five years younger than Harper.

"Sweetheart, if you want to go to Miami, I can manage just fine while you're gone. I don't want you to feel any obligation to keep me company. I have a big summer ahead of me."

"Nah, I don't want to go." He sighed. "I don't hate him, Mom. I just don't like him and don't want to be around him. He needs to be saved, but that isn't my job. I try to remember him in my prayers, but it's hard to keep my heart in the right place."

Stratton knew that road all too well. She'd spent decades pleading and begging with the Father to help Dexter. Dexter used his license of free will to the fullest and lived for himself. Stratton never asked her children about Dexter, but they often shared, usually when he did something hurtful, like missing a special event or bringing a new girlfriend to a function. Stratton was careful not to speak ill of him but simply listened and consoled her kids. Her heart ached for Noah's hurt when he received the piece of paper. Why couldn't Dexter see their son like she did? Noah was so sweet and loved to laugh. He was hardworking and was thriving on the farm. Why couldn't Dexter celebrate that his son was content and didn't need to follow in his steps as a banker? Noah was created with different interests and talents that Dexter didn't understand, appreciate, or embrace. Stratton doubted Dexter would ever come around, but she would hold out hope for Noah's sake.

"I gotta go move some hay for some folks. I'll be back for dinner." He pecked her cheek. "And I'm OK, Mom. Don't spend the rest of the day thinking about this. Think about that cool Revolutionary history stuff." Noah smiled. "See you later on." He knew her well.

"Bye." Stratton rested her hands on the white marble countertop. She wasn't going to think about Dexter. Noah's suggestion about Revolutionary stuff took her back to Pennsylvania and her encounter with Everest. She had forgotten to get his contact information in a hurry to depart from his cottage, but he was probably easy to google. She wondered if he would reach out when he came to town.

Her phone buzzed. She thought it was Everest for a moment and immediately clipped the wings on every butterfly in her stomach. It wasn't Everest.

"Hey, Willodean, " she answered. Yes, I am making the pies for the next meeting." Stratton was a member of the Daughters of the American Revolution, and they had an upcoming meeting in a couple of weeks to discuss their Memorial Day plans. "Sounds good. OK, thank you. Goodbye."

She checked her phone to make sure that she had that meeting on the calendar. It was there, along with the American Historical Association annual meeting, she would attend in late summer.

She decided that she should also figure out a time to visit Harper in Arkansas over the summer. She hoped Finley and Noah could come. She enjoyed trips to the ranch. It didn't hurt that it was always a guaranteed time of opulence and grandeur with the in-laws. They spoiled Stratton whenever she went; she knew that's how they treated her girls. She loved Whitten's mother for embracing Harper and her girls, Scarlett and Daisy. They shared a multi-generational home, not just with Whitten's parents, but his grandmother also lived with them. Stratton could not give her grandbabies multiple in-tact marriages and plenty of family members, but she was thankful for them to be surrounded by a family who could.

Stratton decided to unpack and then see about finding and meeting Cully the Cat.

* * * * *

"These essays are really good. I'm having a hard time choosing the best ones for scholarship contenders," Stratton mentioned to Willodean as they sifted through scholarship applicants at her dining room table. A plate of fruit and vegetables rested between them with a couple of homemade dips Stratton had made that afternoon.

"This one reads like a story. He even tied in some fascinating facts about river pirates." Willodean handed it to Stratton, lifting her glasses above her eyes and pushing them atop her short, curly blonde hair. She dunked a piece of celery into the dill-flavored dip.

"And treasure, I see!" Stratton laughed. Stories about treasure were always appealing.

"Hey, Mom. Hey, Ms. Willodean." Noah came into the dining room. "I got the mail." Noah handed over the stack of envelopes.

One caught Stratton's eye. "A wax seal?"

26

"You don't see that every day," Willodean said as she returned her glasses and picked up another essay.

Stratton looked at the envelope. Written in flawless calligraphy was Stratton's name, and the return information bore the name Everest Galloway.

Stratton blushed. Why had he written her a letter? She opened the letter.

Dear Stratton: I've finished the job at Valley Forge and am spending some time with my folks in Pennsylvania. After combing through some family records, it looks like our families enjoyed a grand Independence Day celebration a decade or so after the war. I've enclosed a copy of the article from a small PA newspaper that mentions our families hosting quite a soirée. I hope you are enjoying the sabbatical. Feel free to write if you find anything in your family records. I am still in awe that our families are connected and curious to know if the Cokerill's mentioned the Parsons.

Take care,

Everest

"Well, do share. If it's got you smiling, it must be good," Willodean said.

"Oh, I met this historical society guy who worked at Valley Forge. He had found a letter a soldier wrote about how my ancestor, his captain, had led him to the Lord during the Revolutionary War. It was quite a touching letter."

Why did she flash to Everest, holding her hand when she said the word touching? *Focus, Stratton.* "Come to find out that this soldier was one of his ancestors. Our families stayed close for several years, and here's a copy of the article about them celebrating together on the Fourth of July. Isn't that sweet?" But that wasn't why she was smiling. Sure, it was sweet, but the sweet who man had taken the time to track down that copy and send it to her in a letter that made her smile.

"Looky there. How fun." Willodean glanced up from reading the article. "I may have to do some ancestral research and see what I can discover, too. I knew enough to get into the Daughters of the American Revolution, but I'd really like to find out this kind of stuff."

A journey like that might just lead to an evening at a stranger's cottage on a stormy night with a hot meal, relaxing music, and engaging conversation. Stratton wouldn't admit she replayed that evening over and over in her head or how she daydreamed about Everest's hands locked with hers at his bedside. What if she hadn't been the first to pull away her hand? How long would they have stood there together? It was sophomoric to keep dwelling on it. It wasn't going to manifest into anything, so it wasn't worth reliving. But if it wasn't worth reliving, why did she allow it rent-free space in her mind when her thoughts traveled?

Six

"Noah! I'm headed out to the parade. I'll see you there!" Stratton picked up the container of homemade cupcakes she had just frosted and headed toward the front door. There was a tailgating party hosted by the ladies of the DAR who were marching in the Memorial Day Parade Lynnville was having. She'd dressed for the parade in jean capris with a red, white, and blue cotton T-shirt and white tennis shoes.

She placed the cupcakes on the foyer table as she took a final look in the mirror. As she ran her fingers through her hair, she glanced down at the two letters on the table. Everest had sent them, and she had yet to respond to him. Besides the article he'd enclosed with the first letter, he'd sent a copy of a photograph of their two families from the late 1890s. Stratton had appreciated the research and the photograph but wasn't sure how to respond. She'd pulled out her family papers and sifted through them, trying to see if there was something she could send to him about their families. Maybe after the parade, she could finally sit down and write him back, at least to say thanks.

Picking up the cupcakes, she opened the door to leave. Startled, she jumped back.

Everest, wearing a baby blue polo shirt, jeans, and navy Sperrys, stood before her with a hand held up in a knocking position.

She would have dropped the cupcakes if not for his quick reflexes. "Everest, oh my goodness, I didn't expect to see you." *What's he doing here? Do I look alright? How's my hair? Did I put on my lipstick? Not that I care; it's only Everest, but one should always be ready to have company.* She'd already forgotten what she'd seen in the mirror thirty seconds before.

"Well, you said to stop by when I was in town, and I'm here now."

She took a step back, "Oh, did you find a place to stay?" hoping he'd forgotten her former offer.

"I did, and that's why I'm really here." Everest pulled out a piece of paper. "I rented a barn apartment, but it wasn't until yesterday that I realized it was the same address as yours. Am I in the right place?"

Noah! What have you done? Stratton recognized the pictures Everest held on the paper and was equally embarrassed and angry. "Everest, come in, please. Make yourself at home. I'll be right back." Stratton ran upstairs and rapidly knocked on Noah's door.

"It's open."

"Noah!" She closed the door behind her. "Did you rent out the barn apartment to someone?"

"Yeah."

"That barn apartment isn't ready."

"I said it was rustic in the ad."

"Rustic! Does the plumbing even work? Do you have air conditioning out there? Insulation? A certificate of occupancy?"

"I said it's like camping." Noah tossed a couple of shirt options on the bed.

"Well, your new tenant is here."

"OK, I'll go show him the apartment then."

"No, no, no. He's not staying out there. You're not putting renters in an unfinished barn apartment with your livestock right there."

"Mom, it's actually really popular for farms right now. I researched the trends."

"If your renter were anyone else, I would let this play out, but that's Everest."

"Who?"

"Everest, the man I met in Pennsylvania who sent me the letters I showed you about how our families knew each other in the War. Anyway, I know him, and he is not staying in your barn apartment." Stratton sighed, "I guess I'll let him stay in the basement."

"Well, alright." Noah buttoned a short-sleeved yellow plaid shirt over his white undershirt, unphased by Stratton's obvious frustration.

"And you take down that listing right now."

"Sure thing. I gotta finish getting ready; I'm doing the fishing contest before the parade. Do you mind?"

Stratton shook her head and went downstairs.

Everest stood at her French doors, looking out at the deck.

Why did he have to look like he was the model they chose to advertise the windows or those jeans? "Sorry about that. My son listed that barn apartment, which doesn't have many amenities. Would you like to check out the room downstairs instead and see if it would work for you?"

"I don't want to put you out, so I'm fine going to Mister Walters' rental, really." His eyes conveyed nothing but honesty and sincerity.

"No, it's OK. Come this way." She led him to the door just off the kitchen, which opened to the fully finished basement. "Let me give you the tour." They went downstairs. "This is the media room here, the bedroom off to this side, the bathroom is through there, and a small kitchen is out here, but you're welcome to use the one upstairs if you prefer. You should have everything you would need. The towels, extra blankets, and pillows are in the closet. Did you bring a lot of stuff?"

"Whatever fit in the truck." He looked around and nodded. "I'll take it if you're sure it's OK. Do you want me to pre-pay? I've just been corresponding via email with your son, and he said he just wrote $600 there as a starting point for the negotiation. This is clearly worth a lot more than that."

"No, we can talk about all of that later. I'm so sorry, but Noah didn't tell me you were coming. Otherwise, I would have been way better prepared." She turned to head back upstairs, "I have to go; I've got a parade to get to. You know how our families love a good celebration."

"Speaking of our families, I would have written and shared more of my research, but I wasn't sure you got my letters."

"Oh, I did get them, thank you. I just haven't had time to respond."

Everest stretched a little. "Well, I'm glad you got them. I'll unpack and get settled in here."

"Great." She started towards the door.

He reached out and touched her hand. "It's really good to see you,

Stratton."

She had a flashback to their last encounter and blushed a little at the memory of how she had felt in his embrace. Stratton had somewhat hoped that their paths wouldn't cross again, but here they were, their paths crossing once more.

She quickly moved her hand and patted his shoulder. "You, too. Welcome to Lynnville, Everest. I'll check back with you when I am home. Send me a text so I can save your number."

"Sounds good. See ya later."

She felt like she needed some fresh air, as flustered as she was. Why was she so warm? Was it because she was still angry at Noah, or was it because Everest's fingers had touched her hand? What would people think now that he was living in her basement? The good thing was she wasn't the one who invited Everest. This was Noah's idea, and things still might work in her favor for introducing Everest to Finley after all.

She gathered up her things and then left for the tailgate party, knowing that she had left a total stranger free access to the entire home and didn't go back to lock up anything of value. The more she thought about it, the more this all sounded like an intro to a true crime TV episode. Her phone rang, interrupting her thoughts.

"Hey, Willodean. I'm on the way. See you in five!"

Stratton made the short drive downtown and lined up her SUV with all the others for the tailgate party. For now, she'd simply enjoy the fellowship with her friends before marching in the parade down Main Street. She'd deal with the fallout of Noah's decision and her new roommate situation afterward.

* * * * *

The sun hugged the tree line before slipping below the tops, creating darkness throughout the homestead. Stratton entered the kitchen with an empty cupcake carrier and discovered Everest and Noah at the table eating dinner.

"Saved you a plate, Mom. This bass is delicious." He grabbed another piece of fried fish from a platter stacked high.

"Congrats on your big win, Son," Stratton said. She grabbed a plate and joined them at the table. "So, what have you two been doing?"

"Noah and I have been talking, and he's shared a few things about your work."

"Oh yeah?" She raised a brow.

"You were a National History Teacher of the Year winner and received the Eugene Asher Distinguished Teaching Award your second year at the University of Tennessee Southern."

"Just missing that Pulitzer," Stratton quipped. Had Noah pulled out her diplomas and awards from the box they were in and showed them to him? There's no way Noah had remembered the details of her accolades. He had probably taken Everest all over the entire house. At least it was clean and tidy.

Everest stabbed at the salad in his bowl as he smiled.

"Well, I gotta go check on my goats." Noah stood up from the table.

"Goats?" Stratton asked. "When did you get goats?"

"Ol' Kenny said the market is good this year for Nigerian Dwarf goats. I found a good deal on a starter herd."

"Noah..." Stratton sighed. This wasn't the time or place to have that conversation.

"Relax, Mom. I've got this. Everest, just leave your plate, sir, and I'll clean up when I'm back." Noah made his exit.

Everest exhaled. "Stratton, I talked to Noah, and I know you offered the basement out of the goodness of your heart and to make up for Noah's impulsiveness with renting the barn. I don't have to stay here. I haven't even unpacked so I can find something else."

Stratton reached over and patted his hand, "No, it's fine."

"I don't want you to feel uncomfortable or put out." Everest glanced down at their hands.

Um, Stratton, your hand is holding his. Stratton, let go! She had only meant to pat his hand, but somehow, her hand had closed around his, causing a wave of electric energy to surge between their entwined hands. "Our family histories demand I carry on the long-standing tradition of practicing hospitality."

Everest nodded and tried to stifle yawn, using his free hand to cover his mouth. He didn't move the one she was holding.

Stratton, still holding his hand, stood and led him to the basement door." "You need a good night's rest. Come on." As they reached the door, Stratton paused. "Everest, I want you to stay." *What if he reads more into that than I meant?* She felt the heat rise up her neck as she blushed from not carefully choosing her words.

"You sure?" He looked intently at her but didn't let go of her hand.

His thumb was gently brushing the top of her hand, sending electric currents pulsing through her hand, up her arm, to her chest. *I feel like I might pass out.* "Well, I'm not giving you my bed, but you can borrow my toothbrush." She attempted to lighten the mood.

Everest chuckled. "Thanks for helping a wanderer out. I made the whole drive in a day, so I am ready to sleep. Do you want me to help clean up the kitchen first?"

"No, I've got it." *Hands still together, Stratton.*

"Then, I'll see you tomorrow, and we can discuss my lease."

"OK, sounds good. Rest well."

Everest slowly released her hand, turned, and went downstairs to his room.

Stratton spent the next hour expending the electric charged-up energy she felt on making the kitchen spotless and texting Finley, asking her to please come for a visit.

Seven

"So, you manage the entire homestead?" Everest asked as Noah was showing him around the farm.

"Yes, sir, I do. Took me a while to embrace farming after being raised in the city, but I've had some good teachers and had some great summers with some family to help with that early education, so it's all coming back to me now." Noah turned out the goats from their stall. A silver doe and a buckskin doe made their way out to the open area of the barn, where they could come and go as they pleased, grazing and relaxing. Noah had a separate buck pen for the two bucks he acquired. He let them out into their own paddock.

Stratton, sitting in the back of their UTV, had joined them on the tour. She found the goats adorable and appealing and was glad Noah had gotten them.

"Got me some clover I'm gonna plant in this field here, and then I'm going to do oats and barley there," Noah continued as he pointed to the north. "I'm running late on planting the garden, though."

"Oh, I can handle the garden," Everest offered.

"Well, sure, you gotta earn your keep somehow." Noah and Everest shared a laugh.

Stratton noticed they were forming a bond. *This will be good when he meets Finley; they'll all get along so well.*

"Mom, you oughta take him to town and show him around. He's gotta start work tomorrow at Milky Way," Noah commented as he drove back toward the barn.

"So soon?" Stratton asked.

"Yeah, I've got Orientation at eight in the morning. I'd love some insight on the best grocery store and eateries in case I don't have time to come back for lunch."

"Oh, I can pack you a lunch when I pack Noah's." It was so easy taking care of others. Though he wasn't her responsibility or her ward, here she was, offering to do what she always did for those in her life. She wondered how long it would be before she did his laundry.

"I couldn't have you do that."

"Don't fight with her. You won't win when it comes to the kitchen," Noah said with a laugh.

"Well, then, it's settled. I'll take care of the lunches."

After they arrived back at the house, Stratton made them a quick lunch of tuna salad sandwiches before she took Everest on a tour of the town.

They parked downtown and began the short walking tour. There were 59 homes and businesses on the National Historic Register in Lynnville. The small downtown had a row of buildings close together, reminiscent of the towns of yesteryear when life moved at a slower pace for most. Lynnville still captured the wonderful simplicities in so many ways. Every face beamed a smile, and most folks waved at them as they walked along the sidewalk.

As they entered into the Lynnville Fried Pie Company's establishment, Everest held the door for Stratton. "Fried pies? I've never heard of these, but I have to try them."

Fruit and pastry dough filled the warm air with fragrance as they headed toward the counter.

"Hello, Stratton. What can I get for you? Is this Noah's friend I've heard so much about?"

Had Noah told the whole town about Everest already? Words spread faster than any wildfire ever could.

"Everest Galloway, miss, and I'm new to town working at Milky Way Farms."

"Nice to meet you. I'm Jessi, proprietor of this local enterprise." Jessi, with her 1950s-inspired blonde hairdo, sported a red ribbon headband with her thick curled ends flopping forward. Her lips looked painted with her bright red lipstick. It was a retro look that endeared her to older generations and made her stand out with the new. The black and white polka dot dress she wore today, cinched tightly by a red leather belt, fit her like a glove.

Stratton subconsciously stood straighter.

"The place looks very nice," Everest said.

"I took over for my grandma about two years ago and recently added some new recipes, including a pomegranate syrup that goes great over our orange rosemary crepes. It is out of this world. What can I get for you?"

Everest looked over the menu. He turned to Stratton, "What would you like?"

"Nothing, I'm good, thanks." She was hyper-vigilant. She watched to see if anyone was watching them. Small towns love to gossip, and she didn't need any of that to get started. Everest was already a hot topic, apparently, so there is no need to add to it.

Finley's name showed up on her phone as it vibrated. "Excuse me." She quickly stepped outside. "Hi, honey, how are you?"

"Noah got a roommate? He sent me a text saying that some dude is living in the basement. Mother, what is going on down there? Are you hurting for money? Because Gabriel, this guy I'm seeing, has some really smart investments in cryptocurrency he's been telling me about, and we could totally get you set up."

What happened to Austin? "No, we aren't struggling, Finley. Noah was just trying out a new business venture."

"OK, well, did you do a background check on him?"

"I already knew him."

"You did? Noah didn't tell me that."

"He's from Valley Forge and was working for the historical society when I met him. Our families go way back to Revolutionary times."

"Oh, so like some academic, history connection. Got it. Anyway, I checked with Gabriel, and he said we could come down this weekend but just for a couple of nights with a late Sunday return flight."

"And you shared my rules with Gabriel?" Stratton was refreshing Finley's memory on the one-person-to-a-room-unless-married rule.

She sighed, "He booked us an Airbnb, and just so you know, when we stay in the same place, it doesn't always mean what you think it does."

"Finley, you both can stay at the house. I have plenty of rooms."

"Gabriel's allergic to cats, and Noah said you have one now."

Then leave Gabriel in Denver! "We do."

"And where would you put him anyway? Noah's friend is in the basement, and you probably wouldn't want us on the same floor."

Stratton let the dig slide. Though she had initially wanted Finley to meet "Noah's friend," the more she dwelled on it, the more she realized that wasn't what she wanted. It wasn't that she didn't want Finley to find someone amazing; she truly did, but she didn't want to do this to Everest. He had been nothing but polite, a real gentleman, and she didn't want Finley hurting him. She wanted to protect Everest. Call it motherly instinct because she wasn't ready to face calling it anything else.

They ended the call shortly thereafter, and Finley kept the Airbnb booked.

"You've got to try this. It's sensational." Everest came out holding a fried pie, enthusiastically offering it toward Stratton.

"No, thank you." *Oh, the scandal if anyone snapped a picture of him feeding me a pie on Main Street! Social media posts would be making the circuit in record time.*

"Jessi was so nice. She said she knows of this Civil War cemetery with some original plants from that era still growing that she would like to show me." He sounded enthused.

"Did she now?" Stratton started walking slowly down the sidewalk away from Lynnville Fried Pie Company and Jessi.

"Yes, she gave me her number, so we can hike through it sometime." Everest joined her, matching her stride.

Stratton forced a laugh and stopped to look at him. "Everest, she was totally hitting on you." Which, why wouldn't she? Tall, dark, handsome, single, witty, polite, generous. *Oh, Stratton, dear, dear Stratton.* She had only considered connecting him with Finley, who knew the house rules. What if Everest wanted to date someone while staying at her home? How would she even approach that topic? She had placed herself in a potential pickle alright.

"No way. I think it was just that Southern hospitality I've heard so much about." He stared intently at her longer than necessary. Stratton, unsure if the electricity she felt between them was real or imagined, wondered if he felt the charge in the air. She matched his gaze a second longer before slowly turning to continue strolling down the sidewalk.

"A store full of leather-made goods?" Everest paused at a window.

They stood in front of Colonel Littleton's storefront.

He scarfed down the remainder of his pie. "Come on!"

Stratton entered and inhaled the intoxicating smell of leather. The place was decorated with leather and art from floor to ceiling. The items were made in the back of the shop, then brought up front and displayed.

Everest already had on a leather vest that looked as though it was made for his frame.

Stratton didn't know what Daniel Boone or Davy Crockett looked like, but she thought they probably looked like the scruffy-bearded man standing before her.

"This is nice." He slipped it off, then walked over to look through the luggage that was for sale. As he strolled around the store, he stopped to pick up some coasters. "Do you need anything?"

"Need? Have you looked at the price tags, Everest?" Leather goods aren't cheap, and with quality comes expense.

"Well, let me know if you see something you'd like." He looked at the owner, "Do you mind if I touch these wallets? My hands are clean."

The owner nodded his permission.

Stratton watched as Everest gently ran his fingers over several of the leather wallets on display, handling each one as a delicate work of art.

Finally, deciding on a vintage, cognac-colored one, he walked to the checkout counter. Looking back over his shoulder at Stratton as he paid for the wallet, he smiled. "My dad will enjoy adding this one to his collection."

Stratton nodded, holding out her hand to carry the bag.

Everest soaked it all in as they continued walking through the shops and stores.

"Everest, is this your first extended stay in the South?" Stratton asked as they explored the 1927 Baldwin Steam Locomotive, which rested next to the Lynnville Train Depot and the quaint museum, which could also be toured.

"It is. Everyone has been so nice today. Nothing feels rushed here. I can see why you never left the South."

"Well, when I was married, I lived in Miami, which was hardly considered the South." Stratton stood next to Everest, overlooking the small downtown area from the train.

"I thought Noah said you were a Jaw-juh girl. Did I say Georgia like a true Southerner would?" Everest asked with a smile.

Stratton scrunched her nose and shook her head. It was awfully cute how he tried, though. "I was born and raised there but spent my married life in Miami."

He turned around, leaned back, elbows resting on the rails, and looked at her. "I don't need to know the details, but I know your ex didn't deserve you, nor did he treat you right."

Stratton bristled and reacted. "You're right, Everest. You don't need to know the details. We barely know one another." *Said the girl who slept in his clothes and bed and is now sharing a home with him.* "I am trying to show you around so you feel settled, and then you unsettle me by saying this. Honestly, you have no idea what my marriage was like, so I don't need you telling me he didn't deserve me or that he didn't treat me right. It's legitimately none of your concern nor any of your business. Speaking of business, that's all this needs to be between us. I don't need another friend or a confidant." Stratton was fuming as she climbed from the train and stormed back to the SUV. She watched as a pensive Everest approached and climbed inside. She was ready for a fight and already had several zingers on standby.

"I apologize for speaking out of turn, and I can keep things strictly business," he said calmly.

Her anger was immediately diffused. She thought he'd bring a knife to a gunfight; instead, he brought humility and understanding. Her flesh prickled, but her spirit softened. "I don't know what Noah's told you, and that's not your fault. It's one thing to connect personally with our shared ancestors, but I'm not ready to confide in you about my past."

"I relate to that, and I am sorry."

"Thank you, and I'm sorry for flying off the handle like that. That wasn't called for." *And I hope no one witnessed that.* "Let me show you where the grocery and hardware stores are, then we can swing by the road that leads to Milky Way Farms so you're all prepared for tomorrow."

"Thank you. I'd appreciate that."

Eight

After showing Everest the rest of the town, they returned to the homestead. They were driving up to the house when they saw Noah erecting a round pen with panels in the front field.

Stratton rolled down the window. "What are these for?"

"Oh, Mom, I've decided to host a horse show."

"Noah, buddy, you gotta pick one thing."

"I did. Farming. This is all a part of the package. Agritourism is really popular right now. Everest and I talked about it last night. Right, Everest?" Noah looked at Everest in the passenger seat.

Why was Everest telling Noah what to do on the farm? He didn't have a say in what went on at the homestead. He was a tenant, and it was her land and her son. Though she didn't spend too much time working the land, Stratton was still in charge. She glanced over at Everest but decided this was not the time or place to discuss it.

"Don't throw me under the bus," Everest protested.

"Noah, I'm going to make sure Everest is settled, and then I'm taking some time to catch up on some reading."

"Sure, Mom. I'll be seeing you all later." Noah got back to work.

As they pulled into the garage and went inside, Stratton caught Cully on the countertop. She had a zero-tolerance policy for animals on countertops. Cully would be a barn kitty before nightfall.

"Is everything downstairs to your liking? Do you need anything? Is the temperature good? It's not too noisy with us upstairs?"

"It's very welcoming, Stratton. I think I'll get a little rest this afternoon since I won't have much time after today. Would you like me to cook dinner for you guys?"

His hospitality rivaled her own. She was just about to say no, but she was going to be making breakfasts, lunches, and dinners for the three of them, so why not accept the invitation?

"You may."

"It'll be ready at six."

"Attire?" She was halfway joking.

"Formal."

She laughed. "Are you serious?"

"How often do any of us get dressed up anymore? So, show me formal."

She smiled. This was what playfulness felt like. It had been so long since she'd done something that sounded so silly. Nevertheless, she'd oblige.

She spent at least an hour rummaging through her closet to find the perfect dress. She chose one that she had worn to the Kentucky Derby, a blue floral patterned below-the-knees V-necked white sleeveless dress. Light blue strappy sandals finished the look, and she added a decent amount of makeup since it was formal, after all. Her hair, straight with a little volume added to it from a round brush and hair dryer, enveloped her face and touched just below her shoulders. Taking one last look at herself in the mirror, Stratton decided she was ready and headed down the hallway towards the kitchen.

As she entered, Stratton spun once with a playful smile, enjoying the whistles and applause from the two men at the table wearing their black-tie ensembles.

"I can't believe you got Noah to do this." She said as Everest pulled out her chair for her.

"Not only that, but he also left me in charge of the honey garlic chicken you have before you, ma'am," Noah said. "Oh wait, Mom, don't sit down. I gotta get a picture of us. The girls are going to wonder what on earth we are doing," Noah laughed. "Let's give them something to wonder about in our group chat. You two get together so I can see if I got it framed right."

Stratton stood next to Everest, feeling awkward at having a picture taken with him.

"You look like statues. Mom, lean in."

She leaned closer to Everest, and he put one of his big arms around her. Immediately, Stratton noticed a charge in the energy between them and felt a bit lightheaded at his touch.

"OK, smile!" Noah took the picture. "That's great. Now let me set the timer." He fiddled with the phone, placed it on a shelf, and approached the pair. "Smile again."

The phone made a noise like a photo was taken, and Noah inspected it. "That's awesome." He showed them both.

"We look like something out of The Great Gatsby," Stratton quipped, causing both men to laugh.

"Let's get some food before it gets cold," Everest said. "Oops, I almost forgot." He walked over to the record player and chose a collection of jazz. "For F. Scott Fitzgerald."

Conversation was light and peppered with laughter as they dined. Noah shared some of his humorous farmer stories, as well as his plans for the farm.

Stratton loved seeing Noah so talkative and how his face lit up when he talked about his plans. Had Everest been responsible for drawing this out of Noah? Surely not. There hadn't been enough time for him to have that kind of impact on Noah, had there? She didn't spend too much time thinking about how one evening with him at Valley Forge impacted her. As the meal continued, Everest told them more about some of the gardens and estates he had renovated, and then Noah shared more ideas he had for the farm.

"One thing I want to do is put a cat door in the barn apartment for Cully since he loves being out there. I just need to figure out how to finish it out."

"I'd be happy to lend a hand. I'm pretty good with a hammer," Everest offered.

"Much obliged," Noah said.

By the time Stratton yawned, it was nearing ten o'clock. "It's getting late, and you both have an early morning. I'll get up and make everyone a big breakfast tomorrow and have lunches packed, too."

"You don't have to do that." Everest began clearing the table, and Noah followed suit.

"Boys, just leave the dishes. I'll get them in the morning." Stratton slipped her shoes off and let out another yawn.

"You don't have to tell me twice, Mom. Goodnight, y'all. Thanks for a fun evening. Everest, that was a great idea." Noah grinned and went upstairs.

"Yes, goodnight." Stratton, carrying her shoes, started for her room.

"Not so fast," Everest said. "By my calculations, there's still one more song on that record."

Stratton was puzzled but then heard the orchestra music begin.

"Nat King Cole? *The Very Thought of You?*" Stratton shook her head with a smile.

"Will you do me the honor of one dance?" Everest bowed and held out his hand.

She was too tired to debate. "One dance, but not with these shoes." She placed them on the floor and took his outstretched hand.

He wrapped his other arm around her waist and pulled her close to him while her free hand found its way to his shoulder. They started moving in time with the music.

He must have taken lessons at some point. His footing was sure, and his hand placement was just right on her back. As she and Everest swayed to the music, Stratton listened to the song's words. Why couldn't it have been *Pennies from Heaven* or something more upbeat? Why did it have to be such a romantic song? Why did she have to agree to dance? She should have just gone straight to her room.

Nat serenaded on as they continued to move as one. Stratton felt the warmth of his hand on her back, pressing her closer, and breathed in deeply.

Everest smelled so clean and fresh with that same bergamot and sage fragrance emanating that she'd inhaled the last time they were this close.

Could he smell the ylang-ylang essential oil she'd dabbed on when she readied in front of the mirror? Why had she put it on?

"What's next on your sabbatical, another trip?" He asked.

Did he press her in even closer, or did she move closer?

"Well, I want to see my sister in Georgia, but I don't know if I should go there or have her come here. I also wanted to do some research for a publication I'm working on about online education, too."

"I'd like to hear your ideas sometime." He took a step back as he twirled her during an instrumental interlude.

When they came back together, Stratton labeled it as dangerously close. There was so little space between them that she was sure she could hear his heart beating in time with hers.

"We still haven't figured out my rental agreement, and since I can see you don't need any dance lessons, I can't offer to tutor you in exchange." His voice was low, and he was almost whispering.

She felt his breath warm on her neck as he spoke. Could he see the goosebumps it caused on the back of her neck? She closed her eyes as his cheek pressed against hers. This was one of the sweetest gestures and moments she'd ever experienced. A simple slow dance in her dining room was the perfect ending to the evening. It was a struggle not to let all of this go to her head. She wanted to analyze it, but her cognitive functions were impaired by being this close to Everest as he held her tightly to him. She knew the song would end soon. She reentered the room from her thoughts. When had she rested her head on his chest? Should she have gone with a backless dress so she could feel his fingertips against her skin? Why did it seem that the electricity zinging between them was intensifying? Why did this man holding her in his arms make her feel so special?

She cleared her throat, trying to shock herself out of the daydream. "Say, when does a man from your generation make the time to learn to dance like this?"

"Does it bother you?" His mouth was by her ear. His lips seemed to gently caress her lobe in sync with his thumb as it gently brushed along her back.

She felt herself tilt her head, moving her neck a little closer in case his lips wanted to graze along its terrain.

Was the air conditioning broken? Why was it suddenly sweltering in the dining room? And why was her stomach in her chest? How was that even anatomically possible? Where was that thump-thump, thump-thump sound coming from in her ears?

"Does what bother me?" As the music slowly faded, she leaned slightly back and looked at him, seeing the quiet intensity in his gaze as he traced her face, mere inches from his, with his eyes. *How can anyone's eyes be that crystal clear blue?*

"My age."

"Why would that bother me?" Stratton wasn't sure if she was even breathing any longer. She should be able to hear herself breathing because the music had stopped, but they were standing still with only a whisper between them while that thump-thumping in her chest was growing louder by the minute.

"Stratton, I…"

"Sorry, forgot my phone." Noah entered the room, and Everest stepped away from Stratton, breaking their connection.

Noah picked up his phone. "And forgot to turn off the record player." He walked over as the record moved silently on the turntable. He walked over and turned it off. "Night."

"Night." Stratton leaned over and picked up her shoes, heading to her room. "Everest, no, your age doesn't bother me. Goodnight."

"Goodnight, Stratton."

Stratton felt Everest's gaze following her as she made her way to her room down the hall and closed the door. *What was he about to say? Was there any possibility he was about to go somewhere we can't possibly go? No, that doesn't make sense. We were caught up in the moment, that's all.* Stratton hung up her dress and put away her shoes. She slipped on a silk nightgown she hadn't tried on in years, not questioning why she felt like putting on such a dressed-up form of sleepwear.

She'd analyze the evening more tomorrow when she called her sister. A chat with Savannah always helped clear her mind and ensure she was on the right track.

She quickly took off her makeup and slipped under the sheet, half wondering if Everest would knock on the door to finish their conversation, half wondering what her response would be if he did.

Nine

"How was the beach?" Stratton asked Savannah while they chatted on the phone. Stratton, who struggled sitting still and relaxing when inside, used the time to catch up on laundry and do some light cleaning.

"It was marvelous. We had the best time. I told Charles that all of us should go with our families, including grandkids, and get several beach houses beside each other. I think it would be amazing. We spent a lot of time in the water, snorkeling, looking for sand dollars, and wading out to the sandbar. We even found a great charter for a dinner cruise."

"It sure would give us some lasting memories, and I'd love to spend more time with the grandkids. It's been hard having Harper and them so far away. Those years they lived with me on the homestead were so precious."

"Speaking of the homestead, Noah sent me a picture."

Stratton knew exactly which picture he sent, so why did she suddenly feel like a kid with her hand caught in the cookie jar? Noah had texted her both pictures from last night, and no one knew that she had looked at the one of just Everest and her longer than she should have. Was she more afraid of what Savannah would think about that picture or more afraid of the feelings that surfaced when she stared at it? "Oh, He did, did he?"

"Yeah, he did. Do you have something you want to tell me about?"

"Savannah, it's not what you think." *Noah! He probably laughed when he sent it. I knew I might have to worry about gossip from outside of my home, but*

I didn't realize I had to worry about it from within! "Everest's just a guy I met when I was in Pennsylvania. He's working down the road, and Noah got involved. Well, long story short, he's staying in the basement."

Savannah laughed. "Stratton, Noah sent me a picture of his new herd of cattle and the goats, but please, tell me more about your new roommate."

Noah! Why didn't she think to ask which picture he had sent first? Time to simply acknowledge Everest and not make a big deal out of last night. "He's a gardener who focuses on restoring historic gardens. Our families go back several generations to the Revolutionary War, and through that connection, he's become a friend."

"And how good of a friend has he become?" She teasingly asked.

She knew Savannah was smiling on the other end of the line.

"Savannah, I barely know him. I'm letting him rent the basement because he helped me out in Pennsylvania, and I couldn't let him stay in the barn, which may be fine for animals but is not habitable for humans."

"Oh, is he that random stranger you mentioned who gave you shelter for the night during the storm?"

Stratton's mind flew back to that conversation with her sister. She had briefly told her about meeting Everest and their conversation about their ancestors, but she had left out some details of that evening, such as how he had made her the most delicious dinner, had given her his clothes and his bed so where she was snuggled up warm and cozy all night, holding his warm hand by his bedside. She knew that she had not mentioned how the air had filled with electricity as chemistry was building between them. Yes, these things had happened, but were not worth mentioning because there was no use planting seeds that could sprout into anything with little imagination.

"Yeah, I think so."

"Is this the same random stranger you've managed to bring up each time we've talked since you met him? Who's written you not once but twice with, as you put it, impeccable handwriting of yore? Are we talking about him?"

"Um, Savannah, I don't really remember saying all of that." Rambling never served her well.

"Stratton, I've known you my entire life, and you know that I know you, right?"

"Of course, I know that." Stratton found her duster and began cleaning her decorative tables. *Why is it so hot in here?* She made a mental note that she really needed to get an HVAC person over to inspect the unit.

"I also know how you're going to react when I say this."

"Really, Savannah, I don't know where you're going." Oh, yes, she did know, and she was ready to reject anything that Savannah said.

"Stratton, hear me out. Stop whatever you're doing and listen to me."

Stratton dropped her arm and stood still.

"It's OK to like someone. You're terrible at hiding things, and you don't have to hide that from me. I didn't want to ask you about him because I knew you were scared. I also knew it would take a lot for you to ever like someone, let alone commit to a relationship, after your divorce. Charles and I have met some great guys but have never pushed or rushed you because I know you."

Stratton felt as if a huge weight had been lifted from her shoulders. She had been telling herself that what she had been feeling was not real, but that lie was beginning to take its toll on her. She felt the tears building as she moved to sit down on the couch.

"Sis, if you like this guy, then I will be your biggest cheerleader. We are entering the autumn of our lives on this earth, so if you have one more chance at summer love, I will tell you to pursue it."

"He's forty-seven." She waited for the reproach, but the line was quiet. "Savannah, are you still there?"

"Do it."

The rest of their conversation centered around their children and the family beach trip. They promised to talk again later in the week. Savannah didn't press her about Everest, though she'd given Stratton so much to think about.

After she hung up from talking to Savannah, Stratton stayed on the couch, reflecting on their conversation. She thought back to the day she had met Everest. They had realized they were connected through their relatives, and if it hadn't been for the storm, she would have simply thanked him for the copy of the letter, and everything would have stopped there.

But it hadn't stopped there. That blasted storm had forced them together, and while he was under no obligation to take care of her, he did. He had prepared and shared a meal with her, given her some of his own clothes, as well as his bed to sleep in, and provided a safe, warm haven from the storm raging outside. Why had he done it? Was it possible his kindness was more than just kindness? Was he feeling something between the two of them, too?

She let her thoughts continue to flow freely. *I could get it all out there.* She thought about their embrace as she parted, holding his hands, dancing, tucked close to him. *Could it be that he was just being nice, or was there more to it?* She could simply ask him, but she'd be absolutely mortified if she was reading things wrong. Maybe it would be better if she intentionally dropped a few hints and let him know she was interested. *How do you even flirt at sixty?* She knew acting like an infatuated schoolgirl around him wasn't appropriate, but why did she catch herself feeling that way? None of it made sense. *This is ridiculous.* He was 13 years younger than her and probably wasn't interested in a romantic relationship with her. She doubted she could ever be with someone much younger than her.

Her thoughts wandered down the path of commonality, doubting there was much they had in common. Similar taste in music: check. Love of gardening: check. A relationship with Yehovah and a commitment to His ways: check.

Trying to analyze everything was getting confusing. Stratton knew that she had only one place to turn: to the One who knew her best, her Creator, for peace about the situation. She spent the next hour in Scripture and prayer. Feeling more at peace yet still a little unsure of her next steps, she decided that some light strength training with some free weights would help expend some energy and provide some ideas for how best to move forward. As she worked through her program in one of the guest bedrooms, she forced herself to think about what activities to do when Finley came to visit and not about the intriguing, handsome, blue-eyed man living in her basement.

* * * * *

Everest's morning was jam-packed with a whirlwind of information and touring Milky Way Farms with Lyle and Bernadette Turner, the husband-and-wife team who were taking over the operations from his parents. These folks wanted him to accomplish a lot in a short period of time. They had planned a summer festival and needed multiple themed gardens representing different countries, with indigenous plants exhibited from each country.

Everest had been given a team of twenty people to help him get the gardens ready, and he had already met with each of them. Lunch was fast approaching, so he decided to drive into town and try out the company credit card at the hardware store. Then, he found a quiet place to eat the lunch that Stratton had packed for him.

Though he had only been in town once, Everest had no trouble finding the hardware store. He parked his truck under a tree and headed toward the store's opening.

"Hey, Everest!" Noah hollered from the parking lot, where he was talking to some other men.

Everest approached them. "Hi, fellas."

"Everest, these here are my buds, Ralston and Harlow."

The two ball-capped men each gave Everest a head nod.

"Everest is our family friend staying for a spell."

Everest was touched. Noah didn't call him a renter or a tenant but had said he was a family friend. He sure liked that boy.

And he sure liked that boy's momma but hadn't the foggiest idea of how to tell her. He'd been trying to think of a way from that moment he took her hand and led her to his bed. He'd wanted to share that he was stirred by her, not in an inappropriate way, but in a way that had intrigued and surprised him. Gobsmacked by the likes of an unassuming woman he saw as just that. He honestly thought they were the same age when he first saw her, and he still didn't see the age difference she had alluded to last night. She didn't look a bit older than him, especially not wearing that dress she had worn to dinner, nor in the way she danced or how she instinctively moved closer to him when he placed his hand on her waist. The way she rested her head on his chest had made him dizzy with delight. He had almost blurted out that he liked her right then and there. For him, age wasn't even a factor, other than, they were both losing time because he was not finding a way to tell her what he was feeling.

He felt that she was picking up on the subtle hints he was throwing down, but she always blew them off as inconsequential. She'd already shown a propensity for that when he fumbled his words at the train.

He just needed to be clear, not vague.

He felt that this was something quite unique, and Everest wanted to make sure he was walking with integrity and uprightness in pursuing a woman's heart. His first phone call after she had left his cottage in Pennsylvania had been to his parents. He needed their advice and guidance. His father's counsel had been to be honest with his intentions to pursue her. So, he had to show her his intentions and prove he was worthy of her affection.

He was going to need to step up his game and find the right time to tell her about his feelings and the thoughts he was wrestling with. Perhaps she, too, was feeling some of the same things. *What if she wasn't interested in him?* If, after letting her know what he was feeling, she really wasn't interested in him, then he would need to move on; it'd be too hard on him to continue staying in the basement.

"I see you brought your lunch." Noah, interrupting his musings, gestured at Everest's small cooler, packed by Stratton.

"I did. I was just going to have a quick bite after I do some shopping."

"Heads up, if she put a note in there, she's been known to quiz you about it later. She's a lifelong educator and can't seem to stop instructing."

"Thanks for the advice." Everest's phone buzzed. He glanced down at the text message from one of the new team members asking for help on where to put a fountain for the Italian garden. "I've got to get back to work now. I'll let you gentlemen get on with your day. Nice to meet you both. Noah, I'll see you later."

"Have a good 'un!"

Everest sat on his tailgate and opened his lunchbox. He secretly hoped there was a note and couldn't wait to read its contents.

He saw she had packed him a hearty lunch of two turkey burgers, broccoli salad, an apple, and some almonds. He moved them around, looking for a note. There it was! Like a piece of delicate treasure, he lifted out the napkin with a passage from Psalm 90 written on it in beautiful handwriting:

Let the favor of the Lord our God be upon us.

Establish the work of our hands for us —

Yes, establish the work of our hands.

Everest nodded and smiled to himself. He knew that Scripture well, and as he bit into one of the turkey burgers, he wondered why Stratton had chosen that passage to give to him.

His resolve was to pursue her at a patient pace and prove to her that he wasn't like the other men she'd known. Though he'd never dated a divorced woman before, he figured the trauma probably ran deep, which meant there would be challenges in winning over her heart. He knew enough to know she would be hesitant and overly cautious. He also knew her children would initially circle the wagons until they knew him and realized he meant no harm to her.

He anticipated resistance, insecurities, and anxiety as initial roadblocks that would have to be delicately handled, as delicate as the hand he'd held onto by his bedside, or at dinner his first night in her home, and just the night before as they swayed to the music. He could still envision their dance and feel how she felt in his arms. He had used it as a way to memorize all he could of her. They were close enough that when he breathed, he could smell the fragrance that was uniquely her. He didn't know what floral fragrance she had on, but it was intoxicating and hypnotic, as well as slightly risky because it conjured up thoughts of what might have happened if he had kissed her ear lobe instead of just brushing his lips along it. Had she noticed? Had she felt something? Was he imagining things when it appeared she had moved her head so he could access her neck and pepper it with kisses? His lips were headed that way when she moved to speak to him. Perhaps Noah's untimely entrance as the song ended was more of a rescue. Everest wasn't sure that he would have known how to react if Stratton had been receptive if he had followed his instincts and kissed her. The daydreaming swirled around him while he ate his meal, a meal that had been prepared by hands he couldn't wait to hold onto again, even if he wasn't sure how that occurrence would come to pass.

As he finished his lunch and hopped off his tailgate, Everest was determined to be focused, clear, mindful, and prayerful about each step moving forward with Stratton. He didn't know exactly what the next steps would be, but he vowed to remain in constant communication with the One who did. That realization made him smile to himself as he turned and entered the hardware store.

Ten

"Were you at a costume party?" Harper asked in her phone conversation with Stratton. "Noah sent me the pic, and I guess that other guy was the rando you met in Pennsylvania, and Noah decided to rent to? Mom, you don't even know him. Let Finley and I at least run a background check." Protective Harper had shown up in full force.

"Harper, he's harmless."

"Yeah, I was just listening to a podcast, and that's exactly what these people said about the serial killer that had been living among them."

"Come and meet him then. Did you google him? You can find out all about him from his resume and reputation right there on the Internet."

"Mom, I don't have time to come out there and vet him. Anyway, Whitten and I want you and Noah to come here for the Fourth of July. We're doing a massive week-long festival with the town, and I've been working really hard on the entertainment. I think you'll like it."

"I'm sure I will." Her first thought had jumped to Everest, and unlike in the past, when she would have pushed it down to the fathoms below, she let the thought surface this time. She wanted to include him. "If Noah and I haven't become Everest's victims yet, do you mind if we extend the invite to him?" Did Harper suspect anything? Had she asked casually enough that her real feelings for Everest were hidden from her daughter? Now that she knew she felt something for him, she felt an obligation to let Everest know before anyone else, though; he at least deserved that much.

"Whatever, he's Noah's friend, I don't care. I just really want you to come, OK?"

"Of course. I will be there."

"Good, well, I have to take the kids to their piano lessons now."

"I love you, sweetheart."

"I love you, too, Mom. And just so you know, you don't have to drive. Whitten and I will buy your plane tickets if you want to fly."

"Noah hates flying, so we will just make a fun road trip out of it."

"OK, bye."

"Bye." Stratton ended the call and let out a sigh of relief. She metaphorically patted herself on the back. No one suspected a thing, not Noah, not Harper, and she was pretty sure she could keep it from Finley.

She knew that if she and Everest became an item, there would be some serious sit-down conversations with her grown children. No one had witnessed the trauma and stigma divorce had wrought on Stratton during those early years other than those precious children of hers. No one had brought her more joy and comfort through those years than those same children. She knew she wouldn't have survived without them, but she had survived and was now thriving, so much so that she faced a possible opportunity to have a relationship with someone. She wanted to share her heart with her children so they understood she didn't need protection any longer. She was ready to give love a try again, which caused her to be equally thrilled and terrified at the prospect.

The rest of the day was spent doing the things that she normally did, with one subtle difference: Everest was constantly invading her thoughts. She went through the motions of tidying the house and getting dinner started, but today, one thing was different: she was going to attempt to flirt with Everest, and for that, she needed just the right dinner outfit. The one that Finley had chosen for her was perfect.

As she pulled the outfit from her closet, she could see Finley's influence shining through, which was how she ended up buying the dark-washed skinny jeans to begin with. Paired with a loose button-down pink cotton shirt, she fiddled with how high to button it. She didn't want to come off prudish, but she also didn't want to look like she belonged on the streets of Las Vegas. She settled on leaving the top two buttons open. Though she had vowed not to be the schoolgirl type, she snapped a picture of herself in the mirror and sent it to Savannah.

Titanic never would have sunk if
you'd been on board. Glacier woulda
melted right away!

Ha, thx. I'm gonna go for it.
Pray I don't mess it up.

Hello?! He's living in your house. He could
have literally chosen anywhere else and he
showed up at your door. He is definitely
giving off some strong signals. Go for it, Sis!!!

I'll let you know what happens.

A drop of jasmine essential oil on each wrist, light eye makeup, and there she was, barefoot in the kitchen, in her Finely-influenced outfit, making dinner for the three of them. As enlightened and as educated as she was, she didn't buy into modern feminism's screams for what a modern woman should be; she believed that The Creator had made them, man and woman and that they both would be more empowered and content in their respective roles when following His Design as laid out in Scripture. She wanted this night to be a perfect reflection of His Design and could think of nothing more rewarding than preparing a meal for these two men and preparing to let Everest know she was interested subtly.

Noah entered the kitchen. "Shew boy, them cows can kick!" He was holding his wrist.

Stratton went from Chef to Doctor instantly. "What happened?"

"I's messin' with the herd and got a calf away from its momma. I knew I shouldn't have done it, but I reached to grab it, and she got me."

His wrist had already doubled in size.

"Noah, this looks bad. As in, E-R bad." Stratton glanced at her open recipe book. *So much for trying to take that first step.* She was going to make a colonial-styled turkey and see what Everest thought. Maybe he'd had it before, maybe not. It was her way of sharing their initial connection. She quickly put away the perishable ingredients.

"Nah, some ice will help." He winced as he wrapped the ice pack around his wrist.

"No, it won't. I'll get my purse." She went to her room, put on her slides, and came back out. "Let me text Everest."

> **Change of plans for dinner, assuming you were dining in. Noah hurt his wrist. Nothing life-threatening. Headed to get it looked at. Help yourself to anything in the house or there are a ton of gift cards in the kitchen drawer closest to the garage. Plenty to go and do especially in Franklin.**

She got into the SUV. Her phone buzzed. It was Everest.

Do you need me to meet you?

She paused. Her heart had stopped after the word "me." Do you need me? She hadn't depended on a man since her marriage dissolved, and when she had depended on Dexter, it had ended in disappointment almost every time. She knew curbing her independence wouldn't be easy if she entered a relationship.

> **No, we will be fine. Be back later. Hope your first day at work was enjoyable. Can't wait to hear about it.**

Stratton and Noah entered the house hours later.

Her phone buzzed.

Busy day at work, but I picked up enough Chinese for you two. It's in bags in the oven, probably still warm.

> **Thanks.**

"There's Chinese food if you want some." She told Noah as she started down the hall and went to her room. "I'm not hungry. I'm just going to go to bed."

"Thanks, Mom."

Stratton closed her bedroom door and leaned her back against it for a moment. Letting out a heavy sigh, she pushed herself forward and headed to the bathroom to prepare for bed. Everest text just as Stratton started getting changed.

Noah OK?

> **Not even a sprain. Just going to be a bad bruise.**
> **How was your first day at your new job?**

Grinning to herself, she hit 'send,' then grabbed her silk nightgown and pulled it over her head.

I felt like He established the work of my hands. :)

She smiled at his text and started brushing her teeth.

> **Did you get to tour the grounds?**

Practically skipping to her bed, Stratton turned down the covers and grabbed some pillows, propping herself up against the headboard. She felt herself getting excited as she held her phone, eagerly awaiting his next text.

I did. Gorgeous property. It's a mighty big
undertaking. I didn't know I'd have a large
staff to manage. Might need you to teach me
some of your management skills, you
being a department chair and all.

> **And here I was, thinking I'd have a**
> **sabbatical from all of that.**

You can take the girl outta the university, but
you can't take the university outta the girl.

Her heart fluttered. *He called me a girl. He thinks of me as a girl.*

My best tips for management are true servant
leadership, ensuring everyone feels listened to,
not just heard, and managing expectations
from the start.

Wise words.

Thanks for coming to my Ted Talk. :)

Thanks for taking me on as a pupil.

Happy to encounter someone eager to learn.

When the instructor is enthusiastic, it helps.
Great reminder for my job at Milky Way.
   I need to remember to be excited about the
project to keep them engaged.

I'm sure that won't be a problem.

Why?

*OK, Stratton, this is your chance. You can do this. You can send a
text letting him know you are interested.*
   "Because you are mesmerizing." She sent the text, proud
of herself for actually taking that first step, and waited anxiously for
his reply.

Sorry, I don't understand.

Stratton stared at her phone. *What didn't he understand?* She
looked back at the text message she'd sent to him. Somehow, it had

auto-corrected to: Because you are a merman. Stratton was mortified. There was no way to pass that one off and recover from that mistake coolly. She needed just to shut it down.

> **Sorry, auto-correct. I need to go to bed.**
> **Goodnight.**

Ha, I get it. Goodnight.

She would never try to flirt via text again. As she settled into her bed, she realized that today had been a total wash. He hadn't seen the cute outfit, hadn't eaten a dinner made especially for him, and hadn't received her flirty text. *Guess that's three strikes, and I'm out!*

She needed to dedicate some more time and brainpower to figuring out ways to overcome these types of obstacles. Was there an art to all of this? Could it be simple? Or were matters of the heart always so complex?

Eleven

After a long night of tossing and turning, Stratton began the morning in full-on reality mode, with no makeup, gray cotton shorts, gray T-shirt, and glasses. She looked drab and dull in a conscious effort to separate herself from that nightie-wearing texting temptress she clearly was not. The internal chastisement would only increase in volume when she had to face Everest, so it was best to meet it head-on in frumpy clothes and with some gray hair showing through.

He would see her for who she really was, aged and out of touch with his generation. She thought that she had put enough distance between them in her mind, but as soon as Everest entered the kitchen, her heart betrayed her and sped up when she saw him. Could he hear it beating against her chest? Did he hear the sharp intake of breath at the sight of him?

Dressed in khakis and a mint green polo shirt, he made everything look dangerously attractive. He had a backpack in tow and appeared hurried. "There's a water pipe burst, so I have to get over to the farm early."

"Oh, I haven't made the lunches yet." *Like this dowdy lady does for all in her home.*

"Don't worry about it. I'll pick up something. I'm happy to make us dinner."

"I've got a DAR meeting tonight, but I can get dinner started for you and Noah."

"No, it's fine. We'll manage. I need to run. Have a good day."

"You, too."

Everest exited, leaving her standing there feeling slightly dejected that they wouldn't have breakfast together. She liked being around Everest, but who wouldn't? Even though they would never be romantically involved, they could still be friends, couldn't they?

Stratton, still pondering the events of the last 24 hours, heard Noah up and moving, so she cracked some eggs and put the turkey bacon on, then made his lunch, though she wasn't sure he would be going anywhere today with his bruised wrist. Noah assured her he could still do his chores and headed out after breakfast.

Stratton cleaned up the kitchen and then headed to the couch to give Savannah a call.

Savannah answered on the first ring. "Tell me everything!"

"You mean how Noah hurt his wrist, and we spent hours at the E-R last night? How Everest never got to see me in the outfit I spent too much time choosing, or how I bumbled a flirty text and proved to him I am closer to being an elderly woman than a datable option? Where should I start?" Her voice betrayed her true feelings.

"Oh, honey. I'm sorry."

"Savannah, I was a fool. Did I tell you I pulled out a silk nightgown? Not even one of those long ones, and I'm pretty sure it needed a pair of shorts to go with it. It was a gift from my bridal shower and still had the tags on it. No one is ever going to see me in that, so why did I think wearing it was a good idea?"

"Because he's making you feel something." There was a musical tone to her voice.

"Foolish is what I feel."

Savannah laughed. "How many love songs involve foolishness in the lyrics? I'd say you're right on track."

"And I'd say you give bad advice. All that summer, autumn deep-thinking drivel."

"Stratton, if you really don't want to be in a relationship with him, I support that, but if you're sabotaging it on purpose because you don't believe that you deserve a chance at happiness, then I'm not your ally in that. When Charles found me crumpled on the floor with three kids under the age of four running wild through our house, he picked me up and asked what he could do. At that point, I was done with it all. I was so overwhelmed and felt like everyone wanted a part of me, and I had nothing of myself left. I didn't want to be married. I didn't want these needy kids that kept me up sometimes, literally twenty-four hours a day. I was supposed to be preparing to go back to work, but I didn't know how to do it. We would be rubbing nickels together if I didn't go back to work. I felt like I had made the biggest mistake of my life by marrying and having a family. I had put all of this pressure on myself to be perfect and to perform everything flawlessly. I wanted to be the perfect wife, mother, and employee. Charles was scared but took charge of things. He called Momma and his mom, who both showed up and helped me for the next three months. Their help saved my marriage. I wasn't honest with Charles before they got there to help. You know how Charles is. Cues and innuendo don't work. He needed me to come right out and say that I didn't want to go back to work. He also needed me to say that I needed help at home. Those three months were hard ones, but in the end, I learned I had to be honest with myself and ask for help. I also learned that I had quit trying to be what I thought everyone around me expected to be or wanted me to be. I know you don't have Momma to talk to about this situation, but I love you just as much as she did, and I want you to know that you can be honest with yourself and Everest."

Stratton's cheeks were wet, and she wiped under her eyes. "I honestly don't know if I'm ready. I keep getting cold feet, and nothing seems to be working in my favor."

"Has he shown you any interest?"

"Well, I didn't want to read into it, but we held hands, shared a long hug when I left his cottage and slow-danced to Nat King Cole."

"Oh my gosh, Stratton! He likes you! And I'll bet he doesn't want to mess it up, so he's waiting for you to let him know you're ready. Don't let one text flub it up."

Stratton had a lot to ponder. Savannah was right; one mess-up didn't mean she should stop altogether. She'd go to her Father and search His Word for what she should do, then prayerfully find a way to let Everest know she was ready for the next step.

* * * * *

The following week was a busy one for the whole house. Finley was due to arrive on Friday, and between the DAR meeting, Noah's projects, Everest's schedule, and Stratton prepping for Finley, the three housemates hadn't shared a meal since Monday.

On Thursday, Stratton went shopping to get everything she needed for the Sunday afternoon cookout she planned to host. She'd already invited some of her friends, as well as some of Everest's co-workers, along with a few folks from the community. The early part of the weekend would just be low-key, enjoying a Shabbat dinner on Friday night and relaxing on Saturday.

Stratton had the challah bread baking when Finley and Gabriel walked through the door.

"Mom, we're here!" Finley announced, looking as though she had just stepped off the runway, in white shorts and with a purple denim shirt tucked in.

Stratton greeted Finley with a hug and a handshake for Gabriel. "Come on in. I've got a veggie tray for snacking if you want."

"Sure!"

Finley and Gabriel came into the kitchen and found seats at the island. "So, we're all checked in at the Airbnb, and I want to take Gabe downtown before dinner. We saw Noah on the way in, and he wants to give us a ride around the farm." Finley took a bite of a celery stick.

"Well, I'm just going to finish making dinner. It's a colonial turkey."

Finley, being Finley, didn't offer to help, but Stratton wasn't surprised. "Yeah, that sounds delicious, Mom. So, by the way, Gabe actually has a family history here. Where's that guy that knows history?"

"You mean Everest?"

"Yeah, we wanted to ask him about Gabe's family."

"Baby, he's not a historian. He restores historic gardens."

"Oh. Well, maybe he knows someone who can help."

Did she really not remember that Stratton was a history professor?

"You could swing by the library and look through the archives," Stratton suggested.

"Yeah, I guess we could do that, too."

Stratton noticed Gabriel had hardly looked up from his phone, which made it hard to start and carry a conversation.

"Did you get the pool started yet?" Finley stood and walked over to the French doors opening to the deck. "No garden, either? What have you been doing on your sabbatical?"

Oh, Finley, if you only knew. Hair, makeup, clothes, just regular high school behavior, with an emphasis on that senior year. "I've been busy with the DAR. We are planning to visit Harper for the Fourth of July. Are you able to come?"

"Gabe doesn't know if he can take that much time off, so it's up in the air."

Why, Finley, why?! Why do you let Gabe dictate what you do with your time? Though it wasn't an exact parallel, Stratton admitted to herself that she allowed thoughts of Everest to occupy a lot of her time. She was constantly thinking about him when making their meal choices, thinking about him when she chose her clothes, thinking about their interactions, and he always seemed to be the last person she thought about as she drifted off to sleep each night. At that moment, Stratton knew she had come to the point where something needed to be done; she couldn't keep ignoring the energy she felt between them. *I am done with hinting. I'm just going to tell him I'm ready, and if he feels the same way, then let's go for it.*

Stratton, realizing that Finley had been talking about the other things she and Gabriel planned to do while here, focused back on the conversation. She visited a bit more with Finley and sort of Gabriel before they took off for a tour of the small town.

She decided to text Everest.

Hope you're hungry. Have a fun surprise for dinner.

Sounds great. I'll pick up dessert.
See you later.

Stratton combed through her closet, trying to locate the perfect summer outfit. She settled on a belted, green foliage-printed, sleeveless dress. It wouldn't be too dressy to catch Finley's attention, but perhaps dressy enough to catch Everest's.

Twelve

The savory smell of colonial-style turkey and fresh bread filled the air. Potatoes au Gratin, sautéed asparagus, and fresh salad rounded off the photo-worthy spread atop Stratton's dining room table.

"Smells delicious, Mom," Noah said as he entered with Finley and Gabriel.

"Thank you."

"All of my favorite sides. Thank you, Mom!" Finley said, giving Stratton a side hug.

Everest came in shortly thereafter, and the Shabbat meal began in the dining room.

Stratton thought she saw Everest glance her way when she shared she'd prepared a colonial turkey. The glimmer from his eyes and his smile as she served him made her think he must have known she'd done this for him. She let her hand briefly brush over his as she placed his plate before him, hoping that he realized that it was intentional. After all, it had been a while since their dance in this very dining room. Was her touch able to send signals to Everest like he did to her? The surreptitious graze on his hand thrilled her, but he didn't seem to react. She found it trivial how she had almost hoped he'd give her hand a pat or maybe one to her arm or even maybe to her hip.

Everest opened with prayer. Everyone was also given a time of reflection if they wanted to share anything they found praiseworthy. The conversation flowed as everyone got to know one another.

"How did you all begin the path of exploring the Hebrew roots of our faith?" Everest asked.

"Mom said we were going camping for a week, and it was actually a Sukkot celebration," Finley answered for the group, even though Stratton felt the question was more directed toward her. "She ate up the Bible study sessions, and when we got home, she totally eliminated any traces of pagan influences, her words, not mine, and started weekly Shabbat dinners."

Stratton had taken the kids to celebrate that Fall feast with a group of new friends, and it had been life-changing for her. She reordered her life to fulfill as much of Scripture as she could and took to learning, studying, and meditating on the proper context of Scripture.

"What about you, Everest?" Stratton asked.

"A professor in college planted some seeds, and I took them to my folks for some deep discussion. Come to find out, they were wrestling with understanding Scripture from the Hebraic mindset as well, and we began the journey together. We went a little far at first and had to back off the temptation of becoming legalistic. What was the spirit of the Torah, not the letter? Scripture says the Torah gives freedom, but a lot of teachers have taught differently and do not understand the proper context. We had to find out for ourselves, and I feel like those were times of tremendous scales being lifted from our eyes and embracing what it means to be set apart."

"Well said," Stratton nodded.

"Interesting. So, legalism isn't a good thing," Finley mentioned.

Stratton knew that was directed toward her and her rules about cohabitation between couples.

"But boundaries are," Stratton patted Finley's hand.

Finley rolled her eyes and then started talking about new listings she had in Denver, which carried them through until the end of the meal.

Everest presented a Chantilly cake decorated with berries and edible flowers for dessert.

"That looks wonderful," Stratton said.

"Let me grab some plates and clean forks." Everest disappeared into the kitchen.

"Yeah, it was the funniest thing. We were getting fried pies and met Everest, getting this cake from Jessi. She is so talented. I can't wait for our hike tomorrow," Finley offered.

"Hike?" Stratton asked.

"Yeah, we're doubling with Jessi and Everest. I guess they're like a couple or something. There's some cemetery with flowers or plants that they want to see. She thinks she's seen Gabe's last name on a headstone, so it's going to be so cool to check it out."

Everest returned with the forks.

Stratton didn't look at him as he sliced the cake, putting a piece on each plate. As he passed around the plates, Stratton didn't look in his direction. *You waited too long on that one, didn't you? Now he's gone and made a date with Jessi. And why shouldn't he? She's adorable.* She took a bite of cake. *And she makes excellent cake.*

Stratton tried to stay engaged with the group conversation, but she couldn't bear to look at Everest.

She felt so ridiculously foolish. She had actually begun to think he was interested in her, but maybe he was just being polite. Or he was just a Don Juan making his rounds through the town. Either way, she needed to let go of the idea that she could have a life of romance and excitement like the characters from the fiction faith-based books she read. Real life was what was real. It wasn't like those romance stories or movies where her demographic was noticeably absent as the main character. Maybe there was a reason for that. Could it be that passion and ardor were only meant for a season, one that she had long passed?

Stratton gave an inward sigh as her shoulders seemed to sag just a little from the weight of everything. Maybe she was just meant to simply have a supporting role in her own story moving forward, the aging grandmother on her homestead trying to serve the community and avoid becoming a shut-in or a crazy cat lady.

She sat up with the group until she couldn't stifle a yawn. "I've got to get some sleep. Will you be over for breakfast?" She asked Finley.

Shabbat breakfasts often included honey poured over leftover challah bread and fruit, as well as Greek yogurt smoothies.

"I think we'll have time before our hike," Finley said. "Goodnight, Mom."

"Night." She gave Finley a quick hug, then walked to the kitchen to get a bottle of water.

Everest followed. "Hey, are you OK?"

"I'm fine." *Not true.*

"This is not how I wanted this to go, but..."

"Everest, I'm gonna stop you right there. I just want to go to bed. I'm really, really tired." *Don't cry now. You knew this was all too good to be true, so just take a deep breath and get away from him.* "I'd really like to enjoy the rest of the weekend with my daughter, so could we talk about whatever you want to talk about after the party on Sunday?"

"OK, then. Goodnight." He looked deflated.

"Who's up for a game of Monopoly?" Stratton heard Noah ask as she took her water and went to her room. She could hear the sounds of uproarious laughter filtering down the hall as the younger generation continued on with the camaraderie into the night.

* * * * *

He had to do something to get Stratton's attention.

Everest sat in the media room in one of the comfy chairs with his Bible opened on his lap. Focusing on reading was hard. *What had changed during dinner?*

He replayed the evening's events. *She made that turkey with me in mind, didn't she? She looked like she was trying to tell me that she was interested with her smile and that dress. Was I imagining it, or was that sweep over my hand meant to convey something deeper? Was she invading my space on purpose?* He'd noticed how the dress hugged Stratton's figure in all the right places, and with as close as she'd been to him, he'd wanted to give her an affectionate touch.

Somewhere between when he went to get the plates and forks for the cake and when he had returned, something had happened, causing Stratton to not look at him.

If it had been just him and her, with Noah, he would have reached out and patted her hand and asked what was wrong. He was comfortable in Noah seeing his early pursuit of Stratton. He didn't want to hide it from Noah that he was interested in her. There were times it even seemed Noah knew that he liked Stratton.

But he couldn't pat her hand in front of Finley and Gabriel.

Finley seemed to be one who might swiftly jump to conclusions, and though those conclusions might have been accurate, it wouldn't do for Stratton to find out he was interested in her that way.

70

He just didn't understand why she wouldn't look at him the rest of the evening. There were no side glances, shared looks, or smiles; nothing. He admitted that he enjoyed those moments with her and realized without those things, it hurt a little when she ignored him.

He glanced over at his phone on the table beside his chair. He could text her. He could ask what had happened, but she was probably already asleep and might not respond. She said it had to wait until Sunday. He knew he needed to respect that, reminding himself Stratton would tell him when she was ready. Breaching a boundary she had set could wreck everything. He didn't want to do that.

Keeping silent about what he was feeling had gone on long enough.

It was time to share his interests with Stratton, but it had to be special, something from his heart to hers. He smiled as he thought of how to best share this with her. He knew that he needed the right timing and the right setting, which, for him, meant a garden setting, but how could he create the perfect atmosphere without her noticing?

He worked through his thoughts and ideas and even drew out a few sketches before deciding that the best course of action would be to pray about it.

* * * * *

It was late afternoon when the crew returned from their hike.

Stratton was sitting on the couch when they came through the door. She noticed that Everest and Noah were missing from the group.

"Where's your brother?"

Finley made a face. "Oh, it was too weedy for us, so we left Noah with Everest and Jessi. I just wanted to come by and see if we could take you and Noah to dinner tonight in Nashville."

"That's fine." *Because I have no plans and probably will never have Saturday night plans ever again with anyone.*

"Great. We'll go get showers and be back to get you and Noah at six," Finley said as she and Gabriel headed back out the door.

"I'll be ready."

Stratton text Noah to be home and ready for dinner by six. She didn't bother texting Everest to let him know that he'd be on his own for dinner. Let him and Jessi figure it out. She went to find something suitable to wear to downtown Nashville.

* * * * *

Finley had chosen a trendy rooftop grill where they had spent the dinner hour laughing and sharing plans for the summer. Gabriel spent most of the time playing on his phone but did join in the conversation a little. The group decided to walk around downtown, where they took plenty of pictures and selfies to document the excursion.

Stratton picked up on Finley's boredom with Gabriel, especially after seeing her flirt with a couple of guys while they waited in line for the bathroom. Though she thought about asking Finley for some tips on flirting, she realized that would cause unnecessary drama. Besides, there was no need to get flirting pointers from her daughter since she'd already decided she wasn't moving forward with Everest. Hadn't he actually made that decision when he made the date with Jessi?

Stratton glanced down at her watch. *How could it already be after eleven?* "Finley, it's after eleven, and we still have an hour's drive home."

Noah chimed in, "Yeah, I need to get back since I've got to be up early to deal with the animals." They headed to the car and back towards Lynnville.

Finley and Gabriel dropped off Stratton and Noah at the house and promised to be over to help set up for the party by ten o'clock the next morning.

As Stratton got ready for bed, she decided it was time to let go of her fanciful ideas of having a relationship with Everest and place things back in their proper order. The fantasy had gone on long enough. She didn't have any more time to waste.

Thirteen

Stratton knew how to throw a party. Most of the people she had invited were here, along with some neighbors who had dropped in to join in the fun. As she walked around speaking with each person, Stratton noticed Finley laughing with her brother while enjoying some watermelon. She hoped it reminded Finley to appreciate the simple things in life and remember what truly is important.

She noticed that Jessi, who had shown up bringing fried pies, had cheered the loudest for Everest during the fishing contest at their pond. She wasn't even upset as she watched Jessi be the first to hand him a towel when he took a misstep on the dock and fell in the water. She barely noticed the way Jessi laughed and looked at Everest, her hand lingering on his arm. She didn't care that Jessi loitered as the guests started leaving. *See, I am totally over him already.*

"Mom, our red-eye leaves at ten, so we gotta get down to the airport." Finley hugged Stratton.

As she held her daughter, she breathed in the special scent that only belonged to Finley. "Come back soon, honey. I miss seeing you here."

"Well, I've been talking to Harper, and there might be a spot near Little Rock where I might be closer."

What prompted that? Little Rock has never been on Finley's radar. Stratton didn't question her because she didn't want to scare her off. Arkansas would be a closer drive than Denver, so that was a plus.

"Keep me posted on what you do. Let me know when you land. I love you."

"I love you, too." Finley released herself from her mother's embrace and finished her goodbyes.

Noah had already closed up the barn and headed upstairs, so when the last of the guests had left, Stratton decided that the rest of the cleaning up would have to wait until morning; all she wanted was a hot bath and a few minutes to unwind from the busy, but fully rewarding, day.

She wondered if Jessi was downstairs in the basement with Everest. She was certain nothing immoral would happen, but she was curious if they were downstairs talking. *Would they be sitting close together? Would he be holding her hand? Would he be looking at Jessi with those gorgeous blue eyes of his? I need to not think like that; it's not any of my business what they do.*

Stratton dried her hands on the kitchen towel, then turned to head to her room.

Everest appeared in the kitchen.

So close. Another thirty seconds, and she would have been in her room for the night. She hadn't talked to him the whole afternoon and, right now, didn't really want to have the conversation that she knew they needed to have.

"Can I finish now?" Everest sounded a little salty with his request.

"With the clean up? Sure." *Tit for tat, Everest.* Stratton started to walk past him, a slight bounce in her step.

He reached out and lightly touched her arm, "I have something you need to see."

Stratton paused before him. That's how their relationship began at Valley Forge when he took her to his cabin. "What is it, Everest?"

Standing this close to him, she tried not to notice the smell that she had come to know as individually his or that he looked so good in that well-fitting t-shirt and jeans. She inadvertently took a small step back.

Looking at her, he said, "Come with me," and he held out his hand.

Last time. I'm only doing this one last time. It drove her crazy how she couldn't refuse him, how he could get her to do anything he wanted. *What was wrong with her?*

He led her out the deck doors, down the stairs, and toward the barn.

The night air had a slight crisp chill to it as they walked along, but she didn't feel it. Even though he was holding her hand, she was not reciprocating. She wondered why he was leading her to the barn. Where was Jessi? She hadn't seen her leave, so maybe she was in the barn waiting for them. Stratton hoped that whatever it was he wanted to show her would be over soon; she was beginning to get a little unnerved by the heat radiating from their hands up her arm, causing her to feel warm inside.

They neared Noah's barn apartment and paused just before the door.

"You've obviously been giving me the silent treatment for two reasons, which are actually one and the same, and I think I know why: you're jealous of Jessi."

Stratton yanked her hand away in a flash and abruptly turned to go back to the house. Before she could get fully turned, Everest reached for her arm and turned her to face him.

"You need to see why I didn't ask you on the hike." He opened the barn apartment door.

The space was bathed in a soft, golden glow from dozens of flickering candles scattered throughout. In every corner were bouquets of roses of various colors: deep crimson, blush pink, and ivory, tied with satin ribbons. The flowers' delicate perfume mingled with the warmth of the candlelight, creating a romantic, almost ethereal atmosphere. Everest earnestly watched Stratton's face as she glanced around the room.

"I don't understand," she whispered as she looked at him.

"On our hike the other day, we saw this gravestone of a fallen Civil War soldier with roses planted all around his resting place. On our way back, we met the property owner, who told us that every year after the soldier died, his widow would plant a new rose bush in his honor to remind others of the love they had shared. I asked him if I could get some cuttings at some point. So, Noah and Jessi, who means absolutely nothing to me, helped me cut these roses and bring them here. We set up everything this morning, and I told Noah that it was for work. After we had everything arranged tonight, I made it very clear to Jessi that I am not interested in her and nothing is going to happen between us." Everest gently took hold of both of Stratton's hands and slowly turned her to face him.

"Here's what I've been working up the courage all week long to say to you: Stratton, I had countless conversations and encounters with hundreds of people every day at Valley Forge, but it was different when I saw you. I was caught off balance from the moment we met, and I haven't been steady since." Everest paused, searching her face.

"I've been trying to subtly let you know, but I don't think I've been very good at it. I don't really know how to tell you this other than to just say it: there is a force that keeps pulling me to you, and I can't resist it anymore. I find myself drawn to you and want to be close to you, so I want you to know that I intend to pursue you and your affection."

Stratton looked up at him with tears in her eyes as relief encompassed her. "So, I wasn't imagining it?"

Everest smiled as he gave her hands a little squeeze. "Not at all."

"I've spent this entire week trying to think of how I could show you that I am interested in you."

"You have?"

Stratton shook her head with a light laugh, "Everest, this is a big step for me, and I wasn't sure how to tell you that I was ready to like someone again. I tried flirting with you in a text, but I bumbled it; I had this amazing dinner planned the other evening, but Noah's injury stopped it. I've been obsessing over my outfits all week, hoping you would notice, but I couldn't tell."

"Oh, I noticed, I really did."

"Then," Stratton continued, "I thought the whole hike idea was your way of letting me know you weren't interested and that I was making it all up in my head."

Everest beamed. "No, I went out searching for treasure to bring back to you." He rubbed his thumbs over her hands. "I knew that I wanted things to be special when I told you what I'm thinking and feeling."

Stratton looked coyly at him with a twinkle in her eyes, "So, what are you thinking right now?"

He grinned. "Hmm, let's see. I'm thinking of several things. First, I'm thankful to have told you how I feel and that you feel the same. I'm thinking that we have some of the basics down already, like we know how to carry on a conversation, how to hold hands, how to hug, and we're pretty good at dancing. So, what am I missing?"

"A kiss." Flirtatious Stratton entered the conversation.

Everest tenderly brushed her hair back from her shoulders, his fingers lingering for a slight moment on the soft curve of her neck. He gently cupped her face and lifted her chin. His gaze held the depth of emotions he was feeling. His breath brushed against her skin as he leaned in, his voice a low whisper. "Do you want this?" The question seemed to hang for a second between them like a promise of good things to come.

Stratton could hardly breathe. Afraid to break the connection, her eyes remained locked with his. The air surrounding them was electric, filled with anticipation. "I do." Her simple reply quivered with uncertainty and desire.

Everest closed the remaining space between them, covering her lips with his. His kiss was unlike anything she had ever experienced. She felt heady with the sensations she was feeling. The faint glow of candles and the fragrance of at least a hundred roses clinging to the air around them enhanced the sweet taste of that first kiss.

Just when she thought her heart might stop beating, Everest lifted his lips from hers and held her tightly against him. His lips brushed across the top of her hair as he tried to steady his breathing. "I'm sorry about that day when we were in town on the train. I know that I messed up what I was trying to say. I want to be someone worthy of pursuing you. Will you be willing to allow me to prove it to you?"

"At first, I was flattered thinking you were interested in me, but then I was scared when I realized I was interested in you. Everest, I have been back and forth in my head and spent time praying about you, so yes, I am willing."

His mouth covered hers again in unspoken approval. Held closely to him, she could feel his heart beating in time with hers. Nothing else mattered at that moment. Time seemed to stand still. *Remember what Savannah said about being honest.* The thought effectively brought Stratton back to the present, and she broke their connection. "Everest, I'm not sure what your expectations are for us, but this right here is my limit as far as getting physical." *And at sixty, Stratton, it may already be your limit no matter what.*

He smiled as he softly touched his lips to her forehead. "I would only cross certain thresholds with His blessing."

She drank him in as he looked deeply into her eyes. His eyes, a mixture of enthusiasm and joy, sparkled as their gaze held, silently sharing what had just happened between them. As Everest's eyes wandered from hers and down to her lips, Stratton felt herself tingle with anticipation of his lips claiming hers once again.

"You know, there was a moment in the cottage, beside my bed, when I thought about kissing you, but I'm not that kind of guy. I had really enjoyed our time together and I didn't want that night to end. I couldn't believe that we had so much in common and a shared history. I was totally enamored with you."

Not holding back, Stratton reached up and held his face in her hands. She initiated the kiss allowing her instincts to guide her. He had liked her from the day they had met and had not taken advantage of her or the situation at the cottage, though he had thought about it.

Everest released her lips and inhaled deeply. He lightly kissed her brow. "And full disclosure, the storm wasn't that bad. I could've gotten your rental car and sent you on your way, but I wanted you to stay. I wanted that night with you." His thumb traced invisible circles on her left cheek.

Stratton had to ask. "How many women have stayed over in your cabin?"

"Only one: you."

She drew him to her and let her lips express the feelings that she had tried to hide from Savannah poorly, yet she cleverly assumed she was hiding from the children. All those feelings came bubbling forth, crashing down, and rising up again, billowing like an overwhelming force pulling them into a swirling whirlpool with the two of them unable, nor wanting, to escape. Their kisses intensified, and intimacy deepened, threatening to suffocate her as passion burst forth, acting as a tutor to the zealous apprentices at its door. When she pulled back to catch her breath, she noticed she wasn't the only one.

"That was incredible." Everest ran a hand over his head. "I need a little break." Everest walked farther into the barn and started blowing out the candles.

Moonlight filtered through the trees, casting soft shadows on the barn floor. The hum of katydids filled the night with a soft song. The sweet, intoxicating scent of fresh roses filled the night air, a silent reminder of the moments they had just shared.

Even when she was married, she had not experienced anything like this. This form of expression was foreign to her, but that didn't mean she didn't like it.

Watching Everest extinguish the barn light source, Stratton was thankful Noah hadn't put a bed in the barn apartment. It was one thing to state where the boundaries were, but it was entirely something else to adhere to. She wasn't accustomed to thinking along those lines, and that rattled her slightly.

"Do you want any of the roses for the house?" He asked as he walked back to her.

"Leave them for now. We'll get them tomorrow." She reached for his hand, the look in her eyes intentional, and drew him to her.

He gathered her in his arms and kissed her in the darkness.

The hibernation of her heart halted. The glacial thawing had been expedited by molten emotions. On a mission to explore every part of Everest's mouth, she voyaged along, learning the contours of his lips as they met with her own, which positions felt more natural. She could feel him smile as she discovered what he liked her to do in a kiss, and she reveled in all of it. Isaiah 35 popped into her mind: *The wilderness and dry land will be glad. The desert will rejoice and blossom like a lily. It will blossom profusely, will rejoice with joy and singing.*

She felt the full force of that verse in the vigor of Everest's kisses. With each one, she felt as though feelings long dead were being brought to life again. With the candlelight gone, the cozy envelopment of roses and evening sky invigorated Stratton. This was the same Stratton who was consistently asleep by nine PM most evenings. She now felt as active as any nocturnal creature moving about the homestead, seeking to devour a meal, except she sought to devour every affection she could ascertain from Everest. She was thankful there wasn't a bed in the barn apartment.

The pair reluctantly stepped apart, releasing rapid breaths into the night air as their lungs replenished all of that oxygen lost during their exchanges.

"If I'd known this was how things were gonna go, I'd have brought you flowers sooner," Everest said with a grin and playful little tap to her nose.

"Just curious, but what would you have done if I would've kissed you that night at the cottage?" It was the first time she admitted out loud she had been thinking about initiating a kiss with Everest on their first night together.

"Same thing you'd have done if I kissed you the other night while dancing. The timing wasn't right before tonight."

She knew that she would have pulled away immediately and asked him to leave. It would have startled her and been too soon the other night, but not tonight. Tonight had been the perfect timing for them both.

"Were you trying to tell me all of this the night Noah interrupted us?" She ran a thumb over his short beard, detecting a dimple when he smiled.

He moved his lips to kiss her palm. "I think so. I really didn't know what I was doing. I just knew that I wanted to be near you." His mouth closed over hers, a testimony of what he was feeling.

The world around them ceased to exist as she felt herself pulled into the intensity of the moment. Stratton tried to remember if there was a hay loft because it didn't matter that there wasn't a bed. As his lips left hers, Stratton started to say that they should be heading back to the house but stopped when his lips kissed the nape of her neck. Stratton was sure she had stopped breathing. How could that impact the pleasure center of the brain while clouding its ability to think logically? With his lips caressing her neck, she didn't have the brainpower to analyze why she could hardly breathe. She could only tilt her head and let his lips press against her nape and throat as his mouth forged its own expedition.

A pack of coyotes chattered from the woods, breaking the spell between them.

Stratton stopped short of letting out the intense sigh of passion that had been building inside her, a desire so strong it would have left no doubt as to how she wanted to spend the rest of the evening. "We should get back to the house." She took in some deeper than deep breaths.

Everest joined her in the breathing exercises as he nodded. He closed the barn apartment door, then took Stratton's hand as they walked by moonlight to the deck stairs. That's where they should have parted; Everest's door was right there, and Stratton's room was just up the stairs, through the kitchen, and down the hall, but he followed her up the steps to the deck where they found a spot on the loveseat rocker.

They sat next to each other with Everest's left arm around her shoulders, holding her close, her left hand resting lightly on his chest.

They were content for the time, to simply listen to the sounds of the night. It was as if Yehovah had precisely orchestrated the soft mooing of the cows, the rhythmic chirping of crickets, and the crooning of frogs to perform a sweet, melodious symphony meant just for them.

"Do you mind if we don't tell anyone about us right away? I want a little time to just enjoy the time with you. When I tell the kids, it will be overwhelming for all of us. They are definitely a part of my life, but I want it to be just us right now. Does that make sense?"

"We will do whatever you want to do. I personally think sooner is better. You don't want them to feel like you've been keeping anything from them."

"I know. It's just that I selfishly want time with you by myself. I'm not ready to share you with them yet."

Everest turned slightly to face her. "Stratton, there are parts of me only you will ever have, starting with this."

Stratton welcomed the feel and warmth of his lips against hers. Would it always feel like the first time every time?

The fireflies lit up the field beyond her deck while the night continued playing its familiar tune, interjected every now and then by a whippoorwill call.

Stratton sighed. "I want you to always be upfront with me about how much time you expect us to spend together. We both have jobs and family responsibilities. I know how quickly outside factors can ruin a relationship, so I think we need to have a plan to prioritize us. I want you to share with me what you want and what you expect from our relationship and to be honest and truthful with me."

Everest inhaled and slowly exhaled. "I know our jobs keep us busy, and oftentimes, my volunteer work assisting in disaster relief takes me out of the state at a moment's notice. I don't have children, but I do have aging parents and a responsibility to do what's in their best interest, which may mean moving them in with me at some point. Do you understand that I'm not looking for a fling? I don't know what I fully expect or want, but I'm here for the long haul. You and I have lived extremely independent lives, and that's bound to create friction at some point," he looked at her with a smile and a wink, "but we've been creating some pretty strong friction all night, so it really depends on how we channel it."

"Oh, Everest, I get your double entendre, and while it's true, I'm having a hard time staying within my limits tonight." Maintaining boundaries and limits wasn't something that Stratton had ever struggled with. She could blame it on the moonlight or those intoxicating flowers, but she knew that would be unfair. She knew her inability to maintain those limits was due to the magnetic appeal of the man sitting next to her. The intimate way he looked at her, the way he held her close to him, the way he made her feel when he kissed her, he was the reason she was struggling to keep her boundaries intact.

Everest smiled. "I'm sorry. I'm not trying to wear you down. I have done enough in my life to dishonor Him, and I don't want to do that again by dishonoring His commands or dishonoring you. I won't put us in that position," Everest winced. "Sorry."

Stratton laughed.

He wrapped an arm around her and brought her in close again.

She snuggled against him with a contented sigh.

He kissed her temple. "You tell me what you want from me, too."

"Right now, I just want this moment with you."

They rocked together. The symphony Yehovah designed continued playing softly in the background. Everest trailed his fingers through her hair and occasionally paused to place a kiss on her temple.

"Can you see the Big Dipper?" He asked.

She looked up into the night sky, not realizing her eyes had been closed as she rested against him. "Yeah."

"Did you know the constellations tell the story of the Gospel, but it's been corrupted over time and changed?"

"No, and I guess I never thought about it."

"The Big Dipper, for example, is actually The Greater Sheepfold. In the Book of Job, Yehovah asks Job the rhetorical question, 'Canst thou guide Arcturus with his sons?' to point out His omnipotence and omniscience. The four stars that form what we call today the Big Dipper actually form the sheepfold, and the stars inside are the sheep. If you follow the three stars on the handle, you will see a bright star. That is Arcturus, which is the name of the brightest star in the constellation Bootes. Bootes is the Shepherd-Guardian, with a sickle in hand, protecting the sheep in the sheepfold and is ever-ready to harvest souls. The three stars that make up the handle are the sheep,

Arcturus' sons, leaving the sheepfold following Bootes to share the Gospel. Now, look at the right side of the enclosure. Those two stars point to the star Polaris."

"The North Star."

"Yes, and Polaris is pretty much in direct line with the Earth's axis and fairly stationary, meaning all of the other stars in the Northern sky revolve around it. Do you know whose foot rests upon the North Star?"

"No."

"Cepheus, seen as the seated King wearing a crown and royal robes, with his right foot resting on Polaris. So, the heavens literally revolve around Him."

"Tell me more."

Everest walked through what he could remember and recommended a few books for further reading in between sweet whispers and soft kisses.

Stratton couldn't believe this night was real. Here she was, sitting under the stars, learning more about the One Who calls the stars by name and Who brought Everest into her life.

Her eyes grew heavier and heavier as they rocked in a comfortable silence.

Eventually, Everest stood and took her hand as he led her to her doorway.

"I liked it better when you were only twenty feet away on the couch." She sleepily said, referring to his cottage and the sleeping arrangements they had made on their first night together.

As they reached her bedroom, he whispered with his lips just mere inches from hers, "It's safer for us both that I go to my room." The way the darkness hid his handsome features made Stratton want to step closer and see if she could still find his lips with her own in the shadows. As she took that first step, his lips found and claimed hers. His lips moved along her neck, leaving a trail of tingling sensations.

She was breathless. "I know." Did the rule, no overnight guests, apply to the rule maker?

His lips moved to meet hers in gentle undulations reminiscent of ocean waves spreading smoothly over sand.

How could a kiss so tender start such a stir in her synapses?

She wrapped her arms tightly around him, nuzzling his face with hers. She was astonished that his short beard didn't bother her. Somehow, it made his kisses more sophisticated and masculine, calling to and drawing out the femininity in her.

He touched her wrists and gently moved her arms from around him. "This is where I stop."

She understood and nodded. "I'll be up to make you breakfast and pack your lunch."

"You should sleep in."

"But the Everest of my dreams doesn't hold a candle to the one before me, so I'd rather return to you as soon as I can." Literary Stratton mingled with Flirty Stratton.

"You dream about me?" He leaned in, their foreheads touching.

"I wonder if all of this is a dream." Stratton felt her emotions stirring again. Why was it so hard to breathe when he was touching her?

"It's real." He drew in for a long embrace, one she wished could continue for the remainder of the night.

His touch was so powerful and electric. The progression from hand-holding to now had unlocked a door for Stratton that she thought would forever remain sealed and hidden. Everest was the first man since her divorce with whom she'd shared this depth of affection. It was a bit surprising to realize that she had never felt this level of allurement toward any man.

She instinctively squeezed him tightly as he held her close against him.

"Hey," Everest pulled back as though he could sense Stratton's thoughts. He ran his thumbs along her cheeks. "I know tonight's been a big step for both of us. Stratton, the morning isn't going to change how I feel."

She blinked back tears. "It's hard to trust myself again, Everest. I'm sorry for that."

"You don't need to apologize. Ever. I won't rush this."

She nodded.

He squeezed her again. "I'll see you at breakfast." He left her with a departing kiss. She stood at her doorway, watching him as he disappeared down the hall. The hallway felt suddenly cold as if all of the heat had suddenly been drained away, leaving nothing but silence behind.

The evening had turned out quite differently than she had planned. Different from the quiet bath she'd longed for, but different had turned out to be so much better. Her life just changed, taking a different turn than she was expecting. With Everest beside her, she knew that they would work together to navigate the new currents and tides that they faced. With that peace of mind, she crawled into bed, thoughts of the evening replaying in her mind as she drifted off to sleep.

Fourteen

Stratton was up early and in the kitchen when Everest walked in. She had been running through different scenarios before he came in, but she was not sure how he would act after last night. She decided that being cordial was best until she was sure nothing had changed between them overnight.

"Good morning," she said as she crossed to the refrigerator to grab the milk.

"Good morning. I trust you slept well and had sweet dreams," he replied with a smile.

Her heart leaped in her chest, and her pulse raced. "I did." Turning her attention back to breakfast, Stratton took a moment to take a couple of deep breaths in an effort to ground herself before finishing the task at hand.

Everest wrapped his arms around Stratton's waist from behind and planted a soft kiss on her neck. "I told you nothing would change between last night and this morning."

She nodded at his reassurance.

"What can I do to help?"

Stratton had the eggs frying and bison bacon sizzling. "Don't distract me, for starters." She shot him a sideways smile and didn't unclasp his hands or stop him as he gently swayed and moved her with him. She reveled in the pleasant nuzzling he did against her neck while his lips dotted her collarbone. *I will never wear a turtleneck, a high-collared sweater, or a scarf again.*

He drew her closer to him with a squeeze. She wanted to memorize the feel of his strong arms wrapped around her. He nibbled on her ear lobe. She was slightly distracted as she felt his mouth moving softly along her cheek and neck, causing her to almost overcook the eggs. She leaned back against Everest and lost herself in the moment, allowing herself to be carried away by the simplicity of his delicious affections.

The crackle and pop of the bacon made Stratton stand ramrod straight. "Noah will be down soon. Do you mind pouring some orange juice for everyone?"

Everest kissed her cheek and released his hold by sliding his hands along her hips instead of just letting go. He gave her a little smile as he gathered the glasses and got the juice ready.

Last night really happened. Stratton wanted to spend all morning basking in that truth. Now, this wonderful man was in her kitchen, holding her, kissing her, being so sweet and adoring; it was really real. She wasn't sure how long she could keep their relationship from Noah, and she wasn't sure she wanted to wait either.

Noah entered the kitchen while Stratton was buttering everyone's bread.

"Morning, hon. How'd you sleep?"

"Good." Noah stretched. "Say, I got something I've been meaning to confess. It's only right I let you both know because I like you, Everest, and I love my mom."

"What is it, Noah?" Stratton asked, a mixture of concern and curiosity apparent in her voice.

"You know how Grandpap taught me how to fish? Well, I'm mighty good at it. And, Mom, you just kept bringing Everest up in all your phone conversations. I don't know if you realized that you were doing that or that I heard so much of the conversations. I wasn't eavesdropping; it was just in the regular conversations you had with others, kinda like when we talk out here in the kitchen. I thought maybe there was something there, but I didn't want you to hold back on account of me."

In her peripheral vision, Stratton could see a small grin forming on Everest's face. She wasn't sure where Noah was headed with this but decided to be quiet and let him finish what he wanted to say before she asked any questions.

"So, I knew it wasn't ready, but I listed that barn apartment as bait. I knew the Walters' place was one bad storm away from being condemned, so I figured I had pretty good odds on landing me a big fish." Noah looked knowingly right at Everest. "I declined every renter who reached out until you, Everest," Noah sighed. "I stacked the deck against you both, and I shouldn't have. I apologize for my meddling."

"Thank you for saying something, Son. I appreciate that." She giggled internally, sending a quick glance Everest's way. *Wait until I tell him his plan worked.*

"Yep, thank you, that's big of you," Everest chimed in.

Noah nodded. "Well, I'd better go tend to the animals." Noah started for the door. "Oh, and by the way," He turned back around. "I forgot to tell you that I put security cameras on the barn apartment two weeks ago, just so you know." Noah grinned mischievously at them with big eyes, then turned quickly to head outside.

Stratton was stunned, not sure she had heard him correctly at first, but then was instantly mortified. He saw them last night; her son saw her kissing Everest last night.

"Noah, get back over here right now!"

Noah headed back inside with his hands held high, palms facing out, while innocently looking at them. "I didn't see anything. It was too dark! I swear!"

Everest placed a hand on Stratton's shoulder. "It's OK, Stratton." It was obvious that he was trying not to laugh.

"I'm embarrassed as all get out."

"Mom, it has a motion sensor set to start recording. Once I realized what was going on, I deleted the whole file. I'm the only living witness, besides God, who knows. Besides, I'd like to keep living, so I won't be sharing this with anyone."

How much had he seen? How much did he exactly witness? But then again, hadn't he been seeing the beginnings of their relationship the whole time? Hadn't he been the one to instigate Everest's moving in with them?

"I want to keep it quiet before telling everyone. Do not tell your sisters." She pointed a finger at him.

"I won't say a word, I promise. It doesn't bother me in the least to be the only one to know. I think it's cool, and I'd say that if you pulled me aside in private and asked me what I really thought. I did my darndest to get him here so you could have your chance, Mom, so don't worry about me. Now, if y'all don't mind, moving forward, I'll plan on announcing myself when I enter a room, just to be safe." He had a huge smile on his face.

A new wave of awkwardness washed over her.

"I'll be back inside in about twenty minutes, so if you two…" Noah tapped his watch.

"Go." Stratton's tone was the one that meant Noa was approaching thin ice if he kept on.

Noah left.

Everest started laughing, a deep, uncontainable laugh that filled the room. His shoulders shook, and his eyes sparkled with amusement as he turned to look at her. "Come on, Stratton, you have to admit that's a little funny."

"Did my adult son just see us making out on camera for half the night?" Then, as soon as that thought was finished, another one flashed across her mind, "Oh my gosh, Everest, did it capture audio?" New fear unlocked.

* * * * *

Everest started his workday at Milky Way Farms, where he met the owners, Lyle and Bernadette, at one of the locations for the gardens.

"Since the festival is tied to cuisine, we'd like those chefs who've signed on to prepare food to have a matching garden for people to tour," Bernadette began. "So far, we have The Netherlands, China, Italy, France, and Brazil, and we'd like to feature the United States."

"So, six gardens featuring the flora, fauna, and gardening styles of each country?" Everest was taking notes.

"Yes, that's right," Lyle said.

"Any particular era in time or theme you're wanting?"

"I think more modern," Bernadette offered, "but we're open to ideas."

"OK, I'll have some sketches this afternoon after meeting with the team. I think the best way to approach this is to complete one country at a time. If we split in various directions, more problems and issues can occur."

"I don't have any problems with that. We'll be meeting with

decorators later for the manor, so shoot us a text, and we can meet up to go over your thoughts. Thanks." Lyle shook Everest's hand, and then he and Bernadette headed back to the house.

Everest flagged down one of his team members. As they started brainstorming, his mind continuously cut to scenes with Stratton. He could vividly see him cradling her face, looking into those azure eyes by candlelight. He'd seen the flames from the cottage fireplace reflected in those same eyes last night. The sparks between them ignited a fire that didn't need extra stoking. He'd felt her uncertainty when he'd kissed her soft lips for the first time. How quickly that had faded, and Everest felt Stratton grow in confidence with each successive kiss. They were the most powerful kisses he'd ever encountered. Thoughts of kissing her, holding her, and being with her lingered at the forefront of his mind, while the buildup to future exchanges was almost more than he could bear. *Am I gonna get to replay last night again tonight?* He willed himself to focus on the task at hand, trying to keep himself in the present, if only for just a few moments.

He put out a text to his dad asking for prayers to help with concentration, which led to a short phone conversation that was encouraging and uplifting. Before ending the call, his father cautioned him not to rush and to continue to be sensitive to the Spirit's leading.

Fifteen

The long-awaited bath was worth it.

Stratton couldn't remember the last time she'd enjoyed an afternoon bubble bath. The added Epsom salt and lavender essential oil made it most relaxing.

Savannah's name popped up on Stratton's phone.

"Hey."

"Well? Any new developments?" Savannah asked.

"A few." Stratton smiled as her fingers absently swirled the bubbles around in the tub.

"OK, what are they?"

"He is interested."

"He told you?"

"He did. Well, he actually showed me first. Last night, he took me out to the barn apartment. He had it decorated with lots of lit candles and hundreds of roses tied into bouquets. Then he told me."

Savannah laughed. "That's more than interest, Stratton. He's smitten. And what do you mean I took you out to the barn apartment? Did you stay out in the apartment?"

"Absolutely not."

"Well, I didn't mean it like that. Well, I kinda did," Savannah laughed. "I received an interesting text from Noah yesterday. He attached a picture with the three of you featured in formal attire. You didn't tell me Everest was a chiseled younger man."

"Must have slipped my mind," Stratton added more warm water to the tub. "I'm feeling a very strong attraction to him."

"I can see why. So, is that all that happened?" Savannah asked in a teasing tone. "He showed you some flowers, and then you shook hands and went your separate ways?"

Stratton leaned back, creating ripples in the water. "I've never been one to kiss and tell."

"He kissed you! How was it?"

Stratton's mind flashed back to those moments. She wanted to protect what was shared between them, so she simply replied, "It was pleasant and a little uncomfortable at first for me."

"So, are you like a thing now?"

"Yeah, I guess so. He said that he's in this for the long haul."

"When can I come to meet him?"

This is why Stratton wanted to wait. Everyone would want to meet him. All of them would adore him, and then they'd all want to know more and more details about their relationship and next steps. A mom, or in her case, also a grandma, wouldn't have the luxury of having a private romance.

"Noah knows because he's here, but I haven't told the girls. I want to have a little time alone with Everest. We are entering the third month of my sabbatical, so come June, it's halfway over. We've got the July trip to Arkansas to figure out. I promised to go to the historical association meeting, and he's working five days a week. I really want to focus on building a strong foundation and make sure we are doing this right."

"I get that. What if I invited the two of you down here? Next weekend?"

Savannah was a pushy little sister at times.

"I haven't even asked him about the Fourth of July. I'll check." Stratton heard the oven beep. "OK, my timer is going off. I have to go add some vegetables to the roast."

"Well, let me know about next weekend."

"Will do." Stratton stood and let the water out of the tub. She watched as the bubbles started spiraling towards the drain.

"I love you. Bye."

"I love you, too. Bye." Stratton reluctantly stepped out of the tub, tied her robe around her, and then went to tend to the roast.

* * * * *

The roast dinner was a hit. Both Noah and Everest appreciated the time she had taken to prepare their meal. Stratton felt Everest's eyes following her as she put the finishing touches on the meal and brought everything to the table. She had purposefully chosen to wear a pair of peach-colored cotton shorts and a matching top with a loose collar. She had pulled her hair up in a messy bun, just in case Everest wanted to repeat last night's nuzzling of her neck.

After dinner, Noah and his friends headed to a bluegrass pickin' party, which left Stratton and Everest time to spend alone. Everest excused himself as soon as Noah left, leaving Stratton to clean up the kitchen alone. She was a little surprised he didn't offer to help but figured that he had to do something for work. She had just hung up the tea towel to dry when Everest appeared in the doorway.

"Come with me," he said as he held out his hand.

Stratton wondered where they were going as she took hold of his hand. He led her out of the kitchen and into the den, where he had an opera album playing on the record player. Stratton recognized it as an album of opera love songs.

He ushered her to the cream leather couch, where he sat her down on one side, then sat down next to her, taking hold of her hands as he looked earnestly into her eyes. "I would like for you to relax and let me do something for you if you will let me."

Stratton felt her chest tighten with anxiety at what he wanted to do. In the past, it had always been about what she would do for others, not what someone could do for her, so she was unsure of what to say. What could she say that wouldn't expose her insecurity?

"Well, it depends on what it is," she replied vaguely to cover her nervousness.

His eyes held a quiet sincerity as he looked at her. "You've been standing on your feet most of the afternoon and evening, so I ask that you allow me to care for you." He metaphorically swept her off her feet so he could massage them. "Are you up for a foot rub?"

Stratton was speechless and could only nod her head.

Everest carefully picked up her legs and gently laid them across his lap. His hands were warm as he wrapped one hand around each of her feet, giving them a slight squeeze before running his thumbs across the arches of her feet.

Stratton gave an inward sigh. She felt a touch of self-consciousness mixed with vulnerability at this level of intimacy. No one had ever cared for her in this way. She had spent so many years building up an emotional wall thicker and thicker with each hurt so that keeping her distance was her primary method of protection. Was it possible that the protective enclosure around her heart was finally melting?

With the music playing softly in the background, Everest's fingers firmly pressed into the balls of her left foot, releasing the tightness and tension that was there. With each movement of his fingers against her skin, she felt herself sinking deeper into the recesses of relaxation.

"Everest?"

"Yeah?"

"For the Fourth of July this year, we're planning to go see Harper in Arkansas. I didn't think to mention it earlier, but I already asked her if you could come, too." She peeked at him through her closed eyes, nervous for his reaction.

He caught her looking at him and smiled. "You were planning to take me on a family trip, not knowing if I was interested in you, nor had you told me you were interested in me?" His fingers slowly followed an imaginary track from the top of her foot to her knee and back.

"I figured that might be a big clue." She pulled her left leg back so he'd switch to her other foot.

Her words solicited another smile as he kneaded the bottom of her right foot. "As long as the projects are going well, I can work from the road. How long will we be gone?"

"You'll really go with me?" His lack of hesitation was refreshing, but she wanted to be sure he really wanted to go and wasn't just saying it.

"Of course. I think it will be great to meet more of your family."

He stopped rubbing her foot and then reached over to pull her closer to him. "I mean it, Stratton. I really would love to go with you."

She looked intently at him and could see that he was sincere, then gave him a quick hug. "Thank you." They sat listening to the harmonious sounds coming from the record player for another few moments.

Everest interlaced his fingers with hers. "By the way, I've

volunteered for a disaster clean-up project for the next two weekends to help the tornado victims in Alabama. If you'd like to come, you can, but it's backbreaking work, and we often only have primitive living arrangements."

"No, that's fine. I may go to my sister's in Georgia and visit the family while you're away." Life commitments didn't waste any time in their slow encroachment. What would it be like when she returned to work? Would Everest be content to stay in her basement forever, or would he want to do the long-distance thing as he traveled for work?

Everest slapped his knee with his free hand, bringing her back to the moment. "Say, we never talked about my rent."

"I just assumed you were going to help Noah with the garden and around the farm in return for room and board."

"It is my pleasure to help him, but I figure that the basement space is worth at least a thousand a month plus money for groceries and utilities."

"Everest, no, I don't want any money from you."

"And I don't want you covering my share of anything. That's not how it works."

Well, this was a discussion she did not think she would have with him. She never had this discussion with Dexter because he was a taker to his core. How different it was to spend time with Everest and the abundance of his giving. Giving her shelter their first night together, providing food and bed, and continuing to give more of his heart away to her. His affection, kindness, time, finances. She had never known such selflessness.

For now, she'd diffused the situation by letting him think she would take his money when she had no intention of doing so. "Just keep a log of what you think your bills are, and we'll work it out later." The bills wouldn't noticeably increase, and Everest did his fair share of cooking and cleaning, plus he would be assisting when needed. She'd see how long they could table the discussion.

* * * * *

It was close to six o'clock when Stratton pulled into the garage after running errands most of the day. She paused at the door leading into

95

the kitchen. She could hear the faint sounds of The Bellamy Brothers singing *Let Your Love Flow* coming from inside. She quietly opened the door.

Everest was getting plates together as he sang and moved around the kitchen. The savory aroma coming from the oven made Stratton's mouth water. Everest, even with his busy schedule, had taken it upon himself to make dinner for the household. *He is so thoughtful.* With a small smile, she slipped off her shoes and walked into the kitchen.

Everest looked up, pausing mid-dance step, then spun in a circle with a playful grin on his face. "Oh hey."

"Don't let me stop you."

Everest tapped his phone, and the song started over. He held out his hand, inviting Stratton to join him in the fun.

Stratton accepted his hand with a smile.

Creating their own dance floor, Everest swept her into his arms, singing as they danced from the kitchen to the deck doors and back again. When he demonstrated his prowess for twirling her, Stratton knew that he had taken lessons at some point. Stratton let herself relax and enjoy this moment with Everest.

This was the essence of falling for someone where joy met simplicity, providing a glimpse of someone's character and true self.

Stratton wanted his effortless footwork to be a metaphor for how he intended to pursue and treat her. With tremendous ease, he guided her along and never missed a beat, never misstepped; he also never missed an opportunity to look at her with a cheery smile, indicating he was immensely enjoying dancing with her.

He knew how to blend physical and subtle flirting together in a seamless fashion when he touched her hip to indicate the direction he was leading her. He even changed things up for the last bit of the song by quickly switching into a line dance.

Stratton beamed as she effortlessly followed his flawless lead.
He took a few more wide steps, grabbed her hand, and twirled her once more before ending with a quick kiss just as the oven beeped. "Let's feed you a good dinner before you head off in the morning to visit your sister."

Everest went to the oven and pulled out the baked shredded chicken tacos.

"That looks amazing." She was thankful to have the evening off from cooking, especially without having to ask him to cook. Though she appreciated Everest's efforts to share the responsibility of preparing their meals, she was quick to remind herself that people are the best version of themselves early in the relationship. She remained cautious in letting the wall around her heart fall too soon, too fast.

The newness of their relationship was exhilarating yet unnerving, reinforcing Stratton's insecurities and doubts. Allowing herself to be romanced like this was something she had never experienced, so she didn't have a good reference point for the direction things should take.

Stratton wanted things to go slow, partly so she could savor the progression of their relationship and partly because she was scared of opening her heart again. If she ever wanted to give Everest her whole heart, she would need to take things baby steps and adjust to each step before she could give anything further.

Sixteen

White columns, stately and tall, surrounded the veranda. Rays of sunlight shone through the Spanish moss, reminding Stratton of a familiar embrace. She was home. Her childhood home was filled with memories of her family. Though her father had died when she and Savannah were young, her mother continued to help them make happy memories. Charles and Savannah purchased the mansion from Stratton's mother before cancer quickly ended her life, but this was, and would always be, home to Stratton.

"Will you be having tea or coffee, Miss Stratton?" Chessie, Savannah's servant, called from inside Stratton's room.

"Yes, Chessie, herbal tea and some honey would be nice." Stratton, wearing a long silk robe over her pajamas, sat on the veranda reading Scripture. Visiting Savannah, Georgia, was like stepping into another world that was so different from where she lived in Tennessee. It was ethereal in some ways, nostalgic in others, and always restful and warming to her soul.

Clip-clop, clip-clop, clip-clop, clip-clop.

Stratton looked down to see a familiar horse-drawn wagon coming down her street.

"Howdy! Is that Miss Stratton Sanford I see?" Sanford. Her maiden name.

"Warren? Are you still delivering milk by way of yesteryear?" Stratton hollered down to the man dressed in all white with a hat to match. Warren had been a family friend since childhood. He had started his career by helping his father deliver milk to the wealthier clientele who still preferred fresh milk every day. Even back when most milkmen had switched to vehicular delivery, Warren was the only one she knew of who was still delivering by horse.

"Only on the streets that pay me triple!" Warren waved, and the horse clip-clopped on.

It felt good to be home.

Stratton dressed for breakfast and headed downstairs. She found Charles and Savannah dressed and reading the paper in the breakfast nook.

"Good morning, Stratton. How'd you sleep?" Savannah asked.

"Great, as per usual. Do y'all use Warren for milk?" Stratton could hear it. Her accent was slipping right back into a southern drawl. Her students could always tell when she'd been back home for a visit.

"I don't drink milk anymore, and Charles has been using almond milk for years." Savannah put the paper down. "Say, how do you feel about going to a debutante ball tonight? I thought it'd be a nice throwback to ours."

"That would be fun," Stratton said.

"Hey, we've got tennis in twenty minutes," Charles interrupted. "Stratton, we've got an extra racket."

Had she ever left? "Absolutely! I'll be ready."

They played tennis at the country club, followed by a delicious lunch, then a leisurely chat on the front porch with a plan to leave for the ball by six.

Stratton stood in front of the floor-length mirror, looking at her reflection. She had borrowed an A-line, halter, high-necked, tea-length dress from Savannah for the occasion. The fabric captured the perfect blend of the fuchsia plant's vibrant colors when she moved. Pearl-colored sandals, along with a pair of Savannah's earrings, completed the outfit. She'd even added some curls to her hair and light makeup.

Her hometown transported her back as they went to Victory North, the venue for the ball. Stratton remembered her own debutante ball and thought of the advice she would have told her younger self. *First, don't marry the first man you meet who's different than everyone you've ever known; different doesn't always mean good. Second, don't ignore your gut.* She had photographic proof of what a broken marriage and single motherhood could do to a body. It had taken time, prayer, and self-control to get back on track with her health.

As the trio found their table and took their seats, Stratton prayed none of these young ladies she'd be seeing tonight were ever in the same position she had been. *Don't think you can change him. You can't.* She hated that her first thoughts were negative advice, so she tried to redirect her thoughts and focus on the positive advice she'd pass on to the younger generation. *Cherish the college experience and the wonderful friendships you will find during that time. Be open to new and exciting job opportunities. See yourself as He sees you and speak to yourself like He does.* Stratton was still working on that last one; maybe if she'd done that one a lot sooner, she might have avoided certain entanglements. However, she knew Yehovah could make her mess into a message.

The program began, and the announcer began calling each girl one by one. As their names were called, each girl walked out on the arm of her father, formally being presented to society. Smiles and camera flashes abounded, and after the final girl was presented, they had their first dance of the night with the boys their age. An orchestra played, and the teens demonstrated mastery of their cotillion class lessons in front of the audience.

"I remember my first dance. He stepped all over my feet and even bruised my toe," Savannah said with a smile as she shot a sideways glance at Charles.

Stratton quizzically looked between Charles and Savannah. "Charles, was your first dance?"

"I didn't want anyone else to dance with her, so I figured I had to make my move," he said with a grin.

They were an excellent match, able to both listen and compromise as they kept their marriage a priority. Charles had become a brother to her and a positive male role model for her children, treating them like his own three sons. He held a special place in each of her children's hearts, as well as her own. She would remain eternally grateful for him, Savannah's bruised toe notwithstanding.

As the young couples danced to the music, Stratton let her thoughts drift to Everest. Not that she wanted to seem needy, but she hadn't heard from him yet. She decided to step outside to try and touch base.

The muggy twilight air had been replaced by a cool evening breeze. Stratton took a deep breath, inhaling the sweet yet spicy scent of the dianthus that surrounded her. Stratton walked towards a magnolia tree that stood at the center of the outdoor garden, taking out her phone. She called Everest, excited to hear his voice, but was disappointed when the call went straight to voicemail. *Where was he that his phone wouldn't ring?* Curiosity, mingled with some doubt and insecurity, got the better of her, so she decided to text him.

She noticed that the orchestra had stopped playing, and the instrumental sounds of a familiar song had begun to play.

"Is that Dave Barnes' song, *On A Night Like This*?" She looked inside. "Oh, wow, it's actually Dave Barnes." He started introducing the song before singing, saying something about this first song was for the parents. He said that these kids owed mountains of gratitude for what their parents had done for them. Stratton appreciated his sentiment. She'd forgotten that affluent old money could afford to hire the best performers for this one evening of celebration. She wondered what other musicians were lined up for the night. She started to text Everest.

"Excuse me, miss." That familiar voice.

Stratton turned.

Everest stood before her in a charcoal 3-piece suit and a big grin.

"What are you doing here?" She said, unable to hide the surprise in her voice.

"I wasn't about to let the prettiest girl at the Debutante Ball miss out on the dancing."

Dave's voice carried on the breeze as he started singing.

Everest opened his arms.

Stratton moved to him, and they shared their first slow dance as an official couple. She couldn't believe how perfectly the lyrics matched everything about their night together.

"How did you know where I'd be?"

"I'm sworn to secrecy." He moved in closer, so they were dancing cheek to cheek.

Savannah! "I was just getting ready to text you."

"Been missing me?"

She loved his nuzzling against her cheek. She breathed him in. "I have. Last weekend, this weekend, and we leave for Arkansas next. I feel like we haven't had much time alone."

"I'm here now." His embrace was a little tighter and longer than usual as they continued swaying in time with the music.

She sensed something was not quite right. She pulled back, stopping their dance. "What is it?" She could see tears in his eyes.

He sighed. "The disaster relief we provided was a challenge on this trip. It was an EF4 tornado that hit, ripping through a trailer park and destroying most of the homes. They said everyone was accounted for, including casualties." He shook his head. "They were wrong."

Stratton held his gaze and saw the sorrow in his eyes.

"My buddy and I were picking up a large piece of metal, and there was a little boy lying underneath it. I grabbed him immediately and checked for signs of life, but he was gone. We asked around, and finally, someone who thought he might be the grandson of a lady who was one of the casualties. How did people not know he was missing in that neighborhood? What if we had found him sooner? Did he know he was trapped? Are things that bad that we just don't pay attention anymore or care about little kids?"

"Oh, Everest." She saw the tears spill forth from his eyes.

"I had to get out of there after that. My buddy called to let me know they did identify him. His name was Drake, and he loved tractors."

Stratton pulled him against her and shed tears with him. "I'm so sorry."

He buried his head in her neck and held tightly to her.

Stratton wanted to show him she cared, and she didn't want to fill the stillness with empty words, so she just held onto him and let him hold her. They stood holding on to each other in silence for the next three songs.

He cleared his throat. "Now, back to your question. I got a text from Savannah introducing herself, and she made me an offer I couldn't refuse."

"How did she get your number?"

"Noah."

Noah! "I'm glad you came." She gave him a big smile.

"Me, too." He wrapped his arms around her again and brought her in for another long embrace.

His sensitivity and expression lifted another layer of caution from Stratton's heart. His steady pursuit was progressively earning not only her trust but her care. She cared about his sensitive-to-children heart and found herself wanting to shield him from pain while providing comfort. Right now, that took the form of holding onto him, running her nails softly along the back of his neck as they swayed. She prayed for Everest and anyone mourning the loss of little Drake.

* * * * *

Holding onto Stratton eased the burden he carried and made him forget about the numerous times he'd encountered the darkness of the world while doing his volunteer work. This wasn't the time for Everest to share the other details of his volunteer work. It was one thing to share with her about his disaster relief and recovery but entirely another thing to open up about the full extent of his duties.

Disaster relief extracted a huge toll on emotions. Until now, Everest had leaned on his friends that he volunteered with or his parents as he decompressed and processed the emotions. Now, he was opening his heart to Stratton, which meant sharing those emotions openly and honestly. Tonight, she had been safe and supportive as he told her about finding Drake.

Sharing with her had a dual effect: soothing yet powerful. On one hand, it meant allowing him to drop his guard, welcoming her into the innermost chambers of his heart. On the other hand, it stirred in him a strong resolve to protect her from the disaster and pain that he had seen. He never wanted her heart broken like his currently was, but he also couldn't hide the pain it created.

"Are you OK with me sharing that with you?"

Stratton pulled back and looked into his eyes. "Everest, I'm honored you did. You don't have to keep anything from me. Whatever you feel comfortable sharing about your volunteer work, I will listen and do everything I can to support you and be there for you."

"Thank you."

The music grew louder and more upbeat.

"We can stay here if you want or go find Charles and Savannah. I'm fine with whichever you want to do," Stratton offered.

"Let's go find our hosts. Savannah told me nothing compares to Georgia's southern hospitality. I reckon I need to judge that for myself. Am I getting better at the accent?"

Stratton laughed, "No, it's terrible."

Seventeen

Charles and Savannah's front porch was the perfect spot for post-ball entertaining. Matching white wicker patio furniture, comfortable cushions, and Chessie's pecan pie. The citronella candles and lemon grass potted plants, designed to keep away the mosquitoes, were strategically placed in each corner of the porch.

"So y'all's families knew one another from Revolutionary times?" Charles asked, looking from Stratton to Savannah and then to Everest.

"Yeah, the two families stayed close for several generations but eventually lost touch with each other over time," Everest explained.

"And y'all met each other because of a letter?" Charles inquiringly asked.

"Charles, dear, that's only part of how they met," Savannah said as she gave his leg a loving pat.

"Well, I think meeting because of a historical letter is quite appropriate for you, Stratton," Charles said, giving her a smile.

Stratton laughed, glancing over at Everest, who gave her a quick wink that caused her heart to skip a beat before he mentioned, "Savannah, you and Charles have a lovely home. I would love to know the history behind it."

That was the opening Charles needed, and for the next thirty minutes, he provided a detailed history of the house before the girls lived there. As he began to share about the more recent history, Stratton noticed Everest slipping his hand to his mouth, stifling a yawn.

She nodded toward Savannah, who returned the nod.

Savannah looked at her husband. "Charles, I think it's time we head to bed. Everest has had a long day." She looked at Stratton. "Do you mind showing Everest to the guest room across the hall from your room?"

"Of course not."

Savannah, taking hold of Charles' hand, winked at Stratton as they turned and headed inside. "Goodnight. Everest, thank you for coming."

"Goodnight, Everest. We'll golf in the morning if you're up for it," Charles offered.

"Sure thing. Night."

The couple were alone, save for the cricket orchestral arrangement playing around them.

After several minutes of simply enjoying the quiet time together, Stratton ran a hand over Everest's arm. "We should get you to bed. I know you've got to be emotionally and physically exhausted."

"That's a good call."

Stratton didn't tarry at his doorway; she parted for her room. As she started to change, she remembered that Savannah had helped her with the zipper to the dress. She was stuck if she didn't have an extra set of hands. *I can't disturb Savannah now. I wonder if Everest is still awake.*

She knocked on Everest's door.

He slowly opened it, and Stratton drew in a sharp breath and felt her heart hammering in her chest.

It was the first time Stratton had seen him shirtless. *Seriously, why does this man want to pursue me? When does he find time to maintain this muscular build?* Blushing, she realized she had been staring at him. She cleared her throat. "I promise I don't have a hidden agenda, but I need help with this zipper."

Everest chuckled. "No problem. I don't mind helping."

Stratton turned around and lifted her hair.

Everest's hand brushed lightly against her neck as he took hold of the zipper and slowly started pulling on the slide, meeting with resistance almost immediately. He placed his other hand at the top of her neck, holding firmly to the material. Giving a gentle tug, the slide released its grip, and he continued to pull slowly downwards.

The slide left a trail of tingling nerves traveling from Stratton's neck to her shoulders, then continued down towards her back. Her skin was hyper-aware and sensitive to his touch, knowing exactly where his hands were each second of their descent. *I've never felt like this before. What is wrong with me? How can Everest make unzipping a dress such a sensual thing?* Her heart pounding and pulse racing, Stratton strained to maintain her composure, but her body betrayed her and gave an involuntary shudder, startling her back to reality. *I can't do this; I have to step away now.*

"Thanks. I can take it from here." She turned back around, facing him, suddenly feeling flustered at the intimacy of the moment.

"So that's your old room?" Everest, passion shining in his eyes, nodded toward Stratton's bedroom.

She welcomed the attempt to calm the electricity zinging between them. "Yep."

"Who was in this one?"

"Savannah, but we usually shared a bed when we were little. She didn't like sleeping alone."

Everest smiled, his eyes twinkling with promise.

"No quips, nothing suggestive," Stratton warned as she felt the warmth rising in her cheeks.

"I'm not the one who came over asking for help getting undressed while catching me ready for bed."

"Goodnight, Everest." Stratton quickly turned to go, lest he see her eyes betraying her conflicting emotions, and hoping he'd just forget she had knocked at his door.

He reached out before she could escape, taking hold of her by the arms and pulled her toward him. He planted a soft, borderline-suggestive kiss on her lips, effectively taking her breath away.

What do I do with my hands? With him holding the tops of her arms, she had no choice but to keep them at her sides as they kissed.

The light massaging of her upper arms and the gentle caress of her shoulders brought her back to reality. "Everest, I should go to bed." It was a partial plea offered only so she could say she tried.

"Want me to tuck you in?" He murmured in a teasing tone. His lips landed on her jawline as he gave her three light pecks, making her shiver beneath his touch as he neared her earlobe.

She noticed the invigorating moonflower fragrance drifting in from the veranda, where she'd left the doors open, blending with the melodious tree frogs' trills. The enhanced sweet scent of vanilla mixed with jasmine filled her senses. Filtered moonbeams from the window enhanced the soft glow of lamplight from Everest's doorway, accentuating every detail of the masculinity before her.

"I'm not allowed to have boys in my room," she softly whispered against his lips. His kisses robbed her of breath and thought as his lips peppered her collarbone. Running her fingers through the hair at the nape of his neck, she wrapped her arms around him. She couldn't have boys in her room, but if he had just taken a few steps back, they could have been in Savannah's old room. She couldn't recall any rules about that.

She was slowly becoming putty in his strong and tremendously gentle hands.

Stratton hardly recognized herself in what she was thinking and feeling; feelings that had been smothered, stunted, and cut off over the years but were starting to come alive, encouraging her to move forward, trusting, hoping, and believing.

Moved by the depth of compassion he'd shared at the ball, Stratton knew at that moment that she had no defenses if he wanted to unfasten, unclasp, unravel, or undo anything his hands discovered. She knew she needed to be careful and that her threshold for affection might be much higher than his.

"Stratton," Everest abruptly pulled back and bent over, panting as if he couldn't breathe.

Feeling the lingering effects of his kisses, she asked, "Are you OK?"

Running his hand through his hair, he appeared flustered and upset at the same time. "No, this isn't safe. I've let things go too far."

"Tonight, or us?"

His eyes, as blue as the deepest recesses of the sea, looked as though they matched the passion he felt. Those eyes looked at her for a moment before he stood up straight, reaching to gently touch her cheek. "Do you want me to answer that before or after the cold shower I'm about to go take?"

His words melted her heart and filled her soul. "Down the hall, on the right."

"I'm sorry if you felt this was too much." Sincerity glazed each word from Everest.

"And I'm sorry I didn't." She responded in all honesty.

As she closed her door behind her once they parted, she had to smile at his admission. Grandma or not, Stratton enraptured this man, and it made her feel like the belle of the ball.

* * * * *

Everest splashed cold water on his face and looked in the mirror. "Nope, definitely gonna need that shower." The Book of James came to mind. *For if anyone is a hearer of the word and not a doer, he is like a man who looks at his natural face in a mirror— for once he looks at himself and goes away, he immediately forgets what sort of person he was. But the one who looks intently into the perfect Torah, the Torah that gives freedom, and continues in it, not becoming a hearer who forgets but a doer who acts—he shall be blessed in what he does.*

Everest knew the man he was and wanted to continue to be the man who would flee from sin, not run towards it. He wanted to be the kind of man who walked upright with integrity, which meant he would not put himself in compromising situations.

He knew he hadn't exercised self-control with Stratton tonight. He had let his thoughts wander into a future that he wasn't promised with Stratton. That kind of thinking was enough to start a physical response that could have led to disaster.

The cold shower was a shocking reminder that he had to keep his thoughts in check and honor the biblical boundaries Scripture set forth. He wanted to honor both himself and Stratton and, in doing so, would honor His Heavenly Father.

He penned a quick note to Stratton and slipped it under her door before retiring for the night.

Eighteen

"Miss Stratton, Miss Savannah asked me to wake you. I've brought some tea, and this note was on the floor by your door." Chessie placed a tray on Stratton's lap as she sat up.

"What time is it?"

"Eight AM."

"OK, thank you, Chessie." Stratton could hardly believe she had slept so late. She propped herself up with some pillows and took a sip of tea. She reached for her glasses on the nightstand and opened the note.

We aren't to move boundary stones (Deut. 27:17, Proverbs 22:28). To do so is to steal what isn't rightfully ours. I won't prematurely take what isn't mine. Stratton, I deeply apologize for loosening my guard last night. I renew my pledge to protect and honor the tenets of Scripture and thereby also guard your purity. Boundaries are a good thing. "My boundary lines fall in pleasant places—surely my heritage is beautiful." -Psalm 16:6. I commit to doing what is pleasing to Him, trusting in His design and plan, knowing He will use our courtship to demonstrate beauty and blessing for us and others. Everest

His handwritten confession and pledge made this the single most romantic note she'd ever received. These words were from his heart, spoken from a place of vulnerability, a space in Everest's heart that she never wanted to hurt. His desire to follow Scripture, walking in the way of the Word as he pursued her, was such a stark contrast to her relationship with Dexter, who didn't even believe in the Word.

Stratton knew it was wrong to compare the two men, but she had never met anyone like Everest, so it was hard not to compare.

She took a few more sips and then decided to prepare for the day.

Stratton borrowed a light blue sleeveless polo dress cut pretty high above the knee from Savannah for a round of couple's golf at the club.

* * * * *

The mid-morning sun was bright as it shone above the trees along the fairway. The golf course was hustling with activity as the foursome checked in and loaded their four-seater golf cart, just making their tee time.

She was waiting for the chance to be alone with Everest to thank him for the note he'd left her last night. On the fifth tee, she sliced her ball, sending it right into a group of bald cypress trees. She and Everest, who volunteered to help her in her search, headed off on foot to try and locate her ball.

Finding themselves alone for the first time that day, Stratton glanced at Everest as they approached the thicket of trees. "That was a very touching note you wrote. Thank you." Her voice was soft with appreciation.

"I meant every word of it." He replied with a serious tone to his voice before moving some undergrowth brush around with his club. After a moment, he nodded toward the right. "Why don't you check over there? I'll search this side."

Stratton stepped a few feet from Everest, using her club to scan the ground for her golf ball. A silence settled between them, filled only by the soft rustle of leaves and the distant sounds of the course.

Everest paused, looking at her with quiet intensity.

She felt his eyes on her and stopped, turning to glance his way.

"The foundation of our future should be one that recognizes the Word as the authority. If I mess up and make mistakes, I will immediately ask Him for forgiveness. My intention isn't to sin in regard to our relationship, but I realize how easily our own needs can get to a place that is not pleasing to Him. I'm meaning the emotional, as well as physical, needs."

His eyes never left hers as he began walking slowly towards her.

"Stratton, you have such a servant's heart; caring for others is part of who you are. You have not only taken care of my physical needs, such as cooking, cleaning, and a place to stay, but also have met my emotional needs, like last night at the ball. I would never want to take advantage of you and your servanthood."

Everest rested his club against a large tree trunk. He took Stratton's club from her hands and did the same with it, then took her hands into his. "I see all of the things that you do and give to others: your time, your talents, your resources, your attention, your compassion, just to mention a few." He gently rubbed his thumbs across the top of hers as he took a step closer to her.

"You are one of the most accomplished, professional women I know, with a true servant's heart. The more I know you, the more I realize how amazing you are. I know that anyone who meets you is left wanting to know you more, which is a testimony to your kind heart." Everest, gazing into her eyes, lifted her hands to his lips, placing a soft kiss on each one.

"I'm thankful that no one has pursued you yet and that I have that honor. I know that I can't ever replace the loneliness you must have felt in the years since your divorce. My hope and prayer are that you will find our relationship fulfilling, like a breath of fresh air, and worth the wait."

Stratton blinked back, the tears swirling in her eyes. She was not used to such genuine, honest accolades. While she felt a warmth at his compliments, there was a part of her that was still not willing to trust and believe what Everest said. She always knew that her children and her coworkers expected her to do the things she did, but they had never really said much about it, not like this. *Is this real? Is this what true appreciation feels like? What am I supposed to say? What am I supposed to believe?* "Is that what you really see when you look at me?"

"That, and so much more." He drew her into an embrace.

She let herself relax and soak up the assurance and security those strong arms gave her. She wasn't sure about the future. She was not yet able to fully trust and enjoy where their relationship would go. If it didn't work out, separating from Everest would be beyond devastating to her. "It's still hard for me to open up and share. Are you OK with that?" She feared that even telling him that much might make him back away.

"I am, I really am. Does it bother you at all that I share my thoughts with you?"

"No, it doesn't, and I'm working on how to return it."

"Stratton, there's no rush and no pressure. Take your time." He gave her another hug.

"Hey, are we golfing here or what?" Savannah hollered from the course.

Everest gave Stratton a quick peck on the cheek, then a quick neck nuzzle, sending chills down her arms in spite of the warmth from the sun. He grabbed the clubs, pocketed the ball he'd found lying by the roots, and reached for Stratton's hand. "I will say, golf attire suits you," as he gave her an appreciative once-over and winked.

She kissed his cheek for the compliment, and they walked hand in hand back to Savannah and Charles.

After they finished the final hole, they drove the golf cart back toward the club, deciding that they would have a late lunch there.

As they drove back toward the restaurant, Charles and Savannah filled Stratton and Everest in on all of the upcoming events and happenings as if they, too, were members and spent just as much time there as they did. This wouldn't be a lifestyle Stratton would want to return to. She loved her homestead and watching Noah thriving like he was. She enjoyed everything about the homestead. Those quiet, peaceful mornings sitting on her deck, book in hand, watching the sun rise over the horizon, hearing the cows lowing in the pasture, watching the red and orange hues paint the sky as the sun set through the trees, filled her heart with joy. She was thankful that she and Everest were able to start and build their relationship at the farm and not amongst the bejeweled distractions in Savannah.

"Well, aren't you out early today?" Bitty Barrow, clad in her pink golf wear, asked as they passed en route toward the club.

"Good morning, Bitty," Savannah said, stopping the golf cart.

"I was just telling Robert we should have you and Charles over for cards."

"We're pretty booked," Savannah started.

"But give us a call, and we'll make the time," Charles said.

"Will do. Nice to see you." Bitty moved on.

"What did I miss?" Everest asked as they continued driving.

"That? Oh, that was a Southern woman's grudge on full display," Stratton said. "Savannah, let it go."

"I just find it rude," Savannah said.

"I'm still confused. What happened?" Everest asked.

Stratton shared the story. "After our father passed away when we were children, the insurance money was tied up in probate. I was playing outside on the veranda and fell from the edge into the tree, hitting the branches and landing in the bushes. My mother called the doctor, who was Bitty's grandfather, to help. They moved me inside, where he set my broken arm and treated me for a concussion. The only payment we had was some jewelry until the estate was settled. Savannah thinks that Bitty still has it, and she should give it back since our mother actually did pay the bill."

"It's not like we couldn't or wouldn't pay the bill. I think they looked at us as a charity case."

There it was, Savannah's issue. This was Southern pride at its finest, not wanting to be anyone's charity case.

"Have you all asked Bitty about the jewelry?" Everest asked.

Savannah looked incredulously at him, "Everest, Southern manners dictate that I cannot ask her."

Stratton noticed Savannah laid that accent on thicker than thick and gave Everest's hand a quick squeeze, signaling he should let it alone.

"Have you seen her wear anything indicating she has it?" He asked, missing the subtle cue Stratton sent.

Stratton stepped in, striving to defuse the escalating conversation. "We aren't even sure what Momma used as collateral for the bill. She had this beautiful aquamarine ring that we never saw after my accident, so we suspect that was a part of the bargain. There may have even been a necklace or two. We don't really know. Whatever it was, it's theirs now, Savannah, so don't hold it against Bitty; she had nothing to do with it."

"I don't know why you aren't more upset about it. That was your favorite piece of Nana's, and Momma had promised it to you. I think she once told me it was European, crafted during Edward VII's reign."

Stratton sighed. It had been her favorite piece. She used to play dress up and wear it in front of her mother's antique mirror, imagining herself attending a ball and wearing that ring on her finger. After her accident, she felt guilty that her mother had to part with the jewelry to pay for her medical bill, but her mother never minded. After the estate went through probate, the girls never wanted for a thing again.

"There's a lot of nuances to Southern culture," Everest mentioned with a shrug.

"You don't even know," Charles offered.

Nineteen

Stratton let the barn door slam shut behind her, nearly catching Cully's tail as she strode purposefully across the ground with the needed extra materials. She was a little miffed that Everest's workload had increased. His hours had extended into the evening, resulting in them putting off the task of building the trellis. She paused, taking a deep breath as she watched the sun steadily make its descent behind the trees, ending the day. The forecast predicted a shower early in the evening, so they were trying to finish building the cucumber trellis before the rain started. "Everest, I don't think that's how it goes. You're not running the line taut enough." He had just gotten home and decided now was the time to get the garden going.

"Stratton, I have to get this part in the ground first, then I can tighten the line. This is no different than what we did for the tomatoes," Everest explained, wiping his brow with the bottom of his shirt. "If you'd just let me bring my team over here, you and I wouldn't have to do this."

"I told you that I don't want the whole town talking about us. And, by the way, I also told you we didn't have to have a garden this year. You were the one who insisted we do this!"

"What was all that talk about? 'I can't wait for fresh tomatoes. Hope you like okra'?" he said, repeating the words she had said to him.

Stratton immediately became defensive. "I don't sound like that." It was hot outside, and the temperature was rising. *Is this our first fight?* Stratton was in no mood to analyze that thought right now.

"What are you frustrated about? Do you not want this garden?"

"Everest, I said from the beginning. I just wanted it to be us for a moment. I'm halfway through my sabbatical, and here we are, out here, trying to beat the rain headed our way and working on a project that doesn't need to be done. You spend ten or more hours a day at work while I am stuck here waiting for you to come home at who knows what time. Then we rush just to squeeze in a few precious little moments together before we get up and repeat it all over again. Is this some sort of adult version of playing house? I still haven't told the girls about us, and we are leaving for Arkansas this weekend."

"What do you want me to do, Stratton, quit the project? Insist on part-time?" He was clearly getting irritated. "Besides, let's get this clear right now: I never asked you to stay home all day waiting around for me. I also have never asked you to cook or clean for me. We could just eat cereal, then we'd have plenty of time at night to do something."

"And not have something ready for Noah with as hard as he works?"

"I am not touching that one," Everest sniggered.

"What does that mean?" Stratton's eyes narrowed.

"Well, it means he's not ten years old."

"Wow. OK." Stratton took off her gardening gloves and stalked back towards the house.

"Stratton, wait," Everest said.

Stratton was already out of the garden and heading toward the deck stairs.

"Stratton, come on!" He hollered as she continued walking away without a backward glance at him.

She stormed through the kitchen and marched straight to her room, slamming the door behind her. So, this was a side to Everest she'd never seen. She couldn't believe he had actually thrown Noah in her face like that. *Who does he think he is critiquing my wanting to make sure Noah has a good meal at night?* She had no desire to spend time with Everest right now and intended to stay in her bedroom for the remainder of the night. Stratton picked up her phone and called her sister.

"Do you think I baby Noah?" Stratton asked Savannah.

"What happened?"

"Everest and I are in a fight."

"Over what?"

"Over it sounds like he thinks I baby Noah by making sure I cook healthy food for all of us."

"I'm always on your side, and I really like him, but I can't feed the fire. If you can be objective and tell me word-for-word what was said, then I'm happy to help you. Can you do that?"

"No, I cannot."

"OK, so he struck a nerve, and you're aware you might have overreacted? Does that sound right?"

"Maybe."

"Slow to anger, quick to forgive."

"Thank you, Savannah."

Stratton let those words marinate, running through the conversation with Everest again and again. It was time to apologize to Everest. She went out to the kitchen, expecting him to be there. Seeing a small light and movement out by the garden, she opened the door. In the distance, lightning flashed briefly, illuminating the man still working in the garden. Just as she headed down the steps, a couple of large raindrops pelted her face. The storm was close.

As she got closer, she saw that Everest was wearing a headlamp, which effectively illuminated the ground in front of him.

"What are you still doing out here?" She asked. "There's a storm blowing in. It isn't safe."

"I've gotta finish this garden fencing, or the rabbits will destroy these plants." He unrolled some chicken wire and began clipping. The thunder rumbled, announcing it was coming their way. He placed the final piece and then zip-tied the chicken wire to a small stake.

"Everest, I'm sorry. I shouldn't have walked off angry like that. It was rude, and I was wrong. I won't do that the next time we disagree." *Will he forgive me, or will this be the end of our relationship? How would I react if he says it's over?*

Everest turned off his lamp and looked her way. "It's OK, Stratton, and I'm sorry about the barb I carelessly tossed at you. I didn't think through my words before saying them. I would never want you to feel like I was putting you in a position to defend your relationship with any of your children. I know that being with you is being with them, which I welcome. I am sorry, too."

"Thank you." She felt the sincerity of his words. The raindrops began to fall a little faster. "Can we get out of this weather?"

"No makeup kiss?"

She leaned towards him, quickly kissing his cheek, but didn't make it one step towards the house before he wrapped his arm around her waist, pulling her to him. His mouth captured hers in a tantalizing kiss that made retreating an impossibility.

With his free hand, Everest pushed the headlamp off of his head, letting it drop forgotten into the dirt. He pulled her in closer to him, smothering her with kisses.

As the raindrops began to fall more steadily, she knew they should head inside, but Stratton couldn't make herself leave the comfort of Everest's arms. He was sweaty yet warm, a stark contrast to the chilly summer rain. She felt her insecurity in their relationship matched the vulnerability of being in the midst of the elements, but it didn't deter her from savoring the kisses that matched the intensity of the approaching storm. Everest seemed to sense her feelings and deepened their kiss as an unspoken promise that their relationship was something worth fighting for.

The heavens burst open, and a torrential downpour completely drenched them. She'd never been kissed in the rain. It was a surreal experience.

As Everest brushed his lips across her lips once more, he nudged in closer to her.

Stratton tilted her face toward the sky as Everest's lips traced the curve of her jaw. Each tantalizing kiss was like a soft caress against her skin. The warmth of their bodies mixed with the cool raindrops sent shivers down her spine. *What is this I'm feeling? Is this normal?*

The rain created a wall of water around them, a secret sanctuary of their own. They existed in another realm, hidden by the cascades that washed away their disagreement and renewed their commitment.

Suddenly, a powerful boom overhead shattered the moment, breaking the intensity between them. Everest held tightly to Stratton's hand, then raced for the house and shelter.

They entered the house through the basement door, water dripping from their clothes as they stood on the tiled floor. Everest collected fresh towels from his bathroom and brought one to Stratton.

The combination of the intensity of their kisses and mad dash indoors left Stratton flushed despite the coolness of the room's temperature. She took longer than normal, drying off her rain-soaked hair in an effort to calm her racing heartbeat.

"Are you OK?" Everest asked, looking her way as he worked to dry himself off as much as possible.

Feeling herself blush, "Yes. That was a bit intense," she replied honestly, unsure of how Everest would receive it.

"It was intense, and yet it was perfect." He threw his towel in the corner before moving to stand in front of her. Giving her a knowing look, causing her to blush, he softly traced the shape of her lips with his finger, "This reminds me of our night at the cottage."

It felt like both a lifetime ago and mere moments ago. She smiled at him, eyes sparkling.

His fingers traced the curve of her neck, moving slowly over her shoulders before settling his hands gently on her upper arms. He slowly leaned in, bringing his lips within a hair's breadth from hers, "You're trembling. You need to go upstairs and get dried off."

Stratton felt her words stuck in her throat. "You're probably right," she whispered as his mouth tenderly met hers. She knew he was right; she needed to get out of her wet clothes, but she secretly hoped that he'd offer her his robe and ask her to stay a little while longer, snuggled together on the couch. She didn't dare verbalize those thoughts.

The celestial drumbeat of the thunder was no longer a threat; it was simply a melodious backdrop to the passion igniting between them. A new threat crept in, a temptation that became stronger the longer she stayed in Everest's space. She felt herself glance towards his made bed across the room. Immediately, she felt a wave of conviction, mixed with guilt and shame, wash over her.

Stratton reluctantly took a step back, "I should go."

Everest, still catching his breath, nodded. "I think that is a good idea."

"I'll see you in the morning."

"Goodnight."

"Night." Stratton stood there a moment longer before heading to her own room.

As she dried off and prepared for bed, the storm raged on outside.

He was still here after our first fight. Would he be willing to traverse through any future emotional storms? She felt he was willing, and if all of their fights ended like this, Stratton would face the foray. *But what if he isn't willing? What if I'm not worth the fight?* She wanted to trust him with her heart, but could she do that?

Feeling the tentacles of self-doubt creeping in, Stratton sat on her bed and reached for the one weapon she had against these feelings: Scripture. She opened up the Word and read about the importance of being fully prepared with prayer and supplication to fight the enemy, which in this case was herself.

* * * * *

Everest stood in the middle of his room, watching Stratton as she walked out the door. He was torn between the pull of desire and knowing things needed to stop. He instinctively ran his hand through his still-damp hair, sliding down to cover his face, willing his heart to stop racing. *What just happened?*

Taking a deep breath, he bent to pick up the towels that had fallen, forgotten on the floor, and started towards the bathroom. He paused for a moment to lift the towel she had used, inhaling her scent. Desire assaulted him again, and he quickly threw the towels into the hamper. Knowing and feeling that his flesh was weak, Everest grabbed his Bible from his bedside and began pacing as he sought solace and peace from the Word.

He opened and began reading aloud from 1 Peter, "Husbands, in the same way, be considerate as you live with your wives and treat them with respect..." Everest stopped there. *Had he treated Stratton with respect?* No, he had let his desire for her overrule his thoughts and almost allowed them to cross the boundaries that would have left them feeling guilty, empty, and ashamed. Unable to stand under the weight of his actions, he sat down on his bed and continued reading where he left off. "...as the weaker partner and as heirs with you of the gracious gift of life, so that nothing will hinder your prayers."

Though she wasn't his wife, wasn't that where he hoped that their relationship would lead? He wanted a future with Stratton, but he wanted it only with Yehovah's approval and in His timing. In order to honor their relationship, Everest must fight his desires until he had

His blessing and their time is fulfilled. He turned to the passage that would help keep him grounded during the fight and began reading, "Finally, my brethren, be strong in the Lord, and in the power of his might...."

Twenty

Mount Judea, Arkansas, wasn't a place Stratton imagined even existed, much less any of her children living there, but it was where Harper's in-laws, Marjorie and Zechariah Carter, lived. They ran a 4690-acre cattle ranch that spread over mountain ranges and fertile fields with a main home measuring 16,000 square feet. The French Provincial limestone structure was home to seven bedrooms, nine bathrooms, and a guest house, as well as a 12-stall equestrian barn situated behind the house. Four generations shared the home, including Marjorie's mother, Clementine, along with a married couple who lived on the premises, Darla and Ray, who helped keep things running smoothly for the family.

As Noah pulled through the front gates and headed into the estate, Stratton decided she had to inform him about her plans, which had changed a little since Finley had decided at the last minute that she wanted to come.

"I'm going to tell your sisters about Everest. I just need to find the right time to do it." Stratton glanced in the passenger mirror to the backseat at Everest, wondering what would happen when she told the girls.

Last night, they had spent the evening on the couch discussing how much affection Everest was allowed to show her in front of the girls. He had snuggled close to nuzzle her neck, but as soon as she heard Noah coming through the garage, she pulled away and straightened herself, ensuring there was plenty of space between them.

They'd finally settled on no physical contact in front of anyone that would indicate they were a couple. Stratton apologized in advance if she couldn't always make eye contact; if she made even one look at Everest in just the right way, then everyone would know.

Noah pulled up to the front of the house and parked the SUV.

"Mimi! Mimi!" Scarlett—8, Daisy—6, Levi—4, and Caleb—3, came racing toward Stratton's side of the car. Stratton's heart was full as she was smothered in hugs and sticky kisses, and four little voices were talking all at once about everything they wanted to tell her.

"Mom, it's so good to see you." Whitten greeted Stratton. She loved that he called her that, just as Harper called Marjorie "Mom." "Harper's getting something out of the oven. She'll be right out."

"Mimi, come see our new tree house Daddy built," Scarlett pleaded, dragging Stratton by the hand. She and Daisy still saw their biological father on occasion, but Whitten had become as much of a father to them as possible.

"I even have my doll house in it!" Daisy said.

"And I can show you I know how to use the swing," Levi added.

Caleb just reached his arms up, and Stratton picked him up. "Hold me." She remembered when Noah used to do the same, and her heart was flooded with precious memories.

"Mom!" Harper came out the door, and the two embraced. She took Caleb from her mother and held him. "I was just making Nana's chess pie bars. They're cooling now."

"Uncle Noah, will you take us fishing?" Scarlett asked. "Who's that?" She looked at Everest, noticing him for the first time since they had arrived.

"This is my friend, Everest," Stratton said as they grabbed their luggage and headed into the house.

Closing the door behind them, Stratton glanced appreciatively at how the creamy beige walls complemented the honey-toned hardwood floors. Harper had added a long, crimson runner with bronze, navy, and white geometric motifs, creating a warm and inviting entryway.

"I see you added some more paintings since I was here last." Stratton nodded to the wall on her left. Harper, still carrying Caleb, smiled. "Yes, I found them in an art gallery that specializes in vintage paintings."

"You did a great job. It's beautiful." She gave her eldest child a hug.

"Thanks, Mom." Harper looked at them," Just leave your things against the wall. We'll get them later."

"Come on, Mimi," Scarlet said as she grabbed Stratton's hand and pulled her down the hall to the kitchen, with the rest of the group following.

Sunlight streamed through the large double French doors at the back of the kitchen, casting a warm glow across the room. The kitchen was a seamless blend of timeless elegance and country charm, where soft, cream-colored walls served as a tranquil backdrop to the blue accents in the tiled backsplash, marble countertops, and cabinets with gold accents. The kitchen island was filled with a glorious-looking buffet of vegetables, crackers with cheese, potato chips, brownies, cookies, and other goodies. Harper, opening the refrigerator, pulled out a platter filled with Darla's amazing turkey sandwiches and placed it at the end of the island by the paper plates.

Harper motioned for Everest to go first, then turned to her mother. "So, Marjorie said Noah and Everest can have the bunk bedroom. You and Finley can have the one with the queen bed. Does that work?"

"That's fine, honey. Where are Marjorie and Zechariah?" Stratton asked.

"Mimi, I colored this for you." Daisy interrupted as she ran into the kitchen, handing Stratton a picture.

Levi was fast on her heels, "This is for you, too," as he also handed her a picture.

"Oh, thank you. These are beautiful." She leaned down and hugged them both. She missed this. "Let's go sit down and eat." Maybe it was time to consider moving closer to them. Noah could handle the homestead, but what about Everest?

As she pushed Daisy and Levi up to the table, she glanced to her right, where the family room opened off the kitchen, to see Everest sitting on the couch, Caleb already in his lap, Scarlett educating him about all of the different breeds of chickens she had, even reciting them in alphabetical order. *Why would me moving to Arkansas have anything to do with Everest? Why is that one of the first thoughts that occurred to me?* She knew that she must have thought their relationship was quite serious if Everest was one of her top considerations when entertaining the idea of moving.

"They are literally out on a cattle drive but should be back for dinner." Harper brought her back into the conversation.

Stratton laughed, appreciating how those two typically did those things together, taking off on their adventures or excursions. *It's all about companionship.* She hadn't realized she'd longed for companionship until Everest. A lot of sentences could begin or end with that phrase until Everest. Until Everest, she'd never stayed over at a stranger's home. Until Everest, she'd never so quickly entered into a relationship. She'd never been romanced with such gusto and care until Everest.

Now, to find the time to tell Harper.

"Just so you know, I did invite Dad for Fourth of July, too, but he isn't coming," Harper mentioned as she placed food and drinks for each of the children on the table.

"Honey, you can always ask your dad to come to anything. It doesn't make me feel awkward." *Actually, yes, it did.*

Harper propped her hip against the kitchen island, looking at Stratton. "If he was coming, I would have put him in the guest house and let you know well in advance." She was apologetic in her tone.

Everyone lost in divorce. It put Harper in a difficult position, especially during holidays and special occasions. It made Stratton act like things didn't bother her when they absolutely did. Of course, she never wanted to live in the same zip code as Dexter ever again, but she would never let her children or grandchildren know that. Though she was grateful he wouldn't be there, she would never decline an invite just because he was going. He always seemed to find a way to make a dig about something, making it hard to be polite to him. Eventually, she knew the girls would let the news about Everest slip, which would give Dexter more ammunition to try and hurt her. She could already imagine what he might say to Everest. She knew that because she cared so much for Everest, she'd do her best to shield him from anything that Dexter did or said.

"Anyway, I don't even know why I bother. We only see him if we go to Miami, and that's usually just on his birthday. So, I guess we'll see him in October."

It hurt Stratton to see her children hurting over Dexter's absenteeism. She knew she had done her own disservice to them, especially after the divorce, but she'd sought His forgiveness and wisdom in order to develop a healthy relationship with all of her grown children. "I'm sorry, baby."

"I keep thinking that maybe he'll change someday." She looked around quickly and lowered her voice, "He doesn't even send Caleb and Levi birthday cards. I told him I was in the process of legally adopting them, but he only sees two more people to add to his trust, which he doesn't want to do."

"Mommy," Levi called from the table, "may I have more milk, please?"

It broke Stratton's heart. How could Dexter not embrace these boys as his own? They had taken up residence in her heart the moment she met them.

"Sure." Harper crossed to the table and filled his cup. "Be careful not to spill it."

"Thank you." He took a sip, which created a cute white mustache, before he pushed back his chair and walked over to Everest, Whitten, Noah, and the other children.

Stratton turned as she heard a door open and saw Darla walking into the kitchen. "I've gotten all the laundry caught up. Miss Stratton, I am happy to take your bags to your room now." Darla, wonderful Darla. She was probably close to Stratton's age and had embraced the gray hair, cut short yet with a modern style.

"Thank you, Darla, and I'll grab my own bag."

"Nonsense, come on. I'll show you to your room and make sure you're nice and settled."

They walked through the house and entered the bedroom. Stratton smiled as she paused at the threshold of the room, taking in the sight. Light spilled through the window, enhancing the soft pastel pink hues of the room and giving it a peaceful, tranquil feeling. The queen-sized bed, sitting at the center of the room, was adorned with a plush comforter in a pale, almost ethereal pink dotted with subtle lace accents. Soft, silky cream, pink, and lavender-colored pillows were artfully arranged at the head of the bed. As she entered the room, she saw that Darla had placed fresh flowers on the desk.

Stratton crossed to the desk and delicately lifted a bud to smell its sweet fragrance. "Thank you for the flowers, Darla. They are beautiful."

"You are welcome. I know how much you love flowers."

Stratton moved to place her bag on the bed and noticed that Marjorie had left gifts for Stratton lying there: a gorgeous white Stetson cowboy hat, some lovely honeybee-themed jewelry she knew was handmade, and two nonfiction books about local history. Marjorie knew her so well.

"I have enough towels for you and Miss Finley. Would you like the sheets changed daily?" Darla asked.

"No, we will be fine."

"Every other day, then it is."

House rules. Who was Stratton to argue?

Darla opened the French doors that led to the pool and the back garden area. "You can leave these open at night if you'd like for some fresh air. As I recall, it's usually one of your favorite parts about coming to the mountains. The pool gate is always locked even though the children are all excellent swimmers."

"Thank you, Darla."

"Happy to oblige. The red button here on the intercom system will ring to me should you need anything, day or night."

"I appreciate it."

"Alright, I'll let you get settled, and I'll show the gentlemen to their room." Darla exited.

Stratton basked in the splendor and pampering. She was still quite nervous about telling the girls about Everest and prayed they took the news maturely and calmly.

Twenty-One

When Marjorie and Zechariah returned, it was only long enough for quick greetings and a fresh change of clothes before heading to town for the hoedown, which included bringing Great Grandma Clementine, who was a lively, lovely eighty-year-old.

Stratton entered the family room wearing black jeans tucked into cream boots and a turquoise shirt embroidered from the shoulders to the chest with fringy chenille. She noticed that Finley had arrived and was on the floor playing with Scarlet.

"Finley! I didn't hear you arrive!" Stratton walked over to give her daughter a hug and a quick kiss.

"Wow, Mom, you look adorable." She complimented, standing up and brushing off her shorts.

The doorbell rang, sending Scarlet racing off to beat her brother to answer the door.

Stratton appreciated that Finley chose to wear a flannel shirt with jean shorts and a little less makeup. "You do, too, darling."

Harper entered the family room with an older gentleman trailing a few steps behind her.

"Mom, this is Lewis Townsend from the next ranch over. He is going to be joining us for the hoedown."

Stratton extended her hand to the older gentleman before her, noting he wore his gray hair longer as it peaked out from under the cowboy hat. Speaking of cowboys, where was her cowboy?

Hearing laughter, she glanced toward the kitchen, where she saw Everest sitting at the table with Zechariah and Noah. His gaze met hers, sending a wave of warmth rushing through her. She averted her eyes and focused on the grandchildren as they ran into the room, clamoring for her attention. She could feel Everest's eyes watching as she turned to compliment them on how cute they were in their outfits, hoping no one noticed how red her face had become. She didn't know if he'd borrowed that denim shirt he had on or if he had brought it, but it clung to his frame. If he flexed his muscles, she wondered if it would rip the seams. She had to not think about all of the times she'd been cuddled in those arms because it created a longing to go there again.

"I think we're all ready!" Harper said.

As they exited, Harper directed everyone to load up in one of the three vehicles. Somehow, she worked it out with Stratton being left to ride with Lewis in his nice-looking, new-appearing white Chevy Silverado.

Oh, Harper. I should have told you about Everest. Stratton realized Harper had subtly set her up.

"Harper tells me you're on a sabbatical. How's that been?" Lewis began as they followed the other cars.

I'm spending all of my time falling head over heels for the most wonderful man I've ever encountered while losing all sense of time or the list of things I'd hope to accomplish. "It's definitely a change of pace, but it's very nice to have some time away from the university." Stratton hoped the drive would be quick. "So, you own a ranch, too?"

They drove through the property and onto a road with a thick forest on either side.

"I do. My two sons have mostly taken over the daily operations. It's been about two years since their mother passed, and I haven't felt up to getting out much. I ran into Harper picking up my grandkids at piano lessons. She insisted I come to the hoedown with everyone."

Harper, you picked a nice widower who is probably lonely and wanting companionship, but it isn't with me. She wondered if Everest hadn't entered her life when he did, if she would be open to a relationship at all. Had she been destined for a summer of love no matter what? By his weathered skin and hair color, she guessed him around 70. If she hadn't met Everest, would she consider going ten years or so in the other direction? She couldn't answer it because it was a nonsensical question. She wasn't interested in Lewis. She was in a committed relationship with Everest, and she wanted to progress with him.

*****

As they walked up to the hoedown, fiddles, banjos, basses, and mandolins could be heard coming together to create foot-stomping, yeehawing, hands-clapping, loud-cheering music. The large barn was decorated with fairy lights twisted on the rafters and bales of straw strategically placed throughout. On the stage up front, a singer began giving out square-dancing instructions on how to do-si-do. Folks started clapping and hollering along with the music.

Stratton, unable to keep track of Everest's whereabouts, obliged many-a-dance with Lewis throughout the evening and made sure that she danced with the grandkids.

Standing by a table off to the side with Marjorie, Stratton opened a bottle of water. "What do you think of him?"

"Who?" Stratton innocently asked, but knowing full well who Marjorie meant.

"What do you mean, who? Lewis! I told Harper he would be a fabulous match for you. Not that you're even looking, but I selfishly would love to have you closer."

Marjorie continued without giving Stratton a chance to respond. "His family made it big in oil, but he really is the salt of the earth. I haven't seen him out much since his wife died, but he seems to really be enjoying himself tonight, though." Currently, Lewis was two-stepping with Clementine and seemed to be having a lot of fun.

"I think it's a very sweet gesture on your and Harper's behalf. I want to be open to anything the Lord has for me, so thank you for thinking of me." She had to tell her daughters. They deserved to know.

But it wouldn't be that evening.

Harper, carrying a sleeping Caleb, walked up to join the two women.

"Mom, I'm sorry to interrupt, but we're going to go home." She looked down at Caleb. "He's already asleep, and Daisy says she has a stomachache."

Stratton's gaze followed Harper's as she saw Whitten sitting at one of the tables across the way, holding a teary-eyed Daisy.

"Do you want me to send Whitten back up here to bring you back home, or do you mind getting Lewis to drop you off?"

"I'll manage, but would you like me to come with you?"

"It's fine. We've got it. Thank you." Harper kissed her mother and started to leave but stopped and turned back to Stratton.

"Finley and I will be working at the park tomorrow for the Fourth of July show, so you just do what you want. Come down or get one of the stable guys to saddle you up for a ride. I want you to feel like this is a vacation, too."

"Thank you. I'll see you tomorrow."

While the band struck up again, Stratton took a break and sat upon a bale of straw, watching her other two children dance the night away. The years melted before her. She saw two kids dancing, Finley trying to get Noah to square dance properly and Noah laughing every time he made a misstep.

Everest strolled up and sat down on the bale next to her.

"Where have you been all night?" Stratton asked.

"Upon learning I specialize in arboriculture, I've been outside diagnosing tree issues for the host of this here shindig. Even got the ladder out and had some high-powered flashlights so I could show him the cedar rust on some of his apple trees. Then, somehow, I got roped into being the designated dance partner for the entire Golden Circle Ladies group, which is here tonight showcasing their newest dance moves. That's them over there, wearing mostly gold and, I think, a lot of White Diamonds perfume. Then Daisy threw up on my boots, so I've been out back cleaning up."

Stratton laughed. "I'm sorry."

Everest leaned in and whispered, "You know I really want to take you out on this floor and dance with you until dawn, don't you?"

Stratton felt her stomach flutter. "Yes, I do." She looked straight ahead because if she turned to look him in the eyes, those amazing blue eyes, she was a goner. She felt either the external or her internal temperature begin to rise.

"You know I wouldn't be able to settle for just dancing, don't you?" He said with a hint of what he was suggesting in his voice.

"Uh-huh." She nodded as she took a deep breath to calm her heart. She worried his whispering in her ear might create suspicions, yet she secretly liked the thrill of being discreet. Would he try to touch her lower back or graze her hand? Could she pat his shoulder and let her hand linger?

"I should have just held you until dawn for our first dance. If I had, I would at least have that memory to get me through the rest of tonight."

Stratton felt a longing to steal away with him at that moment, to go off alone, hidden from those at the hoedown. If a slow song had been playing, she would have reached for his hand and dealt with the repercussions later of everyone watching her dance with Everest.

"Mom, come on! They're gonna play *The Git Up*!" Finley came over, grabbed Stratton's hands, and pulled her off the bale so they could dance to the popular hoedown song. Stratton gave Everest a quick look as she was ushered to the dance floor.

He head-nodded for her to go dance with a sweet smile on his face.

She stood next to Finley as the song started, and a large group of people of all ages joined them on the dance floor. The song detailed the steps to take in each verse, and it was meant to be a community dance. Finley was a natural and led the large group of dancers, some of whom knew the steps and some who didn't, but none of them could dance as well as Finley. Stratton, being a quick study, followed along, listening and looking, keeping time with the first verse.

She let Finley shine for the first minute of the song with shoulder rolls and the slip and slide but then decided it was time to remind Finley where her rhythm and moves came from. Stratton started two-stepping, and cowboy boogied when the song instructed. Finley's mouth dropped in surprise and then turned into a big smile. It then became a friendly showdown at the hoedown between Finley and Stratton. The pair were as in sync as could be until it was time to slide to the left and right, that's when Stratton pulled away and gave Finley a run for her money. Stratton butterflied, then swung a fabulous fake lasso as she moved around in a tight circle, putting those hips into it. Whistles and cheers erupted from the onlookers, leaving no mystery as to who the superior dancer was. The song repeated the steps, and Stratton spun out Finley when the song called for it. The next additional move was taking it down low, and Stratton could get as low as Finley. They were both all smiles and laughs. Even Noah was laughing and clapping, trying to keep up with them. As they kicked off their last round, starting with the two-step, Stratton glanced around to see if she could spot Everest.

She eyed him slow dancing with a blue-haired lady in her gold shirt, clearly missing the beat of the song. Stratton met his eyes and couldn't restrain a laugh.

He just rocked side-to-side with the older lady, making her night. The look on his face told Stratton he accepted his fate and resigned to finishing it out with the Golden Circle Ladies.

Stratton joined in the line dancing for a few more songs, fully immersed in the Western lifestyle for the remainder of the evening and enjoying the time with her children.

*****

It was after ten PM when Stratton quickly said her goodbyes to Lewis, who made sure she and Clementine got safely indoors since he had driven the both of them home. She thought she noticed a connection between Lewis and Clementine and hoped she was right.

Finley and Noah sat down in one of the living rooms and were talking.

"Goodnight, Kids," Stratton yawned.

"Night, Mom. I'll be in there a bit," Finley said.

Stratton made her way to her room, opening the outside doors to let in the cool evening air. She never tired of the freshness of the mountain air, no matter what season she came to visit. Even in the dead of winter, she'd bundle up and sit out back by the fire pit and let the crisp freshness fill her lungs. Across the way beyond the pool was another wing of the house where Everest and Noah shared a room. She saw the light on through the curtains.

You awake?

It was a text from Everest.

Barely.

Not true. Now, she was wide awake.

We didn't get to talk about the gentleman who kept your dance card so full earlier tonight.

Blame Harper. She was trying her hand at matchmaking.

Seems to run in the family. First Noah with me, now Harper with your gentleman friend. I'm glad she's not as adept. ;)

Stratton readied for bed.

I agree, and tomorrow, I will let Harper know her services aren't needed.

What do you need?

Her heart pulsated, and the room felt as though it warmed considerably despite the cool breeze blowing through the outside doors. She text a kiss emoji. *Will we always flirt like this?* Could a couple keep fun and romance as part of a long-term relationship? It hadn't yet happened for Stratton, but maybe this would be different. She wanted to walk across the back patio area and visit him but knew she couldn't do that tonight.

He text back a GIF of a cartoon Lady and the Tramp sharing a piece of spaghetti, culminating in a kiss.

She wondered if he saw himself as Tramp, a wanderer from job to job without roots in one place. Was he ready to put those down in Tennessee with her? It was too big of a discussion to get into over text.

Besides, Finley came in, so Stratton put her phone on silent and spent the next hour talking with her daughter.

Twenty-Two

"I done got them horses saddled up and ready for y'all." One of the barn workers mentioned.

"Thank ya, kindly, Toothless Billy," Noah said.

Stratton's breath caught in her throat as she gave Noah a strange look.

Skinny in tight Wranglers and a long-sleeved cotton shirt with a cowboy hat that must have seen plenty of figurative and literal rodeos, Billy looked like he was born to be on a ranch.

"Noah! What on earth?" Stratton scolded after Billy had moved on.

"That's how he introduced himself. He likes the name."

Stratton shook her head.

She, Everest, Noah, and Scarlett were saddled up for a ride, Scarlett insisting on leading the way since she knew her way around the property. She took them through the creek and wound her way through the woods. At the top of a flat ridge, she showed them how to race across it. Wind blowing, sun shining, the thunder of hooves, it was a wonderful, freeing moment, and Stratton felt so rejuvenated.

She loved the life her grandchildren were living on the ranch. They would experience a taste of freedom. Not many kids in their generation would. Stratton prayed for their safety in their adventures and endeavors.

She drank in the image of Everest on horseback; every angle should be captured on canvas. He was a natural in the saddle, wearing that same snug denim shirt but with it open a little more at the top. Her mountain man slash cowboy was poetry in motion. Not only was his ruggedness exemplified on horseback, but desire, too.

Back at the barn, Billy took the horses from everyone except Scarlett. Harper's rule was that she had to do everything herself. Noah oversaw Scarlett. Then they headed out of the barn toward the house, where Darla would have prepared a scrumptious lunch like always. Billy was around the side washing one of the horses down, leaving Everest and Stratton alone for the first time on the trip.

He grinned as he stepped close to her. Taking her by the hand, he led her around a corner where they were concealed. He playfully tipped her cowboy hat back and came in for a kiss. Everest didn't need her permission.

She had already assigned her lips as his exclusive territory. This was the beautiful part of their relationship where words weren't needed, where they both sought to steal precious moments together like this.

It felt like ages since their lips had met, but she knew it had just been the previous morning before the drive. How was it possible to taste both sunshine and liberty in a kiss? How was it possible she found the glisten of perspiration across his top lip so appealing? And when had he found time to pop a peppermint in his mouth? He seemed to tease her by kissing her slowly while easing back ever so slightly, urging her to move toward him. She enjoyed the evanescent moment, knowing it couldn't last much longer without someone catching them before she was ready to reveal their relationship. Right now, though, Everest's kiss was revealing that she had gone too long without his lips against hers. She no longer wanted lunch; she only had an appetite for Everest. Her right hand wound its way to the back of his neck. She applied slight pressure to let him know she wanted him to pull her closer to him.

He brushed his lips across her cheek and smiled down at her before lowering his mouth once more to hers.

She cherished these moments with him. She felt his hands move to either side of her face as he deepened his kiss. She was about to suggest they find a more private place when one of the horses in the stall let out a whinny, startling her. She pulled back and noticed the look of disappointment on his face. "I'm sorry." She patted his cheek, then began adjusting her hat and hair, winking at him, "To be continued."

She hated hiding Everest from the girls; she had nothing to be ashamed of. She needed to tell Harper and Finley the next moment they were together, which happened to be roughly in the late afternoon.

* * * * *

"Mom, did Lewis come by today?" Harper asked as she stood at the kitchen island, scrolling on her laptop.

"Lewis?" Stratton sat across from her on a barstool.

"Yeah, is there something you want to tell me?" She grinned at her mother.

"What do you mean?"

"Scarlett said she saw you holding hands. I mean, it's totally fine, but it's not your style at all. I get that you don't wanna waste time. Lewis was Marjorie's suggestion, which I didn't really see then, but I'm cool with it. He's a nice man."

This family. First Noah and that camera, and now Scarlett. Zero privacy. I will never get that man truly alone.

"Lewis did not come over today."

Harper looked panicked. "Mom, it wasn't Toothless Billy, was it? I don't call him that in front of the kids, and I know he's got a Marlboro Man thing going on if you're into that, but no, you can't date Toothless Billy."

How oblivious were her girls, after all? Or was she just that good at hiding her feelings?

"Harper, Scarlett didn't catch me hand-holding with Lewis or Toothless Billy."

"Oh, then why'd she make that up?"

"She didn't make it up." Stratton steadied herself. "It was Everest."

Harper's brow raised, then furrowed, and her eyes squinted. "What?"

"I'm in a relationship with Everest."

"Finn! Finley!" Harper raised her voice.

"What?" Finley answered from her spot on the couch.

"Did you hear that?"

"Hear what?"

"Mom's dating Everest, Noah's friend that's here."

"What?" Finley laughed. "Wait, are you serious?"

"Yeah."

"Whoa, whoa, whoa!" Finley went into a tailspin. She stared pointedly at her mom. "You are living with him, but I'm not allowed to share a room with my boyfriend?"

"Finley, focus," Harper said. "That's not the point. Don't you think he's, like, really young?"

Did Stratton even need to be a part of the conversation? She wasn't going to get a word in edgewise anyway, not with their flapping jaws going back and forth. If she'd only told them earlier, they would have already had this over and done.

"Mom, how old is he exactly?" Finley asked.

She felt like a child before her children, chastised as if she'd done something horribly wrong. "Forty-seven."

"Well, I thought he was younger, but that's still a big age difference," Harper said. It was a small concession.

"Never pegged you for the type to have a kept boy, Mother." Finley's words were sharp and curt. Stratton knew she was hurt for not being told about their relationship sooner.

"I'm sorry for not telling you both sooner, but I'm not going to argue with either of you, and I'm not going to defend my actions."

"You let me believe he was Noah's friend and that Noah was inviting him to my home. You could have just said something when you asked about him coming here."

"Harper, we weren't in a relationship when I asked if he could come."

"But you were totally crushing on him. Wait," Harper appeared to remember something. "Is this the guy you stayed with at Valley Forge?"

How nice of Harper to remember details at the most inconvenient of times.

"Oh my gosh, you hooked up with him at Valley Forge?" Finley chimed in, dramatically throwing her arms up in the air.

"You two can think what you want about my character, but you should know me better than that. I know you're angry and upset with me, but you two need to grow up and be mature about it. Yes, your brother knew, and no, you will not punish him for it because I asked him not to tell you. I wanted this to be something we could celebrate and share together, but it's obvious I was mistaken."

The girls averted their eyes.

The conversation came to a standstill, so Stratton went to her room.

About an hour into reading one of the new books, Stratton heard a knock on her bedroom door. "It's open."

The door opened. All three of her children stood in the doorway.

"Can we come in?" Harper asked.

"Only if you aren't here to assassinate my character."

"We're sorry, Mom," Finley said.

"And we're not mad at Noah. He told us how Everest got there and how good it's been having Everest there. He also said that you've been happy since Everest came," Harper said.

One by one, the children sat around her on the bed.

"And if I'd been paying better attention, I would have noticed when I visited that you both liked each other. I could have helped," Finley said with a wink.

"Mom, we don't care about Everest's age or that the two of you are an item. We just don't want to see you hurt," Harper offered.

Those three adult children became those three little ones right before her eyes. They gave her a similar speech when she told them that she and their father were getting a divorce. They had told her they didn't want to see her hurt anymore. Now, here they were, still trying to protect her. The girls slid in on either side of her, and she wrapped an arm around each.

"So, how serious is it?" Harper asked.

Stratton stroked her hair. "I really like being with him, and I care a lot about him."

"Is it the kind of serious that my children need to call him something?" Harper asked.

"It might be, Harper, eventually. It's still very new."

"Mom, I really didn't think you hooked up with him. I know you're not like that. I'm sorry," Finley apologized.

Stratton kissed her head. "I'm sorry I didn't tell you sooner, I really am. I wasn't sure how to tell you. I wanted you both to like him as a person without any preconceived notions."

"Did he really pick a hundred roses for you?" Harper asked.

"Ahem, I helped," Noah said. "I wasn't exaggerating, was I, Momma?"

"No, it was close to that."

"So, he's pretty romantic?" Finley asked.

"He is."

"Mom, we won't get in the way of your happiness," Harper pronounced for the group. "I'm just glad you weren't interested in Toothless Billy."

They all shared a laugh.

Stratton held onto them as long as she could before they were joined by the grandkids in a giant snuggle fest that transformed into a pizza party by the pool. Later that evening, the grandkids insisted on bringing their sleeping bags into Mimi's room and sleeping with her.

Stratton's heart was full with the scene before her.

Tomorrow would be different once the household knew of her relationship, but she already felt freer.

Twenty-Three

Stratton slipped out before the household awakened.

She went to the barn and found her favorite strawberry roan mare, Tilly, short for Tillamook, named for the type of strawberry.

"Ma'am, you want me to saddle her for ya?" Billy appeared, and Stratton noted the strong smell of tobacco coming from his direction. How could Harper have even thought she would have been interested in him?

"Yes, thank you."

He soon had Tilly ready to go, and Stratton took to the trails.

She had spent her childhood taking English riding lessons, but when she went trail riding with a friend, she fell in love and went as often as she could. She and Dexter had lived in the city, so she never got to have a horse of her own during her marriage, so she relished the rides with Tilly when she visited Harper.

Sunlight filtered through the trees, casting soft rays of light on the trail. As she and Tilly rode along, the tranquility of the woods settled deep in her soul as she prayed for her children and grandchildren. They made their way through the woods to the top of the ridge, where Stratton paused. She looked out over the valley below that seemed to extend for miles in all directions. From her vantage point, Stratton could see how the creek wound its way through the fields, fields that had colorful wildflowers interspersed among the luscious, green grass. She inhaled the fresh air, giving thanks to the Creator for His marvelous works. Her heart's desire was to honor Him and share His love with others. She wanted to pursue Kingdom work and more so pursue it with Everest. *That is something to continue to lift up in prayer.*

"What do you think, Tilly?"

Tilly nickered and moved her head a little.

Stratton gave her neck a pat and made a clicking noise to get her going again.

She was famished by the time they returned and eager to see what Darla had for their morning spread.

* * * * *

Darla was bustling around the kitchen as she prepared breakfast. Everest, already seated at the table, lit up when he saw Stratton enter the kitchen. There were some packages wrapped in butcher paper sitting on the table.

"What are those?" She asked as she walked over to the table and sat down next to him.

"I know you already gave Marjorie and Zechariah some very nice seats at the Celtic concert next month, but I have something to give them from us, too."

"That's very sweet of you."

"Waffles or pancakes, Miss Stratton?" Darla asked as she put a plate in front of Everest with eggs, chicken sausage, and two of the fluffiest waffles.

"I'll have the same as Everest, minus a waffle."

Marjorie and Zechariah came into the kitchen and joined the couple.

"How was your ride?" Zechariah asked Stratton.

"A little faster than your jog." She said.

"Maybe we'll race next time." Zechariah joked.

"What are these?" Marjorie asked as she touched the brown paper packages.

"Gifts for you and Zechariah from us," Everest said, handing one to each of them. He reached over and took hold of Stratton's hand under the table, giving it a little squeeze.

Marjorie sat down at the table. "You know you're going to have to tell the story of how you two got together. I highly doubt Everest just showed up at the homestead." She began untying the jute twine and opened the paper. The first package was a convertible leather backpack purse. "This is gorgeous. Thank you."

Darla brought coffee to Marjorie and Zechariah.

Zechariah opened his package, revealing a leather grip bag. "Wow. This is a wonderful piece of craftsmanship. Thank you both. Are these from that leather store Harper mentioned?"

"Yes, they are." Everest looked Stratton's way. Her eyes were as large as saucers. He knew she was probably adding up the total in her mind. What was a couple of thousand dollars anyway? She wouldn't accept rent money so he'd done this as a partial substitute.

"So what's the story?" Marjorie asked, sipping her coffee.

Darla brought Stratton's plate to the table.

Everest shot Stratton a smile and launched into the story of how they met.

"What a delightful story!" Marjorie laughed.

"It didn't take long before I let her know I was sweet on her, and thankfully, she agreed to take a chance on me."

"Please forgive me for not giving you both the proper introduction when we first arrived; I had not yet told the girls," Stratton apologetically explained.

"Nonsense! You're entitled to a little mystery in romance. It's what keeps a relationship interesting," Marjorie said with a smile.

*****

Everest clicked through the checklist in his mind for the fifth time.

After asking Zechariah for some of the most romantic spots the homestead had to offer, he'd chosen the hay loft. At first, he had chuckled at how cliché that sounded, but it was the perfect place to take Stratton. Dimly lit with the right blanket and cushions, it became a romantic retreat.

He stood in the middle of the loft, making sure he had everything in place to make this evening special. He glanced around the loft once more, then checked to make sure the song he'd chosen was ready and would play easily.

So many thoughts coursed in his mind. He wanted to ensure they had a strong foundation upon which to continue to grow in their relationship, yet he felt pulled in opposite directions. On one end, he was struggling with his flesh to hold back his desires and not rush headlong into temptation. On the other end, he felt compelled to treat her as the treasure she was, one that was special and cherished.

Since Stratton had told Harper and Finley about their relationship, the girls had been extra attentive and somewhat overly polite to him throughout the day, so he'd decided to retire to his room later in the day, giving Stratton time with her family. He'd texted her, asking her to meet him in the barn after dinner.

"Hello?" Stratton called from below right on time.

Everest came down the ladder.

"No, you did not." She had her hands on her hips, acting like she was annoyed, but the twinkle in her eyes spoke of a different message.

"Didn't what?" Everest held up his hands in innocent surrender.

"Do you have that hay loft all fancied up and something special planned for the two of us? You know that Whitten did this for my daughter when he was courting her?"

Courting. He loved when she used that word. It was a throwback to an era nearly forgotten, and he reveled in the wistfulness of it.

"I know it's overdone, but come on." Everest took her hand. He glanced down at their hands. He liked the way she wrapped hers around his, fitting perfectly in his.

They climbed up the ladder to the loft.

"Oh, Everest," she exclaimed, her hands covering her mouth as tears filled her eyes.

It was the reaction he wanted.

He had converted the loft into an inviting and warm haven. The gentle fragrance of the fresh lavender springs that he had scattered around the loft created a sensual yet peaceful aura. He'd covered broken-down bales of straw with double blankets and tossed some comfortable cushions on top. Mini solar lanterns were strategically placed around the loft, emitting a soft, ambient light throughout the loft.

He reached up and wiped away the tears that softly fell from her eyes. "Wait here. I have a surprise for you," he said as he moved quickly around the loft, turning off a couple of the lanterns, leaving only a few lit. He untied a rope and used a pulley to open the top of the loft, revealing a midnight blue sky filled with stars. Taking her hand, he guided her to the cushions. "Have a seat."

"Oh, Everest, this is lovely." She commented as she sat down, still looking at the night sky.

"And, I've got a song." He gave her a quick wink.

"Of course you do."

"Wait for it." He brought out his phone and hit play.

Stratton laughed. "Conway Twitty? *I'd Love to Lay You Down.* Everest!"

"It's perfect. Conway, Arkansas. We're in Arkansas. Just listen."

Stratton smiled, tapping her foot to the beat while looking around the loft. By the third verse, which speaks of age not fading the singer's love for his wife, Stratton glanced over at Everest.

He smiled. "I like this song because it celebrates the simplicity and inevitability of what time does to both parties, but his desire for her doesn't dwindle or get tarnished by time."

"That's a sweet sentiment, but I have to tell you, it does make me wonder why you chose this song."

"Stratton, I never want to pressure you into expressing anything unless you feel you want to share it. I'm committed to our relationship without seeing an end." He reminded himself she'd been hurt deeply in the past, and trusting him and their relationship with him was a huge step.

The song ended.

"I like the song and the sentiment. Thank you for the reassurance."

Everest put on some classical music from his phone. "I take it things are settling down with the girls after you told them about us. They've been paying me more attention and being quite inclusive." Everest gave a little chuckle. "Harper and I spent an entire hour poolside talking about my life, and Finley's been making sure I've had a plate, napkin, or a full cup all afternoon."

"I noticed. It's going to take some adjusting. Marjorie told me that Clementine couldn't figure out why I rode with Lewis the other night when it was obvious you and I were an item."

"She knew?"

"Everest, we're terrible at hiding it. Noah knew. Savannah suspected. If anyone pays close attention, I guess it's easy to pick up on."

"I suppose most folks are oblivious. I can't imagine not noticing you the first time I saw you. If it wasn't part of His plan, you could've been like all the other tourists and faded from my memory."

Stratton pursed her lips, a playful smile trying to escape. "Speaking of things fading from memory. I don't remember how your kisses taste."

Everest, noticing she had become more playful lately, scooted toward her. "Then let me help you remember," he said in a low voice right before his lips pressed against hers.

Stratton wrapped her arms around his neck, pulling him closer to her as their kiss deepened.

With one arm around her, he slowly eased her back against the cushions, lavishing her with a multitude of kisses that rivaled the number of stars looking down on them from the heavens. Stars burned with nuclear fusion; Everest and Stratton burned with their own fire each time their lips met.

Everest paused for a second, his lips slightly suspended above hers. He looked down at her, the desire in his eyes reflected in hers. His mouth covered hers again.

He envisioned the rest of his life with her. He knew that they had both experienced lonesome times, waiting and wondering what Yehovah's plan might be, and now He was revealing it in His perfect timing. *Is it possible I'm not just falling in love with her, but I actually love her?* He silently asked Yehovah to examine his heart. He had to know if what he was feeling was genuine or just a result of what a decorated hay loft on an Arkansas ranch in the middle of a moonlit summer night could do to a fella.

He turned his attention back to Stratton. She was a beautiful woman, both inside and out. Seconds turned into minutes as they became lost in their desire for each other, unable to control the flame that continued to grow with each touch, each kiss, each breath.

Everest released his hold on her lips and leaned slightly away from her. Tracing his thumb over her cheek, he let his gaze travel over her face as if memorizing each feature. Unable to stop himself, Everest leaned in and placed a tender kiss on her brow. "I could stay here all night with you."

"Oh, Everest. I can't be out here all night. Finley will never let me hear the end of it. I have to go." She began fixing her hair and brushing the straw off her clothes. "This was really wonderful. Thank you for tonight and everything."

"I'm glad you enjoyed it." He was confused at the sudden change in her.

"Are you coming?"

Everest shook his head. He needed to spend time with Yehovah and get answers about what he was feeling.

"You go on. I just want to gather some of this up beforehand. Here," he handed her a lantern, "this one has a little left in it."

"Well, goodnight."

"Night."

Twenty-Four

Stratton felt like she had let him down.

With age, there were a lot of changes, both physically and emotionally, as well as memories of her past. While Dexter's venomous vitriol was no longer paralyzing, there were times that his voice and words popped into her head, but he was wrong on all accounts. Someone did want to be with Stratton. Someone did find her beautiful and attractive. Someone did value her. She first knew the Father was the One Who would never leave or forsake her, and she was learning to accept that Everest was nullifying every negative word Dexter had spoken to her throughout their marriage, during their divorce, and any chance he got since.

She made her way back to the house.

Clementine sat in a chair with a book in her hands when Stratton walked through the living room. "You've got some hay in your hair, dear."

Stratton ran her fingers through her hair and found a piece of straw. She blushed.

"You don't need to try and hide how much you care about him and enjoy being with him."

Clementine's words caught her off guard. Stratton paused, unsure of how to respond.

Clementine continued, "You worry too much about upsetting the apple cart when you should enjoy the bountiful harvest set before you."

"It's hard for me. I've been divorced since my 40s. I told myself I'd never let anyone get close to me again. It's one thing to care for Everest, but letting him get close to my children and grandchildren is a different story."

"Are we talking about the same man who chased imaginary dragons around the garden with those children for half a day today? Are we talking about the same man who took your son to the picnic table to have a Bible study and discussion before he prayed over him?"

Stratton didn't know that. She hadn't witnessed it, but it demolished another wall around her heart.

"Darling, give yourself permission to love." She closed her book. "I'm off to bed, honey." She stood and placed her book on the table next to the chair.

"Thank you."

Clementine opened her arms, enveloping Stratton in a warm hug as she kissed her cheek. "I should be thanking you. My daughter may have had you in mind when she invited Lewis to the hoedown, but I'm the one he's taking out next week; apple carts be darned!"

Stratton gave her a big squeeze. She had been right about the two of them being attracted to each other. Clementine was a beautiful example of living to the fullest no matter where one was on the earthly timeline. She let those thoughts sink in as she made it to her room.

Finley was scrolling on her phone when Stratton entered. "A little late, aren't we missy?" Finley asked. "I can't believe I'm the one saying that to you." She laughed and shook her head as she said it.

For the past thirteen years, those were Stratton's words to Finley.

Finley sat up, looking so beautiful without a stitch of makeup. She removed the glasses she wore when her eyes were tired and ran her hands over her face.

"We were just...," Stratton started.

"No, I don't wanna know details, Mom. It's weird to me, but Noah is really happy to have him there and says you are, too. I'm still trying to adjust."

Stratton moved to the bathroom to brush her teeth.

"And I'm gonna take a job here in Mount Judea."

Stratton poked her head out of the bathroom. "You are?"

"Yeah, I've been talking to Harper, and everyone is telling me the market is thriving. There's a property in foreclosure I could get for really cheap and, I don't know, turn it into a venue or something."

Stratton came back into the room and changed into pajamas. "It's a big decision." She got under the covers next to Finley.

"I just want to find my own place, Mom."

Stratton took her daughter into her arms and held her close. "I know, sweetie. I know you do. You've moved around so much that this could be a really big, scary, wonderful, amazing adjustment for you." Stratton was so happy. Finley would be here with family, and so far, there has been zero talk of any boy leading her up to this decision. Could this be the start of long-awaited answers to prayers?

"You're not upset that I don't want to be at the homestead?"

"No, unless you want to come there."

"No offense, but you see where we're staying, right?"

Stratton kissed her daughter's head. "I do."

"OK, well, the market is a bit more on fire here, and I want to be with the kids more. Besides, I'm not sure I'd be able to stomach the kind of security footage you have at your place."

Noah! "What did your brother say?"

"Mom, it was innocent. He just told us the story. And just so you know, he has trail cams set up, too."

They shared a laugh, then turned out the light.

Was it possible that multiple prayers were being answered before her very eyes? Stratton knew that she needed time to sift through her feelings for Everest. *Could it be more than infatuation? How could she feel so strongly for Everest after such a short time?* The more she thought about her relationship with Everest and analyzed her feelings, the more she realized that there was quite a bit of items on the Scriptural checklist being checked off.: Patient; kind; doesn't envy; doesn't brag; isn't puffed up; doesn't behave inappropriately; does not seek its own way; isn't provoked; keeps no account of wrong; does not rejoice over injustice but rejoices in truth; bears all things; believes all things; hopes all things; endures all things; never fails.

Love. *Was it possible she loved Everest?* More importantly, was it possible she was ready to let her love flow freely? No more drops. No more trickles. Stratton had much to pray about.

* * * * *

It was the Fourth of July, and Stratton had been on Grandma duty, ensuring the grandchildren who needed a nap received a nap before they would head to Jasper, the next town over, for festivities and fireworks. Harper and Finley had left earlier in the day to put the finishing touches on whatever it was they had planned. Stratton assumed it would be a cute patriotic song with the children.

Everest, Noah, and Zechariah had been taken along to assist. Whitten stayed behind so he could drive everyone after naps.

"Mom, I want you to know that while Harper is still adjusting to Everest, I am really happy for you," Whitten said to Stratton while she enjoyed a lemon poppy seed muffin at the kitchen island.

"Thank you."

"And, though she didn't remember it, we had prayed about your sabbatical, and she had specifically asked for you to partake in an adventure that spoke to your heart. I gently reminded her of that when she told me about Everest." How many sons-in-law, like precious Whitten, prayed like he did for their mothers-in-law?

Whitten's words were touching. "That's so sweet. Thank you for telling me." *Harper. How sweet of them to offer such a prayer. It certainly has become an adventure, one I never expected. Now we're halfway through, and I haven't spent any time on the things I thought I'd be doing, but I have plenty of time on things I'd thought were over and done with long ago.*

She recalled the time Whitten had come to her house before he proposed to Harper. He had openly and honestly shared that he didn't know if marrying Harper was right because he still loved his deceased wife, Alana. He never wanted her to feel compared to Alana. She had responded to his concerns with a question: when Caleb was born, did he feel like he wouldn't be able to love him as much as Levi? Whitten said, of course not; his heart had grown larger. As Whitten answered, he realized that he could love Harper and her girls and that his heart would only grow larger. He felt the guilt lifting from his soul and thanked Stratton for her wisdom. Harper had called home within the week to share the news of her engagement. Married shortly after that, and they continued to work together, creating a family that was filled with love. Harper had never mentioned that she was being compared to Alana or that she was living in her shadow.

"We just wanna see you happy, Mom, and if that means Everest is joining the family, we welcome that." Whitten pulled her out of her head.

"Daddy, can we go now? Everyone is awake." Daisy said as she entered the room, effectively ending their discussion.

* * * * *

The park was filled with food vendors, craftsmen, artisans, and crowds of people when they arrived. Seas of red, white, and blue moved about the grounds. In the center was a large stage, currently curtained with stagehands preparing for what looked like a concert. Stratton, with her blue and white striped seersucker dress with three-quarter sleeves, held tightly to the girls' hands as they looked for the others.

Marjorie and Clementine had been helping prepare food for a family-style meal of BBQ chicken, fried okra, biscuits, corn, mashed potatoes, and green beans for those who wished to join. It was a joyous feast set before the folks.

Everest, looking handsome with his jeans and button-down, short-sleeved shirt made to look like the American flag, approached Stratton and gave her a quick hello kiss. She felt her cheeks warm. It was their first public display of affection, and she knew all eyes would be watching.

Harper walked up, saying that she needed the children directly after dinner to prepare for the performance she'd planned.

"Mom, you have reserved seats down front. I have our names on them."

"OK, thank you. We'll get down there in plenty of time."

After eating, they were eager to see the performance, so they made their way to the stage.

A young teenage girl started the ceremony by singing the National Anthem and, at the end, welcoming everyone to the celebration.

It quieted as a wonderfully familiar song played on the speakers: Ray Charles' version of *America the Beautiful*. The drums began, and as the instrumental piece started, the curtain raised to reveal the entire stage filled with at least a hundred men and women, all of whom were veterans, some in uniform, some not. Those veterans who could stand did. Some were in wheelchairs in the front row. Two large screens began showing pictures of uniformed soldiers throughout the ages, photos taken during wartime and peacetime.

Everyone in the audience stood.

Stratton felt the tears falling from her eyes as she listened to the words of the first verse and looked at these veterans before her. The stage was filled with living history, those men and women who had loved their country more than themselves. Each one of them was a hero. These were the ones who had secured their freedoms through their service. It was one of those indescribable moments known only to those who have partaken in such a unifying moment.

Stratton knew not everyone in the pictures was standing here today nor made it back from deployment. She looked at how youthful these veterans once were in the photos, some yet unaware of the hardships and horrors they would witness in times of war. Yet time hadn't diminished their value and worth to their country nor to the people who stood in their honor before them. Her heart swelled with emotion. Her daughter had planned this beautiful moment to honor the veterans.

In that moment, Everest instinctively placed an arm around her and drew her close to him. Just as Ray's voice asked someone to help him sing, the children, all wearing red, white, and blue, entered the stage, singing along. Stratton cried tears that were a blend of happiness, pride, and respect as cheers erupted from the crowd.

To see those men and women on stage and hear those children, her grandchildren, singing those words, knowing that because of their service, it meant they could be doing just exactly what they were doing, was awe-inspiring. The next generation. Scripture spoke so much of the next generation, and there those kids were, taking part in something they wouldn't understand for years to come. If not for Everest's strong arms holding her as they swayed and sang in unison, she wouldn't be standing.

She could feel Everest's embrace, a silent pledge that he would be a fighter and preserver for her and her family, seeing them as his own. She didn't know how she knew it, but she knew it. She also realized without a shadow of a doubt that she loved him. It was an overwhelming, surreal feeling, realizing that she was choosing to love

Everest and wanted a life with him.

Seeing the glistening eyes of the servicemen and women on stage, seeing emotions bubble forth from some, hearing those tiny voices sing about His grace upon their homeland, Stratton soaked in all of it from the safety and security of Everest's arms.

It was a ten-minute round of applause with more tears. How could there be a dry eye among them? She'd seen the tears in Everest's eyes, and they naturally endeared him more to her.

She couldn't wait to congratulate Harper on such an impressive job.

When she found her after the performance, she held her so tightly. "That was amazing, sweetie. You did a fabulous job."

"Mom, that was Finley's idea."

Stratton felt the earth move. *Finley? My Finley?* Hadn't Stratton been praying for something exactly like this for Finley? "It was?"

"Yeah, she told me about it, and I got most of it ready, but we worked on it together."

Finley was laughing and talking with Noah and Everest on the other side of the stage.

Stratton went to her, dragging Harper with her. "Finley, that was wonderful. You two created something so spectacular and moving that this could be life-changing for so many people."

"OK, Mom," Finley said, "don't overreact."

"Honey, listen to me. That was powerful. That was a gift that you two need to lean into more. This is a way to reach others with a message of hope and appreciation."

Finley was speechless.

Stratton hugged both of her daughters. "I love you two so much."

Before the fireworks began, there was a procession to meet the men and women from the stage. Everyone wanted to express their heartfelt gratitude for their service, which continued right up through the first boom and crackle of color lighting up the night sky.

Stratton had never enjoyed a more hallowed celebration than the one she had at this moment.

* * * * *

After returning to the ranch and tucking in some very tired kids,

Stratton bade her children goodnight. It warmed her heart to see the three of them talking together and enjoying one another's company. That might not have always been the case when they were children, but she was grateful they had become friends in adulthood.

As she made the walk down the hall to her room, Stratton continued to lift up her prayers of gratitude. She entered her room and opened the doors leading outside, as was her nightly ritual.

She saw a lit sparkler by the pool.

Everest. She smiled and walked through the doors towards him. "What are you doing out here?"

"Celebrating." He moved his sparkler around and made light circles. "Got you one." He offered her one.

"I'm good. Thank you."

"That was an amazing show your girls put on, Stratton. I'm sure if anyone recorded it, it's already gone viral."

"I hadn't even thought about that."

"It was quite moving." The sparkler died.

Everest looked at Stratton. "Since our night in the hay loft, I've been doing some thinking and searching my heart. You know that I waited longer than I should have to tell you I liked you and wanted to pursue you, and I don't want to wait to tell you what's on my heart now."

Stratton didn't mean to hold her breath. It just happened.

Everest placed the spent sparkler on the rock wall and took her hands in his. "Stratton, we've been having a lot of fun together, and I don't want that to change. I told you I was in this for the long haul. At some point, you have to confront the possibility that feelings already run so deep it can only mean one thing."

Stratton readied herself. She knew where he was headed.

He looked at her, his emotions evident in his gaze. His voice was soft and confident, "Stratton, I love you."

She'd planned to dismiss his words because it was too soon for either of them to feel that way, yet if she hadn't just had the experience of the previous hours with him, she just might have dismissed it. But she didn't. She knew she felt the same way, too.

"Everest, you know you're not just getting me, right? To love me is to embrace all of my family, which is easy to do in Arkansas when we're here, but it also applies when we're back in Tennessee. I don't want you to think I come without baggage because I absolutely do. I know it's a big ask to take that on, so I just want you to know what it entails."

Everest squeezed her hands and pulled her into his arms. "I love you, and everyone you love will fit into my heart just as they do in yours."

Stratton didn't want to ask, but she felt if she didn't, she wasn't doing her due diligence. She took a step back from him but kept hold of his hands. "Everest, we haven't talked about this before, but I think we need to discuss it before things go any farther. You are entirely capable of having children of your own." He started to interject, but she lifted one of her hands, placing a finger over his mouth to silence him before she continued. "Listen to me. If you feel that you want kids, even the tiniest amount, I do not want you to give up that dream for me." She felt the tears pool in her eyes, but she refused to let them spill down her cheeks.

"Stratton, you're a lot of firsts for me. I have never been in a relationship with someone who has had kids before you. I also have never gotten to a point with someone where I thought of actually having children with them. I know how biology works, and I've known that from the day we met."

"Please don't remind me that Sarah was ninety, so it is possible." She referenced Sarah from Genesis, who miraculously conceived and birthed Isaac in her old age.

Everest laughed. "I wasn't going to. Do you love Levi and Caleb?"

"Of course I do."

"Do you view them as less deserving of your love because they aren't biologically yours?"

"Absolutely not."

"When you refer to them, do you call them anything different than your grandsons?"

"No."

"Stratton, it doesn't have to be an either-or situation; it can be both. I don't have to choose between either being a father or not. Choosing you is choosing fatherhood." He paused as he ran a hand over his eyes, wiping away the tears that had gathered there. "Granted, it may not look the way I thought it would in my youth, but that doesn't mean I will love your kids and grandkids any less."

She knew he meant every word. He wasn't giving up the dream of fatherhood for her. He was embracing that role with her and the family that accompanied her. The tears welled up. "Everest?"

"Yes?"

"I love you."

His arms enveloped her as his mouth covered hers in a kiss that was full of hope and a future.

She was doing it. She was letting love love like Clementine suggested.

Their future shone as brilliantly and beautifully as the twinkling gems overhead.

Twenty-Five

Stratton sat at the dining room table with her laptop open and paperwork strewn all about it.

Everest entered after seven PM, walked over, and pecked her on the cheek. His work shifts had been continually extending as the festival neared.

She remained intently focused on her computer.

"I've got some items of interest when you have a moment." He flashed a folder in front of her.

"I'm just trying to finish this article I wanted to write, but I should be done in a bit. Your plate's covered in the oven."

"Thanks. I'm famished." He left the room.

She went back to writing, but after fifteen more minutes, her eyes were blurring. She wanted to see Everest.

Since returning from Arkansas two weeks ago, their routine had been Stratton focusing on writing but kept coming up short each time she sat down to write. Her days were spent in the garden, learning about animal husbandry from Noah and meal-prepping for the home. She was reserved with Everest in public appearances, not ready to be the summer subject of local gossip.

She sighed as she closed the laptop and went to find Everest.

He sat on the couch, an empty plate on the coffee table, an open folder in his hands.

"I'm sorry I was distracted," Stratton apologized. "This sabbatical is winding down, and I feel like I haven't accomplished anything that I'd hoped to."

Everest opened his arm for her to come to rest against him. "I'd say you're doing all right." He kissed her cheek. "I have something you'll find very interesting. Look at this," he showed her some letters. "Lyle and Bernadette, let me borrow these family letters from Milky Way Farms detailing Morgan's Raid. Are you familiar with it?"

She knew about the raid. During the Civil War, in 1863, General John Hunt Morgan rallied over two thousand Confederate cavalrymen to march northward into Union territory to raid and terrorize those they encountered.

"I know some about it." She looked at the letter Everest handed her.

It was written by the owner of what became Milky Way Farms in 1863. Having heard a rumor about the raid and fearing what the men would do, the owner claimed to have buried the family silver and gold on the homestead.

"Everest, a lot of these Confederate gold stories are just that. Whimsical tales without factual basis spun on fanciful rumors and hope."

"Well, I thought it might be something worth looking into. Want to go treasure hunting with me? Fifty percent finder's fee."

"So, you think I should stop working on my article and go treasure hunting for the remainder of this sabbatical?" She chuckled.

"I think you should look into the validity of these claims and see if there's something to it."

Stratton mulled it over. What was one more absurdity added to her list? She'd already entered into a relationship with a younger man, spent all summer giving and receiving the most wonderful affections from said man, and now had the opportunity to hunt for buried treasure in close proximity to this man. It almost read like a work of fiction.

"Are there more family letters?" She asked.

"There are. They are housed in the family library. This was just to whet your appetite."

"OK, I'll look over them. By the way, did you save room for dessert?" She asked, changing the subject.

"What's being featured this evening?"

"Kisses a la carte." Stratton did enjoy this special time with him each night. *Does he think about the future? Will there be a time he will want more than simply kissing?* He'd never crossed their mutually agreed-upon boundary. Stratton honored that boundary by keeping their times together similar to the times in the past, though she had thought about what would happen if she didn't honor that boundary.

Though she struggled about what to write in the articles, she would have no trouble writing page after page about Everest's touch and kiss. Could she win a Pulitzer for that? Those fingertips gently rubbing her neck, his other hand resting firmly on her back, providing a sense of comfort. Between the sprinkling of kisses to her neck, the tiny nibbles to her ear lobe, and the whispering of some attribute he adored about her, she felt how much Everest cherished her and their time together. Their passion would build each time, but Stratton never felt like the dam would burst. She wasn't sure if it was because of Everest's staunch commitment to not letting things go too far or if things just looked and felt different at sixty.

She didn't have much time to dwell on it. Everest exercised exclusive occupation over her lips and only stopped after they'd both burned a hundred calories. It was energy well spent.

* * * * *

"Here's all of the family letters and diaries we have, ma'am," Lyle said.

Everest and Stratton stood before a large oak executive desk in the manor house at Milky Way Farms. Several stacks of letters and a few books were piled on the desk. A sizable antique Persian rug covered most of the hardwood floors, and the built-in shelves were filled with books ranging from antiquity to modern times. The south side of the room was an entire wall of windows offering a full view of the gently rolling meadows.

"Everest here said this would be a rather large job. I'm convinced there's something we've missed. See, I think my ancestor left behind clues we just aren't seeing. If he was willing to hide it, and the raid never happened, there must have been some interruption in the recovery of it. He doesn't say what it was, and I don't know enough about our family history to make a guess. I'm hoping someone with your background can assist."

"I'll do my best."

"Thank you, ma'am."

Lyle turned toward Everest, "We wanted to add some piping for this water feature Bernadette saw when we visited New York last week. Can I tell you about what we want and show you where?"

"Sure." Everest looked at Stratton. "Are you all set?"

"I'm good. I'll be in full-on research mode. "

"OK, I'll come get you for lunch." His eyes said he wanted to kiss her farewell, but he gave a small wave instead. "Bye."

The two men left.

Stratton wondered what Lyle would think or if he would tell anyone if he saw Everest kiss her. She realized she still wasn't ready for anyone outside of the family to know about her relationship with Everest: the tall, dark, handsome stranger from out of town, the younger man endearing himself to all he encountered who was renting a space from Old Lady Davis.

Stratton dismissed that thought. She gathered the letters, moved to sit down in the brown leather office chair behind the desk, and started reviewing the documents before her.

* * * * *

"Find anything interesting?" Everest asked, sticking his head into the room.

"Possibly."

He crossed through the room to where she was still seated. "It's time for lunch, so let's take a break and eat."

Stratton marked her place, stretching before she stood.

Everest held out his hand for her to take. They walked outside to one of the large maple trees overlooking the estate, where she saw he had a cooler sitting on top of a picnic blanket he'd spread under the tree.

He unpacked the cooler, then fixed her plate.

"Chicken salad, mmm. Did you make this?" Stratton asked as he handed her a plate. He'd insisted on preparing some of the meals and had been in charge of making lunches today. He'd even inspired Noah to start pitching in more at meal times, too.

"You didn't think I was cleaning all night, did you?" He asked, adding three large scoops to his plate. Everest led them in prayer,

162

thanking Him for the day and the food.

"So, are you ready to share what you found?"

"Yes," she replied after taking a bite of food. "There are a few family trees with Lyle's ancestors listed. Interestingly, all but one have the same people listed, except for one, Solomon Turner, that I found in the pages of Merrick Turner, who was the owner during the time of the raid. Solomon Turner isn't listed as a son on any of the other family trees, and I've yet to encounter him on any of the pages in the diaries. I suspect he was a child who may have been stillborn or died quite young."

"No mention of the money yet?"

"I'm not up to that point in the diary. I just wanted to get my bearings, but I will look at those entries after this delicious lunch."

After they finished and had cleaned up their picnic, Stratton returned to the library and returned to reading until it was time for them to head back home.

Twenty-Six

"Say, Mom, you reckon we can have Ralston and Harlow stay over for supper? We're working on the finishing touches for that horse show I'm putting on, and I hate to break for dinner to go somewhere," Noah asked.

"That's fine. It's Italian beef and should be done shortly," Stratton responded from her place at the dining room table, where she was perusing the copies she'd made of the letters from Lyle's ancestors.

"That's great because we're hungry."

Stratton looked up to see Noah standing there with his two friends. "Of course, you asked with them right there. Noah, you boys, go get washed up, and I'll get the plates set on the deck. I'm not moving my paperwork."

She hadn't heard from Everest but figured he'd be home later.

She readied the sandwiches and joined the trio of men on the deck, a surprising breeze cooling the warm July night.

"So, Noah says you're working with Everest at Milky Way." Harlow began.

Are people already talking about us? What has Harlow heard?

"Yes."

"To hear my great granny tell it, our two families were almost related."

"What do you mean?"

"Great Granny said one of them Turners almost married our relative. She was a house slave at the Turners, and Mister Turner sold her away when one of them boys had an idea to marry her."

"Harlow, do you know which son that was?"

"No, ma'am, but Great Granny might."

"Does she still live in town?"

"Yes, ma'am. You can catch her sitting on her front porch most any summer night."

* * * * *

Stratton, having filled Everest in about her conversation with Harlow, had asked him to come with her the next night after dinner to go speak to Harlow's great-grandmother.

"I love seeing you sparkle." Everest held her hand as he drove the two of them into town.

"What do you mean?"

"Doing this kind of thing. You're really enjoying it."

"It is interesting; I'll give you that."

Everest brought their locked hands up to his lips and kissed her hand at a stop sign. "I'm glad."

A few minutes later, they pulled up to a tiny brick ranch home on High Street. Sure enough, an elderly woman sat on her front porch, wearing a robe over a gown with hair already in curlers for the night.

"Mrs. Reed? Did Harlow tell you I was coming by?" Stratton asked as she exited the SUV.

"Stratton, right? I believe we've met a few times before. Come on up."

She and Everest walked up to the porch. "I don't know your husband, though."

"I'm Everest Galloway, ma'am." Everest extended his hand. "We aren't married yet." He winked at Stratton, causing her heart to skip a beat.

Yet and Ma'am. He called me miss when he met me. Either the South is rubbing off on him, or he really thought I was a miss when he met me. And then there's yet. I'm not ready to even think about marriage, but is he? This wasn't the place to analyze that one word. Was he really planning to marry her? Sure, she loved him, but could she marry him? This was a summer full of surprises. She could imagine the look on her students' faces if she walked into the classroom as a married woman.

"Well, you two have plenty of time for all that. Now, have a seat here and tell me what an old woman like me can do for you two."

"Mrs. Reed, I'm going over some family letters from Lyle Turner's ancestors. They own Milky Way Farms, and Harlow said one of the Turner boys almost married a relative of yours. I'm not finding any references to that in any of my research or their family papers. Do you have any insight into this?"

Mrs. Reed closed her eyes and sighed. "Oh honey, it was a different time for them." With her eyes closed, she seemed to travel back in time. "I heard the story at the feet of my great-grandmother. Her father, Meriday, had been a house slave of the Turners, along with his sister, Daphne. They were close companions of the Turner children. Young Solomon Turner, especially, took an easy friendship with them."

Stratton stared ahead and let Mrs. Reed take her back in time, too.

"They were just about eighteen, all of 'em when the War started. That Solomon was the youngest of the Turner children, and Mister Turner did not let him leave for war, which suited him just fine. He was secretly courting Daphne, planning to take her away to New York, where they could marry. He planned to stay up there and was going to take Meriday with them.

Mister Turner got wind of it somehow; I suspect Daphne's mother spoke up, being afraid of what would happen if they were caught. Besides, she didn't think that there would be a future for the two of them." Mrs. Reed breathed in deeply. "When Mister Turner caught wind of it, he sold Daphne, and she left the only home she'd ever known, thinking that would end the relationship, but that wouldn't stop Solomon. He was devising a way to go and get her when the rumors of the raid happened. They said the Confederates were going to pillage their own people or enrage the Union soldiers to retaliate against civilians. Mister Turner took ill, and he told Solomon to take the family silver and gold and bury it on the property. Solomon was ready; he'd been waiting two years for this opportunity. He was going to take the money and go after Daphne." Mrs. Reed paused. "Only when he got to where Daphne was, she had taken ill. She'd always been a house slave, so when she had been sold, the new owner had put her to work outside to keep their estate going. They had her farming hard, and she contracted malaria. She passed before Solomon could buy her freedom. I suppose the only consolation was he was with her when she passed. He immediately took off to fight for the Union as his last act of defiance against his father and died in battle shortly thereafter. He had secured Meriday's freedom before he went to war, and it was a well-kept family secret that the homestead Meriday purchased was the result of the stolen fortune Solomon ran off with. Meriday always said that he refused the full portion because it had equally belonged to Daphne. No one knows what Solomon did with the rest, but I don't think you'll find any answers at Milky Way Farms."

Stratton could see that even in modern times, the family might not want the world to know that Solomon Turner had stolen the family fortune and defected to the North. It didn't matter that he had done the right thing by joining the Union, and now she knew the reasons he wasn't included in the family line.

"However, you might find some answers here." And just like that, Mrs. Reed pulled out a bundle of old papers.

Stratton's jaw dropped.

"Meriday saved Solomon's letters to Daphne. We used to think we'd found clues in there to tell us where the gold was. My kids were the last ones to even look at these. No one else has asked about it in years."

They probably didn't need to since Meriday's original farm had tripled in size and was one of the top-producing cotton farms in the state.

"Could I borrow these?" Stratton asked.

"Sure, honey. And if you find that missing money, do something good with it. Those two were gonna change the world if they'd just had a chance."

"We will. Thank you, Mrs. Reed." Stratton took the bundle of letters. After shaking Mrs. Reed's hand, she and Everest made their way back to the car and headed home.

Twenty-Seven

Before going to bed that night, Stratton had spent time reflecting on what Mrs. Reed had shared. There were a lot of dynamics to unpack, so she had created a list of the themes she was encountering: Forbidden love. Traitorous action. Felonious theft. Untimely death. Generational mystery. Denied freedom.

The next morning, she sat on the deck watching the sun rise over the horizon, casting shades of pinks and yellows over the field in front of her. She reveled in the peace of the morning as her only companion, except for the occasional sound of the farm animals stirring...and the flock of chickens exploring the perimeter of her garden. *Noah!*

Stratton had the bundle of Mrs. Reed's letters sitting in front of her, planning on opening them after the mini quiches she had made for breakfast finished baking.

"Morning, Mom." Noah opened the deck doors and came outside. "Did you start reading the letters?"

"I will as soon as we finish breakfast. However, I might be having some chicken for dinner if that rooster I see wakes me up too early."

"Somebody posted 'em and had to get rid of 'em. They'll keep all the ticks away, promise." Noah looked at the stack of papers. "You think that boy left clues behind in the letters?"

"Possible, but probably not probable."

"Well, I'm gonna get to feeding. I'll be back for breakfast." Noah returned indoors, passing Everest, who was on his way out to the deck.

"Good morning." He walked to Stratton and leaned over for a kiss.

She inhaled his scent, crisp and fresh like the morning air. "Morning."

He placed a hand on her shoulder. "With the festival happening at the end of the week, I may be working some nights longer than usual."

"I expected as much." She patted his hand.

"Looks like you've got some things to occupy your time with, though." Everest nodded toward the letters.

"That I do."

Everest hesitated. "I know you've been thinking about the story Mrs. Reed told us. Would you like for me to take the day off and stay here reading through them with you?" He rubbed his thumb over her shoulder.

His offer warmed her heart. He always made her feel like she was a priority. "No, you go finish making that place as amazing as I know you are. I'll let you know what I find out."

"Alrighty, I'm gonna head out and get an early start so I can hopefully get home early tonight."

"Oh, I haven't made your lunch yet."

Everest leaned over and kissed her. "That'll hold me over." He winked. "The vendors are starting to show up. I'm sure I'll find something there."

"Can you wait til the breakfast is ready?"

"Not today, I'll just grab some hard-boiled eggs. I'll see you tonight. I love you."

"I love you."

Everest went back inside.

Stratton was so thankful for the natural ease of having Everest in her home. Their everyday rhythm was as harmonizing as the morning birds singing praises to their Creator. Everest added peace to her days and promise to her future.

Stratton looked at the pile of correspondences, excited that she was about to head into a different era. It was time to see what Solomon had to say to Daphne.

Dearest Daphne, my Beloved. I've learned today, upon returning from visiting relatives, that my Father has dismissed you from this estate. Your mother is beside herself in anguish, not realizing the depth of his hatred for our love.

I presumed you were mine since we were children. You've been afforded almost every luxury next to us, from sitting under our same tutors and being clothed in the same fabric to traveling on almost every excursion. How was I to think of you any differently than being the one my parents betrothed me to?

Father says you are a youthful indiscretion and struck me in anger when I raised my voice. I won't win against him by shouting or fighting in the traditional sense, but I will fight for you, for us, for everything I've promised to provide for you.

I'm aware your new family has strict instructions to keep me away from their property. For now, I shall use couriers to send word to you.

Write only if you can devise a way not to get caught. One so delicate as you isn't meant for such harsh treatment.

Yours Affectionately,

Solomon

She cried for Solomon. She imagined him as a child, not knowing and understanding what slavery was, growing into a small awareness as an adolescent, and hating it by the time he was an adult. He and Daphne had been together almost their whole lives, spending every day together, so it was natural that they would fall in love. It was easy to see how Solomon thought that they had his father's blessing, never thinking they'd be separated. There he was, pledging to fight for her. There was no stopping a young man in love.

Stratton wondered if Merrick Turner was so angry because Daphne was his illegitimate daughter. She wasn't sure if she'd find that answer in the letters.

She picked up the next letter and continued reading.

My Beloved: I'm asking Father to allow me to join the War and will try to gain a promotion as soon as possible. With enough pay, I can then secure our passage away from here, and we can continue our future as planned.

Meriday has promised to bring you some fabric I purchased when I was in New Orleans. I had hoped it would be a bridal gown for our wedding this summer, but those plans must remain on hold.

Your mother will tell you to forget me just as she is telling me to forget you every day. She is more hurt than angry, and I am on the receiving end of her ire. She blames me for daring to tell you my feelings, for laying open my heart. I would have kept my feelings to myself if it would have kept you near to me and near your mother.

Daphne, the pain of not having you here is most unbearable.

There is an emptiness and sorrow that fills the halls and floors. Gone is your laughter that echoed throughout. Gone is the peace and joy your presence added to every room you entered.

I often take to the outdoors to find you, but you're not at the pond, the creek, or our tree in the woods, yet I still search for you.

I will try to make plans to see you in the weeks to come.

Yours Always,

Solomon

Her heart was broken for Daphne's mother. Here was a woman in an impossible situation. She was not a free woman, and she had to watch her own children endure the same hardships and sufferings as she had. When Solomon, being the master's son, had professed his love for her daughter, it added another layer of conflict within her. She and her children had already been robbed of so many choices that no matter how she viewed this situation, she had to have known it would only end in tragedy.

Stratton grabbed another letter.

My Sweet Daphne, I've received your letter, and I've spent hours reading and rereading its contents. Your words bring me comfort, and I am thankful you are finding ways to make yourself useful and occupy your time. I should like to see you caring for the young children of the home. It would only show me a glimpse of what it will be like when you care for our children one day.

This War can't go on for very much longer, Father says. However, I do not spend much of my time with him. I am beginning to oversee the estate here since my brothers are gone. They've yet to see any battling and also believe this War won't last long.

The outcome doesn't change my plans for us.

We are going to leave Tennessee and move to New York.

Meriday says we will convince your mother to go and might be able to find and track down your father. She said he was separated in Kentucky and sold to a family in Illinois, which means there is a strong possibility he is a free man. This could have grandiose implications for you and Meriday.

I will send word as soon as I can.

Stratton's phone buzzed.

"Hey," she said. It was Savannah.

"Did you find that Confederate gold yet?"

"Not yet. But I did learn that the youngest son of the man who owned the farm during the Civil War, Solomon Turner, loved a young woman, Daphne, who was a slave. They never had a chance to love each other freely, Savannah. Noah's friend, Harlow, said that his great-grandmother is a descendant of Daphne's brother. We went to see her, and she shared the oral history of the story, which is how I found out about the relationship. She let me borrow the letters that Solomon wrote to Daphne. It's heartbreaking to read."

"How many letters do you have to get through?"

"A fair amount."

"I'm really glad you listened to Everest and decided to look into all of this. I'm sure you're finding plenty of inspiration now to write about."

"I am! So change of subjects. When we went to see Harlow's great-grandmother the other night, she thought we were married. Everest told her that we weren't married…yet. Do you think he's thinking about marriage?"

"If he's abiding by your house rules, marriage is the only way he's ever going to get to stay upstairs," Savannah laughed.

"It just isn't something I've even thought of."

"Hello, first comes love, then comes marriage."

"All in the span of one summer?"

"There aren't too many women who get this type of opportunity. I'm not telling you that you have to be ready for his proposal or even ready for marriage, but from what I've seen and what I hear, you hold his heart. I hope you can find a way to not hold back yours."

"Why do you have to know me so well?"

Stratton knew that she loved Everest, but she still had reservations. Before she had been married, no one had explained the importance of being equally yoked, not just spiritually and physically but emotionally as well. Even after her divorce so many years ago, Stratton knew that she had some emotional damage that still lingered, things in which she continually prayed for healing and release from the bondage that emotional damage had caused. She knew that she and Everest were equally yoked, walking in the way God had designed and had outlined in Scripture, but was that enough to free her from the chains that bound her to her insecurities and fears from the past? She prayed that it was and knew that total release from her emotional bondage would only come from One Who extends His saving grace.

Twenty-Eight

"Mom, are we doing takeout tonight?" Noah entered the dining room.

Stratton sat at the dining room table with her laptop open, surrounded by property map printouts and other papers. She pushed her glasses up. "Sorry, I lost track of time." She had been unsuccessful so far in trying to locate the farm or even the name of the family to which Daphne had been sold.

"It's not a problem. I can go get us all something to eat."

"Check in with Everest and get his order. I don't know what time he'll be home." *Can't you see yourself married to him, Stratton? Doesn't it feel right to say this is his home? Doesn't it feel like his home is with you and Noah?* It did. He was a constant in her days, and it felt like it had always been this way.

"Alright, I'll call him on the way."

After dinner, Stratton took her work to the family room, intending to work for a bit longer until Everest got home. She awakened to a light kiss on her lips. She opened her eyes to find Everest kneeling beside her, her laptop still open and her glasses in her lap.

"I must have fallen asleep," she said with a sheepish grin.

"Is that research wearing you out?" He asked.

Stratton nodded as she yawned and sat up. "What time is it?"

"After ten. I just got home. I called and texted but figured when I didn't hear back that you might be asleep."

"Did you eat? Do you want me to heat something up for you?"

Everest smiled. "I'm totally fine. I ate some white fish this evening from The Netherlands, but I appreciate the offer. I hated to wake you up, but I thought you might not want to spend the night on the couch, so I just popped in to check and see."

Stratton stretched, then took his outstretched hand as he helped her off the couch and into his embrace. "Goodnight. I'll fill you in on everything tomorrow."

She could feel her eyes getting heavy again as his embrace made her feel warm and secure. This is where it would be nice to be married to Everest, she realized. They could retire to one bed where they could talk and share about what happened during the day while they drifted off to sleep together instead of heading to separate bedrooms. She envisioned how comfortable it would be to have him sleeping next to her. Tonight was not the night to pursue that thought, though. Besides, she had to remember they were committed to adhering to biblical standards.

Stratton knew at that moment that she genuinely wanted to hold nothing back from him; she wanted to give him her whole heart.

He held her until she nearly fell asleep standing up, then planted a kiss softly on her lips before sending her towards her own room down the hall.

* * * * *

"So, you're trying to find the property of the family Daphne was sold to?" Everest asked. He sat next to Stratton at the dining room table, sifting through the piles of papers she'd accumulated. He'd arrived home early for a change, read through most of the letters, and then heard Stratton's summaries.

"Here, read this final letter." She handed him a worn piece of paper.

How do I address this letter? Your breaths are labored and weak. Will your eyes soon behold what I have penned as you are recovering, or will your eyes behold Our Savior?

The doctor says you need rest and time, but I saw how quickly he dismissed himself.

Why can't they see you like I do?

Why won't they treat you like they treat me?

My privilege is a curse. I shall bury that which has contributed to this curse and leave for the Union if you perish.

I will leave it among the lilies in our special place by the sea and, if needed, will die for freedom.

Yours For All Eternity,
Solomon

Everest looked at Stratton. "You think that this is a clue to where he buried the silver and gold?"

"I would like to see the business records from that time. Do you think Lyle will know where those are and give me access?"

"Great questions. Why don't you ride with me to work tomorrow and see what you can find?"

"Mmm hmm." She was deep in contemplation.

"What's bothering you?"

"Solomon loved her so much. Everest, there weren't any Scriptural reasons the two of them shouldn't have been able to have a life together." She let the tears build as she recollected what she had read in the letters. A love so pure and innocent had been crushed by the society in which they were born. "He spent his boyhood thinking one day the girl at his side was going to be the one he would have a family with, grow old with. Then, in a moment, she was removed from him, from her mother, and from her home, but he still held onto hope. He fought for her, but then she died. It just seems so wrong, so unfair."

Everest stood and took Stratton's hands. "Come here."

She stood and let him hold her. "It just breaks my heart to think about it."

"That's why you need to share this story. There's so much to learn from history, from those who've gone before us, like Solomon and Daphne. There is so much their stories can teach us."

"Well, this story seems to teach that you should never give your heart away, or it could be broken beyond repair." Her tears fell on his shirt sleeve.

He held her against him and kissed her head. "That's not the take-home lesson, Stratton. I see two people whose love transcended the confines that their family, as well as society, placed on them. I see a man determined not to give up, one committed to pursuing his beloved, though it cost him his fortune, his reputation, and ultimately his life. The value that he placed on securing freedom for the future was worth more than his own life. I see a story of a nobleman that should be shared."

"That's quite eloquent and beautifully said." Her voice cracked.

"You've looked at these papers long enough for the afternoon. Let's go see what fun, new things Noah's been up to on the homestead."

Stratton looked quizzically at him, "What do you know that I don't?"

They found Noah and took the UTV out to a wooded area that Noah had cleared. In its place were rows and rows of sunflowers, swaying gently in the late afternoon breeze, their yellow petals vibrant against the violet and coral hues of the setting sun. It was breathtaking.

"I've got folks signed up online for photo sessions all summer. And don't worry, I already made sure with the insurance man; it's perfectly fine."

Not that that was Stratton's first question; she was relieved to know he had checked. It was lovely to see a sea of vibrant colors of the blooming sunflowers before her. *What if 'sea' didn't mean actual water in Solomon's letter? What if 'sea' meant something like a field?*

* * * * *

Later that night, Everest, arms folded behind his head, stared at the ceiling of his basement bedroom, thinking about Daphne and Solomon.

Daphne spent her life in captivity, treated no differently than domesticated livestock.

It was easy to armchair quarterback what he thought he would have said if he were the one who had to confront Mister Turner. Everest had actually confronted someone before who was just like Mister Turner and taught that guy a lesson, a lesson that ended up backfiring on Everest in the long run. He probably needed to share that with Stratton, but was it something she needed to know? *Wasn't the past best left in the past?*

Immediately, the verse from Psalm 51 about God desiring truth from his inner parts came to mind. He hadn't been honest with

Stratton. He hadn't detailed everything about his past or divulged the particulars of previous relationships, as short and insignificant as they were. He also hadn't shared why he hated the concept of slavery so much with her, and he hadn't told her about his childhood friend, Emma Rose.

Scrappy and sweet, Everest had met her on the way to school one day when he walked by the run-down trailer park where she lived. She had jumped in front of him before a snarling dog could get any closer and told that dog to go home. Third-grade-Everest thought she was the bees' knees.

She had stringy blonde hair and brown eyes and smelled like strawberries. They walked together to and from school every day but were never playmates beyond school hours. He had returned her life-saving act by giving her a Snoopy necklace with their initials carved on the back with his pocketknife. She was appreciative of that small token and wore it all the time.

Time doesn't stand still, and over the years, they grew apart. At fifteen, Emma Rose had chosen a path different from Everest. Hers was a path filled with drinking, drugs, and casual sex. Though she had earned a bad reputation at school, he still had a soft spot for her.

On her 16th birthday, Everest had given her a Bible. His parents had taught him that all of life's answers were right there in that book, and he wanted to help her find a way to get back on the right path, but she didn't seem to appreciate his gift.

Within a few months, Emma Rose started missing more and more school. On his way home from school, Everest would see her with older guys talking to her on the porch. He'd wave, and she'd give a head nod, then go back to her discussions with whoever was on the porch.

And then, one day, Emma Rose was gone.

Everest had knocked on her door, but there was no answer. He had asked neighbors, but no one knew anything.

He finally asked one of her girlfriends. All she knew was that Emma Rose had told her that her boyfriend had been trying to get her to move away with him to Philadelphia. She wasn't sure she wanted to leave, but her friend figured since she was gone, she must have agreed and was with him there.

Two weeks later, Everest saw a box next to the trash can by Emma

Rose's trailer. It was a box of her stuff, and on top of a sweater was the Snoopy necklace, so Everest took it.

Over the years, he'd used the Internet to try and find her, but he'd had no success. She had seemed to vanish, except for a few rumors here and there. Once, a high school friend of theirs had said he'd seen her on the streets. Another friend said Emma Rose had called her, saying that she was living in a high-rise with her rich boyfriend taking care of her. Everest hadn't had the resources or time to look into any of the leads.

He had never been sure why, but he'd kept the necklace as a reminder of her.

Several years ago, he learned about human trafficking and realized that it sounded similar to what might have happened to Emma Rose. He knew he'd never liked that she had just disappeared, and no one knew where she was or where she was living, and now he had a strong possibility of the mystery. He knew he had to do something to fight that kind of darkness for Emma Rose and the others like her.

Stratton would definitely understand that kind of passion, and he needed to share that with her sooner rather than later.

He had a partner, a companion, a beautiful helpmeet who deserved to know how much, and why, he hated the concept of slavery and exactly how much that righteous anger had once cost him.

Twenty-Nine

"These are all of the family business records we could find for that timeframe," Lyle said. He had a couple of large books on the desk in the manor library. "Have you found any clues as to if there really is buried treasure somewhere on the property?"

"I'm still doing some research, but I think these can help me narrow down things quite a bit."

Once Stratton was alone with the business records, she carefully opened the first book with a mixture of excitement and anticipation. She paused as her hand touched the fragile, worn pages from another time. She glanced thoughtfully around the room, wishing the walls could share their stories. *How many choices and decisions had been made in this very room? How many lives and generations were impacted by the ruminations made by Merrick Turner? Did Solomon confront his father in this very room and tell him of his plans? Where did Mister Turner strike his son? Was it over by the windows, or was it close to where she presently sat? What did Solomon do after he was hit? What was Mister Turner thinking when he looked Solomon in the eye?*

Stratton couldn't imagine being so enraged at her own children. Maybe, deep down, Mister Turner wasn't as angry as he was afraid; afraid of what people would think, afraid of what they would do, or afraid of what they might find out. She decided it was actually fear that spearheaded his decision to remove Daphne from the estate, fear that made him gather the family wealth to hide it from pillagers, and fear that ultimately, though indirectly, cost two people their lives.

Stratton leaned back in the chair with her hands still on the open book, thinking about her own insecurities and fears, which were not that different from those of Merrick Turner. She feared what others thought about her relationship with Everest, she feared letting the protective wall around her heart fall, she feared being hurt emotionally again; she feared losing her children, and she feared letting herself love Everest. Unlike Mister Turner, her battle was with the voices from the past that occasionally still rattled around in her own head.

She shook her head slightly to bring her thoughts back to the record book in her hand.

Written in neat penmanship was a list of the slaves that Mister Turner owned in 1860, seventy-three in total.

Stratton knew that owning that many slaves would have meant he was an extremely wealthy man, one of the upper percentiles of the privileged class from that period in time. Most Southern families did not have any slaves, but those families having more than ten meant larger estates and plantations and greater operations to run.

She began reading through the list of names.

Primus. Abel. Venus. Sarah. Murray. Marcus. Lettia. Bartlett. Ann. Eula. Woodson.

She respectfully touched the page. So many lives. So many generations.

She kept reading.

Winney.

Then, her name was written below, and indented were two more names, Meriday and Daphne.

I found them.

The record reflected that Mister Turner had purchased all three in 1848 when the children were 5 and 6, children standing with their mother on an auction block like animals.

This realization brought on a new wave of tears as Stratton reverently touched the page where Daphne's name was written. Winney couldn't have done a thing about it even if she had known what was to happen. It felt fatalistic reading the record.

Stratton wiped her eyes with her hands and continued reading.

She read through business ventures, ledgers, and accountings and followed the chronology until she finally made it to 1861.

Her hands began to tremble slightly. Torn between needing to know and not wanting to know, she was hesitant to look at the records. She knew the story that Mrs. Reed had told her, that Young Solomon was going to return from a trip and Daphne would be gone, but part of her wanted to find that Daphne was still part of his father's household.

Taking a deep breath, Stratton mentally steeled herself for what she would find and began to review the records from 1861. About halfway through a group of papers, she found the record she had been searching, yet hoping not, to find.

Daphne, age 18, was sold to Andrew Wessyngton of Wessyngton Farms.

What must Winney have felt? She'd tried to demonstrate loyalty and was rewarded by having her daughter taken from her. She'd only been trying to do what she thought was right. How her heart must have broken when her child was sold. No one could have known that Daphne would be dead within two years.

Stratton knew that she had found an important piece of the puzzle, but the toll extracted ran deep. She felt the weight of her emotions crushing her lungs, making it hard to breathe. She pushed back the chair and stood, tears falling down her face. She turned and walked to the window, lost in her thoughts.

Daphne and Solomon would have played together just outside this very window. Stratton could almost see the two of them as kids running back and forth, playing on the green grass. Unfettered by societal mores, they were free to be playmates and friends.

Stratton had so many questions that she knew would never be answered, but she had to ask. Had Winney stood right here through the years, looking out this very window, watching the two bond? Had she watched as they went from chasing one another as children to awkward adolescent flirting, then young adult love? Had someone warned Solomon to hide his feelings for Daphne? Had they tried to hide their love from his father?

Even if they hadn't developed a romance, Solomon would have been hurt to return home and find that he was missing his dear childhood friend. It was unfair on so many levels. It was unfair that society at the time dictated who could be with whom. It was unfair that Daphne had been sold. It was unfair that they had to be separated. It was unfair they had to fight so hard to keep their love alive. It was unfair that Daphne died, and they didn't get a chance to marry and have a family.

She had to take a break. She walked over to the desk and closed up the books, then went to find Everest. She needed him right now, and she needed him to know that she needed him.

She found him helping hang a banner over the Italian-themed garden. His eyes found hers, and he smiled. She waited patiently as he finished the chore and walked to her.

"How'd it go?" he asked softly, his tone filled with concern.

She knew her eyes must still show signs of the tears she had shed. She couldn't hide the raw emotion she felt.

"I was about to suffocate in that room. I was so overwhelmed with emotions for these two strangers, and I couldn't help but think of us. Just a few months ago, we were strangers, and now I can't imagine my world without you. Poor Solomon knew Daphne most of his life, and then she was yanked away from him. He knew her as a friend and a touchstone, an anchor, and the loss of her must have been soul-crushing. I've only known you for a much shorter time, but I would feel the same way as Solomon did if I lost you."

Tears were flowing again as she poured out her heart. "I keep putting myself in their place, and their story just breaks my heart. I had to find you and tell you that I love you."

She reached out and grasped both of his hands. "I love you, Everest. I love your courtship of me without demands. I love how deeply you care and strive to understand my emotions. I love how you make me feel safe when you are around, not just physically safe but emotionally safe." She released one of his hands to wipe at the tears streaming down her face. "You are an amazing example of leadership and servanthood. I love you as my friend and companion. I cannot imagine never having a conversation with you again or hearing about your thoughts. Those are my treasures. The openness of your heart means so much to me."

"Hey, come here." He pulled her close to him and put his arms around her. He kissed the top of her head. "It's OK."

The tears came afresh again for Daphne and Solomon, for her and Everest.

She didn't care who saw. She almost hoped someone was watching so they could see how wonderful it was to be loved.

He kissed her cheek. "I love you, and I think you need a break from the research. The festival is tomorrow, but we are hosting a soft opening for the family and a few of their friends tonight. I want to take you all over the world this evening. Will you come with me to Paris and Rome and anywhere else we fancy?"

"I'll go anywhere with you." As she heard the words come out of her mouth, she meant it, every word. Travel the world or travel through her emotions. There wasn't any territory she would keep from him.

He gave her a quick kiss. "Great. Let me finish up here, and then we can get ready." Even though they were in public, she didn't shy away from his kiss, and she wasn't going to anymore. She was ready to let everyone know that she was in a relationship.

Thirty

A garment bag was hanging on Stratton's door when she and Everest came home.

"Who put this here?" She asked. "What is it?"

"You should probably open it," Everest suggested with a slight chuckle.

Stratton unzipped the bag and pulled out a navy blue knee-length, off-the-shoulder satin dress. "Oh, my goodness. This is gorgeous. Everest, did you get this for me?"

"I'll admit I had some help from Harper."

She was so touched that he had gone to Harper for help. She was pleased Harper had shared her favorite color with him and that he had made the time to find the dress.

She leaned in and gave him a kiss. "It's lovely. I can't wait to wear it tonight. Thank you."

"You're welcome. I'm going to get ready, then we can head back to Milky Way for some dinner."

And that's exactly what they did: Everest in a light beige tweed three-piece suit, Stratton in her dress with her mother's pearls. They arrived just as twilight settled over the farm. As they walked the cobblestone path around the manor towards the first garden setting, they paused to have their picture taken at the 360-photo booth that was all the rave at current events throughout the country.

They started their tour in The Netherlands.

"Did you import these?" Stratton asked as she looked at all of the tulips on display.

"Yep, I suggested a few other flowers, but they said that money wasn't an issue, so here you have your spring flowers in July."

They held hands as they walked around sunken tiers of rectangular beds of flowers, including lilies and irises.

"Did you design all of this?" Stratton asked.

"Most of it."

"This is so intricate and detailed. I had no idea you were working so hard up here. I'm sorry if I ever made you feel torn between coming home and here."

"I never felt that pressure coming from you. Besides, I always had you close to my heart every day here." He lifted her hand and tenderly kissed it.

They continued walking toward France, where they were greeted by a two-story replica of the Eiffel Tower, which was made entirely out of roses.

"Did you think of this as well?" Stratton asked, stunned at the beauty displayed.

"I did."

She was so impressed with his creativity, knowledge, and skill. She knew that she had done nothing deserving of such a wonderful partner. He was a gift from her heavenly Father, Who provided more than she could have ever asked for or imagined.

They had their picture taken at the Eiffel Tower replica and toured the wonderful-smelling French garden filled with fruits and vegetables intermingled with plants.

In each country they visited, it was evident that Everest was quite popular. Rounds of shoulder pats, handshakes, and congratulations ensued everywhere they went. Stratton enjoyed hanging back, watching him in his element. He would catch her eye in the middle of his greetings, and if the greeting lasted too long, he'd reach for her and bring her in. She was thrilled to see people appreciate his talents and to see him shining because of his hard work.

Italy was next, and Everest had kept it very traditional with evergreens, geometric hedges, and topiaries. There was a large fountain in the middle with lion statues surrounding it, water bubbling forth from their mouths.

"We will stop and have an appetizer here," Everest said as they came to a few tables. He pulled out her chair, and Stratton sat.

"What can I get for you two?" A waiter asked.

"We'll take the polenta crostini with tuna and two limonatas."

"Right away." The waiter dismissed himself.

"I feel like I'm actually in Italy with you," Stratton said as she looked around.

"I feel like I'm in heaven with you."

"Think that line is gonna work?" She said with a smile to her voice and on her face.

"I'll bet it gets me in the front door later."

Stratton blushed. "Everest, will it always be like this? I feel like I am in a fairytale with you. I know that I have guarded my heart and myself for a long time, and I don't want to be that way with you; I want to enjoy life with you." The sound of the water from the fountain and the violin players warming up from a section of the garden continued to set the stage for an authentic Italian experience.

"I want us to go at the pace you want to go. Am I making you feel rushed?"

"No."

The waiter brought their drinks and appetizers.

"Wow, this is good," Stratton said after a bite. "We should make these at our next party." There it was, the playing house portion, even though they weren't married. Stratton winced. "Sorry, I didn't mean to assume anything. It doesn't make you feel rushed, does it?"

Everest leaned in. "Stratton, there are times I want to jump forward and speed right along, but I really want to focus on us. I want to memorize every part of you. I want to see the sunrise, the sunset, and the stars reflected in your eyes; I want to know how your kiss tastes in all the seasons and in all types of weather, and I want to take you back to that cottage in Pennsylvania and spend another evening together with a few adjustments." He winked. "I aim to savor the sweetness of slow."

Stratton felt hot and was thankful the limonatas came with ice.

Had she really initially tried to dismiss this relationship with Everest? What would she have missed out on had she done that?

They next toured an American garden with hydrangea, roses, and astilbe mixed with ferns, coral bells, and vegetables growing throughout. It was a melting pot of plants, much like the country.

Dinner was in Brazil. It was styled like a jungle full of colorful hibiscus and music. There was even a samba instructor teaching those who wanted to learn some basic Brazilian moves.

The two ended their walk in China with a replica of The Great Wall made of azaleas, begonias, camellias, and chrysanthemums. In the center of the garden, Chinese dancers clad in colorful, traditional garments performed.

Stratton rubbed her upper arm, a little chilled.

Two seconds later, Everest placed his jacket around her shoulders and pulled a gardenia from the Great Wall, tucking it in her hair.

At the end of the performance, the dancers released sky lanterns, and they gently floated higher and higher in the night sky, resembling sparkling stars as they drifted across the night sky.

Everest and Stratton stood alone in the shadows near the flower wall, watching the lanterns.

"Everest?" she whispered.

"Yes?"

"Have you kissed me by lantern light?"

Everest smiled. "I have not."

"Would you like to?"

"I would." He moved in closer.

"Go slow." She smiled.

"As you wish," he replied as his lips lightly brushed hers.

Stratton felt the slowness of their kiss create an ache in her, which demanded she compensate for it with added fervor. Her hands moved from his chest to behind his neck, pulling him closer to her. Her lips pressed in closer to meet the passion in his kisses.

The earthy, spicy, and sweet, intoxicating fragrances from the flowers were so close that her senses could pick out each scent.

Was it just the newness of their relationship that brought this passion forth, or was she in love for what felt like the first time in her life?

Applause from the small gathering of folks near the Chinese performers brought Stratton back to the present. She pulled away to catch her breath.

Looking at Everest, she smiled at him, eyes twinkling. "So that's how slow feels."

*****

Everest breathed in and out as he ran his fingers through his hair. It was becoming more of a challenge to exercise self-control when he was with Stratton. Each night, parting upstairs or at her doorway was growing even more difficult. He wasn't sure how much longer he could wait before he had to ask her to marry him. He wanted her as his wife.

It wasn't that he merely wanted to be physical with her, but he wanted just to lie next to her, hear her final thoughts about the day as she fell asleep, and hear the first thing on her mind when she woke up. He wanted to have a bath ready for when she returned from teaching. He was drawn to the way her mind worked, so he wanted to share intellectual discussions with her. He wanted to have surprise weekend getaways and take her to places she'd dreamed of going. Yet, he knew he would only have the level of intimacy he desired with Stratton when he was her husband.

He wanted her partnership and companionship for the rest of his days. He knew she was hesitant and scared, but slowly approached the idea of the two of them having a life together. He knew, though, she wasn't ready if he fell to a bent knee right now and proposed to her. She might freeze or flee; she might turn him down or even accept out of kindness. Her kindness was what made her irresistible.

He needed to spend some time in prayer. He needed to pray to find the right timing, as well as the method to communicate his desire for marriage so as to solicit an unconditional yes from this woman who was just as ready for the next step as he knew in his heart he was.

"Hey there!" Lyle hollered, walking up with Bernadette.

Everest placed a hand on Stratton's lower back, indicating he wanted her to stay next to him. He hoped he was conveying the concept of partnership to her, always giving her an opportunity to feel integrated into his work. "Good evening, Lyle. Bernadette."

"This was amazing. I can't believe the feedback we are getting. I've actually got a couple of other venue owners interested in having you help them with some of their ideas. I hope you don't mind that I passed your info along. I'm thinking this is going to be an annual event for sure, so we'd like to discuss our ideas for next year after this event concludes. What do you think?"

He could finally find a spot to rest and focus on one location. No more suitcases, no more renting. Just permanency and roots. He would have continued regional work so that he could have stayed here near Stratton, but this was much better.

"I think we should have a celebratory meeting next week if the scheduling works." Everest and Lyle shook hands.

"Say, did you find any locations to dig for treasure?" Lyle asked Stratton.

"I'm working on some leads, but it looks like it might be on a different property if it exists at all," Stratton said.

"Yeah, Daddy said it was a fool's errand to chase after it, but I just thought it was cool and would make a great story."

"Lyle, we promised to do some promo pics in Italy." Bernadette reminded him as she started to whisk him away.

"That's right. Well, thanks again, and we'll be in touch."

The couple moved on.

"Congratulations," Stratton said.

"Thanks."

"Sounds like you have a lot of new opportunities headed your way."

He knew she was feeling apprehensive about him taking a job away from her. Long distances always bring challenges, especially for a budding romance. He turned toward her. "Whatever the future holds, I want you to know you're a part of my decision-making process. I'm not planning on going anywhere anytime soon. Should a job arise that would take me away from here, you and I will discuss whether I'm taking it because you're coming with me or I'm passing it up because we're staying home."

Home. That was it; she felt like home to him. All he wanted to do was to go home and hold her all night. Then to spend all day with her just being at home. He knew he would share his time with her, with her children, and grandchildren, but he would make sure they had time for them. There would be times when they would retreat with one another to a private place long enough to share the things a biblically-based marriage offers to a submitting couple.

Everest stopped himself from dipping that weak knee and forging ahead with a proposal. He needed to work up to it. He didn't know when that perfect time was, but he knew that only knowing each other for nearly four months just wasn't enough time yet for her.

While he had zero doubts and reservations, he knew more time was needed for Stratton. He prayed and readied himself for the endurance it would demand on his part. All he seemed to think about was how wonderful it would be to refer to Stratton as his wife and finally know her completely.

Thirty-One

"Noah, I do not want all of those people coming into this house during your horse show," Stratton said.

"Relax, Mom. The waste management guy just texted, and they are pulling in now. He'll be back tomorrow to get everything, so nothing will be sitting on our land. Everest and I have all the electricity pulled and available for the food trucks when they arrive this afternoon. Permits are in place. Everything's in order."

"OK."

"Just let me do my thing. You can sit back and enjoy the show. We're having a bonfire afterward, so it might be a late night around here."

That was usually the case with Noah and his gatherings, but Stratton didn't mind. It never disturbed her sleep, and Noah's company never destroyed anything or left a mess.

Everest came in from the deck door carrying a bouquet. "Good morning, my sweet. These are for you." He handed her a bouquet of zinnias and kissed her.

"Thank you." Stratton got a vase from the cabinet and placed it in it before displaying it on the kitchen island.

"Well, I'm going to go get things set up. Everest, will you…" Noah raised his eyebrows and nodded at Stratton.

"I got it, bud," Everest said.

"Got what? Noah?"

Noah walked out.

"What is going on?"

Everest took hold of Stratton's hands. "Sometimes a boy needs to talk to a man about things."

"What things? What are you talking about?"

"There's a girl coming tonight to the show, and Noah likes her."

"Who? What's her name? Do I know her?"

Everest looked at her, eyebrows raised. "Do you maybe have an idea why I'm here telling you this and not Noah?"

She did.

She would have asked a thousand questions and made a million suggestions. She didn't know how she'd feel about Noah bringing someone home. This was a different situation than when Harper started dating Whitten; this was her baby, her only boy. "So, you're here to make sure I don't overreact or embarrass him?"

"I'm here because Noah likes her, wants you to like her, and is so nervous about asking her out. They aren't a couple; they haven't even been on a date. Think back, if you can, to all those days ago in the spring when we met. Can you picture it?"

The handsome, strong gardener carrying potted lilies for planting. The kind stranger who offered her a place to stay during the storm. The gentleman who gave up his bed for her.

"I can picture it."

"OK, now think about when you came home, did you want to be hounded with questions by anyone about our night together?"

"No." She had rather enjoyed replaying it over and over privately in her mind. How grateful she was that she hadn't been mistakenly building it up.

"But you were thinking about me, weren't you?" Everest clasped his hand around her waist.

"Everest."

He delicately kissed her neck and smiled. "You had to have time to quietly work out your own feelings. That's exactly what Noah wants."

"I don't know if I should be sad he didn't come to me or happy because he came to you." She wrapped her arms around his neck and drew him to her for a kiss.

"There's one more thing."

"Yes?"

"Noah said that she was in an accident when she was a little girl and suffered third-degree burns on one arm. She's still self-conscious about it."

"Everest, you both know that I would never say anything."

"I know you wouldn't," he said as he tenderly ran his finger down the curve of her cheek and over her lips. "I think he wants tonight to be very special." Everest's mouth closed over hers.

It was at that moment Stratton knew that she wanted to be a wife again. She wanted to slip away with Everest to the quiet of her room, close the door, and show him how appreciative she was of his fatherly advice to her son. She knew that Everest would call Noah their son if they married. *If? Is it really an 'if,' or is it really a 'when'? Should I even bring it up? Should I say anything? Am I really, really, really ready to do this again?*

Stratton leaned slightly back, looking at Everest. "I'm glad you're home now. Would you like to go to the register of deeds office with me this week? We can dig into their records and see about finding that Confederate gold?" Stratton winked and asked, with a hint of intrigue in her voice.

With a playful smile, he twirled her around with one arm, then guided her into a graceful dip, his arm supporting her arched back, their faces just inches apart. "Who needs gold when I've got the prettiest girl in all of Dixie?"

If you ask me, Everest, I'll say yes.

* * * * *

Noah and his group of friends planned a fun evening before and after the horse show and invited anyone in the community to attend.

Pickup trucks with their tailgates down lined the temporary arena Noah had created. Lawn chairs were set up around improvised tables while games of cornhole and horseshoes dotted the area. The sounds of laughter and friendly chatter could be heard as an impromptu game of frisbee football started while waiting for the events to begin.

The horse show consisted of three events: Reining, Mounted Archery, and a Horse Obstacle Course. The first prize was a special-order leather saddlebag donated by Colonel Littleton.

The sun was just above the horizon, casting its final amber rays over the arena as if waiting for that moment between dusk and dark when the lights would flicker to life, flooding light over the area. The opening of the evening was kicked off with a parade of little ponies and young riders proudly showcasing their horsemanship skills.

Stratton and Everest had set up lawn chairs in the back of Noah's truck, providing them an excellent vantage point for viewing not only the events but the crowd as well. She looked around to see what Noah was doing and if she could see him talking to anyone. *Not yet. I wonder where she is?*

About thirty people had registered to compete in the horse show, which was a strong turnout, in Stratton's mind, for a previously unknown event.

Using the PA system that Noah had set up, the emcee for the evening announced that the reining competition was starting.

As she watched the horses move with such elegance and grace, an invisible connection between horse and rider, Stratton longed to return to Mount Judea and ride across the vast fields of the ranch. She could almost feel the wind blowing her hair, the strength of Tilly underneath her as they moved in perfect harmony and freedom. She could own a horse on the homestead, but she'd need help with care and maintenance. She couldn't add that responsibility to Noah's plate, but what about the man sitting next to her? She glanced over at Everest as he watched the show. He caught her eyes, and he smiled, reaching for her hand.

She accepted it with a shared smile.

After the archery and obstacle course events were finished, the winner was announced. People began gathering their things and headed home for the night, commenting on the success of the event as they left.

Stratton was proud of Noah for venturing out and doing something different. She headed toward the rather large bonfire he had built, trusting that he had a hose on hand or some way to control the fire should it get out of hand, to tell him goodnight.

"Hey, Son. Congratulations, and well done at the events tonight. You did a great job bringing the community together. Everyone had a great time." Stratton tried not to stare at the adorable blonde girl sitting next to Noah on a straw bale.

"Thanks." Noah nodded. "Mom, this is Shelby."

"Hi, Ms. Davis." Sweet, adorable Shelby said with a Southern accent and held out her hand for a handshake.

Stratton obliged. "Please, call me Stratton."

"Yes, ma'am."

"Mom, would you like to stay? Ralston's bringing more chairs."

Right on cue, Ralston walked up with a few foldable camping chairs. "Evening, Ma Davis."

Two summers ago, after his folks' lease was up and they moved to Alabama, Ralston needed a place to stay while he decided what to do, so Noah offered him a room. Over the course of the summer, he'd taken to calling her 'Ma Davis', and it had stuck. The boys spent the summer working around the homestead, mending the fences that were in need of repair, and even finding time to go fishing several times a week. By the end of the summer, Ralston had decided to work with his uncle for his landscaping business, which gave him a very flexible schedule and the opportunity to spend most days outdoors.

"Hi, Ralston."

He got all of the chairs set up. "Have a seat."

Stratton did.

"Did you enjoy the show?" Ralston opened a bottle of water and handed it to her.

"I did. How about yourself?"

"I liked it when that ol' boy leaned over on the side and still hit the target with that arrow. That was cool."

"It was."

"Say, where's Everest?"

Stratton felt a little flutter. *Why is he asking that? Were people talking about us at the show?* Stratton still struggled to accept their age difference but thought that she had overcome the fear of everyone knowing about their relationship. Obviously, based on her initial reaction to Ralston's question, she needed to continue praying about that fear.

"He's here, somewhere." She replied, sending up a quick prayer thanking Him for using Ralston to show her that she still needed Him to help her overcome her fears and insecurities about being in a relationship with Everest.

"Hey, Ma Davis, I told Noah, and now I'm telling you. Everest's a good fit here. It's nice having someone like him around, you know?"

"I do."

"You two are a good match."

"Thank you, Ralston." Stratton smiled, glad that the heat from the bonfire covered the flush she felt moving up her face at his observation.

Ralston's phone buzzed. "Oh, I gotta take this." He left his camping chair as he answered his phone.

"I have to get home. It was nice to meet you, Stratton." Shelby and Noah stood.

"Nice to meet you as well, Shelby." Remembering the conversation she'd had with Everest early in the day, she resisted the urge to invite her for dinner or make any plans.

"I'll walk you to your car," Noah said. He and Shelby turned and walked towards the remaining cars parked around the arena.

Stratton, sitting alone by the bonfire, silently congratulated herself for not asking Shelby a million questions. As she sat in reflective thought, the crackle of the burning wood was the only sound heard in the quietness of the night. She watched, mesmerized, as a soft, gentle breeze blew, causing the flames to flicker and dance in response.

Everest appeared from the darkness beyond the fire's perimeter. He kissed her sweetly on the cheek, then sat down next to her. "Well, I have some news." he softly said as he gazed into the fire.

Stratton braced herself for some bad news. "OK, have you been tapped for a job that is out of the country?"

"No," he reached for her hand as he sat next to her. "My parents are coming to visit."

She felt her stomach take a dive to her feet, then rise quickly to get stuck in her throat, leaving a trail of nausea in its wake. She willed herself to not get sick right there and focused her eyes on the flames in the fire. *Why do they seem to be laughing at me? What am I supposed to say to that news? How awkward is that going to be meeting his parents? Breathe, Stratton.*

Trying to keep the sudden fear she felt from Everest, she took a deep breath and asked, "Are they staying with us?" *OK, so that did not come out like I wanted.*

"No, of course not."

"I mean, they can if they want." Stratton didn't want to seem inhospitable, though she did have a fleeting moment of relief that they wouldn't be staying in her house.

"You don't have to do that with me, Stratton." She felt Everest turn to look at her.

"Do what?" She couldn't face him. She didn't want him to see the depth of fear in her eyes.

"Hide."

She continued to stare into the fire. "I didn't used to act like this, you know? When I first got married. I was so naïve and trusting. I wore my emotions like accessories; what you saw was what you got, but that was before things changed; I changed. Everest, I am really trying to accept the idea and concept of our relationship. But meeting your parents? I feel that things are moving much faster than I had in mind." *Why am I stepping back? I was ready to marry him just yesterday, but now I don't want to meet his parents. Why can't I just trust that I won't get hurt? What is going on with me?*

"Stratton, may I remind you that you had figured out how to secure an invitation for me to your daughter's when we barely knew each other. I've already been to your childhood home and met your family. Plus, I live with you and your son."

She glanced at him with a slight, one-sided smile. "I didn't say it wasn't a double standard."

He reached over and squeezed her hand. "You're going to adore my parents, and they will really enjoy getting to know you."

"I can't believe it. Here I am at sixty, feeling nervous about meeting your parents like some young girl. Do they know how old I am? Do they know we're dating?"

"They know both." Everest looked toward the fire. "They knew before I did that you were special and different."

"What do you mean?"

"When I was last at their house, I reorganized their entire attic, looking for links between our family. I spent most of the time there trying to find a way to stay connected to you. Apparently, I also couldn't stop talking about how coincidental it was that I would already have an acquaintance in Lynnville for the upcoming job. They didn't say anything at the time, but Mom suspected this was more than just a crush. I had already been asking my dad for prayer before our first kiss. After our first kiss, I called them the next morning and told them I was planning on pursuing you with integrity and intention. They were nothing but congratulatory and have been constantly supporting us through prayer."

"They didn't have a thousand questions about me?" She knew that she sure would have had a lot of questions if her son were to start dating an older woman.

"Not really, but I'd been sharing pretty much every impression and thought about you, so they have an idea of who you are, at least viewed through my lens. Stratton, they already feel as if they know you. There's no need for you to change or try to be someone you're not, nor is there any reason to change any part of our routine. I've found them a nice Airbnb in Franklin. They arrive in the middle of the week and will be staying three days and two nights."

"Are you positive that you don't want them to stay with us?"

"They're excited to stay in Franklin and have already found a few touristy things to do around town. Stratton, look at me. I know this is taking you out of your comfort zone."

"Hasn't that been the theme since we met?"

His eyes stayed fixed on hers. "Since we've met, tell me the one outcome you'd change after you got over your initial discomfort."

Her mind raced through their numerous encounters: the first I-stared-too-long-at-you-and-you-noticed look, holding his hand at his cottage, that long embrace when she left the cottage, dancing, conversations, and a first kiss that could still make her blush if she thought about it long enough; every single incident carried an initial amount of discomfort, but Stratton hadn't let that stop her. The reward each and every time was a deeper level of comfort that she had never known. She didn't have to fear being herself around him, and now he was asking her to step out in discomfort once again, meet his parents, and let them get to know her for who she was. She wanted to prove to him that she trusted him and began reflecting on how to do just that.

Thirty-Two

While Everest and Noah were outside working in the barn, Stratton was sitting on the couch talking to Savannah on the phone. "His parents are coming to visit."

"He is so going to propose to you."

"I don't think so. We've talked about going slow, and that's what we both want right now."

"So, are you freaking out about your future potential in-laws coming to town?"

"Savannah, we aren't engaged, so you can't call them that."

"I hear that you were quite engaged in some hand-holding, according to one Miss Scarlett."

"When did you talk to her?"

"Harper put her on the phone when I called the other day, and she volunteered that tidbit."

Did her entire family have nothing better to discuss than her and Everest?

"You clearly see the man these two people raised; they have got to be just as amazing as he is and will find you're perfectly suited for their son."

"I'm just apprehensive. I want them to like me, not only as a person or as the girl who is simply dating their son but someone they would have chosen to be with their son." Stratton paused a minute and thought about what she had just said. "I guess what I really want is their blessing. I know that sounds crazy because I don't even know them. They are part of the package Everest brings to our relationship, just as all of you are part of the package I bring to the relationship. I've thrown him into my world, but I haven't really offered to step into his. I guess this is really more about what our blended family might look like, not about my fears and insecurities."

"Well said, Sis."

Realizing that this wasn't about her as much as it was about them and their future provided a sense of peace and comfort for Stratton. She knew that she needed to embrace his family just as he had embraced hers.

* * * * *

Everest had left to go to his parents' Airbnb in Franklin and would be returning shortly, with them following him to Stratton's in their rental car.

Stratton stood before her mirror, giving herself one last look before checking on the chicken that she had in the oven. She looked at her reflection, pleased that she had chosen to wear a simple short-sleeved terracotta-colored dress with a built-in tie-around belt and taupe sandals. She had pulled her hair halfway up and put on a little eye makeup. As self-doubt and insecurity about her age, her failed marriage, and even herself started to creep in, Stratton grabbed the notecard beside her bed and read aloud what she had written on it a few days prior: "For I know the plans I have for you," declares the LORD, "plans to prosper you and not to harm you, plans to give you hope and a future." She felt the words from Jeremiah calming her soul. *Thank You, Father, for Your Words, Your peace, and Your guidance. I trust You and Your plans for me and Everest.*

She went upstairs to Noah's room before heading to the kitchen, sticking her head in his doorway, checking to make sure he wasn't in farm attire or covered in any number of farm by-products. "Are you cleaned up?"

Noah smiled and rolled his eyes dramatically at her, "Yes, Mom. All ready, and I even put on extra deodorant."

Stratton laughed and closed the door. How she loved that boy!

She placed the homemade veggie tray on the table and lit beeswax candles throughout the house. The fresh scones were cooling, and the roasted chicken was almost ready. She felt everything was in order for their arrival.

She was still nervous but knew she needed to trust that his parents would be open to her and to Noah. She wanted them to accept her, not just as a person but as a potential daughter-in-law.

The front door opened.

"We're here!" Everest called.

Stratton took a deep breath, ran her hands down the sides of her dress, and went to the foyer to meet Benjamin and Sarilda Galloway. She hoped her smile hid her surprise at seeing a handsome older version of Everest and a clear Helen Mirren look-alike standing in her doorway "Welcome."

"Mom, Dad, this is Stratton."

"We'd know you anywhere by Everest's description. You're lovely." Sarilda said, opening her arms for an embrace.

It nearly moved Stratton to tears, but she held it together as she hugged the woman. "It's so nice to meet you both."

Benjamin also gave her a quick hug and said hello. "We are so glad to meet you."

"Come on in, please." She saw Everest give her a quick wink as he closed the front door.

The tour of the main floor was quick, ending with them settling at the kitchen island for some light snacks.

Noah came downstairs to greet them both. While they enjoyed some tea and scones, he shared some of the projects he was working on around the farm. As they were finishing the snacks, Noah invited Benjamin and Sarilda for a tour of the farm. Benjamin happily agreed, but Sarilda declined.

Once the men left, only Sarilda and Stratton were inside, still seated at the kitchen counter.

"Can I refill your cup?" Stratton offered.

"Yes, thank you."

As she poured, she tried to hide her nervous energy.

"Honey, it's OK," Sarilda said with a smile and a pat on Stratton's hand.

With those simple words, Stratton felt herself relax a little. It touched her that Sarilda could read her anxiousness and sought to reassure her.

"I told Everest you would probably be a little anxious to have us come for a visit. We offered to come at another time, which, if I know Everest, he didn't tell you that part. It's not because he wanted you to be anxious, dear; he is just so excited to share you with us, and I can see why."

"I have been anxious, like a young girl in her twenties. Everest has done nothing but reassure me that you two are wonderful, and I see that he was right, but it hasn't stopped me from being anxious about meeting you and finding out what you think about our age difference and my being divorced."

"Stratton, life is too precious and too short to worry about trivial things like age. All we have heard is how wonderful you and Noah are, how much Everest has enjoyed meeting so many of your family members, and how welcoming they all have been. If they aren't making a big fuss over the age difference, why should you? I'm not saying I wouldn't have the same thoughts if I were in your shoes, but we did our best to teach Everest that love is what is important, regardless of any societal imposition regarding age or life status. We feel the same way." Genuineness coated each word spoken. "Now, I'll share something with you. I see before me a beautiful woman who has planned and put together a delightful welcome for us and who clearly appreciates and adores our greatest blessing. Am I right?"

Stratton could feel the tears trickle down her cheeks and could only nod her head in affirmation.

Sarilda came around the counter and wrapped her arms around Stratton in a warm hug. At that moment, Stratton realized that she had just been given a beautiful gift from Yehovah. He wasn't just giving her Everest; He was giving her more family—a good measure, pressed down, shaken together, and overflowing.

* * * * *

By the time the men returned from riding around the UTV, Stratton felt relaxed and more at ease around Everest's parents. Lunch was pleasant, and Benjamin and Noah traded fishing tips. Noah even procured an open invitation to visit Pennsylvania any time for a fishing excursion.

As Stratton was clearing the table, Sarilda looked at her watch.

"We've got tickets to the Grand Ol' Opry tonight, so I think we'll be heading out."

"Alright, we'll be up tomorrow morning to take you two to breakfast and tour around town some," Everest said, and both of his parents thought that was a good plan.

As he and Stratton walked them out, Sarilda paused. "Thank you, Stratton." and gave her another hug.

"For what?"

"For being you, honey. Authentic and true." Sarilda kissed her cheek. "We'll be seeing you in the morning."

They exchanged their late afternoon goodbyes. As his parents backed down the drive, Everest put his arm around Stratton's shoulders, standing next to her, waving to his parents as they left. Stratton's heart was full of love for the man standing beside her and his family. She turned her head towards him and gently kissed his cheek.

"What was that for?"

"For once again, showing me that stepping out of my comfort zone doesn't have to be scary. You were right, Everest. Your parents are delightful, and I am so thankful that you wanted me to meet them."

He pulled her into a hug and kissed the top of her head.

Stratton silently rejoiced at crossing another milestone in their relationship.

Thirty-Three

After Everest's parents left, Everest and Stratton went to the local county archives and register of deeds office.

They focused on the archived records from 1810 to 1900 regarding deeds, wills, marriages, and court records, making countless copies of potential leads and anything that looked promising.

"I feel like I could write so many books on Giles County now," Stratton remarked as they sifted through more papers. She stretched and twisted her back. The metal chairs weren't the most comfortable seats for the amount of laborious work they were doing.

Everest had his phone out, snapping pictures from a cemetery book. "My eyes are tired. What do you say we take our copies and sift through this at home?"

She smiled; how she loved it when he used those words. "Sounds great to me."

They loaded up their research, and Everest drove them home, where they sprawled out on the couch and began going through the day's findings.

"Everest," Stratton sat up, "look at this." She had been going through the pictures that he had taken with his phone. "This isn't a cemetery picture; this looks like a misfiled family reunion. What does that say at the bottom?"

"Wessynton Family Picnic on the farm, 1880, "Wessynton Sea."

"Is that a lake back there, and are those lilies down around the front?"

Everest squinted at the picture. "I think so."

"Could this be what Solomon referenced in his letter to Daphne? How do we find out where this lake was? Did you see any water on those maps?" Stratton started looking again.

"Hmm, lakes don't last forever, and some only last a couple of decades, so I don't know that we can rely on the water. Hold on," he said, putting the picture closer to his face. "That's a tulip poplar on the left, and it looks like it was really big back then. If we could find someone that has one larger than this within the old Wessynton family farm property lines, we might be onto something."

They shared a smile, then gave each other a high five.

"Let's get to work."

They pounded the pavement in the days that followed, asking local arborists and agricultural offices if they knew of any large tulip poplars in the area.

Their evenings consisted of reviewing deeds, looking through records, and trying to fit the pieces of a rather large puzzle together.

A few evenings later, when Everest hadn't yet returned from his meeting with Lyle, Stratton sat on the floor beside the couch in the family room, sifting through news articles that highlighted old trees in Giles County. Feeling the strain on her eyes, she slipped off her glasses just as Everest entered through the front door.

"Sorry, when I texted earlier, I meant to leave right away. We ended up having another mini-meeting by the car for twenty minutes."

"It's fine. I didn't wait to eat. Your plate is in the oven, probably still warm."

He crossed over to Stratton, giving her a quick kiss before heading to the kitchen.

He returned to the couch with a plate of food, a fork, and a napkin.

"What did Lyle say?"

"They made bank on the event and want to do this at least twice a year, maybe more."

"And they want you to be there?"

"They do." Everest took a couple of bites of grilled salmon.

"What about other jobs?"

"Well, these would take at least six weeks each time."

"So roughly three months of the year."

"But the pay is acceptable."

They hadn't really ever discussed finances. What was his definition of acceptable pay?

As if reading her mind, "And just so you know what I mean, here." He handed her the check signed by Lyle.

Stratton's jaw dropped. "That's almost two thousand dollars a day."

Everest smiled. "Is now a good time to settle my rental account with you?"

"No, but I feel like this is a big step with what you just shared. Would you like to see my bank account?"

"Stratton, I want to share everything with you. I know I may seem like a bit of a vagabond in some respects. I also know that entering into a relationship with me without knowing what I could offer financially was a big leap of faith for you. I know you're well-established, but if you ever wanted to explore an alternative career path or take an extended sabbatical, I would support you whichever one you chose."

It felt like he was nearing the proposal territory but had stopped. He was letting her know she wouldn't have to go back to the University if she didn't want to, that she could stay at home, and he would work.

What would it be like to take a longer break from teaching? Was this summer merely a foretaste of a future of treasure-seeking through historical analysis? Could Stratton really open herself up to Everest's offer?

Noah came in from the deck just as Everest was finishing his dinner. "Hey, Y'all. I'm fixing to hit the shower and turn in."

"Hey, Bud. Sorry, I wasn't able to help tonight," Everest said.

"What are you two doing out there in the barn anyway?" Stratton asked.

"You said that the barn apartment wasn't habitable, so we're just getting it fixed up," Noah explained. "Say, I almost forgot. Harlow was asking if you two found that gold yet?"

"No, we keep hitting dead ends," Stratton said. "We're trying to locate this one particular tree, which may or may not have a lake by it now. There are just too many properties to look at and people to contact. I don't know how much more time and effort we can put into it."

"What particular tree?"

Stratton shuffled through some papers and found the photograph of the tulip poplar. She handed it to Noah. "This one."

"Hmm. Kinda looks like that big ol' tree out beyond the woods out back," Noah offered.

"Are you serious? We have a tulip poplar?" Stratton asked.

"I don't know what it is, but it's just about to the property line. It's not a part of the sections I got fenced off, so I don't go back there too often. But that ole tree looks just like this picture."

Stratton could hardly contain her excitement. "Everest, do you think that could be it? We don't have a pond or a lake back there."

"I say we head out at first light and take a look."

Stratton started shuffling through the deeds, her focus on one particular piece of paper. "I guess if I'm looking at this correctly, there once was a small piece of our property encompassed by the Wessynton Farm, but I'm not exactly sure."

"I'll have to bush hog first 'cause there's a large briar patch blocking the way. I can get to it after morning chores."

"Thank you, sweetie," Stratton said.

"Um, do you mind if Shelby comes over for dinner tomorrow?"

"I don't mind." She said calmly, trying to hide her excitement.

"All right. Goodnight, y'all."

"Night," Everest said.

Noah went upstairs while Everest took his dishes to the kitchen.

Stratton sat back, thinking about all of the progress that had been made tonight, not just with the tree but with Everest. She couldn't believe his offer and knew that he hadn't offered it lightly; he meant it.

As he walked back into the room, she stood up to meet him. "I played it cool, didn't I?" Stratton asked.

"Real cool." He replied, coming to stand in front of her.

She traced the rim of a button on his shirt with her index finger. "So earlier, you said something about exploring alternative paths. "What if I like the familiar ones?"

"I think I'll need a demonstration of what you're talking about to make a fair assessment."

Stratton wasted no time in smothering Everest with kisses. These moments were the real treasures to her, precious moments that she kept close to her heart. She tried to stay in the moment, but she couldn't help but think of Daphne and Solomon. Those two never had the freedom to love, no nightly kissing sessions, no parting at the doorway with more quiet kisses, and certainly no public hand-holding or pronouncements of their relationship to others. Having the freedom to love Everest made Stratton's time with him that much more sacred. She vowed never to take one moment with him for granted but to treasure all aspects of his love and affection.

Thirty-Four

Toward the back of Stratton's property, beyond a thick grove of trees, was the briar patch Noah mentioned. After it was bush-hogged, they saw that it opened to a small meadow.

"That's a tulip poplar, alright," Everest confirmed.

"But no lake and no signs of lilies."

"Well, maybe." Everest looked at his watch.

"Maybe?" Stratton asked, curious about what he meant.

"Hello!" Ralston hollered as he walked up carrying a large backpack.

"Maybe," Everest said again, his eyes glinting with excitement

"What does he have?"

"It's called ground penetration radar," Everest smiled.

"Here you go." Ralston handed over the backpack to Everest.

"Why do you have that, Ralston?" Stratton asked, still confused as to what was happening.

"Since there are so many Indian mounds around here, my uncle likes to scan a place before landscaping. They found one by accident, and ever since, if the project is large enough, he won't do it until he gets a good scan." Ralston looked at Everest, "Said you can use this as long as you need."

Everest was already putting it together.

"You know how to use it?" Stratton asked.

"I've got a pretty good idea. I've used this and LiDAR a few times."

"What even is that? Is another person bringing it?"

"Light Detection and Ranging," Everest answered. He quickly put together the GPR device and started scanning.

"Y'all just drop it off at my uncle's when you're through. I've got to get to a job site." Ralston gave a wave.

"Thank you," Everest called as Ralston disappeared into the thickness of the trees.

Stratton began to finally understand what Everest was doing. "Anything?" Stratton asked.

"Not yet. All looks pretty normal."

"Hey, I've got to mow some fields this morning for Willodean, so I'm gonna head out if you two don't need anything," Noah said.

Stratton responded for them both. "We're good, I think, so we'll see you later. Anything special you want prepared for dinner?"

"Shelby likes pretty much anything."

"Well, I'll have something ready around six. Is that good?"

"Yup, we'll see ya then." Noah started the tractor and headed back toward the barn.

Everest had started doing a grid search without the markers while Stratton walked around thinking about where Solomon could have buried the silver and gold.

She thought back to what she had learned from his letters to Daphne. If there had been a lake, it had dried up long ago. Therefore, anywhere it previously existed most likely wouldn't have been a proper burial place for the treasure.

However, if lilies once thrived in this area, Solomon probably wouldn't have disturbed them. She remembered him mentioning a "special place," then it hit her; Solomon hadn't lived on the Wessynton Estate, so he wouldn't have chosen a special place – Daphne would have.

Stratton's mind quickly started putting the pieces together. She walked around the small meadow looking for a place that would have provided the most privacy for a young couple, a place that prevented anyone from discovering their fleeting moments of time spent together. She spotted a small hill with a maple tree growing and headed toward it. She sat down under the tree and looked around. Yes, this spot was fairly tucked away and private, but would it have been so in Solomon's time?

Everest continued scanning the area with the device.

Stratton motioned to him that she would just check something and went to the UTV to get a shovel. She figured a little digging wouldn't hurt while Everest scanned.

She looked at the hill, imagining where the lilies and the lake might have been. She chose a spot halfway down the hill and started digging.

About ten shovelfuls later, she paused for a water break. Glancing around, she saw that Everest was still methodically working through the next grid. The sounds of birds chirping and flitting among the trees blended with the soft rustling of the leaves from the humid breeze. The meadow, blanketed in a golden glow from the mid-morning sun, radiated a subtle energy mirroring the excitement of its current inhabitants.

Looking down at the dirt pile she'd accumulated, her eyes landed on something that caught the sunlight, its luster reflecting back to her. "Everest!" She hollered excitedly as she dropped to her knees and carefully moved her hands in the dirt in case it was just a piece of glass.

Everest jogged over. "What's going on?"

"I'm not sure, but I might've found something." She picked up a clump of dirt and began cleaning the item off with trembling hands.

Simultaneously, their mouths opened in utter astonishment.

Stratton was holding a gold coin. "Everest," she said softly, her voice filled with disbelief, as she handed him the coin.

"Oh, my goodness." He smiled as he took the coin from her, turning it between his fingers to look at both sides. "Let's keep going!"

It was challenging and exhausting work digging into the hillside, but with each gold coin they uncovered, a renewed determination ignited within them, urging them to keep going. When they had a lag in discovery, Everest used GPR to uncover more of the treasures hidden beneath the overgrown hillside. Finally, after not uncovering anything for the past hour, they collapsed, exhausted, and drenched in sweat and dirt, but elated at the treasure they had found: thousands of gold coins and bars, as well as traces of what looked to be a burlap bag.

"Honey, it might be time to call it quits." His last pass with the GPR device hadn't signaled anything, and it was scanning twelve feet deep. Stratton knew he must be fatigued from the constant exertion and the heat. "Have some more water."

Everest quickly downed a quart of water, then pulled her in for a quick hug. "You did it. You actually found it."

"We found it. This is our find, along with Noah, Mrs. Reed, and Lyle and Bernadette. It was a group effort." She sat back, taking a drink of water.

"This is an incredible find. How did you know where to look?"

"I tried to think like a young couple in love would. They'd have wanted a place that was far from prying eyes yet offered some protection and comfort so they could sit and be together. The tree would have also offered an escape from the heat but still give them a view of the lake and the lilies. I can just picture them sitting right here talking about their future." Stratton could feel tears pooling in her eyes.

"My hands are too dirty to wipe your tears, so the best I can do is kiss them away."

Stratton gave him a quick smile. "Thank you, but I'll be alright."

A stillness settled over the meadow in quiet acknowledgment and respect for the incredible find that had been made. The birds had paused their chirping, and the wind had ceased to blow as if granting their silent approval of what had just been discovered.

Stratton broke the silence, "I want to do something meaningful with this discovery. I want people to know how much Daphne meant to Solomon and how much he loved her. I want them to know how he was going to use the money to escape and start anew with her. I want them to know that due to circumstances beyond their control, Solomon considered the money useless without Daphne, so he buried it instead of using it."

"When the time is right, you will get to share their story." Everest took her dirty hands into his. "Stratton, we don't have to escape from societal mores. Yehovah is giving us the chance to start anew with each other."

They shared a tender gaze. "We'd better get things gathered together and taken back to the house. Let's wait until after dinner to tell Noah. I'm not sure we should shout this one from the rooftops until we have a plan. What do you think?"

"I agree. I think we should have a plan figured out for the best course of action. There's some sensitive history to discuss, and we also don't want trespassers coming here thinking there's more gold to find."

Stratton stopped short. "I hadn't even thought about that."

"That's why oftentimes folks remain anonymous when they make discoveries like this." Everest, estimating the gold to weigh about fifty pounds, placed the last gold bar in his backpack and put it on his shoulder.

"There's so much to consider, but right now, let's get back so I can get dinner going."

They finished loading the UTV. Stratton sat lost in thought as Everest drove them back towards the barn.

What would this discovery do to their relationship? How was she going to balance work responsibilities and this amazing discovery? Would she be given a night class when she returned from her sabbatical? When would she ever see Everest, then? Would a small amount of fame and fanfare be more competition for their alone time?

The summer was whizzing by, and she still felt like they had not been able to spend much time alone, just the two of them getting to know each other better. *What could I have done differently? Where could we have had more quality time for us this summer?* Stratton had to stop her mind from going back to the cottage, back to Savannah, back to Mount Judea. Instead, she had to try to create more memories and moments like those with the time she had left.

"You can put the backpack in your bathroom, and we'll bring it up later to show Noah," Stratton suggested. She quickly made her way upstairs, washed her hands, and decided on chicken cacciatore over a bed of rice and a Greek salad for dinner.

The clock was somewhat against her, but she pulled the meat out to thaw in the cool water of the sink and flew to the shower to wash off the remains of adventure and discovery.

Thirty-Five

"I don't need to be a part of the meeting, do I?" Noah asked, relaxing in his recliner near the window. "I really don't want to be in front of any cameras or have to address a group of people."

The next evening, the group migrated to the family room after dinner to put the finishing touches on a proposed meeting with Lyle, Bernadette, and Mrs. Reed regarding the gold coins they had found. Stratton, her laptop open on the coffee table in front of her, was seated on the couch across from Everest, who had taken up residence in the winged, high-back loveseat with his laptop perched on his knees.

"If you don't want to, you don't have to," Stratton assured Noah, knowing that he was not comfortable speaking to groups of people. "This is just an idea I want to offer them before we officially decide what to do with the coins," Stratton clarified.

"Well, I don't think you should keep all that gold here since it's worth a little over two million dollars," Noah commented.

"That is exactly why we need to involve all of the folks who have ties to this treasure. It really belongs to all of us." She and Everest, too, excited about finding the gold, had stayed up late last night brainstorming ideas about how to handle the treasure best. "We have a good plan if the others agree to it. We think that the coins should be part of a traveling exhibition and include each person's story about their ancestor," Stratton said.

Stratton closed her laptop and then walked around the coffee table, taking a seat beside Everest. "Are you sure you don't just want to talk to them in private? I don't have to be there."

"Babe, this is your thing." Everest shut down his computer, too. "This is where you shine. I'm just there to support you." He opened an arm, and Stratton nestled against him.

"You can loop me in, but keep me out of the spotlight. I've gotta go call Shelby. Night," Noah made his exit.

"Speaking of Shelby, neither you nor Noah has shared how they met." Tucking her legs underneath her, Stratton snuggled a little closer to Everest.

Everest ran his fingers along her arm. "He swung by to have lunch with me at Milky Way, and I saw him look at her with a look that I knew well."

"What look is that?" She draped an arm over his chest as she grew more relaxed and comfortable.

"The look when time freezes. The look when you see the most beautiful creature your eyes have ever beheld. So, I thought, how can I help?" Everest gave a half-smile." It just so happened that I may have had Noah take her some insignificant paperwork so he could talk to her. Then I may have just set up a fake meeting so the two of them could be alone."

She chuckled at his ingenuity and matchmaking skills. "Are you for real? How can you care about him so much?"

"Stratton, everyone you love will have room in my heart. I don't care to know the details about how their father interacted with them in the past or how he does now. What matters to me is that your kids will benefit from seeing someone like me love their mother like I do. My commitment to you is to work on having a relationship with each of them, not to take the place of their father, but to enhance their relationship with you, with us. I know the girls may feel threatened by my presence, but that's just because they aren't here to see how much I love you. I know that your divorce has caused damage, and you have baggage from it, but, Stratton," he paused a second to tilt her face up to look at his, "I'm not shying away from courting you. I plan on continuing to know you, and that means knowing all of 'you,' including your children and grandchildren. I know what the full package is, and I am not here to compete for your affection. I'm here for all of you." She could see the depths of sincerity mixed with passion in his eyes, eyes that told her this was his promise to her. Oh, how she loved this man.

"Everest, I want to make sure we prioritize us. I know my children and grandchildren can easily consume my time, but I want you to feel important. I commit to you to be the best partner and companion to you I can possibly be."

He leaned down and kissed her. "Stratton, I already feel that way, and I have no doubt you will be."

"You do now, Everest, but I'm not working, and you're not off on a job. It's less of a challenge when we're able to spend so much time together."

"No amount of distance can change my devotion and love for you."

Stratton hugged him and snuggled up against him a little closer, silently wondering if those words would, one day, be put to the test. With her first marriage, there had not been any physical distance but an emotional distance, which eventually contributed to her divorce. She knew that her divorce had left more of a negative emotional impact than a positive one on her. She still struggled with her own insecurities and self-esteem, as well as, deep down, being genuinely afraid to trust and fully love again. Her biggest fear now was that the happiness she felt with Everest would not last.

Even though Everest hadn't given her any indications that he would eventually tire of her, she feared that the possibility might exist, causing a knot to form in her stomach. How would she ever survive a breakup with him? Would she be strong enough to avoid the darkness it would bring?

She silently prayed for deliverance from these negative thoughts and thought of the Scripture from Romans about being transformed by the renewing of the mind in order to know and accept the perfect will of God. She'd experienced so much self-growth over the summer due to Everest and wanted to focus on the positive while seeking His will for their lives.

* * * * *

The annual Blackberry Festival, a favorite event each July, was held in Lynnville over a two-day period. The town would swell from three hundred to five thousand over the course of the weekend. Vendors, food trucks, a farmers' market, speakers, homemade craft booths, and music filled the streets, providing enjoyment for the young and the old.

Throughout the venues, blackberries were served in every way imaginable. Everest and Stratton chose to attend on Sunday, along with what seemed to be the whole town, as well as many locals and tourists.

Stratton and Everest stopped by the DAR booth during Willodean's shift to visit before heading for some blackberry pie.

"Willodean, this is Everest. He's the one who assisted with the festival at Milky Way Farms earlier this summer."

"Nice to meet you."

"And," Stratton felt her heart skip a beat as she reached over and took hold of Everest's hand, "we're seeing one another." She was ready to let the people know they were dating.

Willodean smiled. "Honey, that's been the scuttlebutt since someone saw y'all talkin' on that train."

"What? That was like his first day in town. Who started that rumor? We were not together then."

Everest leaned into Willodean as if sharing a big secret, "But I was totally into her."

Stratton blushed.

"Does it matter who started it? You knew better than to take a handsome fella like him into town."

She totally did, but she thought she was being careful.

"Well, I didn't want folks talking."

"Who cares? Bless 'em for not having anything better to do with their time."

"I suppose you're right. I really don't have any control over what folks think or say. I've been concerned about that all summer, and it sounds so silly to me now." She felt Everest squeeze her hand. She smiled as she realized that he wasn't going to let go of her hand for the rest of the day.

"We need to run. Thank you, Willodean." Stratton gave her a quick hug as they turned and continued to wander through the vendors, headed for the blackberry pie.

The couple stood in front of Jessi's pie tent, which was abuzz with patrons. Jessi looked at Stratton and made her way toward her. "Hi, Stratton, could I talk to you for a minute?"

What on earth could Jessi possibly have to say to her? "Sure." She turned to Everest. "Give me a moment."

He nodded and walked over toward a blacksmith exhibit.

Stratton followed Jessi to the side of her tent.

"What's up?" Stratton asked.

"I didn't know you two were a thing the day I met Everest; I just wanted you to know that. I wasn't trying to steal him or anything."

"Jessi, we weren't dating then."

"Well, he let me know at your party he was pursuing someone. It didn't take me much time to figure out who that was. Anyway, honestly, if I had known he liked you, I wouldn't have asked him on the hike or invited myself to your party. I'm sorry."

"Oh, Jessi, you have nothing to apologize for. Those flowers you helped him pick were beautiful and are now a sentimental part of our story."

"I'm glad. I also wanted to get your advice."

"On?"

"Ralston's been doing some landscaping at my place. He's been finishing up right about suppertime, and I've been preparing dinner a few times. Well, two evenings ago, he asked me out."

Stratton smiled. "And?"

"I just wanted to know if you have any advice since he is younger than me."

"Honey, I wouldn't let his age cause you any reservations; that's something I am learning. Don't let what townsfolk talk about dissuade you from going on a date with Ralston."

Jessi gave her an impromptu embrace. "Thank you."

"Anytime, sweetie."

Stratton found her beau waiting patiently for her. He held out his hand as they resumed walking through the vendors, heading home after sampling different blackberry soda flavors and sharing a piece of blackberry pie.

* * * * *

As they got out of the car, it warmed Stratton's heart to see Noah and Shelby having dinner on the back deck. From their vantage point, it looked like Noah had made the dinner and had everything properly set on the deck.

"What do you wanna do? Play cards in the dining room? Start a puzzle? The couch may already be spoken for tonight." Everest nodded toward the young couple.

"Do you think he's going to kiss her?" Stratton's heart welled with emotion.

"I don't think he will if we're around, so if you're not ready to say goodnight, we'd better make ourselves scarce."

"My place or yours?"

"Ha, neither. Let's take a walk under the stars."

Everest took her hand and led her toward the pasture, away from the warm, golden glow of lights emanating from the house. The rhythmic chirping of crickets, the high-pitched drone of cicadas, the haunting hoot of an owl, and the distant howl of a coyote blended together in a symphonic melody that only the Creator could orchestrate. The mid-July sky seemed to stretch endlessly, sprinkled with twinkling stars that grew brighter the farther they walked from the house.

"The stars seem so bright tonight. It's so beautiful."

Everest paused their walk and turned towards her. He leaned in close, his breath warm next to hers, "Almost as beautiful as you," he said, stealing a kiss before returning to their walk.

Stratton looked upward as they walked. "This reminds me of what Scripture says: The heavens declare the glory of God, and the sky shows His handiwork. Day to day they speak, night to night they reveal knowledge."

Everest nodded in agreement. "The stars are his handiwork, creating and naming each one; not one is missing from His sight. Just like us, His children. He created each one of us, and knows us by name, and knows where we are at all times; none of us are missing from His sight."

Everest settled them down on a soft patch of grass. He leaned back, one arm behind his head, while the other gently cradled Stratton's head. The stillness of the night was a calming balm for their souls.

"Everest?" she asked softly.

"Mm-hmm."

"Did you help Noah plan the menu?"

He shot her a sideways glance before answering. "Maybe."

"I can't tell you how much it means to me that you're helping him. His father has not been that kind of an example, and Charles can only do so much when he is here. There's no substitute for a consistent, positive male role model in a young man's life. He looks up to you and admires you. I know that you've boosted his confidence and made a huge impact on him already. Thank you."

"You've raised him to be a wonderful, caring, loving, kind young man. I think he's pretty serious about his intentions with Shelby. I also know that he thinks about his duties here and the responsibility he feels toward you. He's asked me if I mean to take care of you, and he let me know he approves, and it's fine if I am."

"I can take care of myself. I don't need Noah or you."

"That's not how he meant it, and you know that. You are capable, no one is going to argue that. He's been a rock to you, and he just wants to make sure you don't lose your bearings as he and Shelby get closer."

"So, are you going to take care of me?"

Everest leaned up on his side, facing her, and intertwined his fingers with hers. "I told him I was here and that I have no intention of leaving."

"What are your expectations in staying?"

"They change from day to day." He brought their linked hands up to his lips and kissed her hand.

"Well, on a day like today, for example, what would your expectations be?"

"I'd say we hit the mark today."

"What about your expectations at night?" Stratton flirted.

"Stratton, if you get the fire started…"

"Nothing a dip in the pond won't cure, and we aren't that far from it."

"Then get ready for a barrage of kisses."

Magical moonlight kisses made for a marvelous close to their night, with one thought lingering: would she have joined Everest in a moonlit swim if he'd jumped in?

Thirty-Six

The morning sun was still low in the sky, its golden rose aurora streaming through the windows, casting streaks of light throughout the kitchen. Outside, two squirrels skittered along the top of the railing while butterflies flitting around the back deck. The soft lowing of the cows drifted up from the pasture out back. Stratton hummed softly as she put the finishing touches on breakfast. Checking to make sure everything was ready, she called for Noah and Everest, but neither of them responded.

She headed upstairs first. Noah's bed was made, and his room was empty. *He must have been up really early today.*

Next, she walked down to Everest's room. She was met with the same sight: a neatly made bed and an empty room. She headed back upstairs; she wondered where they were.

When she neared the top of the stairs, she heard low voices coming from the kitchen. As she entered the kitchen, she saw Everest and Noah talking while filling their glasses with the fresh-squeezed orange juice she had left on the counter.

"Where have you two been?" She asked.

"We have something to show you if you'll come with us," Everest said.

He and Noah shared a look with grins.

"So, help me, Noah, if you've added one more creature to this homestead."

"Just come on, Mom." Noah opened the door, grabbing her by the hand.

They walked towards the barn, Stratton paused when she heard a distinct whinny. She turned and looked quizzically at Noah and Everest, who just innocently shrugged their shoulders at her, not saying a word.

She quickened her pace, reaching the barn before them. As she reached for the door handle, Stratton heard the whinny sound again. Feeling both uncertain and excited, she pushed open the barn door and stepped inside.

"Tilly, what are you doing here?" Stratton ran over to her favorite horse and stroked her head and mane. "I don't understand what is going on?" She looked back at the smiling men.

"Harper made me an offer I couldn't refuse," Everest said

An amber champagne horse tossed a head over the stall.

"Is that Bartlett?" She asked as she eyed the gorgeous gelding, she also enjoyed riding when she was at Harper's

"It is."

Noah's phone rang. "Excuse me." He stepped outside of the barn to take the call.

"How did you orchestrate all of this?" Stratton, still trying to take it all in, stepped over to pet Bartlett.

"I know you, Stratton." Everest came and stood before her, taking hold of her hands. "I know your look when you're happy, when you're sad, when you're upset, and even when you're deeply touched. I know you." His gaze fixed on hers, the truth behind those words evident in his eyes. He lifted her hands and tenderly kissed each one.

"I've seen you ride and know how much you love riding. You talked about it almost the whole time on our drive home from Arkansas. On the night of the horse show, as we sat in the back of the truck watching the horses, you had this look about you. You were mesmerized and enthralled, your face filled with passion and excitement, and I knew that look. I spoke to Noah later and asked what he thought about adding a couple of horses to the homestead."

"Oh, I'm sure that was a hard sell." She rolled her eyes.

Everest grinned. "He answered yes before I even told him what I was thinking about."

"I don't know if I can care for both of these on my own, and last time I checked, I'm the one with the most horse experience."

"Honey, you won't be burdened by their care, I promise. I've got it all planned out. The farrier is coming over to teach me the basics. Then, Lyle's groomer is coming to give me some lessons. I've even got a local holistic vet lined up should we need anything." He smiled at her.

"You can't possibly be real. I'm touched to my core, Everest, that you cared enough about me to invest in them. Thank you." She embraced him. No man had ever invested himself in a hobby of hers. What could she do for him that showed how much she loved him? Could she ever find a way to reciprocate?

"I love you, Stratton, and want you to be able to ride whenever you want. It was easy to see how much you loved it when we were at Harper's." He gave her a knowing smile. "Besides, I caught how you looked at me when I was riding, and I kinda liked that." He winked at her with a mischievous tone to his voice. "But I was thinking we should ride double at first, my arms around you, so I don't fall off, that sort of thing."

She leaned back, a sultry look on her face. "Do you know this look?"

"I do, but Noah is just outside."

She playfully tapped him on the shoulder. "How do you know that look doesn't mean I just wanted a quick kiss?"

"Because I know you, Stratton." His eyes turned a deeper blue, reflecting his emotions, as they locked onto hers, "and the look you're giving me right now tells me that you need kissing badly. In fact, you should be kissed often and by someone who knows how."

Stratton laughed at his Clark Gable impersonation, his voice capturing the confidence of Rhett Butler. He was right. She did want those wonderful kisses, needed them, but was it worth the risk of being seen by Noah? Her mind told her, no, but her face conveyed the opposite.

Everest gently lifted her chin to look at him, his eyes searching her face, silently asking the question while simultaneously looking for her answer.

Unable to resist him, one soft word escaped from her lips, "Yes," before his mouth covered hers in a kiss that kindled the fire between them. Her arms tightened around his neck, pulling him closer to her, forgetting her earlier reservation of being seen. The energy between them exploded as Everest gently pressed her back against the edge of the stall, the heat threatening to consume them. Would she ever not feel this way when she kissed him?

His hands tenderly cupped her face as the soft caress of his lips traced an imaginary line from her lips to her nose and her brow before returning to cover hers in a kiss that spoke of the depth of his affection. Overwhelmed by the intensity of his kiss, Stratton felt as if an electric jolt had ignited the connection between them, awakening every nerve in her body.

A loud meow shattered the moment, causing Everest to leap back, and Stratton instinctively placed a hand over her heart.

Cully, clearly agitated with the two new animals in his abode, darted between their legs before jumping on one of the bales of hay in the corner.

They looked at each other, then at Cully sitting there grooming his paw, unaware of the panic he had ensued. As relief washed over them, they began to laugh at the irony of the situation and the sudden release of the tension that had been building between them.

Noah returned to the barn as the laughter dwindled. He looked from Everest to Stratton, who was wiping tears from her eyes. "What did I miss?"

Everest and Stratton shared a look and burst into laughter again. "Looks like Cully decided to assert his dominance over the barn," Everest said, trying to stifle his laughter. He clapped Noah on the back, "Let's head back. It's time for breakfast."

Thirty-Seven

Early August in Tennessee brings warm, humid days with the occasional thunderstorm, and it was no different this year. The vegetable garden was bursting with its bounty; tomatoes hung heavy on their vines, squash, and zucchini plants with their over-sized leaves sprawled over the garden floor, while the peppers and cucumbers welcomed the heat. The cattle and horses were enjoying the lush and green pastures after the evening rains last night.

"I can't believe this is happening." Stratton, clearly annoyed, unloaded the dishwasher while Everest stood at the kitchen island. "It was no small feat making sure everyone could meet here tomorrow, and now you're up and leaving!" She haphazardly tossed the silverware in its drawer.

"Stratton, I told you my volunteer work is often at a moment's notice. I have zero control over the hurricane that hit Louisiana. People are counting on me."

"What about me counting on you?"

"Is that what this is really about? Do you feel like you can't count on me? If that's the case, then I'm going to need some very specific examples." His tone was firm.

She continued putting away the dishes, deciding that it was best that she did not respond right now. She was amped for a fight, already riled up over the upcoming meeting with Lyle, Bernadette, and Mrs. Reed, and now she had to conduct it by herself since Everest was leaving.

When she didn't respond, he came up behind her, placing his hands around her waist.

"Do you really feel that way?" Everest asked.

She took a deep breath, loving how his strong arms fit perfectly around her, then turned toward him, seeing the concern mixed with sincerity slayed across his handsome features. "I'm more upset that I can't stay upset with you." She responded rather sheepishly.

He hugged her tightly, kissing the top of her head. "I know the timing is terrible. I really wanted to be here, but this has to come first right now. That doesn't mean you or this meeting aren't important to me."

Stratton sighed, taking a step back to look at him. "I know that, and it's not fair to you. I realize I'm overreacting based on how I was treated in the past like I didn't matter. It's wrong for me to compare what others did to me back then with you. You don't deserve that. I would have thought that by the time I turned sixty, I wouldn't still feel this way, but here I am, letting those feelings rule my actions. I'm sorry, Everest."

"Honestly, sweetheart, I know how your past has impacted you, and I respect the feelings you're having. This has nothing to do with you not being important, you are very important to me. So much so that I can't be sure that I'm making the right choice by leaving." He ran the back of his hand lovingly down her cheek. "For so long, it's just been me making decisions about what I do. I haven't really thought about how my volunteer work would affect you and our relationship, so that is something that I need to pray about. It may be time to reconsider some of the commitments I've made. I have already promised to be on call for these types of emergencies, so I can't go back on that now."

He slid his hands down her arms and gently took her hands in his. "But I can promise you this: I will never, ever let the sun go down with anger between us. You have my word." He gave her a tender kiss. "I've got to hit the road in an hour, but I'm here now, and I want to spend that time talking this through and working on us. I'm willing if you are."

"Isn't there an 'or'?" She looked up at him with a sparkle in her eyes.

He smiled. "Or we can spend it on that couch kissing."

Knowing that Noah was at a movie with Shelby, she took Everest's hand and led him to the couch in the family room. "Or it is then," she told him before she kissed him.

Stratton had grown bolder in touching Everest as the depth of their emotional intimacy was starting to breach other barriers. She let her hands freely explore those strong muscles in his torso and shoulders. *How is it that this gorgeous, marvelous man loves me?*

In the past, she would have doubted it, telling herself that it was too good to be true, but tonight, she chose to savor this moment. Her fingers lingered at his shoulder blades, feeling his muscles contract as her hands moved along his back. She also didn't recall pressing her lips against his with such fervor before, but there she was, matching his passion with her own and even exceeding his at times.

Usually, they sat next to each other on the couch, but tonight, as Stratton moved closer against Everest, he reclined slightly so her head rested on his shoulder. Stratton imagined them continuing this in her bedroom and thought her body might also be agreeing. A sudden surge of sheer panic ripped through her at the thought, along with the Scripture she knew by heart about not awakening or arousing love until the timing was right; she didn't have time to process those thoughts at the moment, as Everest's phone buzzed bringing her back to reality.

Everest bolted upright, reaching for his phone. "Ugh. I'm sorry. I set an alarm. I have twenty minutes before I must get on the road." He stood and reached for her hands, pulling her up toward him. "I'd rather stay here with you." He brought her into a tender embrace and held her.

"I'd rather that myself." She felt her heartbeat gradually slowing down, a testimony to how caught up in the moment she had been. The heat she felt was so intense that she was sure steam must be rising from her. Slightly embarrassed at her reaction to him, she was thankful that his alarm had kept her from acting on the impulsive thoughts that had run through her mind a few moments earlier.

"You can try to call me after the meeting if I have cell service. I'll get word to you as soon as I can, but I should be back by Thursday at the latest." He leaned in and brushed his lips over the curve of her neck. "I'd better go finish getting packed."

She squeezed him tightly and released. "Sounds good. I'll pack a lunch for you." *After I down at least two glasses of cold water.*

Stratton couldn't recall if Noah had cameras where the cars were parked, but she didn't care. Urging him to be ready to leave ten minutes earlier than planned, she spent that time saying her goodbyes, not so much with her words but with her actions. She made sure to send him on his way with enough marginally suggestive kiss maneuvers to keep his thoughts occupied for the next seven hours.

* * * * *

Stratton had spent most of the night before the meeting tossing and turning in prayer about the idea of placing the coins in a traveling exhibition until about 4 am when a new idea occurred to her. She had tried calling Everest to share it with him but couldn't get him. The news reports said that the cell towers were down in New Orleans, and it could take weeks to get electricity to most of the city again.

After getting out of bed and making herself a cup of hot tea, she walked to the back deck, taking a seat in one of the chairs to watch the sunrise and read through Scripture. As the morning light began to peak through the trees, casting its golden rays across the pasture, her eyes landed on Proverbs 3:6, "In all your ways acknowledge Him, And He shall direct your paths." Stratton paused as a peace washed over her; she knew that this new idea was from Him. She continued to pray that her thoughts and actions would be directed by the Spirit because she was about to make a suggestion that, if implemented, was going to change the course of peoples' lives in Lynnville and Tennesseans.

Thirty-Eight

Stratton had taken great care to ensure that this meeting was a success. She had decided that they should meet in the dining room since it would give them the best lighting and give her a place to unveil the gold. She had prepared some light snacks, as well as set out tea and coffee on one end of the table. She had placed the gold, covered with a piece of satin cloth, in the center of the table.

Lyle, Bernadette, and Mrs. Reed had arrived right on time and sat around the table waiting for her to start. Stratton glanced around the dining room once more to make sure everything was in place.

"I want to thank the three of you for coming today. I want you to know how much I appreciate the input from each of you in my search to find answers about the possibility of hidden treasure. We have all had a hand in the journey that has led us to today, and I'd like to show you what I found."

Stratton lifted off the satin cloth, revealing several stacks of the gold coins and a few of the gold bars.

Audible gasps could be heard as the guests took in the enormity of what they were seeing.

"I know that you'll have a lot of questions, which I am happy to answer, but first, you should know that the value of the gold is around two million dollars."

"That's amazing!" Lyle said. "You found it."

Bernadette jumped into the conversation, "How did you do it?"

"Two million dollars?" Mrs. Reed was astonished.

"I couldn't have found it without Mrs. Reed. Lyle, I don't know what you know or don't know about your family's history, but in the mid-1800s, you had a relative, Solomon Turner, who was told by his father to bury the family gold, which he did. However, he didn't bury it on the family's land; he buried it on what is now my land."

"I've never heard that, and his name isn't even familiar," Lyle commented.

"That doesn't surprise me since it appears he was erased from most of the family records."

"Why?" asked Bernadette.

"Well, I was at a standstill until Mrs. Reed helped with fitting the pieces together. Solomon was the youngest son of Merrick Turner, who was a wealthy plantation owner. He had two young house slaves, Meriday and Daphne, who were raised and tutored alongside Solomon. Being about the same age, they spent a lot of time together, and when Solomon turned eighteen, he expressed his intention to marry Daphne."

"What?" Lyle was visibly astonished.

"Mister Turner didn't want that to happen, so he sold Daphne to a neighboring landowner, Mr. Wessynton, but that didn't stop Solomon from continuing to love Daphne. About two years later, in 1863, there came an opportunity for them to escape to the north. Rumor had it that Union soldiers were planning to raid the nearby plantations, so Mister Turner entrusted Solomon to bury the family's money to keep it safe. However, Solomon took the money and went to the Wessynton farm where Daphne was. When he arrived, he found that she was too sick to travel and died shortly thereafter from malaria. Solomon took a portion of that money and buried it on what is now my homestead, which used to belong to the Wessynton family. He then enlisted with the Union army and was killed in one of their first skirmishes." Stratton paused to give them time to process this huge amount of information before she continued. "Mrs. Reed is a descendant of Meriday, Daphne's sibling. Her family had kept some letters that Solomon had written to Daphne outlining not only his plans but his undying love for her. Without those letters, I never would have found the gold."

The room was so quiet that Stratton could hear the ticking of Lyle's watch. She could almost feel their thoughts pressing against her. "I've had a lot more time than all of you to process this and have two proposals; one is that we split the coins evenly three ways and do what we want with our third." She paused and looked around the room.

She noticed Bernadette's eyes were filled with tears while Lyle sat there speechless. Mrs. Reed seemed overwhelmed by everything. *Give me Your words to say, and guide my steps in the direction You want me to go.*

She took a breath before continuing. "The second idea I had needs a little explaining first. Solomon and Daphne were at that transitional time between childhood ending and adulthood beginning. They weren't equipped or empowered to handle the pressures from society or their families."

Stratton leaned in a little closer. "Last night, I was praying about what would be the best thing to do with the gold. I kept asking how this can be put to good use in honor of Solomon and Daphne, and He gave me the answer. Do you know that in Tennessee, each year, around 1,000 children age out of the foster care system, and 97% will end up in chronic poverty? These young adults are also more likely to be incarcerated, attempt suicide, and are at risk for homelessness. Many of the young women become pregnant, thus repeating the cycle of foster care."

She knew that she was giving them a lot of information but felt she needed to continue moving forward with this idea. "With all this said, my second proposal is that we invest a portion of the coins and build a faith-based homestead for these children. I don't know how many kids we can take; I don't know the criteria of what we would look for in taking those kids. We will be the founding members and can work out all of those details. The homestead would be a place for learning life skills and partnering with colleges and trade schools for scholarships or auditing classes. We can decide how best to handle the rest of the coins while getting the word out about our homestead, and eventually, we could support and teach other groups around Tennessee how to do the same thing, assuming our model works like I pray that it will."

"We're in," Bernadette said without hesitation, tears spilling uncontrollably down her cheeks.

Lyle reached over and held her hand as he explained the reason for her tears. "We haven't told anyone, but we're in the middle of adopting two biracial children whose mother and father, both products of the foster care system, cannot care for them."

Bernadette wiped her tears and added, "Also, we haven't told anyone that we're pregnant. We found out right after we met and fell in love with the children. There never was a question of not going through with the adoption. All three of them are our future children."

Stratton looked at Mrs. Reed, who nodded with tear-stained cheeks. Even Stratton sniffled and used the back of her hand to wipe her eyes.

Mrs. Reed stayed behind after Lyle and Bernadette departed. "Choosing the orphans was the right decision, Stratton. The Good Lord is going to use you to change lives, and in so doing, yours will be changed. You can't walk away from an encounter on the Mountain of God without it showing." Mrs. Reed patted Stratton's hand.

"Thank you so much for helping and agreeing to be a part of this."

"These children need to learn about Him while learning skills they can use, like those in the old days, and this old woman right here is glad to help." Stratton knew that she was right. This was going to be quite the undertaking, and its success depended upon the support from the community. She prayed that she could gather enough supporters and volunteers to see the vision come to life.

Stratton walked Mrs. Reed to her car, waving to her as she left the drive. She thought about the meeting as she cleaned up the dining room. How wonderful was God to use Solomon and Daphne's tragic story for good? She thought of the verse from Isaiah about how He makes beauty from ashes and realized she was seeing Scripture come alive right before her eyes.

* * * * *

She tried to reach Everest as soon as she had finished cleaning up. She tried again as she locked up the house for the night and again after she had gotten ready for bed. There was never an answer. *I'll try one more time before turning out the lights.* She propped herself up in bed, intending to read for a bit, but fell asleep with the phone in her hand and forgot to put it on silent.

Around 11 PM, the phone rang, startling her awake.

"Everest?" She answered before her eyes could adjust to see who was calling.

"Mom, it's me," Finley said.

"Sorry, honey, I was asleep."

"Why would Everest be calling you? Doesn't he live downstairs?" There was a distinct edge in her voice.

"He's not here."

"Did you get in a fight?"

Why did Finley sound hopeful? Stratton dismissed it as she tried to wake up.

"No, he's doing some volunteer work."

"And he often calls late at night?"

What is with her and all the questions? "Finley, he doesn't have much cell reception. He's in New Orleans, where the hurricane hit. Why are you calling so late? Is everything OK?"

"I wanted to come see you while the movers take my things to Mount Judea, but if you're too busy…"

"I'm not busy, and I'd love for you to come."

"Sure doesn't seem that way. Noah doesn't hardly text me back. What are you all doing all summer anyway? Aren't you supposed to be resting or something?"

So it appeared that Noah hadn't told his sisters about Shelby; Stratton wouldn't either. She found it a bit ironic that they both withheld any information about their summer loves from Harper and Finley.

Stratton looked down at her phone, blinking her eyes so they would adjust. *Nope, no missed text or call from Everest.* Her heart sank. She missed his company, his conversation, how he looked at her, his kisses. She sighed. *I guess I just miss him.*

"So I'll be there tomorrow, OK?"

"That's perfect. I'll be here. I love you."

"I love you, too. Bye."

"Bye." Stratton ended the call. She took a drink of water. Just as she plugged her phone into the charger, it buzzed.

Her heart leaped; it was a text from Everest.

Bad cell service. Be home tomorrow. I love you.

She smiled, thankful he had gotten a text through to her.

Be safe. I love you.

She was so excited he was coming home. She couldn't wait to share the latest news about the gold with him. She grabbed a post-it note from her nightstand and quickly wrote out a hearty dinner menu for his return and started thinking about something cute to wear.

Thirty-Nine

"Mom, I'm here!" Finley announced.

Stratton, already dressed for Everest's arrival in white skinny jeans and a light denim button-down shirt, came from the kitchen and greeted her with a big hug.

Finley looked beautiful when she was wearing hardly any makeup. Stratton was thrilled to see there wasn't a guy in tow this time. These were praise-worthy changes she was seeing.

"How was your flight?" Stratton walked back to the kitchen and opened the lid of the Crockpot, stirring the contents.

"Fine. What are you making? It smells wonderful." Finley sat at the kitchen island.

"Everest is on his way back today, so I'm making his favorite turkey recipe and some vegetables."

Finley's brow narrowed. "You didn't want to make my favorite?"

Finley was the first to express jealousy over Everest. Stratton didn't want things to get ugly. She couldn't take back what she just said, but she could make amends. "I will make yours tomorrow."

"I mean, if there's time. I'm probably only in town for the night. The movers will be at my new place soon. I wanted to see you before I get settled in Mount Judea and invite you out. Can you come and spend the rest of your sabbatical with me?"

"Sweetie, no. I've got a lot going on here." Stratton suspected Finley mainly wanted assistance in unpacking.

"What do you have going on?"

"Well, for starters, your brother, Everest, and I found buried treasure."

"OK, sure. Like what? One of those Indian mounds filled with old pottery?"

"No, we found some old coins."

"Cool," Finley said as she started scrolling through her phone.

"They're worth a lot."

"Yeah, so I wanted to share some things with you." Finley was still Finley, always focusing on herself.

"I'm back!" Everest announced as he came through the door.

Stratton's smile brightened as she went to greet him. "Hi, Finley just arrived." It was a subtle message to let him know they weren't alone, so their greeting needed to be kept in check, though she ached for him to sweep her into his arms, giving her a deep, passionate kiss.

He gave her a knowing look as he embraced her and gave her a quick kiss.

Instantly, Stratton yearned to be alone with Everest, showing him how much she had missed him.

"What are you cooking? It smells amazing," Everest asked.

"Just a little something special for you." She whispered so Finley wouldn't hear.

"Hey, Finley. How are you?" He asked as they walked into the kitchen.

"I'm fine. How are you?"

Stratton knew from that tone that she wasn't fine.

"Glad to be home."

"Oh, I thought you were from Pennsylvania?" Finley flippantly observed.

Stratton shot her daughter the reprimanding mom look.

"I am. I mean that I'm glad to be back here," Everest corrected.

"Since the turkey won't be ready for a while, let's go sit down, and I'll tell you how the meeting went," Stratton offered.

"Yes, I've been waiting with anticipation to hear this."

Stratton and Everest left the kitchen while Finley stayed seated, looking through her phone; the two settled on the couch.

"Tell me everything," Everest said.

"I spoke from the heart. I couldn't sleep the night before, so I spent almost the whole night in prayer. Super early in the morning, this idea came to me, so I shared both ideas with them. One was the original idea of splitting the coins, or the second idea was that we could use them to make a homestead for kids aging out of the foster care system so they would have a positive start into adulthood."

"That's wonderful. What did they say?"

"All three of them were on board. Lyle and Bernadette are actually adopting two biracial children soon, and they have a baby on the way, so hearing Solomon's story really touched their hearts. It was a wonderful meeting."

"I'm so proud of you." The proud look on his face matched his words, but she also saw the passion in his eyes as he looked at her.

She knew he wanted to lean over and kiss her, not a quick kiss on the cheek kiss, but the kind of kiss that was meant only for them. The kind of intimate kiss that wasn't rushed but was savored in privacy. "Thank you. I was nervous and unsure, but I just trusted that this was His idea. I felt like He blessed the meeting for me, remaining truthful to the historical account."

"Absolutely."

"Well, tell me about the clean-up." Stratton looked towards the kitchen. "Finley, come hear about Everest's volunteer work." She motioned for Finley to come to the living room, doing her best to include her.

Finley came and sat down in Noah's chair, seemingly disinterested, still scrolling on her phone.

It bothered Stratton that she was acting like this. "So, Everest volunteers for disaster relief clean-up throughout the Southeast when needed. He just got back from helping with the hurricane that hit New Orleans."

"What about any other extracurricular activities?" Finley asked.

Stratton didn't like her tone. She detected a touch of skepticism and just a hint of an I-know-something-you-don't-know attitude.

Everest hesitated. "Like what?" He sounded confused.

Stratton didn't like the look in Finley's eyes. "OK, Finley, I think you should take your bags to your room." She couldn't believe she was having to speak this way to her adult daughter.

"And leave you two alone so you can just ignore me from my room instead of out here to my face?"

"Finley, please."

"Don't you even want to know the kind of guy I'd be leaving you alone with?"

"Finley, now." Stratton stood up and walked over to the chair Finley occupied.

Finley jumped up. "Well, I'd sure want to know if the guy I was dating had been arrested for assault."

Stratton saw the anger in Finley's eyes. She turned to look at Everest, who had turned white. Finley had found something out about Everest that he hadn't shared. What was he hiding? *Oh no, was it really the perfect backstory to a true crime podcast all this time?* No, none of this made sense. Finley had to be wrong. Everest wouldn't hide something from her, would he? No, he wouldn't have kept a secret like that from her.

"I'm just gonna go downstairs." Everest hurriedly left, looking like he had been kicked in the gut.

Stratton stood before Finley. "I honestly don't know what to say."

"How about thank you?" She said with a smug look on her face.

"Finley, if he hasn't said anything, then he had his reasons."

"Oh my gosh, he has totally brainwashed you, hasn't he? This is why I offered to do a background check on him in the beginning, Mom, don't you remember? When you were hiding him from us, but not Noah, oh no, never Noah."

Stratton threw up her hands. "If I failed you as a parent, Yehovah, have mercy on me. I tried so hard to be there for you, Finley, and to teach you right from wrong, to love others, to forgive, and to trust Him first. I tried to teach you how to make good choices. I did the best I could in our circumstances to show you that you could have a fulfilled life. Don't you want me to be happy, too?"

"I'm trying to protect you! Can't you see that? Oh, wait, you're too busy waiting around for his call, waiting to cook his dinner, dropping everything for his schedule, or whenever he snaps his fingers to care that I'm trying to help you. I don't know who you are anymore. I'm looking out for you, and you're making me into the villain."

"You could have shared this with just me. You didn't have to do it in front of Everest."

"When was I supposed to do that? Like right before your wedding?

Toast to the new bride and groom?" Finley said sarcastically as she held up an imaginary glass.

"I am going downstairs to talk to Everest and clear this up." Stratton walked to the crockpot and moved the knob to the warm setting. With that, she went downstairs.

Forty

She tapped lightly on Everest's door. There was no response from the other side. The quietness was almost suffocating as she hesitantly turned the knob and opened the door, a slight creak breaking the silence. "Everest? Can I come in?"

Stratton stepped across the threshold and closed the door behind her. The amber and violet rays of the sunset filtering through the French doors brought in some light to the quickly darkening room.

Everest sat on the corner of his neatly made bed, elbows resting on his knees, head hung low as if the weight of his thoughts were too much to bear. He didn't look up as she entered.

She crossed the room and sat next to him on the bed. "I'm really sorry about that." She said softly. Her voice, barely above a whisper, was filled with regret.

He sat motionless, not saying a word.
"Everest, I know you must have your reasons, and you don't have to share what happened if you don't want to." *Of course, it would be nice if he shared why he was arrested for assault. Was it a man? Was it a woman?*

Everest, head still bent low, took a deep breath. "She must know a skilled hacker. That arrest was from a sealed record."

Stratton's heart sank. So it was true. Not sure what to say, she just waited in silence.

He straightened and turned his head to look at her. "This isn't how I wanted to tell you. I will tell you about the arrest, but I need to tell you more about where I volunteer first."

She nodded.

"Disaster relief is one part of our job as volunteers. The other part involves assisting local law enforcement or civilians in the community in a different type of emergency. How much do you know about human trafficking?"

"I know it exists, and it's absolutely horrific."

Everest nodded. "It is horrible." He looked towards the French doors, watching the sky fill with dusky indigo shades as the sun reached the horizon. "I believe that a girl I once knew ended up in a trafficking situation. I used to walk every day to school with Emma Rose." He gave a wry smile. "Nine-year-old me definitely had a crush on her. At that time, the only thing of value I had to give her to show I liked her was this Snoopy necklace. She wore it all the time. About three years later, she started changing. Emma Rose used to talk about her mom having new boyfriends every week and how she couldn't wait to get away from that once she grew up. I didn't really understand what she meant since I had a loving two-parent home."

He paused, bent his head, and took a deep breath. "She started smoking cigarettes on our way to school and told me that her mom's new boyfriend liked to give her gifts. About that same time, she started dressing differently and wearing heavy, dark makeup. I no longer had a crush on her, but still considered her a friend. When we were around 15, I noticed that Emma Rose was getting a lot of attention from older guys, guys that weren't in high school. She started missing a lot of school, which, by then, was the only time we had ever talked."

Everest ran his hand through his hair. "Supposedly, she took off with a boyfriend around that time, but no one is sure; she just disappeared. From time to time, rumors popped up, but nothing was ever proven. After she was gone, I found the Snoopy necklace in a box next to the trash. I'm not really sure why I kept it, but I did, as a reminder of Emma Rose, I guess."

Stratton's heart ached watching the man she loved broken by his sorrow and regret. She reached over and gently took his hand, giving it a slight squeeze, offering him her support and strength.

He stared at their entwined hands. "When I learned about human trafficking, I immediately thought of her and felt this righteous anger well up in me. I knew I had to do something, so I volunteered with a group of people who were part of the disaster relief work for natural disasters but who also provided assistance in human trafficking situations. Every case is taken seriously. Sometimes, law enforcement relies on our intelligence, and they take action.

Everest glanced up, still holding tightly to Stratton's hand. "Are you OK?"

How she loved this man! "I'm fine, promise."

He gave her a knowing look, then glanced at the ceiling, lost in the memory. "It was my first mission. We were called out to a compound to rescue a group of kids who were being trafficked. We got them out." He cleared his throat, clearly struggling with his emotions.

"We held the guy who was the trafficker until the local police could arrive. He was standing off to the side, in restraints, just watching us remove the children. Suddenly, he burst out in this totally demonic laughter, then started shouting obscenities at us and asking if any of us wanted to hear the details of what had been done to the children." He swallowed hard, visibly trying to hold back the tears, but failed to do so.

"I had just carried out a petrified child, trembling in fear, yet clinging to me as if I was the only hope to be had. I could not imagine the trauma this child had experienced. It pierced my soul and shattered my heart in a way that's never been the same."

Tears streamed unabashedly down his cheeks. "I thought back to Emma Rose, who seemed to almost always have an underlying sad expression. I know I was just a kid and didn't know what was happening, but after being part of the trafficking rescue work for quite a while, I know now that someone was hurting her."

Stratton could no longer hold back her own tears and felt them fall softly on their clasped hands.

"That night, I snapped, jumped this guy in rage; rage at what he had done to these children and rage at whoever had done the same thing to Emma Rose. I swung my fists, pummeling his face with all of my strength, until my buddies pulled me off."

Everest inhaled deeply and let his breath out slowly, noticeably reining in his emotions from the memory he just shared. "He filed charges immediately, and I was arrested. I was told the entire thing would be under seal, and no one would ever know. Obviously, I believed that and agreed to it, yet here we are. Though I was willing to tell you about my volunteer work, I wasn't sure if I could, or even should, share the trafficking aspect of my work. I've repented and never touched another perpetrator again, so it's over and done in my mind. Since then, anytime the situation feels too much, which is very often, I depend on Scripture and prayer to get me through it."

Everest turned slightly towards her as he reached for her other hand. "Maybe that was wrong of me to withhold that from you," he said quietly, his voice full of remorse, "But I'm not the same guy that I was on that first mission. I don't want this to affect your trust in me, but I know it probably will. Can you forgive me?"

Stratton softly exhaled, not realizing she had been holding her breath. Her mind raced to process his words, but only one thought emerged: she was in love with a real hero.

That realization washed over her, quickening her pulse and making her heart beat faster. She could only think of one way to show Everest how deeply she loved him, and she was ready. Standing, she released his hands and walked silently to the French doors.

"Well, I didn't figure you'd be so quick to walk away."

"I'm not walking away." She glanced over her shoulder as she pulled the cord, closing the blinds.

"What are you doing?" He looked confused.

She walked back over to the bed. Leaning down to face him, she placed her hands on the bed on either side of him. She let her gaze search his face before brushing her lips across his. "I'm going to stay the night with you."

"Stratton," but he didn't get another word out.

She covered his mouth with her own, letting passion guide her. Stratton realized that being sixty was not a hindrance to love or desire. It might change with age, but it was still there. Though desire might no longer happen instantly, taking more time to build and burn, it was still there. These sensuous, impulsive, explosive feelings that she was experiencing were proof of that.

Everest breathlessly pulled back. "I really thought this could be a deal breaker. I'm sorry for not telling you sooner, Stratton. It's a hard story to share."

Stratton moved to sit beside him on the bed. "I know you felt forced to tell me, but I want you to always share things with me. You were a source of light and joy to Emma Rose. You don't know what your prayers may have done in her life. You've helped save so many others, and I admire your service and sacrifice. So, trust me, I am not going anywhere; I am staying by your side."

He embraced her. "Thank you."

Since they were opening their hearts, Stratton felt she needed to share what was on hers. "I need you to know I really enjoy kissing you," she stated, her voice thick with vulnerability, "but at my age, anything beyond that may need patience, tenderness, and understanding. Are you OK with that?"

"Oh, Stratton." He gently tilted her chin up, his eyes full of warmth and love. "From the moment I saw you, I only saw a beautiful woman. The same beautiful woman who puts the needs of others before her own, the same beautiful woman who has a heart for the Lord, the same beautiful woman who has a fun-loving, adventurous spirit, and the same beautiful woman I've kissed a hundred times and will kiss a million more. You are a woman to me and with me, and this man is man enough to deal with anything if you're by my side. I mean that, Stratton. Anything that comes up or happens, we will face this together." He tenderly kissed the tears that were slowly trickling down her face.

"Let me come home to your embrace from these missions. Let me hold you with gratitude as I process my emotions. Let me pledge that the things I've witnessed won't be experienced by our family."

"Our family?" Stratton couldn't stop herself. A family was all she ever wanted, with a husband and father just like Everest. Her hands cupped his face as she let her lips find his. Previously dormant emotions surged through her like a dam bursting free, creating a sense of urgency in her kiss. Stratton moved a fraction back, breaking their kiss. Memories of their time in the hay loft in Arkansas filled her mind, and she whispered with longing in her voice, "Lay me down."

Everest wasted no time gently laying her back on the bed as he propped himself up with one arm to the side of Stratton. His free hand gently brushed the hair from her face as his gaze traveled from her eyes to her lips several times in a silent request for her approval.

Stratton felt as if she would lose herself in the depths of his gaze, drawn in by his desire. She could see his eyes darkening with a longing that rivaled her own.

Unable to help herself, she ran her fingers along his jawline, down his neck, and across his chest, feeling the muscles tighten in response to her touch.

Everest, still on his side, leaned slightly over her until his lips were but a breath from hers. "I love you," he said just before he lowered his mouth to cover hers in a kiss that matched the hunger she'd seen in his eyes.

As their kisses deepened, Stratton felt as if her breath was trapped in her lungs, the anticipation building, threatening to suffocate her.

Stratton tilted her head back, a subtle hint of what she wanted.

He chuckled softly as he kissed the nape of her neck, sending a shiver through her before his mouth returned to capture hers once more.

She felt his hand explore her body as it moved the length of her, coming to rest upon her cheek.

"You're so beautiful."

Stratton was powerless to stop the emotions spilling forth. "I felt lowered inhibitions in Savannah. Everything about that evening was like a dream. I've never been romanced this way before. I didn't know a love like this was possible." She drew her to him for another kiss.

He reluctantly pulled away. "Stratton, I can't do this."

Instantaneously, feeling rejected and inadequate, tears gathered in her eyes. "I'm not sure what you mean."

He reached and turned on the nightstand lamp. He turned to look her in the eyes. "What I mean is I can't because it's too tempting to move forward into territory that isn't mine."

She took in a few deep breaths as the once-crashing waves of yearning receded to gentle, harmless laps.

Everest moved from the bed, his back to her as he opened the nightstand drawer and turned back to face Stratton.

With a slight protest from her flesh, she sat upright.

"Stratton, this isn't exactly going the way I had planned, but," he dipped to one knee, "There's only one person I will move forward with, and that one person is my wife." He opened his hand, revealing an aquamarine ring surrounded by precious stones.

Stratton looked intently at the ring, its design a familiar memory from the past. "Is that my mother's ring?"

"Yes, with some special touches. I had the jeweler add every gemstone mentioned in Chapter 21 of Revelation as a reminder that it is my intention to spend forever with you." He cleared his throat and took hold of her hand.

"Stratton, from the moment I saw you, I was taken with you. I believe Yehovah has been working behind the scenes throughout our lives, knowing we would encounter one another at that exact moment in April. When the summer started, I anticipated that it would be a season filled with romance and love, and yes, even some adventure. Now it's time for that season to come to an end and for us to start a new season— as one. A season that will align with His purposes and helps us grow more as one more intimately and spiritually, as laid out in Scripture. Stratton, will you accept my proposal to become my wife and enter into a marriage covenant with me?"

"Yes!"

He slid the ring onto her finger.

She dropped to her knees and hugged Everest before smothering him with kisses. "How did you get this?"

"If you can control yourself, we can talk about it." Everest stood and helped her up. "Come sit with me." He propped up the pillows and sat up against them, then invited her to sit next to him in his arms.

Stratton scooted in next to him, holding her hand at arm's length, looking at the ring, her mother's ring, with the most meaningful and beautiful modifications. Jasper, sapphire, chalcedony, emerald, sardonyx, carnelian, yellow topaz, beryl, topaz, chrysoprase, jacinth, amethyst.

Her thoughts raced from surprise to excitement to overwhelming love for the man sitting next to her. She never thought she would marry again, yet here she was—it was like a fairytale come true. She couldn't wait to share it with everyone, but first, she wanted to know the story behind the ring.

"Everest, how did you find it?"

"I stopped in to visit Savannah and Charles to learn more about this mysterious missing ring and took it upon myself to ask for a meeting with Miss Bitty Barrow since Savannah was adamant her family had the ring."

"What?" Stratton sat up and looked at him. "Are you serious? Did she have it?"

"Sit back and relax; let me tell the story."

Stratton snuggled back down against her fiancé' chest. "Proceed." She said with a little giggle.

"Bitty agreed to meet with me at The Olde Pink House, you know, the place with the most delicious Southern cuisine."

Stratton nodded, "Yes, I know it."

"I started by telling her I was trying to track down this ring because it was special to your family. When I described the ring, she said that she wanted to help, but she didn't remember her family ever having a ring like that. I thought maybe I had hit a dead-end, but after a moment of thinking, she said that she did recall admiring a ring fitting that description that the daughter of the dean of her college had. She said that this lady was still living in Savannah. She and Bitty were still quite close. Clearly, I thought this might be a wild goose chase, but why not go two for two? We'd already found Confederate gold, so why not try to find this lost ring? So Bitty gave me the lady's name, Mrs. Avery Morrison, so I reached out to her, and she was willing to meet with me at her house."

She gave him two quick pats on his thigh. "One look at you, and no one would refuse you."

Everest smiled and lightly tapped her on the nose with his finger. "You already had your chance to say 'no' to coming to my cabin, but I admit, I did kinda lay that swagger on pretty thick."

Stratton thought about how every decision has a consequence. Had she said 'no' to him, her life would look very different than it did now. Her life had changed for the better when she said "yes" to going to his cabin, and now, after a series of 'yeses,' she was saying 'yes' to his marriage proposal. She lifted her hand again, the ring beautifully reflecting the light from the lamp on the nightstand.

"Anyway, when I arrived, Avery invited me inside, and we sat down in her library. I explained that I was hunting down a specific aquamarine ring after learning of its story, and Bitty thought she might know its whereabouts. Avery cut right to the chase and asked me why I wanted the ring. I hadn't practiced a response, but I told her the truth that since it was originally a family ring, I wanted to show the woman that I love how much by finding the ring and proposing to her. Apparently, this endeared me to her, and she produced the ring. She told me that it was given to her by her mother, who later told her that the ring had paid the tuition for a student who, at the time, couldn't afford to go to college. That student was Bitty. She showed me a photograph of three cute kids: her grandchildren and Bitty's. Bitty and her husband met at that college, and their firstborn son had married Avery's daughter. Avery said that she treasures her son-in-law, who is a faithful husband and father, and that he wouldn't have been born if Bitty hadn't gone to college. She also said that she knew your family by reputation; it was your mother who introduced her to the man who would become her husband. Her parting words to me were, 'It is time for the ring to be a blessing to someone else.' She gave me the ring."

"That's the most astounding story I think I've ever heard," Stratton laughed to herself. Matchmaking was in her family's blood, alright.

"So, I found a local jeweler in Savannah to make the modifications." He kissed the top of her head. "I may have fudged a little about my volunteer work dates. I was actually helping with disaster relief, but I padded a few of those days so I could get the ring ready for my proposal."

"Did you have it planned already?"

"I've known for a while that I wanted to ask you to marry me, so I've been working on it and have a few ideas, like horseback riding, picnic at the park, and hot air balloon ride. I was more worried it was too soon for you."

Stratton nuzzled against him. "I've known for a while that when you asked, I was going to say 'yes'."

"I think we've already established that you don't know how to say 'no' to me." He chuckled and kissed her temple.

She glanced up, giving him a mischievous look. "Maybe we're living awfully close to danger right now, me not being able to say 'no' to you."

"It might be a little more of the other way around. I was about to demand we call the preacher a little while ago. I haven't seen you that caught up in the moment before."

Stratton blushed as she looked at the ring again. "If you wanted to get a preacher over here today, we could. I know several."

Everest laughed. "Believe me, I would love that, but I also want to honor our families. They should get to celebrate with us as well." He tenderly stroked her hair.

As her head rested on his chest, Stratton closed her eyes and listened to his heartbeat, grateful for this moment and this man.

"So I suppose I won't be staying with you down here tonight?" She raised up off his chest, eyes sparkling as she gave him a slight pout.

"I think you've got to go talk to Finley."

"How about this? We spend five minutes celebrating as an engaged couple, and then I'll go upstairs." She moved to kiss him.

He gazed at her, placing a finger over her lips, preventing them from coming any closer. "Five minutes?"

She nodded her agreement, though the longing in her eyes conveyed the exact opposite.

Everest broke the look they shared. "I think it best that we both flee from temptation. Your presence alone in this room makes my heart race and takes my thoughts to places they don't need to go. I'm struggling right now. I want you to stay more than you know. So many nights, I've wanted that, but I promised God and you that I wouldn't cross those boundaries. Stratton, I can't do that to Him or to us."

"I understand, but it's just I haven't felt this way in a very long time. I wasn't even sure I still could."

"Well, now that we know you can, we need to keep those boundaries." He ran the back of his hand tenderly along her cheek. "You know that I really want you to stay, but you know you can't, right?"

"Logically, I know it isn't right, but physically it's challenging."

"It isn't right tonight, but soon it will be." He briefly brushed his lips against hers. "Since tonight isn't going at all like I envisioned, can we at least listen to the song I would have worked into my proposal?"

"Yes."

"We need to get off the bed and start making our way to the door, though. The longer you're here, the harder it's going to be."

Stratton raised a brow.

"I wasn't even thinking like that!" Everest moved off the bed and picked his phone up from the nightstand.

Stratton sat up and scooted to the edge of the bed.

Anne Murray's *Could I Have This Dance* started playing.

"Come on," Everest held out a hand.

Stratton begrudgingly took it and stood.

Everest drew her into his arms, singing the words to the first chorus softly to her, words that spoke of being dance partners every evening and for the rest of their lives.

She wrapped her arms around his neck and swayed with him. It was a song that made Stratton reflect over the many times she'd danced with Everest: upstairs when he first arrived, in Savannah under the moon, rocking beside him singing *America the Beautiful* in Arkansas, and now, in the serenity of his space. She knew she wanted to be his forever dance partner.

Everest kissed her. "You aren't upset, are you?"

"I just want to be with you."

"You are with me."

"Everest, you could have any woman you want. I don't know why you're choosing me. I struggle not to over-analyze it, but I feel that if I'm not as responsive to you as a younger woman, you'll lose interest, which would break my heart. Tonight, for the first time in a long time, I felt what it was like to truly desire someone, and I don't want to lose that. I never thought I would love you like I do, which scares me in a way and probably will, to an extent, even when we are married. Then we have a night like tonight, and all I want to do is stay with you and give myself to you. I love you and genuinely want that more than anything, so right now, I'm having a hard time seeing how that's wrong."

Everest kissed the tears in her eyes. "First, I don't want any other woman but you and that will never change. I promise to be as gentle and understanding as possible until you truly believe my words. I fell in love with you, Stratton. You're who I want. There isn't a part of you that I am not attracted to." He kissed her sweetly. "Second, it's about the timing. It isn't wrong for you to want to stay here with me all night when it's the right time. If you really think that the timing is right tonight, then let's make that happen with a quick few phone calls."

Taking a couple of deep breaths, she leaned closer into Everest as they danced and let him lead her towards the door. She thought about what he said. She wanted it to happen tonight, but then she thought of Finley and Noah. What would they think of her getting a Justice of the Peace to come to their home just so Stratton could spend the night with Everest in good conscience? When she put it that way, it sounded silly. She paused as they reached the doorway and looked up at Everest, "OK, I agree, the timing isn't right tonight."

Everest smiled. "Why don't you go upstairs and talk to Finley now, but," he leaned close, his lips hovering just above hers, "let me send you off with a little something more to remember this night by."

"I'll never forget any part of this night." she managed to say before his mouth covered hers.

His kisses were tender and achingly slow again.

Stratton, feeling her body respond quicker than usual, leaned in to kiss Everest's neck and softly brushed her lips across his ear lobe.

He reacted by quickly pressing her against him, moving his lips along her neck.

"OK, you've proved your point," Stratton breathlessly said.

He pressed her tighter to him and kept going. "What point is that?" His warm breath against her neck sent a shiver down her spine.

His fingers slipped under the back of her shirt, slowly tracing the curve of her lower back. Stratton felt herself surrendering to the pleasurable feelings of his skin against hers. "I'm there again." *Keep going, Everest, please keep going.*

"What?" He stilled.

"You're going to have to kick me out or take me."

"And here you thought it might only happen once. Do you see that it's all going to work out?" His eyes twinkled with promise.

"Everest, I'm not kidding. Open that door and make me go."

He smiled and opened the door. "Do you think you can manage to get upstairs alright?"

"I just need a second." Stratton took in a deep breath, hoping it would slow her racing pulse. "OK, I can do this."

"Babe?"

"Hmm?"

"You might wanna button up."

Stratton looked down. Somehow, she had managed to undo the buttons on her shirt in the heat of the moment. She felt her cheeks turning pink. *How could I have done that and not remember?* She started carefully re-buttoning, making sure each button was lined up perfectly, or Finley would never let her hear the end of it.

"I'm going to go talk to Finley. Feel free to help yourself to dinner whenever you want."

Everest kissed her. "I love you, Stratton Davis, and I can't wait to marry you."

"I love you more than you could ever know." She whispered, feeling tears begin to build. As she hugged him, she realized that there was no returning to a life before Everest; he held her heart. The emotional growth she had made over the course of a summer had transformed her. She kissed him once more before turning and heading upstairs, trying her best to cool the lingering heat from his touch.

Forty-One

Stratton paused at the top of the stairs, looking at the ring sparkling on her finger, before going to find Finley. She stopped by the family room first but didn't see her there. Thinking she must be in her room, she quietly opened the door, but it was empty. *Did Finley leave?* Stratton headed to her room to get her phone so she could text Finley to see where she was. She opened the door to her room and there was Finley, curled up on Stratton's bed crying.

"Finley, what's wrong?"

"Why do I have to compete with a man for your attention?" Finley sat up, eyes bloodshot, nose running; she looked pitiful.

"Finley, that's not true, but why do you think that?"

"All summer, you've been too busy to come to stay with me or even let me know what's been going on. You've had this secret romance building, and I tried to be supportive at Harper's because you said you were just dating. You said you didn't know how serious it was, but I come home and see that it's way more than dating."

Stratton felt the color rising to her cheeks. Had Finley heard them in the basement? Of all times for Stratton to be in such high demand with her family. If it wasn't Noah and his cameras or Scarlett spying from the barn, it now might've been Finley overhearing something she certainly meant to keep private.

"I see how you look at him. You're acting like you're married or something; always taking care of him, cleaning for him, cooking for him—and you like it! So does he. Before, whenever I came home, you always made my favorite meals, but this time, nothing. Is this what it's going to be like from now on? You just forget about us? Like how can you forget you have kids? Well, I guess not Harper or Noah. You went to Harper's this summer, and you tell Noah everything, but you don't come to see me, and you don't tell me anything anymore. Everest texts with Harper and hangs out with Noah, but he doesn't text me. Doesn't he want to get to know me? Harper already told me he's planned a fall trip for you to go back to see her, but no one asked me to come."

He's planned a surprise trip to see Harper and the grandchildren. Her first instinct was to run downstairs and throw her arms around Everest, but that would have to wait. Finley needed her right now. Stratton didn't want to exacerbate Finley's emotional state, so she moved her hand behind her back, slipped the ring off, and pocketed it before Finley could notice.

"Mom, what's wrong with me that no one wants to include me or spend time with me?" Finley's voice cracked as she began crying again. Stratton's heart broke at the sight of her daughter hurting so much. Knowing this could not be farther from the truth, she stayed silent, letting Finley have this time to share what she was feeling.

"I asked Dad to come out three separate times this summer, and he wouldn't. He said he was too busy at the bank, but his new girlfriend posted their trips on Instagram. Mom, they went on three trips this summer: Europe, the Caymans, and they even took her kids with them to Las Vegas. He wasn't working. He was traveling. He spends more time with her than us! You didn't come to visit me either. You asked me to come here in the spring, and I did. You wanted me to go to Harper's, and I did. I've done what's been asked, but no one wants to accept my invitations. What is wrong with me?"

Stratton climbed into the bed and pulled a still sobbing Finley into her arms. Finley had a point. She hadn't been as supportive as she could have been. Normally, Stratton would have spent at least a few weekends in Denver, and she would have helped organize, paint, and unpack when Finley moved. If she hadn't been swept up in a summer romance, she would have been more involved in Finley's life. However, Harper and Noah seemed to embrace Everest and didn't feel like she was neglecting them. *What was really going on with Finley?*

Stratton stroked Finley's hair. "Finley, nothing's wrong with you. We all love spending time with you. You've had a busy schedule, so that's been a challenge for us trying to find the time to see you, but we should have tried harder. I'm sorry." She handed Finley a tissue from the nightstand. "Also, this is the first time in a long time you've been single, and that is a challenge in and of itself. It'll take a little while for you to get used to being alone, but look at this as an opportunity for you to grow and rediscover who you are."

"I just thought my family would be there for me. Mom, please come and stay with me. I need you."

This is when Stratton was torn between what to do. She could see both sides of Finley: the adult daughter asking for help and her little girl who needed her mother. "Honey, I have the annual historical meeting coming up next week, and you'd be all moved in by the time I get there."

"Why won't you leave him?"

"Finley, don't." Trying to stick with the path of de-escalation, she explained, "It's not about leaving anyone. And who do you mean anyway? Everest or your brother?"

"What does it matter? You won't come stay with me either way."

"Baby, you don't need to be jealous of Everest. I told him from the beginning that being with me means being with all of us, and that includes you. He isn't trying to steal me away from you three if that's what you think."

"Maybe he's just hoodwinked you. I mean, he didn't tell you about the assault. I, for one, don't trust him."

"You don't know him and haven't tried to know him."

"I don't need to or want to. He's a liar."

"Finley, he didn't lie to me. You don't know what happened."

"Omission, Mom. Same difference."

"Baby, he hit an evil man who hurt a child. That record was supposed to be sealed, but you found someone who was able to locate it."

"Well, if you'd have agreed to that type of background check earlier, then you would've already known."

"And if I didn't have all the information, I may have ended our relationship based on a limited perspective."

"So you're still going to see him? Even after he hid the truth from you?"

"Finley, look at me. I love him. Do you know that love covers all transgressions? He loves me and is willing to love all of you. Do you know how rare that is?"

"What I know is that I always knew I'd have you even if I didn't have Dad. You were always there, and it feels like you're not anymore. I feel so left out. I don't want to be included with you and Everest, as if you two are some package deal now. I just want my mom. You said when you divorced Dad, you would never, ever choose a man over us. You promised!"

"Finley, I'm not choosing him over you." The tears flowed from Stratton's eyes.

"Yes, you are!" Finley sobbed. "You just don't see it."

Stratton couldn't tell if Finley was being genuine or manipulative or a mix of both, or if Finley was even right, but she felt the doubt and guilt creep in as Finley wept against her. Uncertainty washed over her, and she began to question everything—her judgment, her relationship with Everest, as well as with her children, her priorities.

Stratton had no defenses for this ambush of emotions and questions filling her mind. *Have I broken my word to Finley? Have I subconsciously chosen Everest over my children? Have I inadvertently taught them that they should always come first? Have I overcompensated the lack of their father's presence by elevating their activities? Have I craved Everest's attention because I've been used to having so little?* She didn't feel she was capable of making a fair assessment now.

She rested her head against the back of the bed.

Finley had finally stopped crying and started falling asleep.

As she gazed tenderly at Finley, Stratton was flooded with memories from when Finley was little and shy, hiding in her apron when company came over and refusing to leave her side for the children's Sunday school class. She remembered the teenage Finley who had brought her crackers and ginger tea for her migraine after a fight with Dexter. She thought of the adult Finley, who always made sure that Stratton's hair, makeup, and outfits were fashionable and in style. Finley had always been the most sensitive of her children, looking to take care of others and wanting the best for them, so Stratton couldn't discount what Finley was feeling now.

Stratton felt drained of emotions and thoughts as she held her daughter and let her sleep. She knew she would have much to discuss and deal with in the morning, so she closed her eyes in an effort to sleep but feared it would be quite a while before rest would come.

Stratton prayed for guidance because this was too much to handle. One thing she knew for sure was that she couldn't share news of an engagement with anyone until she had sorted out her own feelings.

Forty-Two

The morning sun streamed through the window, its golden rays casting a warm glow throughout the room, waking Stratton from a fitful sleep. She stretched, trying to get the kink out of her neck, careful not to wake Finley, who slept soundly next to her. Looking down at her rumpled shirt and jeans, she thought of Everest, and her hand gently touched the ring that was still in her pocket. *Last night wasn't a dream.*

She quietly slid off the bed, grabbed some clothes, and went into the bathroom to change. She pulled out the ring and placed it on her finger, admiring how it caught the light, sending shimmering rays of radiance across the walls.

With a heavy sigh, she removed the ring and placed it in her pocket. *I need to talk to Everest.* Stratton quickly changed her shirt and quietly walked back into her room. She paused beside the bed to check on Finley, who was still sleeping peacefully. Leaning down, she placed a light kiss on her forehead before tiptoeing out of the room. With a soft click, she closed the door and went to find Everest.

As she walked past the family room, she noticed something beside the front door. Pausing to take a second look, she froze, confusion evident on her face. *Why is there luggage here?* Realization dawned as anxiety mixed with fear left a knot in her stomach.

She quickened her pace to the kitchen, where she saw Everest calmly buttering an English muffin as if he wasn't just about to leave. *Maybe there is a disaster, or he has to go out on call.*

Stratton exhaled a slow, steady breath as she approached Everest.

Everest smiled. "Good Morning. Did you and Finley have a good chat?"

"Are you leaving?" She blurted, ignoring his question.

Everest sighed, his shoulders slightly sinking.

"Oh my gosh. You're moving out." Stratton's voice trembled as she felt the tears well up.

Everest raced to her and grabbed her hands. "Whoa, whoa, whoa. You need to hear me out before getting yourself all worked up."

"Why are you leaving me?" Every fear and insecurity she had about opening her heart to love again came crashing in, threatening to suffocate her.

Everest breathed deeply, remorse registering on his face. "Because I was ready and willing to cross to a place that wasn't mine. I saw you unbuttoning your shirt, and I didn't stop you. I waited until you had it unbuttoned, then brought your body close to mine. Feeling your skin next to mine was more than I could handle, so I put my hand under your shirt. Stratton, I wasn't just innocently rubbing my hands along your lower back; I was going to unhook your bra."

As he paused, Stratton stood motionless, absorbing the enormity of his words.

"Stratton, I'm really sorry. Last night was incredible, overwhelmingly so. I was so caught up in the heat of the moment that I almost crossed the line, which was wrong of me. The only way I can maintain self-control is to remove myself from being downstairs and also make sure that we are not alone for very long." He reached up to run his hands through his hair and over the back of his neck. "I'm confessing my struggle with this, and I need a short engagement period."

Stratton exhaled, feeling a deep conviction about her own lack of self-control. She had pushed things too far, thinking Everest would stop if it became too much, not realizing how foolish and risky that was. She hadn't considered how her actions could have led to a situation they would both regret. *Yehovah, forgive me. He is right. He can't stay here.*

Stratton gently touched his arm. "Everest, you are not the only one at fault. I'm sorry. It was wrong of me to tempt you. I completely lost my head. I understand why it's best for you to go and I agree. It's going to be too difficult for us to stay within His boundaries if you stay."

"I'm gonna stay at Milky Way Farms until we figure out the details and the timing. I can stick around for a bit this morning if you want us to tell Noah about our engagement."

Stratton felt torn, her heart melting for his consideration of Noah yet breaking under the weight of what she needed to share, which would test them both. "About our engagement," she began as she reached for his hand and guided him to the couch in the family room.

"Finley and I didn't have a good conversation. She's really upset. She feels like I'm putting you before her, which I promised my kids I would never do."

"Stratton…" Everest started to interrupt.

"Please hear me out. I don't believe that's the case, but she feels like it is. She made some valid points that made me hesitant to share our engagement, which is not fair to you."

Taking a moment to process what she said, Everest looked at her left hand. "I see you aren't wearing your ring."

"No, I didn't want to explain it to her last night since she was so upset and emotional. She was hurt that I thought it was you when she called the other night, disappointed that I didn't have her favorite meal ready when she arrived yesterday, and frustrated that she didn't know that things had grown more serious between us. Everest, she just feels left out."

"I know what you meant when you said I'd be getting a package deal: you and your kids. I feel like I've done right by your kids, so I have to admit, this feels slightly unfair like maybe you're catering a little too much to Finley's emotions."

"Everest, I agree with you. It is totally unfair."

He looked a little surprised at her response. "So you're OK with it being unfair, just as long as it's unfair toward me but not toward them?"

Stratton couldn't help slipping into fight mode. "She's my daughter, Everest, and you know what? I'm OK with that."

Everest pursed his lips and nodded as he stood. "I'm gonna go, Stratton. You need to take some time and decide what you want. I'm not interested in hearing about what your kids want or what your kids want you to do. I want to know what you want for yourself.

When you can answer that, let me know."

Stratton stood facing him, chin lifted, a silent challenge in her eyes. "So, are we still engaged then?"

"Nothing has changed for me. My 'yes' was, and still is, a 'yes.' You need to be sure yours is as well," he said, his eyes steadfast, filled with resolve. "Because that bare finger is telling me that your 'yes' isn't really a 'yes' for you."

"You're not being fair. I haven't had time to process everything, and there's much to think about."

"I just told you to take all the time you need, though it's a fleeting commodity."

"What is that supposed to mean?"

"Interpret it how you want." Everest started towards the door. "I'll be at Milky Way Farms."

Stratton moved in front of him, hands on her hips. "How convenient that you're leaving now, right when I have this work trip coming up and can't just drop everything to figure things out."

"Then just figure out what you want. I want a biblical marriage with you, and that's my offer, but I'm not sure you even understand what that means. For this to work, our marriage isn't about catering to your kids' emotions, whims, or crises. Our marriage needs to be the foundation, the bastion, and anchor to our family structure according to His order."

"With you as the leader?" She retorted, raising her eyebrows.

His jaw was set, his face tense, as if he wanted to say more but simply shook his head. "Like I said, Stratton, you need to figure it out. You know me and what I'm offering." Everest stepped around her, his movements sharp as he made his way to the front door. "I've got everything packed up, so I'll see you later." Everest picked up his luggage and walked out without glancing behind him.

Stratton stood frozen, dumbfounded by what had just happened, her emotions mirroring the confusion and disbelief in her thoughts.

* * * * *

The tension radiating from Everest was almost palpable as he tossed the luggage into his truck, the force echoing his frustration. He opened the driver's door and hesitated, knowing he was at a crossroads that would impact his future with Stratton. Should he go back inside and try to smooth things over or stand firm in his resolve? He started toward the house, uncertainty plaguing him. If he went back inside and apologized, she might be upset enough to push him away, but probably not. He knew he could kiss away her anger, but to do that would exploit her emotions. Two steps in, he turned back, knowing that while his actions were unpleasant, maintaining his resolve was essential to their future.

He sat in his truck, hands gripping the steering wheel, as thoughts raced through his mind. He knew that Finley was prone to bouts of manipulation, so she would likely see this as a victory.

He could stay and show her he wasn't like her father; he wasn't going anywhere, but deep down, he knew that this really wasn't his battle to fight.

There was no question in his mind that he loved Stratton, but he wanted her to know, for herself, that she loved him. She needed to be willing to enter into a marriage with him, accepting him as head of the household according to the Scriptures.

He started his truck, his thoughts drifting back to last night.

He had tried to convince himself that since he wasn't the one undressing her, then it was OK, but that was just a lie the enemy wanted him to believe. In all honesty, he should have stopped her hands, but they were so quick and deft with those buttons. One glimpse of her exposed skin, his longing outweighed reason, leaving him vulnerable to emotions he could not control.

Thankfully, she had been the one to put on the brakes, helping him see they'd gone too far. Everest hadn't even realized brakes were needed at that moment. That was the problem; he had already visualized picking her up and taking her back to the bed. He had moved those boundary stones in his mind, and his actions would surely have followed had Stratton's words not stopped him.

He put the truck in gear and slowly started down the drive, glancing at the house once more in the rearview mirror. He could have given in, letting Finley's emotions dictate hiding their engagement, pretending like it wasn't a big deal. Then he'd probably be inside Stratton's right now having breakfast with her and planning their wedding, but that would have been disrespectful to his and Stratton's relationship and wouldn't do Finley any favors.

It was time for Finley to rely less on her mother and foster a relationship with the One Who would always be there for her, loving her and guiding her into truth. The same One Everest was now crying out to with all of his heart, praying he hadn't just lost the woman he loved.

Forty-Three

Finley stretched as she walked into the kitchen, yawning. "Did you make breakfast?" She asked, acting completely normal.

Stratton, standing at the kitchen island with a mug of black tea, bristled at her daughter's question. Maybe things felt normal to Finley, but they certainly weren't normal for Stratton.

"No. There are ingredients in the fridge and pantry if you'd like to make something for yourself."

Sitting down at the kitchen island, Finley asked, with a sharp edge to her voice. "Usually, you make a big breakfast when I'm here. What, you didn't make anything for Noah and Everest?"

"Everest isn't here," Stratton replied, staring into her mug.

"Where is he?"

Stratton sighed, her voice flat and void. "He left, Finley."

"What do you mean?"

"He moved out."

"Guess he couldn't handle lying to you," she said with a little snort.

Stratton snapped her gaze toward Finley. "I'm tired of this. You know what? This is why he left." Stratton pulled the engagement ring from her pocket, slipped it on her left ring finger, and stuck her hand out to Finley.

"He left because of a ring?"

"He left because we're engaged, Finley. Last night, I came to find you and tell you, but you were too upset, and I was afraid my news would make things worse." Sorrow filled her voice, "Finley, I've babied you for a long time, always putting your needs before mine, but you are

265

not a child anymore, and we both need…"

"But why would he leave you?" Finley interrupted, still fixated on that part.

Stratton sighed, not sure her daughter would understand. "We've reached a point in our relationship where we want to save ourselves for marriage, the way Yehovah designed. That means we cannot put ourselves in a position to be tempted. Everest loves me enough to leave so we won't be tempted."

"Do you still plan to marry him?" Her words dripped with indignation.

"That's what I have to decide. Marrying Everest means that he and I are unified; we are as one. We become each other's priorities above all else. Last night, I let your emotional needs come before Everest, and if we marry, I cannot let that happen."

"So you would be choosing a man before us."

"I would be choosing unity with my husband, which ironically means I have to think of you three first in order to make my decision. I have a lot to think about, Finley, because," she choked back the tears, "honestly, I don't know if I want to get married right now."

"Well, do we get a say in your decision then?"

Stratton slapped her hand on the counter, "You know what, Finley? You go ahead and tell Harper and Noah about my engagement—and that Everest left." Holding back her anger and her tears, her voice was strained. "I'm not in the mood to share anything with anyone right now. All the joy of announcing this engagement has been taken away." Stratton stormed out the back door, letting it slam behind her.

Once outside, she paused, tears trickling down her face. She inhaled slowly and wiped her eyes, trying to regain her composure. The morning greeted her with the remnants of a stunning sunrise, birds singing, butterflies flitting, and the bright, blue sky dotted with fluffy white clouds contradicting the storm inside her. She squared her shoulders and headed to the barn.

Tilly and Bartlett both tossed their heads over their stall doors and blew as she entered their domain.

Rubbing each one on the nose, she said, "I'll bet you're hungry."

She grabbed a bucket, gathered their feed, and placed it in their stalls. "Oh, I won't be burdened by their care, will I, Everest?" She muttered sarcastically, mimicking what he had said, as her anger resurfaced.

She quickly whipped out her phone to text him, knowing that it would cause a fight, but at least they would be talking. It distressed her that he had left like he had, and she just wanted him to come home. She didn't want to be left alone facing the insecurities plaguing her right now.

Irrational thoughts of how to get him to come back raced through her mind, but she dismissed each one as none of them would honor Scripture. *What am I to do? What is the right choice?* Tears streamed down her face as she stood silently convening with her Father, seeking His guidance. *Yehovah, impart Your wisdom on what You want me to do. You've been with me my entire life, through it all: the highs and the lows, the good and the bad. I've had the best summer of my life with that man, and I have no doubt that You brought us together, but I'm scared. You know the scars left from my first marriage make it hard to respect Your order for a marriage, so speak to my heart because I need to hear Your voice; I need Your guidance. I don't want to make another mistake.*

As Stratton absently ran her hand over the gate to the stall, a young woman's voice broke the silence. "Hi, Good Morning. I'm Delaney," she said as she walked inside the barn. "I'm one of the groomers for Lyle and Bernadette Turner. Everest hired me to come over a few times a day and take care of the horses. I'm sorry I'm late, but my tires were a little low, so I stopped to put air in them."

She wiped her eyes as she cleared her throat. "Good morning, I'm Stratton. I just gave them some breakfast."

"Thanks. I'll let them finish, then get them to their space. I'll be back and have them turned in by nightfall."

"Thank you," Stratton uttered as she walked out of the barn and back to the house, thankful that she hadn't text Everest in anger. Then, the thought hit her; he had hired someone without consulting her, then approved Delaney's coming on her land and taking care of her horses. She felt her anger start to rise but took a deep breath to calm herself down. *Think before you act, Stratton.* She thought back to the day Everest had surprised her with Tilly and Bartlett, telling her not to worry about their care. Realizing this was further proof that his 'yes' was a 'yes,' she felt tears slip down her cheeks.

She didn't see Finley when she returned, so she retreated to her room. She needed time to sit quietly and sort out the events that had taken place in the last 24 hours.

Her heart leaped when her phone buzzed. *Everest!* She looked down at the name, disappointed that it wasn't him.

"Hi, Harper."

"Mom, what's wrong? Finley told me I had to call you."

"She didn't tell you why?" *That has to be a Finley first.*

"No, she just said you were upset. What's wrong?"

"Everest proposed to me last night, and I accepted."

"That's wonderful! Congratulations! But wait, why would Finley say you were upset?"

"Because I have to decide if that's what I really want."

"Well, why wouldn't you want that?" Harper asked, clearly surprised.

Stratton took a slow breath as she rubbed the bridge of her nose with two fingers, not wanting to explain herself or her reasons. "Harper, I do want that, but there's more to consider. First, I have to think about the three of you, and second, I've been independent for quite a while, so entering into a marriage means there will be a lot of changes. I just have to work through all of it."

"Well, I wasn't supposed to say anything, but just so you know, Everest has already planned this really cool trip for your fall break. I already told the kids, and they are really excited. Mom, he just wants to add to our family, not take away from it. I know Finley thinks he's trying to pull you away from us, but she just doesn't know him well enough yet. So, don't let that be a factor in your decision."

Easier said than done, Harper; of course it was a factor. She had promised her children never to choose a man over them, and now it seemed she was breaking that promise.

"OK, sweetheart. I just have a lot to think about. I appreciate your calling and your support."

"Do you want me to come out there?"

"No, it's fine."

"Do you want to come here?"

Yes, and escape from it all! Anything to not have to face this current situation.

"No, but thank you, sweetie. I have my meeting in New York coming up, so I've got to prepare for that."

"Alright. Well, I'll check in later. I love you."

"I love you, too."

"Bye."

"Bye, darling." Stratton ended the call and leaned back on her bed, staring at the ceiling and thinking back over her conversation with Harper. What if choosing Everest meant she could still choose her kids, too? What if the real struggle was grounded in her own deeper issues and not the kids? She sat up, deciding that a hot shower would help clear her head; trying to answer these questions felt too challenging for her to tackle right now.

* * * * *

Stepping out of the shower, Stratton wrapped herself in a towel. The hot water had washed away some of the fatigue, giving her clearer insight into her conversation with Harper. She had said fall break, which meant that Harper would be foregoing a trip to Miami to see her father for his birthday. Stratton let that thought settle in her mind. Harper had chosen a visit with Everest and Stratton over a possible visit to Miami to see Dexter. She never wanted her children to feel they had to choose sides, but this spoke volumes about Harper's willingness to bring Everest into the family fold.

Harper and Noah were taking an active interest in getting to know Everest. If only Finley could do the same. *Why did she have to be so emotional and needy last night?*

Stratton glanced at her mirror, smiling at the small picture Noah had printed out and taped in the corner. It was from their formal dinner party. She looked at those three smiling faces, all glamorously dressed, not a hair out of place. She and Everest weren't a couple yet, not envisioning what would transpire over the next few months. Her thoughts wandered back over the past few months with Everest—laughing, holding hands, snuggling, dancing, kissing.

Stratton sighed, her eyes filling with tears. She wouldn't be kissing Everest anytime soon. There would be no more cuddling on the couch, no more foot massages, no more hugs. How she missed his embrace already. She felt like she was still in shock over his departure. So much had happened so quickly since last night that she felt overwhelmed. Needing some fresh air and quiet, she decided to dress and take Tilly for a ride. She needed space to sift through her thoughts and figure out her next steps.

Forty-Four

Stratton returned from her ride to find that Finley had departed without saying a word. She grabbed a bottle of water before sitting on the couch in the family room, feeling dejected.

"Hey, Momma," Noah said as he entered from the garage.

"Hi, Son."

"Finley said I should check in on you. Are you OK?"

Interesting. Finley hadn't told either sibling the news. Stratton wouldn't lie to Noah. "No, Noah. I'm not."

He came over and sat next to her, putting his arm around her. "He told me this morning he was going to have to leave."

Of course, he did. Everest would never abandon her son, even if they were having problems. However, she had to choose marriage with him because she wanted it, not because he was good to Noah. "Did he say why?" Her voice cracked as she asked.

"Told me I should talk to you, but that it didn't change anything between the two of us, which is really good 'cause I signed us up to be partners for a fishing tournament next month." Noah gave a small smile.

Stratton patted Noah's leg. She wanted everything like it was before, with Everest at home, back downstairs, ending her day with him on this very couch. He had become an unshakeable presence in her life, a steady peace, an anchor, supporting her, encouraging her, loving her.

"He asked me to marry him," Stratton said, her voice barely above a whisper.

271

"What did you say?"

"Yes, but then I did something to make him question how sincere my answer was." She turned to face her son. "Noah, he isn't wrong. I gave him the answer I thought I meant at the time, but it turns out that I may be mistaken. My identity as a mother is all I've had for many years now, so the moment Finley needed me, I ran to her, leaving Everest behind. Then, I hid our engagement from her, making her the priority over my relationship with Everest. Finley feels he is taking me away from all of you and that I am choosing him over you, which is something I promised never to do." Stratton paused as she stared down at her hands in her lap. "Maybe she is right, to an extent. If we were to marry, then Everest would be my priority. I need to be willing to follow the principles Yehovah set forth for a marriage based on His perfect design."

Noah's brow furrowed as he thought about what she said. "Mom, I don't think he's trying to take you away or doesn't want us around. He spends time with me and doesn't even correct folks when they say I'm his son. I've heard people say it a few times, and he never said a word. If he didn't want us around, he would make that distinction."

"Noah, listen to me. I am going to pray about all of this and do what I think Yehovah wants me to do. You will not lose Everest no matter what I decide." She knew that Noah felt like he had a father figure in Everest, and he didn't want to lose that bond. "Everest loves all of you, which is part of why I love him and want to be married to him, but this isn't about the three of you. It's about me being willing to change the way I think, I act, and how I have lived for so long."

"Well, I'd move to the barn apartment if that would help so you two could have the house to yourselves."

Stratton's heart swelled, and tears formed in her eyes. Noah was willing to inconvenience himself for her if it would help. She wiped her eyes, reached over, and gave him a hug, "Noah, no, this is your home. If we get married, Everest and I want you here, and if you married and had kids, we'd want you all here."

"OK. I'm fixing to see him later today, so are you OK if I do that?"

Tears threatened to fall again at Noah's sweetness and sensitivity. She would never ask him to avoid Everest, no matter what happened with their relationship.

"You can see him all you want. You're not in the middle of this, so there is nothing wrong with you sharing things with him. He is giving me time to think, and I am taking it. We are still together, sweetheart. His departure is so we can honor Yehovah's will and for no other reason. We love one another and need to proceed with wisdom."

"Sounds good to me, Mom. I'm gonna take a shower and head out for the day."

"OK, sweetie. I'll see you later on."

Noah went upstairs, leaving Stratton alone.

She walked to the window, gazing outside, arms wrapped around her waist as if that would protect her from the uncertainty within. Why couldn't she just make her 'yes' a 'yes' like Everest? *Yehovah, this isn't just about the kids, is it? It's about me, as well, isn't it?*

She let her thoughts drift back over her life. She'd been young, in love, and optimistic about the future when she had gotten married. The first couple of years had been fun and exciting, but everything changed after they had the children. She had prayed and gone to Scripture for guidance on how to be a better wife and better keeper of the home, but it wasn't enough. She wasn't enough. What she thought would be a forever marriage ended in a painful divorce, leaving her with emotional insecurities, issues with trust, and a resolve to never put herself in that position again. Could marriage to Everest end in failure, too? Would it be better to just avoid marriage and the potential risk of subjecting herself and her children to another divorce? If she did marry Everest, would she be enough for him?

Now, she was a successful, educated woman who had raised three children to be accomplished adults and had done it on her own. She had worked hard, paid the bills, made the decisions, taught her children right from wrong, driven them to their activities, celebrated their wins, and cried with them over their losses. She had supported them physically, financially, and emotionally. She had been there for every milestone in their lives, never missing one event. Would she be giving that up to marry Everest? She loved her children and loved being a mother, but would she always be 'just a mom'? Could she prioritize their marriage and still be there for her children?

She had always dreamed of having a biblical marriage. A marriage that had God as the cornerstone, the foundation upon which the family unit is built. A marriage with the husband as the spiritual head and leader, looking to Him for guidance for the whole family.

Everest would be that leader for her and her children. She was tired of making all of the decisions, fixing all the family problems, and tired of doing everything alone, but could she support him and let him lead according to Scripture? What if she wasn't able to let go?

She thought back to the notecard she kept on her nightstand, the one with the words from the Book of Jeremiah: "For I know the plans I have for you," declares the LORD, "plans to prosper you and not to harm you, plans to give you hope and a future."

Suddenly, she felt as if a light had pierced the darkest, most secret places of her soul. Two words from this scripture waged war within her: hope and future. She didn't believe that she was worthy of either, and now that they were knocking on the door of her heart, she was afraid to respond. Why was she afraid? What would she find if she opened that door? Could a divorced woman have a second chance for hope and a future? Could she have hope and a future with Everest? Could she have hope and a future without him? What were His plans for her? For them?

Shaking her head as if to clear the thoughts from her mind, she turned from the window. *I need time to process all of this and pray.* She went into the kitchen, placing her still-full water bottle on the counter. Lost in thought, she jumped when her phone buzzed. She glanced at the name on her screen. *Savannah.* Finley must have called her, too. Stratton went out the back door for a walk as she answered the call.

"Good Morning," Savannah said.

"Hi."

"What's with that tone? Finley said I needed to give you a call, so what happened?"

As she passed the barn and through the pasture, heading to the woods, Stratton was overcome with memories of Everest; his surprise with the horses, star-gazing in the pasture, cutting trails with Noah, walking together through the woods; there were traces of him everywhere she went.

"He proposed," she said, putting her phone on speaker.

"What? He did! And?"

"I accepted."

"Stratton, you're killing me. Why aren't you ecstatic?"

"I was at first, until what happened after."

"Did you sleep with him?"

Stratton stopped, her thoughts flashing back to last night. Images of his face, vivid as if he were standing right there, filled her mind: his mouth against hers, his touch, his embrace. A rush of heat spread to her cheeks. "No, but I had to leave, so we didn't do that."

"Well, then what gives?"

"After he proposed, we came close to crossing the boundary we set, so I left and went to find Finley. I found her in my bed, crying. She was such an emotional mess that I didn't have the heart to tell her we were engaged. I took off my ring, hiding my engagement, and comforted her as she sobbed. She said that she thinks I'm choosing a man over her. It broke my heart, Savannah. She told me she just wanted her mom. I understand how she feels; I wish Mom were here." her voice quavered, tears spilling down her cheeks.

"I just want to feel her arms around me. I want to hear her voice assuring me that everything's going to be OK." She paused, inhaling slowly, trying to maintain her composure. "Savannah, it's been really hard to navigate life without her all these years. There are days that I miss her so much. I know what Finley must be feeling when all you want is the comfort and familiarity of your mother's embrace. I don't want my kids ever to feel like I won't be there when they need me. If I marry Everest, I can't do what I've been doing. I can't hop on a plane or jump in the car anytime they need me." She ran the back of her hand under her eyes.

"Stratton, Everest's not the kind of man who would forbid you from going to your kids if they needed you."

"No, I guess he wouldn't. Finley feels conflicted about him, and I don't want to feel like I'm choosing sides." Stratton stopped, sitting down on a stump at the edge of the woods, the peaceful tranquility surrounding her contrasting with the uncertainty in her heart.

"I just don't know if I'm ready for this. It's a lot to absorb. Over the course of the summer, it's been a whirlwind courtship, engagement, and now possibly a summer wedding as well because Everest said he can't handle a long engagement. I just don't know if I am ready for it — any of it. Am I crazy thinking that this is too fast?"

"Stratton, Charles, and I knew he was going to propose with Mom's ring," Savannah confessed.

"What?" her voice was incredulous. She was glad she was sitting down. *Did I hear her correctly? They knew?*

"Hear me out. We were all for him giving you the ring. He's been staying here while he had it modified, though he wouldn't say what he was having done. He told us he wanted us to know, namely me, so I didn't continue to harbor any resentment towards Bitty. Stratton, Everest is a reconciler. He doesn't sow turmoil and chaos. He seeks harmony, not discord."

Would Finley see that about Everest? Would she see he's not her enemy?

"Marrying Everest is going to change the current dynamic with your children. I think you need to trust him, trust in the fruit you've already seen coming from his life. And, Stratton, if you know you aren't ready for marriage, it's OK. No one is saying you have to get married."

Stratton looked at her ring, still unsure of what to do. Savannah was right. Everest was a man of integrity and worthy of her trust. She knew they could never go back to the life they had before he'd proposed, so she'd either have to accept his proposal and get married, or their relationship was over. "I just need to gather my thoughts and feelings as I pray through this. I would appreciate it if you two would be praying for me as well."

"Of course we will. I love you, Sis."

"I love you, too. Bye."

"Bye."

Stratton turned her phone on silent as she walked toward the back of the property where they'd discovered the lost treasure. She sat down, propping her back against the large tulip poplar, the same place where Solomon and Daphne had spent quiet moments together, hidden from the world's prying eyes and society's restrictions on their love.

Tears formed in her eyes as she thought about their love story. Daphne's choices were so limited. Born into slavery, she would have either been forced to marry a male slave or had to seek permission from her owner to marry a free man. When did she know she loved Solomon? Was it something he said or did one day that made her see him as more than a childhood playmate? Did he make her laugh? Did he comfort her when she cried? Where did they share that first kiss? Was it spring? Summer? Did she know how deeply he loved her? It broke her heart that they never had the chance to marry and create the family Solomon mentioned in his letter.

Daphne's choices were limited, but Stratton's weren't. She knew she loved Everest, and he loved her, but was loving someone enough of a reason to get married? *No, it wasn't.* She had learned from her divorce that love by itself was not enough for a strong marriage. Marriage is a gift from God, part of His created order, so He must be the foundation. The other elements of a strong, enduring marriage, love, respect, humility, kindness, trust, forgiveness, and selflessness, are built on Him as the foundation.

This line of thinking touched deep in Stratton's soul. She had not experienced this type of marriage and wasn't sure she even knew how to be part of a marriage based on God's design. The words inspired by God Himself and penned by James spoke to her: *If any of you lacks wisdom, let him ask of God, who gives to all liberally and without reproach, and it will be given to him.* She knew she needed guidance and had prayed for it, but she needed wisdom and clarity that only God could provide. *Yehovah, You know this decision is plaguing me. I am so confused. I want to make the right decision, the one that is right not only for me and Everest but for my children as well. I cannot make that decision alone. I don't want to make a mistake. I want to know Your Will and have Your guidance.*

She stood up and brushed herself off, heading home. She knew what her immediate next steps would be: fasting and praying. This would be how she would gain clarity and answers from Him, the only kind of answers that truly mattered.

Forty-Five

Everest, no longer asleep but not yet fully awake, was startled by a knock at his door. Sitting straight up in bed, he momentarily forgot that he was staying in one of the manor rooms at Milky Way Farms.

"Come in."

Wallace, the butler, entered. "Sir, you have a caller in the library. Miss Finley Davis is here to see you and insists I implore you to meet with her."

"Thank you, Wallace. You can let her know that I'll be out in a few minutes. Thanks."

As Wallace left the room, Everest reached for his phone, tilting it toward him. *Nothing from Stratton.* His heart sank. He longed to hear from her. Every day, he hoped she'd reach out, even though he knew they needed this time apart. He must have held back from reaching out to her at least a dozen times a day just to let her know that he loved her and was committed to their relationship. However, he knew that he had to trust Yehovah and wait for Stratton.

He sighed, praying that the wait was over soon. *Speaking of waiting, I don't want to make Finley wait too long.*

Everest skipped the shower, opting to simply wet his hair instead. As he ran a comb through his damp hair, his thoughts went to Stratton. He had been fasting and praying for her and their relationship for the past three days, and now he felt the fatigue taking its toll. Placing his hands on either side of the sink, he looked at his reflection in the mirror, reminding himself this was a journey in which he had to remain fervent. He knew this was a huge decision for

Stratton. She had been single and independent for a very long time, and he was asking her to change all of it after only knowing him for a few months. Everest needed to trust God's timing.

He pulled on a pair of jeans and put on a shirt. Checking his phone once more before putting it in his pocket, he headed to the library, wondering what Finley wanted.

Everest paused on the threshold as he quietly opened the door to the library. The midmorning sun streamed through the library window, illuminating the silhouette of a young woman seated at the table nearby, her head cradled in her hands. *She reminds me of Stratton.* His heart ached for Stratton, and he yearned to hear from her. Psalm 37:7 popped into his mind: *Rest in the Lord, and wait patiently for him,* reminding him once again that he needed to continue to wait.

"Good Morning, Finley." Everest steadied himself as he entered the room, taking the seat at the table across from her.

"Hey." She softly replied, not looking at him.

Sensing she needed a moment to gather her thoughts and possibly courage, he waited quietly.

She took in a breath, slowly lifting her eyes to look at him. "I'm sorry about the other night."

Everest nodded but remained silent, giving her space, ready to listen.

"I let my emotions get the better of me, and I wasn't thinking about how I sounded. My mom told me the truth. She said that there was information that I didn't have when I decided to tell her about your arrest."

"Finley, is there something I've done to upset you and make you not like me?" He asked gently, seeing the tears welling up in her eyes.

"My dad hurt my mom so badly. He never physically abused her but was calculating with his words and gestures. Sometimes, after a big fight, she wouldn't be able to get out of bed the next day. We all knew how bad it was for her and how much she wanted to leave him, but she stayed because of the three of us. He treated her so terribly. He would make comments about how she looked or how she didn't contribute anything to the home." She paused, taking a couple of deep breaths and glancing out the window for a moment.

"You know," she turned back to face Everest. "I never understood how my dad couldn't see how beautiful she was. Everyone always said how much I looked like her. Did that mean he didn't think I was beautiful, too? Was he just lying when he would tell me I was?" Her voice trembled, tears trickling over her cheeks.

She swiped at the tear as if trying to erase the memory. "The day he said he wished Noah had never been born was the last straw for Mom. She immediately packed us up, and we left. My mom could handle it when his anger and abuse were aimed at her, but she wasn't going to let him hurt us. Noah doesn't know that my dad said that, and my mom doesn't know Harper and I heard him say that. I don't think she knows how much we actually heard and witnessed."

Everest prayed silently for the strength to stay focused and composed. Listening to the pain Finley carried from what her father had done was a double-edged sword. He wanted to throttle Dexter, but at the same time, he was thankful for the valuable insight about not only Finley but Stratton as well.

"During the divorce, my dad was so angry. He fought unfairly, trying to manipulate us into saying things that weren't true so he would look like the better, more fit parent and gain sole custody. He told us that if we would just tell the judge we wanted to stay with him, we could have whatever we wanted, but that was an empty promise and, as we later realized, his way of trying to hurt my mom. He was constantly telling us that our mom would never be able to afford the kind of life he could give us."

Finley's eyes held a blend of pain and sadness as if she didn't want to share this with him or anyone. "It was bad. He controlled the money, and sometimes, we didn't have enough money to get groceries or pay the bills. Harper and I noticed that Mom would go without new clothes or shoes and, at times, not eat anything to ensure we had enough food."

Finley gave a little half smile. "Harper and I even took back some gifts we received, exchanging them for these really pretty heels she wanted so she could have something nice to wear at our functions and events."

She sat up a little straighter, an unmistakable strength in her eyes. "My dad was often purposely late with child support, so money was very tight until the divorce was settled. That was about the time when I became very protective of my mother. We were all she cared about, and he'd taunt her, saying that he was going to win and take the three of us away. He knew how much she loved us, so he told her that he would move to a foreign country where no one could find us, and she would never see us again. No one would make him bring us back. She knew he had not only the money to do that, but he wanted to hurt her as much as he could."

Everest had to forcibly unclench his fists under the table, his heart broken for Stratton and her children. *Yehovah, when it is the right time, give me words of comfort.*

"At one point, things got so bad that one day, I pleaded with my dad, in front of his divorce attorney while we were at the country club, to let me live with him if he would stop threatening to take us away from Mom. All she wanted was the three of us. She didn't care about the money. I knew if I said that in front of his attorney, it wouldn't look good for him. Right after I said that, my dad stopped fighting, and my mom got full custody." Tears fell freely down her cheeks.

"My mom has never gotten this close to another man since. I'm afraid that you're going to hurt her, and I'll lose my mom if that happens. She wouldn't survive going through that kind of pain again. So, because I want to protect her, I asked a cyber hacker friend to see what he could find out about you." Finley ran her hands down her face, wiping away the tears.

"I ignored all of the commendable things he found about you and your family, bringing to my mom the one thing that he found that could be damaging. I violated your privacy, and I tried to make you into someone you're not. I'm jealous that Noah and Harper have this family unit forming with you and my mom. I feel so left out."

Her voice cracked, and her lip quivered. "I robbed my mom and you of celebrating your engagement, and I'm sorry for the mess I've caused."

Everest could not sit still any longer. "Come here, Kiddo." He stood, walking around the table. He opened his arms and gathered her in, holding her as she wept. His heart broke at the trauma she had experienced as a child, which now dictated a lot of her decisions. He seethed with anger that Stratton's ex had used his children as pawns, threatening to steal them away from her. That was a sign of terrible darkness. Everest knew if he ever encountered this man at family functions, it would be a challenge to maintain his composure.

Finley sniffled and pulled away. "I'm so sorry. I didn't want my mom to be hurt, but I ended up being the one to hurt her." She grabbed some tissues from her purse.

He reached over and patted her hand. "Finley, it's OK. I understand, and everything will be fine."

She gave him a smile. "OK. I need to run to my car and grab my laptop, but I'll be right back. Will you stay right here?"

He nodded as Finley raced out of the library.

His heart softened as he stepped to the window, watching for her as she exited the manor. He may not know everything about being a father, but he knew that if he married Stratton, one of his roles was to be the protector, not only for Stratton but for her children. Finley had wanted to protect her mother from being hurt. Now, he had the opportunity to step in and be the man who treated her mother right, to be the role model that all three children needed, to show them just how much he cherished their mother and would never hurt her. Would Stratton say 'yes' to marrying him, giving him the chance to protect her and her children? For that matter, would she allow him to be a role model for her children and grandchildren?

He continued to watch Finley as she opened her car and grabbed her backpack, his thoughts drifting. From the beginning, he had seen a future with Stratton. He had known that their ages, as well as their careers, could create some challenges as they learned more about each other. The need to compromise and work together, not just on the little things like how to load the dishwasher or separate the laundry, but on the bigger things like balancing their jobs and prioritizing time together, is one of the pillars for a strong relationship. What about his own volunteer activities? What if Stratton asked him not to go on a mission? Shouldn't she be supportive of his missions? Would he be willing to say 'no' to a mission?

He thought of what Deuteronomy 24:5 says: *When a man takes a new wife, he is not to go out with the army or have any duty passed over to him. He is to be free at home for one year and make his wife happy.* According to Scripture, Everest was commanded to make his wife happy by his presence and devotion, without distraction from extra duties. His volunteer work would contradict what God said. He knew he would need to decrease the time he spent volunteering if he and Stratton married, but he hadn't thought of ceasing it for an entire year. Was he willing to commit to that?

Everest envisioned Stratton when he returned from a mission: her smile, her embrace, her kisses. He swiped away the tears rolling down his cheek, the emptiness inside him threatening to overwhelm him. He missed her. He missed hearing her voice. He missed holding her. He missed her laughter. He missed their pace and rhythm at the homestead, but he couldn't stay there until they were wed.

Though Milky Way wasn't the worst place to stay until they had things sorted out, he wanted to be home with Stratton. He missed her cooking and cooking for her. He missed those sweet evenings on the couch, reading together and talking. He missed seeing her reading her Bible on the deck in the mornings, knowing she wanted to start her days with Him. He missed discussing what she thought about Scripture and the wisdom she had.

He missed the real Stratton that so few got to see and know. Barefoot most of the time, except when her feet got cold, she'd put her feet in his lap, letting him massage them until they were warm. He'd walk to her room and kiss her goodnight at the doorway, knowing those kisses would create their own heat and keep her toasty as she got ready for bed.

Taking a slow breath, he rubbed his hand through his hair and down his face, reining in his emotions just as Finley came bounding into the library, looking relieved and surprised.

"Oh good, you stayed."

Why does she seem surprised? Did she think I would have left?

She opened her laptop. "I want to go see my mom at her meeting and apologize, so I'm booking my ticket right now. I want her to know how sorry I am."

Forty-Six

The busy, dizzying noise and sights of New York City circled around Stratton as she waited for an Uber to take her to the hotel.

Last year, she committed to attending the American Historical Association annual meeting before her sabbatical was approved. Normally, Stratton was thrilled to be a part of this 4-day conference with its presentations to exhibits, but this year was different. This year, her heart was back home, focused on what to do about Everest's proposal. She'd been fasting and praying for three days, and the combination of that with the stress of traveling had left her exhausted.

Thankful that she wasn't a presenter this year, she decided to do her best to stay upbeat and positive, enjoying the next four days. She knew that she would meet new people, see fellow academics and professionals, and catch up on the newest research and discoveries. She had been sure to pack a notebook for taking notes since she would be expected to present what she learned to her team back home.

Stratton stepped out of the Uber and walked through the entrance of the Ritz-Carlton Hotel. She walked through the lobby, feeling the contrast between the quiet, inviting atmosphere and the hustle and bustle on the street. As she approached the reception area, she admired how the hotel's design blended classic charm with contemporary luxury. *These next few days might be better than I thought.*

"Stratton Davis, oh my gosh, is that you?" Eugenia Wolff, NYU history professor, came to her with open arms. The pair, who had met at a conference years ago, always caught up with each other at this event. "You look amazing. What have you done to yourself? Tell me your secret!"

It's called being in love—with Everest. "Hi, Eugenia. It's so good to see you," she said warmly.

"Oh my gosh!" Eugenia lifted Stratton's left hand. "You're engaged? Congratulations! I didn't even know you were seeing anyone! We have so much to catch up on!" This prompted another big hug. "I'm already late for a meeting, but we have got to have dinner one night during the conference. Promise me!"

"Sure, Eugenia, I look forward to it."

Someone hollered for Eugenia, prompting laughter from them both. "Gotta run, love! See you later."

Stratton resumed her position in line at the reception area. She couldn't wait to soak in the tub and then bundle up in a soft robe while she relaxed and looked over the upcoming days' schedule.

* * * * *

She finished her bath, wrapped herself in the coziest robe, and stretched out on the bed to read her Bible and pray for a bit. Over the past three days, she had been reading through various parts of Scripture, and today's reading had her starting in chapter 12 of the Book of John.

She paused a minute in verse 24, where He says that a grain of wheat must die when it falls to the ground in order to produce more grain. *Yehovah, what does that mean for me?* She continued reading, stopping once more when she read chapter 15, verse 7: *If you abide in Me, and My words abide in you, you will ask what you desire, and it shall be done for you.*

She closed her Bible and leaned back on the bed, thinking about what she had read today in John as well as yesterday in Exodus, both of which spoke of the importance of abiding in Him and acting in accordance with His will. In order to abide in Him, she needed to be in His Word and in prayer. She knew that prayer was not intended to demand God give her what she wanted. Prayer, where she shared her wants and needs with Him, was the only way to align her heart with His will. When, and only when, her heart was aligned with His will would her requests be granted.

Stratton spent the next half hour in prayer, petitioning Him for answers on what His perfect will was for her life, to be entirely emptied of herself and ready to receive His guidance and plans for her.

* * * * *

She must have fallen asleep. Stratton allowed herself to fully awaken, feeling a calming peace both inside her and surrounding her. She left the bed, sitting down at the desk to let the heavenly download finish.

When the revelation came, she was overwhelmed with the magnitude of it all: she was afraid of entering a biblical marriage. She had believed that her uncertainty about marrying Everest stemmed from her failed first marriage, her feelings of inadequacy, and her being there for her children, but that was not the root cause of her hesitation; it was her fear of choosing the unknown over what was known.

Yesterday's scripture reading from Exodus recounted how the Israelites longed to return to Egypt, even when the Promised Land was right before them, because the road ahead seemed too challenging and unfamiliar. Much like them, she couldn't keep looking back at Egypt when the Promised Land was before her, complete with something new, wonderful, and blessed.

Everest was not only offering her everything he had but offering himself: his generosity, his service, his emotions, and even his quirkiness about playing songs to set the mood.

With tears streaming down her face, Stratton realized that all Everest had asked of her was to marry him and let him love her like Scripture commands. He wanted Stratton to understand the priority of marriage. The children could easily become crutches and wedges, but there wasn't a place for that in a biblical marriage.

She felt foolish for not seeing it before. Everest wasn't going to forbid her to work, forbid her to see, or support her kids; he was giving her a chance to be his wife, to be a mother and grandmother without worrying about a career, to shoulder some of the burdens she carried, and lead their family. He was giving her hope and a future. *Thank you, Yehovah, for your faithfulness, for opening my eyes to the plan You had for me, and for putting Everest in my life.*

Unable to stop herself, she grabbed a pen and opened her notebook.

"Stratton Galloway." She wrote a few times on the notepad, unable to stop smiling as she envisioned life with Everest.

She glanced at her phone to check the time and jumped up, rushing to get dressed. She'd been lost in thought and prayers of gratitude for thirty minutes, so she needed to get to dinner and the lecture. Her wilderness experience was coming to an end. She couldn't wait to share it with Everest.

*****

Day Two of the conference began with scheduled lectures, followed by breaks where attendees could look at exhibits. Stratton kept her notebook with her, writing down new titles of books to read as she perused the exhibits.

It was impossible not to think of Everest. What was he doing? Was he missing her as much as she was missing him? He was a man of his word, and he would wait for her answer, but it was getting harder and harder to refrain from reaching out. Though she longed to hear his voice and share her decision with him, she didn't want to do it via text or a call.

"Stratton!" Eugenia approached. "Dinner tonight? There's a phenomenal jazz club I've been wanting to attend, and I would love to go there this evening if you're up for it."

"Sure, Eugenia. That sounds great."

"Perfect. Meet me in the lobby at eight."

Eight? Stratton hid the internal sigh. At home, she would be on the couch with Everest by eight most nights and parting with him at her doorway by nine. She coveted her sleep and rest and wasn't planning on being a night owl newlywed. "That sounds good. I'll see you then."

Stratton decided to forgo the afternoon sessions, choosing to spend the afternoon relaxing in her room so she could stay awake through a late evening dinner. After a short nap and shower, she felt refreshed for dinner. Stratton, right on time, met Eugenia, and they grabbed an Uber to go to the Birdland Jazz Club.

The hostess sat them at a table about halfway back from the stage. The cozy, dimly lit atmosphere of the club captured the soulful heart of jazz. Stratton was especially pleased to find that tonight, the performer was singing from Dinah Washington's playbook. She thought of how much Everest would love this place. *What was he doing right now?* She hadn't heard from anyone, Noah and Finley were unusually silent, and even Harper hadn't reached out.

"I hear their grilled salmon is excellent," Eugenia suggested, interrupting her thoughts.

Stratton obliged and ordered that.

"So, I've been wanting to get you alone because I just learned we have an opening in my department. We are looking for someone who specializes in Revolutionary and Civil War history. Stratton, you have to apply. I can get you through the first two rounds of interviews, but I'm not directly involved in the final interview. The dean is my son, so basically, this seat is yours if you want it. Oh, please say you want it!"

"You want me to take a job at NYU?" Stratton wasn't sure she heard her over the saxophone.

"I can't think of anyone else I'd rather work with. You'd have an office right across the hall from me. We have partnerships with more conferences and historical exhibits than most universities, so the opportunities to present are endless. We also have these amazing summer abroad classes, but it is always challenging to find qualified professors to lead them even though we pay for the best housing for them. You would have the world at your fingertips. What do you say?"

"Eugenia, I just got engaged. I'd have to talk to him."

"Oh, you're not marrying one of those types, are you? The kind of man you have to get permission from?"

Stratton remained silent, feeling herself stiffen, ready to fight for and defend Everest. It was instinctual to guard her relationship from anyone who would miscategorize or attack their bond.

"My second husband was like that, and he lasted all of four months." She laughed.

Stratton did not find that funny in the least.

"Fine, fine, you see if he will let you take the job."

"It has nothing to do with him letting me do anything, Eugenia. Out of respect for the plans we've made, we would have a serious discussion if this was even something I might see myself doing."

"I can't guarantee this offer will be open beyond the conference,

Stratton, so you'll have to let me know fairly soon."

"I appreciate the offer, Eugenia, I really do. This has just taken me entirely by surprise."

"Hold that thought; my contractor is calling." Eugenia got up just as the server brought dinner and walked away to carry on her conversation.

Stratton listened to the singer as she started performing *Blue Gardenia*. She heard the sorrow of the lyrics, appreciating the fact that Everest loved her and was waiting for her at home. However, if she took the job at NYU, then that would change everything, leaving her with only memories of Everest, like the song speaks of, and nothing else.

Eugenia returned to the table. "Sorry about that. We just got a place in the Hamptons and are having it remodeled. Something else you could do if you took the job."

Owning a place in the Hamptons just wasn't appealing to her. She wanted her quiet mornings on the deck with the sunrise, the bonfire parties Noah threw with his friends, the social outings she threw, and what she was thinking. She had a mission to form a homestead for former foster kids.

She wanted to slow down, not speed up. Besides, with what Everest was offering, they would have the best of both worlds: home and the ability to travel when they had the time.

"Eugenia, the timing just isn't right for me to uproot myself and move to New York right now."

"I can guarantee at least two hundred thousand a year, maybe more."

Everest could make that much by working part-time. *That's it. Time is the key.* She wanted time: time with her family, time as a newlywed, time with her community, time with kids who had been taken from homes, time with kids who had given up and never got their forever families. That was the type of Kingdom work she had in mind and knew that she was called to use the time she had wisely.

She knew her heart was firmly planted in Tennessee and could already envision Everest teaching homesteading life skills to the kids. She smiled as she pictured him in the iconic flannel like a lumberjack. She'd teach the kids skills centered around cooking, sewing, laundry, cleaning, and managing a household. She was already falling in love with the faceless kids.

"It doesn't have anything to do with the money. I have a lot of projects and commitments that demand my attention, so I need to see those through right now. Please know that I am so thankful I was on your list for this position."

"I just can't imagine what could compete with New York, so you can expect me to be making a visit this fall to see what Tennessee has that we don't."

"Anytime, Eugenia. I may even have our barn apartment ready for you by then."

"This I've got to see," Eugenia said with a smile.

Eugenia carried the conversation for the rest of the evening, only pausing when she realized the time. "Oh, I have to get to another meeting. This has been such fun catching up, Stratton. Maybe I'll see you again before the end of the conference."

They gathered their things, and Eugenia gave her a quick hug as they parted ways outside of the club.

Forty-Seven

Since the hotel was only about a mile away, Stratton decided to walk back. What was Everest doing right about now? Was he thinking about her? Was he worried she wasn't going to figure out what she wanted? She could at least text him, letting him know not to worry, but then he'd know her answer. She really wanted to explain to him how she knew when she knew and what she knew.

The soft glow of the streetlights lit the way as she walked. Though it was after ten, people were gathered outside the trendy restaurants, waiting for an open table. She stopped by the Pulitzer Fountain, sitting down on the stone with the fountain on her back, listening to the sound of the water flowing. Stratton wanted to call Savannah, but she couldn't tell Savannah that she was going to accept Everest's proposal. He must know that before anyone else.

Stratton stretched her back and yawned. *It is definitely time to get back.*

"Mom!"

"Finley?" Stratton stood up in surprise.

Finley came running up and gave her a hug.

Stratton stepped back. "What are you doing here? Is everyone OK?"

"Everyone is fine."

"How did you find me?"

Finley held up her phone. "You had us all enable the 'share your location' with you, and you shared with us. I just clicked your name, and I could see exactly where you were. You just never really go anywhere, so I never had to use it before now."

"OK, but what are you doing here?"

"Can we sit down?"

Why does she look nervous? What is so important that it couldn't wait til I got home? Stratton nodded as they sat on the fountain wall.

"I came to apologize."

Stratton looked at her daughter, not sure what she would say next.

Finley drew in a breath. "You're the most loving and wonderful mother in the world. You've sacrificed so much for us and continue to always give to others. Mom, I was more jealous than skeptical of Everest being in your life, which was selfish and immature of me. The only reason I told you about his arrest was to get him out of the picture, not because I thought he was a bad person or anything, but because I didn't want some man coming into your life, disrupting our order, and potentially breaking your heart."

Reaching for Finley's hand, Stratton's eyes filled with tears.

"I know you tried to shield us from so many things when you were married to Dad, but we knew way more than you realized. Do you remember when I tried to help with the laundry and used the wrong detergent?"

Stratton nodded.

"Well, what you don't know is that it leaked all over the floor, and Dad made me wipe it up with my brand-new jeans I had bought with my own money, ruining them. He told me if I wasn't going to respect his things, I didn't deserve things of my own."

Stratton's heart was heavy with emotion as she struggled to control the anger and hatred she felt toward Dexter at that moment.

"I was trying to protect you from his anger over the laundry, especially after that big fight you had had with him. You were in your room, and I didn't want things to get worse. I hated seeing what those fights did to you, and I was scared of what would happen to you."

"I never knew that. Finley, you have no idea how sorry I am or how guilty I feel right now."

"No, Mom, I don't want you to feel guilty. I want you to know why I did what I did. I just wanted to protect you. I saw Everest as a threat, but I don't want to be the reason you do or don't choose to marry him. I went to Everest and apologized."

"Oh Finley…" Stratton started.

"No, I don't want you to make a big deal about it, OK? This made me realize that I need help overcoming some things. I told Everest that and he knows the owner of this faith-based counseling center in Mount Judea. I already had my first session and plan to continue. And Mom, this is the kind of guy Everest is; I told the counselor I wasn't sure if I could afford counseling long-term, and she said not to worry because Everest had already taken care of the bill."

Stratton's heart swelled with love for both Everest and Finley.

"I'm really sorry for how I've been acting. You raised me better and taught me that God is all I really need and that I can be content with Him. I don't want to keep doing the things I've been doing. I want a different life, a better life." She paused to wipe the tears from her eyes.

"I know it's your decision to marry Everest or not, and if you say yes, I will embrace him as family and trust that your marriage will change things for the better for all of us." Finley smiled through fresh tears.

Stratton cried, her heart breaking with a mixture of sorrow and joy, as she pulled her daughter against her. "Oh, Finley. I'm so sorry, honey." Stratton cried for what her children had gone through during her marriage. They had witnessed far more of the emotional abuse than she had realized. She also cried for her children, wanting their father's love but never receiving it. She cried for Finley, seeking help. She cried for Everest paying for Finley's sessions. He was taking care of her children like a father should.

She had known that marriage to Everest wouldn't be just about the two of them, but now she really knew it was an opportunity for spiritual healing and blessing the likes of which she could never fathom. A hope and a future, not just for her but for all of them. Stratton hugged Finley tighter, unable to stop the flow of tears.

"Mom, it wasn't your fault. I want you to know that. The decisions that I made were mine and self-destructive, but I want to make the right decisions from now on. Being with Harper and the kids has really made me see what's important, and I know why you're so proud of her. She's an amazing wife and mother."

Stratton pulled back slightly and looked at Finley. "Finley, I'm proud of you, too. Do you not think I'm proud of you?"

"I've made a lot of mistakes and made some really poor choices. I haven't lived like you raised me and turned my back on God." She said with a broken, shame-filled voice.

Stratton reached and lifted up Finley's chin, searching her eyes. "That doesn't mean I'm not proud of you. You're so talented and accomplished. When others give up, you just keep persevering. You're insightful and innovative, and you excel at organizational leadership. Finley, I could go on and on."

"I want to get my life on a better path, Mom. I'm just not sure if I am good enough to do that."

"Finley, that is the beauty of God's forgiveness; no matter how far you've strayed from His plan and His purposes, you can always begin to obey God right where you are."

"Thank you for always praying for me and never giving up on me. I'm so sorry I ruined your engagement news, and I will make it up to you."

"Baby, it's OK. You don't have to make anything up to me."

"Because love covers all trespasses?" Finley's eyes were wet with tears.

"Love does." Stratton wrapped an arm around Finley as they rested their heads together.

"Mom?"

"Hmm?"

"Do you have room for me in your hotel room?"

Stratton laughed. "Yes, Finley. Come on, let's get to bed." She stood, taking Finley by the hand and pulling her up from the fountain wall.

"Mom?"

"Yes?"

"Are you going to marry him?"

"I need to answer him first before I can answer your question. Can you live with that?"

She chuckled. "That's a Mom 'yes' if I've ever heard one, but I won't assume anything until you tell the three of us at the same time."

"Finley, I promise to be more open with news and happenings."

"And I promise to listen and take an active interest. I know you mentioned it, but will you tell me about the treasure you guys found? I really want to know everything, even the details."

Stratton's heart melted. She absolutely adored this daughter of hers. *I understand it now.* The changes were going to be some of the most monumental redemptive occurrences she would ever experience, and she was so thankful.

Forty-Eight

Finley left the next morning after breakfast, while Stratton finished out the last full day at the conference. She was so excited to return home to Tennessee the following morning that she had a hard time focusing on the last presentations.

She envisioned herself, all dressed up, going to Milky Way Farms to surprise Everest. She'd walk right up to him and give him a big hug, then tell him everything she'd been thinking about since he left. They'd walk the grounds, holding hands, and celebrate their engagement. Maybe she should ask Lyle and Bernadette's chef to prepare something special for the two of them. They'd have a romantic dinner. Then, they would spend some time planning their wedding. *It's the perfect coming-home plan.*

When she landed in Nashville, Noah texted that he had a problem with the cows, so he had arranged to have an Uber wait for Stratton to bring her home. She made her way through the terminal to where the Uber was waiting.

As the Uber pulled up the driveway, shades of orange, pink, and gold were splashed across the sky, creating a stunning display of color as the sun slowly descended behind the treetops. Stratton raced into the house, only to find it empty.

Assuming that Noah was still outside with the animals, she had just grabbed her phone from her purse to text him when there was a knock at the front door. *Noah must have ordered dinner for us.*

She opened the door and immediately felt tears trickle down her cheeks as relief and joy washed over her.

Everest, dressed in a formal, three-piece suit, stood before her, completely stealing her plan to surprise him.

"Why are you all dressed up?" She ran her hand over her cheeks, wiping away the tears.

"I believe you owe me an answer first." He stepped across the threshold and closed the door, then stood waiting for her to reply.

Stratton had been working on her speech to him most of the plane ride home, so why was she suddenly nervous? She took a deep breath and cleared her throat. She reached out, took both of his hands in hers, and looked at him, her eyes glistening from the tears threatening to fall.

"When the Israelites left Egypt, they left behind the legacy of slavery and, though they had the opportunity to embrace the Promised Land earlier than they did, they chose to continually look back, longing for the days of bondage and oppression. I compared my journey over the past week with Egypt, which is a place I left a long time ago. Egypt isn't ahead; Egypt is behind. Everest, you've asked me to entrust the remainder of my life and all that I have to you so that together, as one, we can experience the foreshadowing of the Promised Land, which we can only achieve by following His will, His instructions, His design, and His plan." Stratton felt tears slip from her eyes.

Everest lightly squeezed her hands, encouraging her to continue.

"At first, I thought I would have to choose between you or my kids. I know you don't know all that we've been through, but there was a time when I thought I might never see my kids again. Everest, I would have died if that had happened. I knew that I never wanted to feel that way again, but it's only one reason why I've kept to myself all these years."

Everest released one of her hands, reaching up to gently wipe away the tears silently sliding down her cheeks before taking hold of her hands again.

"I've been so afraid to love and trust someone again, to let someone get close to me, as well as my children and grandchildren. The fear of being hurt again is another reason I've kept to myself. It's safer to stay in my own Egypt than risk having my heart broken again. I knew I would never find the answers on my own, so I fasted and prayed for His guidance and clarity on His will. I realized that I don't have to choose between any of you, but by choosing you means I am choosing family above all and that I'm being given the chance to fulfill His purposes in ways that are grander than I could ever ask for or envision."

Stratton gazed into Everest's eyes, seeing the hope and a shared future reflected in them.

"Everest, my answer remains 'yes'—yes to your offer of biblical marriage. I'm not looking back anymore. I want to be your wife for the rest of my life. I want to marry you to become further transformed to His likeness and bless others, including my kids, by our union."

"Stratton," Everest began.

She placed a finger over his lips. "One more thing; I know you love my children and grandchildren as if they were your own. I see how your presence has already made a positive impact on all three of them. From guiding Finley back on the right path to building confidence in Noah to encouraging Harper to plan things as a family unit, you've been the role model they have not had. So, it's time for me to stop using the word 'my' and start using the word 'our'—our kids, our grandkids, our family. Everest, you have all of my heart. I'm no longer holding anything back from you."

Everest leaned down and kissed her temple before drawing her into his arms. "It broke my heart to walk away last week, and it has not been easy. Please forgive me if I seemed harsh."

"There's nothing to forgive." She snuggled against him, never wanting to leave his embrace. The strength of his hold communicated the depth and fullness of his feelings. She glanced up at him. "Now, will you please tell me why you're so dressed up?" she said with a smile in her voice.

"I took a calculated risk in coming here tonight, but if you say yes, the dividends are immeasurable."

Stratton stepped back. "I'm not following what you are saying."

Everest chuckled. As he looked into her eyes, he dropped to one knee. "Stratton, my 'yes' is still a 'yes,' so will you marry me tonight?"

"Of course, I will," Stratton exclaimed with delight as she wrapped her arms around his neck.

He reached up, unlocking her arms from around his neck, and stood. "Then I have to go now."

"Everest, what? What do you mean?"

There was a quick knock at the door before Willodean popped her head in. "Is it on?"

Stratton looked at Everest, a confused expression on her face. "Willodean, what are you doing here?"

Everest took a step back as Willodean cut through the middle of them.

"For such a time as this," she said with a laugh. "I've kept my cosmetologist license ready for a night like tonight. Come on, girl, we're gonna get you ready for a wedding!"

"What?" Stratton was awestruck.

"I'll get the curling iron and straightener turned on," Willodean said as she disappeared down the hall.

Stratton turned to Everest, "I don't have a dress."

"You'll find you do." His eyes sparkled.

"I want you to stay." She reached for his hands as he started to leave.

He took hers into his. "I'm about to stay with you for the rest of our lives. We can surely handle being apart long enough to get you ready for your wedding."

"I don't know what you have planned for tonight, but I'm ready to be your wife, Everest."

"I can't resist that." He brought her in for another embrace.

Stratton fought to keep her emotions in check, counting it a victory that only two tears fell onto Everest's suit.

"Stratton, come on, let's get you ready!" Willodean hollered.

"I'll see you soon," Everest said as he released Stratton.

She went to her room where Willodean had an elegant, simple, beautiful periwinkle, Bardot neckline, knee-length dress laid out on the bed.

"I'm glad I brought waterproof mascara. This is going to be a night that we all are going to need it," Willodean beamed.

Forty-Nine

"I don't think I've ever seen a more beautiful bride," Willodean exclaimed.

Stratton took a look at herself in the full-length mirror.

With Willodean's expert touch, everything was enhanced. Stratton's blue eyes popped with skillfully applied makeup, and her hair, half pulled up with soft, tendril curls framing her face, allowing for the fullness of the dress to be seen from the front and back.

Stratton admired the glowing reflection staring back at her, the woman about to walk down the aisle and marry Everest.

"I'm sorry I'm a little late." Shelby entered the room bearing a cascading bouquet of colorful lilies.

Lilies were the flower that she'd noticed Everest carrying to the back of Washington's headquarters and followed him. If she'd never seen those brilliant flowers, perhaps she wouldn't be standing here beholding the bouquet Shelby presented.

"You're absolutely gorgeous." Shelby beamed, walking across the room to give her a quick hug before carefully placing the bouquet on the top of the dresser.

"Thank you, Shelby. This arrangement is beautiful."

"I'm glad you like it. I'll see you later!" She replied, smiling as she left the room.

"That's my cue, too, honey. I'm so ecstatic. You'd tell your ol' pal if Everest had a brother, right?" Willodean winked.

Stratton laughed. "I can't believe this is about to happen. Thank you for making everything perfect for our wedding."

"I'll see you out there." Willodean gave her a quick hug before she left, passing Noah as he entered the room.

"Hey, Momma."

Stratton took one look at her son dressed handsomely in his suit and started crying.

"Shoot, the girls bet me you'd cry, and I said you wouldn't." He gave her a hug, which made her cry even more. "Those are happy tears, aren't they?"

Stratton nodded, trying to form the words. "You know that this doesn't change how much I love all of you, right?"

"Mom, the only other times I've seen you so joyful is around the three of us. I know it'll be different when you're married, but in a better way. I don't feel like I'm losing my mom at all. Everest told the three of us that's not going to happen. He knows he's getting three grown kids with grandkids." Noah chuckled, "Momma, you should hear Scarlett working on what to call him. She has an entire list."

Looking intently at Stratton, he asked, "Did you know that he sat all three of us down and asked if we didn't want this for you to share our reasons with him? That may have been the first time that we were ever instantly unanimous about something. We want this for you because you want this, and we support you. So, are you ready for your wedding?" Noah asked, extending his arm and bending his elbow to escort her.

Stratton took it. "Where are we going?"

"You'll see." Noah smiled as he led her out through the kitchen and down the deck stairs. Beyond the barn, she could make out lights in the trees.

Stratton thought she might cry again. *He had planned an enchanted forest wedding.* Icicle lights, weeping willow lights, and fairy lights adorned the various deciduous trees, creating a magical backdrop. A chuppah was ever so slightly tucked into the trees beyond the shorter field, where arranged chairs were already filled by the guests.

As they paused at the start of the runner, Stratton's gaze followed it to the end, where Everest stood, waiting and smiling.

A violin started the first notes of *Canon in D*, followed by the addition of a harp, guitar, and keyboard. *This is one of my favorite pieces.*

As Noah led her down the aisle, Stratton, struggling to hold back her tears, let her gaze sweep over the crowd as they walked. Had Everest invited the entire town?

She glanced at her family, smiling at her as she walked with Noah. *How had Everest pulled this off?* Her children, her grandchildren, future in-laws, and friends had come to her wedding.

Stratton smiled at everyone as they made their way toward the chuppah, which was decorated with a large flower wall drenched in white roses, hydrangeas, and orchids, where Everest was waiting.

This is real; I'm really getting married. When they reached the end of the aisle, she kissed Noah on the cheek as he paused to place her hand in Everest's. Tears threatened to fall when she saw the depth of love in his eyes.

Stratton and Everest stood together under the chuppah as a woman began singing, then was joined by a man, as they led the crowd in the worship song, *You Are My All in All*, as notes from *Canon in D* continued making this a heavenly medley.

Stratton was overwhelmed by the significance of the chuppah and its representation of His presence and His protection. She struggled to hold back the tears, moved by the symbolism of a new home and family the two of them would build—a place filled with His hospitality and grace and the corporate worship of Yeshua, The Lamb of God. "This is absolutely perfect, Everest. I never thought I'd have a chance like this."

"I'd like to take full credit if it was due, but this is mostly the result of our family of wedding planners, especially Finley. She arranged the musicians and song."

She felt Everest gently wipe away her tears with his finger before handing her his handkerchief. As she accepted it, she shared a look that spoke of admiration, appreciation, and love with her daughter. She glanced at the handkerchief, recognizing it as the same one he'd offered her when they first met. She thought of how Yehovah had used everything in her past, even a handkerchief, to bring her to this very occasion. Just as He had promised in the Book of Joel, He had given back the years the locusts ate. With tears trickling down her cheeks, she realized how vastly different the tears today were from the tears before. Today's tears were salty offerings of joy, gratitude, and thanksgiving poured out with humility because she knew she did not deserve this night or this time.

"By wisdom a house is built, by understanding it is prepared, and by knowledge its rooms are filled with every rare and pleasing treasure." Everest gazed into her eyes as he quoted Proverbs to her.

When the medley ended, her nephew, Joshua, stepped into the chuppah to officiate the wedding ceremony, which ended with applause and cheers from friends and family whom Stratton couldn't wait to celebrate with.

After the meal, before the band began playing, Everest pulled her close and whispered in her ear, "I know you want to spend some private time with the kids, so I told them to meet you over by the chairs that are set up by the chuppah. If you oblige the photographer with a couple of shots, you'll also have time to talk with them."

"Thank you," Stratton said, giving him a quick hug before meeting her children.

She and the kids posed for a few pictures before the photographer moved on to take pictures of the crowd.

"Mom, before you say anything or give us a speech, we like Everest, and we are thrilled to have him as part of the family. He's opened his arms to us, and we want to open ours to him and his family," Harper said, speaking on behalf of all three of them.

"I wasn't going to give a speech." She said with a wink, but she knew they knew her well enough she was going to say something along those lines. She let her gaze pass over each one of her children, all grown up, looking at her with love and anticipation in their eyes. "Thank each of you for helping plan my wedding. It's so much better than I could have planned." She wiped at the tears slowly building in her eyes again. "Harper and Finley, you two are so talented, and I hope that you can find a way to blend your talents in Arkansas. Noah, you have been so strong and supportive all summer. I wouldn't be married again today if not for the love and support of you three."

"Mom, don't cry," Finley said, reaching out and giving her mother a hug.

"These are happy tears. I'm thankful that Everest sees we are a package deal. I don't have to choose him over you, and I don't have to choose you over him. You know that you three are my everything, and I was content for it to be just us for the rest of my days. Though I know that Yehovah has forgiven me for the past mistakes and hurts I've caused our family, I was still plagued by the memories. I have realized that I need to let those memories stay in the past and look to the future, one with Everest, a future where I can set the example of a biblical marriage for you three and your children. It won't be perfect, but we will learn and grow together as a couple and a family."

The girls teared up.

"Also, you know this is still your home. You are always welcome here. Noah isn't moving out, but you can come as often as you want."

"We know, Mom and you guys can come and visit anytime, too," Harper replied with a big smile, "especially next year." She pulled out a piece of paper and handed it to Stratton.

It was an ultrasound.

Overcome with emotions, Stratton began crying. "No one had better tell me not to cry."

"It's a boy," Harper offered, making Stratton cry even more.

Embracing Harper, she kissed her cheek. "Congratulations, sweetheart."

"His name is going to be Noah."

Stratton looked over at her son, who had tears in his eyes.

"This night couldn't get any better," Stratton said as she hugged her children.

A slight tug on her dress caused Stratton to release the hold on her children.

"Mommy," Daisy said as she looked up at Harper, "Pops said I had to ask if I could have some cake."

"Yes, that's fine," Harper replied, almost finishing her sentence before Daisy raced off towards the cake.

"Pops?" Stratton asked, raising one eyebrow.

"Scarlett made a list,t and all of them liked Pops the best, so Pops it is. Now I'm pretty sure that you don't have any more tears in you, so you should hydrate." Harper stood up. "I'm gonna go help Pops on cake duty." She hugged Stratton once more, "Congratulations, Mom. I couldn't be happier."

"I'll join you. Have you had a chance to meet Shelby yet, Harper?" Noah stood, kissing Stratton's cheek. "Congratulations, Mom. Finley, are you coming?"

"In a minute."

Finley turned to Stratton. "I hope this makes up for how I messed up your engagement."

"Honey, you have nothing to make up for. I know your heart. You have done a terrific job tonight. The music, the decorations, the food, and everything else are so amazing, but you are more amazing." Stratton lovingly placed her hands on Finley's cheeks, looking her in the eyes. "You've grown and matured over this summer, and that's what makes me most proud."

"I know that I haven't been receptive to how you have told us to make our lives count for the Kingdom, but I'm ready to do that now. I believe that you and Everest together will make a difference for so many. I mean, look at Noah dancing with Shelby, his girlfriend. And look at me. I came alone to a wedding, and I'm not freaking out. We wouldn't be where we are without you and Everest, Mom."

"I'm thankful you're learning to stand on your own and taking time to sort things out. Single or not, serve Him, and He'll take care of the outcomes."

Finley nodded. "I promised the kids we'd dance to a few songs, so I'd better get to it. I'll save a dance challenge for you." Finley winked as she stood and embraced Stratton before going to find the kids.

Stratton glanced over the crowd, her heart full. *Thank you, Yehovah, for tonight, for Everest, for giving me hope and a future.*

Savannah approached, giving Stratton a hug. "You make a lovely bride. Charles and I couldn't be happier for you."

"Thank you. How much notice did Everest give you about this wedding?"

Savannah laughed. "We had a couple of days' notice. Stratton, this was a beautiful blend of worship and celebration. Everyone did a fabulous job." Savannah sighed as she watched people begin to gather on the makeshift dance floor. "You know Mom would have loved tonight."

"She would have, wouldn't she?"

"And she would adore Everest."

The sisters shared a smile.

"Who doesn't?" Stratton looked at her husband dancing with the grandchildren, their grandchildren. "I just want to soak in the entirety of tonight. Can you believe I'm married? This entire summer has been so surreal."

"Are you two taking a honeymoon? What about returning to campus?"

"We haven't talked about any of that. Harper just told me she's having a baby, so I would imagine there will be a lot more trips planned to Arkansas that may be a challenge with work."

"Aw, congratulations! Does this mean you're going to retire?"

"I don't know, Savannah. I haven't depended on a man to financially support me in a long time. I enjoy the university, but now that I have the option to free up my time for other things, I want to be open to that, too. It's something that Everest and I will need to navigate when that time comes."

Charles walked up, giving her a hug. "Congrats, Stratton."

"Thank you."

"I came to fetch you both for some dancing if you ladies are up for it," he said, extending an arm to each of them.

"I think we can oblige," Stratton laughed, linking arms with Charles on one side and Savannah on his other. As he led them back towards the music and dancing, they stopped to talk with an elderly woman from town. Charles and Savannah moved on toward the music. Stratton spoke with the woman while letting her eyes wander over the crowd. Where was Everest?

Stratton felt an arm circle around her waist from behind, causing the woman to pause mid-sentence.

"Excuse me. I need to escort my bride to the dance floor for our first dance," Everest said, stepping from behind Stratton.

The woman smiled and nodded.

Everest escorted Stratton to the floor.

"Attention everyone! May I present Mr. and Mrs. Everest Galloway sharing their first dance as a married couple." The lead vocalist of the band announced.

While forks struck glasses, the couple shared a kiss.

Everest smiled as he led her across the floor. He pulled her into his arms as the music began. Stratton didn't know what song they'd be dancing to, but as the first notes were played, she felt her knees go weak. *Some Enchanted Evening*.

"Who told you?" she whispered, looking at him. It was one of her favorite songs. As a little girl, decked out in a feather boa with a broomstick for her partner, she'd played the song on her record player over and over, dancing on the veranda in her Savannah home, never dreaming of an ending like this.

Everest's gaze was tender as he looked lovingly at her. "This one was all me. It's been playing in my head since I met you."

With tears flowing anew, Stratton thought the lyrics aptly captured so much about their story.

He'd found her across a crowd of people and never let go. Not even when she wasn't sure she wanted to be his wife, he'd never let go. She thanked Yehovah for everything. This was all His composition, a beautiful arrangement and display of His glory and goodness culminating in the merriment and majesty of this moment.

The celebrations carried on into the late evening.

The kids began nodding off just as the band finished its final set.

"Where is everyone staying?" Stratton asked Everest.

"I gave them the house."

"Where are we staying?"

He gave her a mischievous smile. "I'll show you."

Fifty

"Nope. No, sir. Absolutely not," Stratton said as they stood before the barn apartment.

Everest laughed. "Now, wait. You haven't seen what we've done, and I can assure you Cully has been a full-fledged barn cat for weeks now. There are no traces left of him," Everest explained, pulling her by the hand towards the door.

Stratton, looking skeptical, allowed him to lead her. "I don't know about this, Everest."

"Behold," Everest opened the doors, "your bridal chamber awaits."

Stratton caught her breath as she stepped inside, overwhelmed by what she saw. The barn apartment had been transformed into a luxurious, beautifully decorated one-room suite, with gorgeous bouquets of colorful roses strategically arranged on every surface, filling the room with a sweet aroma. Flickering candles were placed throughout, creating a soft glow and enhancing the intimacy of the room. Her gaze traveled from the newly white-washed wood floor entry to the blue pastel rug underneath a wooden bed. The bed, covered with a white comforter and layered with a vast array of pastel-colored pillows, gave the room a romantic yet warm and inviting atmosphere. There was a cream-colored L-shaped leather couch under the window that would be great for reading. The kitchen, nestled in the back corner of the room, not only had the major appliances but a vintage Chambers stove that would make the suite cozy during the winter months.

In awe of what she was seeing, her voice barely above a whisper, she looked at Everest. "Who did all of this?"

"Noah and I mostly. The girls put the finishing touches on things over the past couple of days." He took her hands in his, turning her to face him. "It's all ours for the week."

"The whole week?"

He chuckled. "That's how long our families have decided they needed to stay and celebrate. They even had matching T-shirts made for some of the outings they've planned for all of us."

Stratton walked through the space admiring the little touches everyone had contributed as they worked together, unbeknownst to her, to create the perfect honeymoon suite. She felt the tears pool in her eyes at the love she felt for everyone involved.

"This is beyond exquisite, Everest. Thank you." She touched the comforter on the bed, "Did you have our things brought out here as well?"

"Toiletries, yes, but," he shrugged as he looked around the space, "that's odd. I don't see the bag with our pajamas."

She smiled coyly. "If you recall, I didn't have any extra clothes the first night we spent together. I had to wear whatever you had on hand."

Everest flirted back, "I'm kinda hoping tonight goes a little differently than that night." He walked over to stand before her, reaching up to gently run the back of his hand down her cheek. "I do have one question to ask."

Her breath caught in her throat, but she managed to get out one word. "Yes?"

"How many men had stayed over at your house for the summer, and you ended up giving your heart to them?"

"Only one: you."

With those words, Everest leaned in and kissed his bride with all of the passion and desire that had been building over the summer, leaving no doubt as to what the outcome of the evening would be.

His kiss was like no other they had shared, reigniting the flames that had not been fully extinguished from the last time they had been alone.

The love she felt for Everest exploded like fireworks through her soul, lighting up every part of her heart and fueling her with a fervor that swept away any of the roadblocks she had imagined.

She wrapped her arms tighter around him as he slowly unzipped her dress, moving his fingertips along her upper back. She moved her hands to his shirt, her fingers deftly unclasping each button. "No take-backs after you see what gravity can do to a body in six decades."

He smiled. "No take-backs if six minutes is all a body can offer."

Stratton laughed. She was ready to embark on this adventure called marriage with Everest. She looked forward to the humor, friendship, communication, and openness that was sanctioned by Him as they moved forward as husband and wife.

Her lips just brushed his, "Let him kiss me with the kisses of his mouth!" she quoted from Song of Solomon.

Everest smiled, leaning in to oblige her with kisses betraying the depths of his love and passion as he freed one of Stratton's arms from her dress.

Stratton's heart overflowed with a love that had not only been restored but had been expanded. Unable to contain the bursting wellspring for another moment, she softly moaned against Everest's kiss.

Everest effortlessly scooped Stratton up into his arms as he moved to the bed, speaking the words from Genesis to her, "This one, at last, bone of bones and flesh from my flesh." The intensity in his eyes as he gently laid her on the bed spoke of promises filled with hope and a shared future where the bliss and blessings of union and togetherness in marriage could be explored and experienced by both.

In the afterglow of the consummation of their marriage, Stratton embraced a heart of gratitude as she held a sleeping Everest in her arms. Sixty wasn't too late or too old to marry. Sixty wasn't a barrier to physical intimacy with a spouse. Sixty wasn't beyond the boundary of His blessing, of a summer filled with so many rare and pleasing treasures that would have echoes into eternity of thanksgiving, joy, and proclamations of His ceaseless wonders.

About the Author

Born and raised in the Midwest, Brandi Hudson completed her undergraduate and graduate studies in Tennessee and Virginia before being admitted to the Tennessee State Bar. She teaches law at the collegiate level, maintains an active law practice, and currently resides on a hobby farm in the Nashville, Tennessee, area. In her leisure time, when she's not milking goats or collecting eggs, you'll find her reading, studying Scripture, thrifting, or planning to travel to the next destination, always welcoming the seeds those journeys plant for the next story.

Other Books by Brandi Hudson

Fulfilled in their Time

www.ingramcontent.com/pod-product-compliance
Lightning Source LLC
Chambersburg PA
CBHW061055100726
47911CB00012B/236